GHOSTER

JASON ARNOPP

www.orbitbooks.net

ORBIT

First published in Great Britain in 2019 by Orbit

1 3 5 7 9 10 8 6 4 2

A CIP catalogue record for this book is available from the British Library.

ISBN 978-0-356-50688-3

Typeset in Bembo by Palimpsest Book Production Limited, Falkirk, Stirlingshire

Printed and bound in Great Britain by Clays Ltd, Elcograf, S.p.A.

Papers used by Orbit are from well-managed forests and other responsible sources.

Orbit
An imprint of
Little, Brown Book Group
Carmelite House
50 Victoria Embankment
London EC4Y 0DZ

An Hachette UK Company
www.hachette.co.uk

www.orbitbooks.net

To my mum Jennie Arnopp,
for being excellent

CHAPTER ONE

27 August

Thirty-five days before he disappears off the face of the Earth, Scott Palmer stops licking his ice cream cone and lays that look on me.

That hungry wolf look. The one that leaves me way too keen to be devoured.

The glass sheet of the sea reflects a high mid-afternoon sun as Scott says, "Well, why *don't* you live here, then? I'm serious, baby. Why don't you move down here and live with me?"

He broaches this idea so casually that it feels neither huge nor stupid, despite being both of these things.

My brain pulsates and pops.

The stones of Brighton's beach shift beneath me. The air around us, so thick with salt and sun cream, carries an exotic shimmer. The West Pier wobbles.

The next time I even think about my own ice cream, it's because the thing's melted all over my hand, then down my wrist.

If I were the kind of person who believes in bad omens, I might notice how this cream is chilling the blood in my veins.

I might notice how the skeletal West Pier resembles a burnt-out carcass.

I might even notice how the growing wind has prompted a lifeguard to stride over and plant a huge red flag in a nearby patch of stones.

Not being that kind of person, I notice these things only subliminally, while transfixed by the kaleidoscopic beauty of Scott's eyes.

Hello. My name's Kate Collins and I'm balls-deep in love with a walking question mark whose smartphone will one day show me all of his deepest, darkest secrets.

My grin covers my entire face as I tell Scott, "You know what? I reckon I could just about do that, you lucky fucker."

All I can think about is how I will never, ever, feel alone again.

CHAPTER TWO

2 October

Where the hell is Scott?

I pound my interlocked hands onto Roy's sternum, pressing deep and hard to circulate blood. Each time I release, the suction effect allows his ribs to recoil and fills the heart again.

Too late. Roy's light has already ebbed. Wide and blue, with that unmistakable cataract gleam, his eyes stare clean through me. It's no surprise when there turns out to be no electrical activity in his heart.

Despite this flatline, I carry on for Pat's benefit. I want her to know that we've done everything we can.

She wavers in the living room doorway with one liver-spotted hand cupped over her mouth. My colleague Trevor makes gentle but fruitless attempts to coax her onto the sofa, in case her legs give out.

When life becomes extinct, there's always shock. Makes no difference whether people deny the facts of mortality, or contemplate death on a regular basis, or even actively plan for death, right down to the grim nitty-gritty of graves and urns. None of this makes any difference at all. Because in the end, they never truly believed this day would come.

Hey, here's an idea. What if Scott's every bit as dead as Roy?

I pound on Roy some more. The grating of the ribs I've broken feels horrible, as it always does. But even worse, his face has become Scott's face, because I'm a massive weirdo whose imagination is liable to run away with itself.

Scott goggles blindly up at me, his eyes two blown bulbs. A thick purple tongue lolls in his open mouth.

Pat finally plonks herself on the sofa. "He can't do this, can he?" she says. "November's our fiftieth. The pub's booked. We paid the deposit in August."

August. It's been a little over four weeks since Scott asked me to move in. I told my landlord straight away, handed in my work notice and secured the transfer to Brighton. I've disposed of so many possessions that Marie Kondo herself would consider me hardcore.

Scott can't be dead, can he? He's only thirty-seven.

People die unexpectedly all the time, regardless of their age. If anyone knows this, it's you.

That's enough, brain. Any minute now Scott will text me back, so I must get my head back in the game. I have to maintain laser focus on Pat, whose husband really has died from a cardiac arrest in his late seventies.

Delivering one final compression to Roy's chest, I feel yet another rib crack. Reality regains its grip on my sight, and Scott's lifeless face becomes Roy's once again.

Resting my backside against my heels, I swipe the back of one hand across my brow and claw at the collar of my shirt. This cheap polyester shit never gets any easier to work in.

Joining Pat on the sofa, I hold her parchment-paper hand,

look her straight in the eye and say, "Pat, I'm afraid your husband has died. I'm so sorry for your loss."

Pat studies Roy's corpse, which lies in the middle of the cramped living room where they've laughed, cried, watched TV and bitched at each other for so many years.

"Pat, would you like Trevor and me to move Roy through to your bedroom and cover him up on the bed until the police arrive?"

Her weathered face holds this frozen disappointment, like Roy's genuinely let her down by failing to last until the big anniversary. By having forfeit that piddling deposit.

Everyone handles this in their own way.

Hey, why not tell Pat she can hold the wake in that pub instead?

I squeeze her hand. "Your husband's moved on to a good place, sweetheart."

Pat turns cold, appraising eyes on me. She says, "You don't believe that. I can tell," then returns her attention to Roy.

She's right, of course. Despite having seen countless people die, I've never once sensed their spectral essence coil out of them, destined for Heaven, Hell, Valhalla or anywhere else.

The sorry truth is, dead people resemble complex biological systems that have ground to a random and sometimes ugly halt. What we humans think of as our minds, it's all electricity. All our thoughts, desires and funniest jokes, they're just lightning bolts, bouncing around inside a bag of meat.

"I do believe," I tell her. "I really do."

When Pat does not respond, I abandon these lies and offer to make tea. There's always time for a quick brew when someone's died. Trevor takes my place beside her as I disappear into a kitchen that smells of cooked sausages and fried onions. What would have been Roy's final meal cools and congeals in two pans on the hob.

Once the kettle's on, I feel the burning urge to check my phone. If Scott had texted, I would have felt the vibration against my hip, but I want to check anyway. This kind of compulsive behaviour feels dangerously like my old, bad ways. I really should restrict myself to one check per hour, max, but this is no ordinary day. This is the end of my life here in Leeds and the start of my life with Scott down in Brighton, so I decide to consult my old Nokia once again.

The tiny screen glows into life, opening a restricted window onto the world. This antiquated device shows me calls, texts, low-res photos and little more. Bare bones.

Still no reply from Scott.

He's probably had second thoughts about this whirlwind romance – and can you blame him? If you were Scott, would you honestly want to live with some tedious Miss Average who comes home every night smelling of blood and sick?

I remind myself yet again that it's only been seventeen hours since his last text. This is by far the longest we've ever gone without comms in the four months since we met, but there's got to be a perfectly good reason.

There had fucking better be. What a truly weird time for him to drop out of contact.

Don't you dare ghost me on the day before I move in with you, Scott Palmer.

Don't. You. Dare.

Steam gushes from the kettle spout. The urgent bubble of hot water makes me feel panicked, so I switch off the kettle before it hits the boil, and I make the widow her tea.

CHAPTER THREE

14 February

The first time I ever see Scott Palmer, he isn't really there.

His face has been rendered by one zillion points of light. Untold zeroes and ones. A whole bunch of nothing, which nevertheless ignites chemicals in my brain.

Say what you will about the dating app being the death of romance, but there's such a primal power to swiping left to reject a stranger, then being confronted with a new person who speaks to you. A potential new *partner in crime*, as the great Tinder bio cliché goes.

Half an hour into my tragic Valentine's Day Tinder trawl, Scott Palmer's face doesn't so much speak to me as yell out of the screen.

Some Tinder fuck-boys pose with a big dead fish. *Oh wow, dude, you killed a sentient being by ramming a hook through its mouth and watching it suffocate? Please allow me to cock-worship you forever.*

Other guys present themselves among a group of their mates. *I don't know which one you are.*

And then there are the blokes pictured at their own weddings. *WTF is that trying to communicate – "Hey ladies, someone once liked me enough to marry me"?*

Scott Palmer, meanwhile, has chosen a simple portrait that allows his face to fill the screen. My ovaries *may* be twitching. My inner filth-goddess *may* be imagining how those cheekbones and the wild-yet-somehow-curated stubble would feel against my bare thighs. My fingers *may* be judging how his thin-but-nice, sandy-blond hair would feel. But these eyes, they seal the deal. Apart from being divine pools of azure blue, blah blah blah, their open nature betrays something else deep inside them. Something entirely at odds with the wolfy smirk on his lips.

This guy, whose screen-name is simply Scott, has this real vulnerability about him – one that you only see when you spend more than a passing moment gazing into these peepers. Up until Scott's face entered my life, I'd been swiping with vigour. Having buried the guilt of passing shallow split-second judgements on people based on the configuration and proportions of their facial features, I had allowed myself to enjoy the chemical brain-hits that accompany the anticipation of the new. But I've now become an anomaly in the online world, simply by examining one single image for more than ten seconds.

What is the nature of Scott's secret vulnerability? Can't tell whether it's hurt, or fear, or self-loathing, or whatever, but it makes me want to mother and fuck him at the same time. Yeah, I want to mother-fuck him.

Having fully absorbed his face, I tap the info button to see what he has to say for himself. Turns out he's written no words at all. Hardly unusual on Tinder, but a lack of text is always disappointing. Makes the whole thing feel all the more intensely superficial.

The only information on display is Scott's age: thirty-six. His distance from me is not stated, and neither is his occupation.

How am I supposed to know if we might get along if he tells me nothing about his personality, lifestyle, hopes or dreams?

Ah, fuck him. He's blown this.

So of course, I hit Super-Like. Simply can't help myself, even though Super-Likes on Tinder are a really bad move. Whereas regular Likes are kept secret from the person you've Liked, a Super-Like means the person actually gets notified. So when a woman gives a Super-Like, it's the digital equivalent of doing a handstand and shrieking. While wearing a wedding dress.

See, part of me quite likes the fact that Scott has chosen to remain a man of mystery. An enigmatic array of pixels. Soon as I tap on that little blue Super-Like star, his face gets whisked off my screen, back into the labyrinthine servers of Tinder. Ridiculously, I feel a tad bereft. Why didn't I take a screen grab of him?

Doesn't matter, Kate. He's out of your league anyway. He'll take one look at your profile, with your crooked smile splayed across that weird mouth, your eyes that are too far apart, your short hair of no fixed stylistic abode and your paltry cleavage, and he'll think, "Aw, how sweet, the plain girl loves me." Then he'll move on, hunting for women with perfect teeth, blow job lips and tits that look like they're inflated by a hand-pump twice daily. That's the way of the dating app: everyone's forever holding out to see if someone better lurks one swipe around the corner.

Having dumped the phone beside me on the bed, I force myself to get ready for work. Somewhere out there, across the sprawl of the city, there are people whose lives will need saving. These people currently have no idea, but they're about to have one of the worst days of their lives, often for some cruelly arbitrary reason.

I'm attacking my damp hair with a towel when the phone goes *ping*.

Wow, someone has Super-Liked me on Tinder.

Okay, okay, let's not get excited. This person is highly likely to have tapped the blue Super-Like star by mistake. All too many times before, I've Liked a Super-Liker back, only for them to totally ghost me.

In fact, it's happened every single time.

Still, I may as well enjoy this minor chest flutter for the minutes it'll take me to dry my hair and take a proper look.

Oh God, wait . . .

Surely this can't be . . . what was his name again? Scott?

As much as I try to resist, a new future rolls out before my mind's eye. My mother, suddenly growing a soul and flying back from New Zealand for the wedding. Scott, standing before the altar, grinning back over his shoulder at me and my magnificent frock. That last vision is weird, seeing as I don't particularly want to marry. I suppose I like the idea of someone being there, for good.

Oh. This isn't Scott. This is an altogether more Venezuelan guy named Rudolpho, with a broad brow and even broader shoulders. He looks pretty damn hot, isn't clutching a dead halibut and he may genuinely Super-Like me.

Could be worth riding. I mean, *investigating*.

CHAPTER FOUR

2 October

"Izzy, seriously: where the fucking hell is Scott? Why hasn't he texted? *I'm moving in tomorrow.*"

Tickled by my histrionics, Izzy lays into her rum and Coke. She never used to drink before the accident happened. I wonder if she'll carry on boozing when she can walk again unassisted by the crutches propped up against our pub table.

"Kate, I need to tell you something," she says, deploying frank eye contact. "And I need you to hear me: you're talking like a crazy person right now."

"By the time we finish these drinks," I tell her, checking my watch, "it'll have been twenty-four hours since this guy, the one who *cannot wait* for me to move in with him, last texted. And he hasn't responded to any of my little follow-up prompts. You know: *Helloooo? Are you there?* All that needy shit."

Izzy's braids jostle as she shakes her head. "Crazy, crazy, crazy. So what's going on in that little bauble of yours, mate? What *exactly* do you reckon's happened to this bloke who hasn't replied for a while?"

"Well, worst case scenario, he could be dead." Ignoring what Izzy's eyebrows are doing, I press boldly on. "I don't know any of his friends or family. So there's no one to tell me Scott's been hit by a bus."

She shrugs. "Well, you already know how I feel about the whole friends-and-family weirdness there . . ."

"Yep, you've been expressing that opinion since June. And you're right, it *is* pretty weird, but I honestly think—"

"Yeah, yeah, I know: you *honestly think* that couples often seal themselves in an *insular bubble* in the early stages of their relationship. In other words, you think Scott's been too busy banging you to introduce you to a single friend or family member . . . or even mention any of them. But why have you never asked?"

I blow out a fat plume of air. "Because . . . I suppose . . . if I ask about his family, he'd probably ask about mine. And then, if I tell the truth, he'll have to hear about me never having known my dad. And even worse, about Mum herself and, you know, the whole . . . coma thing. Anyway, we've gone off topic."

"None of that stuff is anything to be ashamed of," Izzy insists, "and Scott will hear about it someday. But all right, moving on, here's an idea: have you checked his social media?" When I frown at the very suggestion, she checks herself. "Of course you haven't. You can't. But surely if you're worried, you won't be breaking your own code by looking at his bloody Twitter for ten seconds."

Temptation triggers a warning sign in my head and makes the back of my neck sweat. My addiction is the only thing in the world I feel unable to properly discuss with Izzy. Back in March, when I destroyed my smartphone, I told her I'd just got sick of the internet.

"I don't think that would be a good idea," I tell her. "Slippery slope, and all that. I've been loads happier since I went off-grid."

"Oh yeah, you look dead happy right now, for sure."

"God, I'm being stupid, aren't I? You're right: Scott's fine. Busy, that's all. Probably getting the flat ready. He's rushing around, buying celebratory balloons."

"Hey, do you want me to look at his Twitter for you? Would that work?"

Seeing me fidget, she adds, "All I want is to see you happy, you know? You're about to move in with Mr Perfect. You should be glowing, man."

The knot in my throat makes it hard to speak or swallow. Despite having laced *Mr Perfect* with sarcasm, Izzy truly does want me to be happy, even though I'm leaving her and Leeds behind. Even though . . .

Even though . . . actually, let's not think about how very badly I let her down, not right now. Let's nod and fight back these infuriating tears.

"Are you nodding," Izzy says, "because you agree you should be happy, or because you want me to check his Twitter for signs of death?"

"Both," I manage to say.

Izzy whoops with relief and whips her phone from her bag. Unlike most people, who feel on edge if their phone isn't on the table right in front of them, Izzy has a healthy, normal relationship with hers. What a total cow.

I gulp my drink as she taps her phone screen and navigates through to Twitter.

"Okay," she says, scrolling down. Then she stops dead and peers at the screen. *Oh shit*. She doesn't look concerned so much as horrified.

I'm waiting for the big fake-out laugh, but it doesn't come. Instead, she says, "Brace yourself."

"What the fuck is it? What the fuck's happened?"

"You know Sarah Harding, who used to be in Girls Aloud? Last night, Scott posted a picture of her and him, saying she's his . . . new girlfriend."

My brain spasms, then snaps back into shape.

"Fuck right off," I tell Izzy, who finally breaks cover with one of her bomb-blast cackles.

"Sorry mate, I couldn't resist."

"Fuck's sake." I'm not even smiling, let alone laughing. "Why did you have to pick someone vaguely plausible? Why couldn't you have chosen Madonna, or Kim Kardashian?"

Seeing my total lack of amusement, Izzy composes herself. "Because I'm . . . evil? Also, Kim's already spoken for by Kanye . . . sorry, I mean by *Ye*."

"So . . . has Scott tweeted?"

"Not since you last heard from him. Shit, I really am sorry." She peers at the drink I bought her. "Is this a double? That *was* mean of me. But serves you right for sodding off to Brighton and leaving me here."

"You've got Jared to keep you busy. You've got plenty of other friends, too, you daft mare. And if you think I won't be in touch, like *every hour of every day*, then you're sadly mistaken."

Izzy knocks back the rest of her drink. "Have you tried calling Scott? Your olde-worlde piece-of-shit phone does do calls, right?"

"Twice so far: morning and afternoon. I mean, you play it cool when you're first seeing someone, but surely when you've agreed to move in together, all that crap's off the table."

She seizes upon a new angle. "Which network is he with? Could the network be down?"

I consider this thin sliver of hope, then brush it aside. "Look, if he'd changed his mind about me moving in, he'd have said so, wouldn't he?"

"Course he would." Even as Izzy says this, I'm painfully aware that she's never met Scott. She has no idea of what he would or wouldn't do.

Neither do you, Kate. Not really. And that's why your stomach feels like you drank bad milk.

"I'm going to miss you so much," I tell her, welling up again. "Sarah Harding or no fuckin' Sarah Harding, you are awesome."

Something diverts Izzy's attention over my shoulder. She says, "You'll love me less in about three seconds."

Wearing his one decent shirt, Trevor leads a grinning, whooping posse of our ambulance colleagues across the tacky carpet towards us. Each of them clutches the string of a bobbing, Day-Glo helium balloon. I barely tolerate half of these people, but apparently they've tolerated me more than I knew. Or, more likely, they'll grab any old excuse for a piss-up.

Izzy and I get sucked into the maelstrom. Everyone wants to hug me, push a drink in my hand and wish me luck on the next step of my journey through the bewilderingly twisty corridors of life.

I'd feel so much better about this little soirée if only my phone would vibrate.

CHAPTER FIVE

1 June

The second time I see Scott Palmer, he comes out of nowhere.

A faint breeze ruffles my hair. I'm cross-legged on one of the blankets the organisers handed out, which in turn sits on the bare earth of this wooded glade.

"And when the black, black obsidian sea tries to claim you," says Tomm, "know that you, and you alone, are your own sparkly little lighthouse."

Is this really a glade? What's the difference between a glade and a clearing, for instance? Being an urban upstart, I have no clue. Also: why am I thinking about this when I should be meditating like the rest of the group?

"Mother Nature, let me feast upon your apples," says Tomm. "For you are my mother too. You are all of our mothers. You are everything."

Would I get any of my £295 back if I wrestle Tomm to the ground while barking the word *Silence*? I've already eaten one of the included vegan meals and heard the first of this weekend's talks from the nice anthropologist woman. That might be fifty or sixty quid's worth, so far.

"You are the trees. You are the hedgerows. You are the living, prancing fire of the Earth."

Tomm probably isn't the type to press charges. He's such a bright-eyed muppet, he'd write the whole incident off as me having become so fired up by his poetry that I couldn't help myself. People express their positive energy via different channels, yeah?

"You are the tiny mice that make homes in the hillside. You are the rabbits, nestled deep in their warren . . ."

These days, meditation feels like a forlorn hope, because life no longer allows you to clear your head. True mindfulness may have been achievable prior to 1980, but that ship has sailed. Our heads are jammed way too full of data.

I've now been without my smartphone for two months, three days, eleven hours and about twenty-two minutes. But hey, who's counting?

Even after this chunk of abstinence, I remain haunted. My skull rattles with the ghosts of old Likes, Favourites, message requests, tweets, retweets, deleted tweets, tweets that weren't deleted but should have been deleted, photographs, videos, memes, bounced emails, emojis and the *pings* of ten million notifications.

Being without my smartphone has felt like acclimatising to the loss of a limb . . . or even the loss of my old self. This has meant trying to figure out who the fuck I am and what I enjoy doing. So far, the answer to the second question has been *helping other people, guzzling booze and wolfing down easily prepared comfort food.*

No longer online? Prepare to feel like you're stuck on the outside, looking in. Prepare to feel intensely alone and isolated, as the world's biggest party carries merrily on without you, barely even sparing a thought for your absence. All those Twitterers who apologise to their followers for not having tweeted in a while, they're kidding themselves. Might as well apologise for no longer pissing in the ocean.

"You are the bees, collecting bounteous pollen and nectar to feed us all . . ."

While passing internet cafés, I've experienced frighteningly powerful urges to slip inside them. On two occasions, I have weakened and found myself settling in front of a computer terminal, preparing to reactivate Facebook. But then, having remembered what went down in the early hours of 28 March, I've left straight away, appalled by myself.

Time and time again, I'll dream up a tweet that's got *viral* written all over it, or I'll mentally frame the perfect Instagram shot. Then I'll pull out my Nokia handset and groan at the tiny screen, the blocky text and the SMS-only bullshit.

When I see the news on TV, my dopamine receptors twitch and yelp through sheer deprivation. I'm no longer part of the online conversation, weighing in with my own "hilarious" hot take on everything that happens in the world.

Maybe, just maybe, the world is better off without one more hot take from a nobody. The world can struggle on without one more person who thinks they can bring down the US president by quote-retweeting them and adding a devastating critique for all thirty-eight of their followers to see.

"You are the ants, the earthworms, the centipedes, even the spiders . . ."

Opening my eyes, just a crack, I dare to bring everyone's silhouettes into view. Perched on the log, our guest poet Tomm reads from his tatty sheets of handwritten paper. Thankfully, our group leader Lizzie has her eyes shut tight. Is she really in a trance, or is she secretly gloating about her success in having lured a fresh consignment of lost, solvent souls to the back of beyond?

Yes, all sixteen of us not only volunteered but even paid to go on this digital detox retreat for an entire weekend, while the rest of society carried on hurling terabytes of data at each other. Are we delusional misfits or enlightened pioneers?

"And when the bold blue ocean rises over your head, know that you are safe in Mother Nature's embrace . . ."

Oh shit. Rumbled. This ridiculously handsome guy is looking straight at me.

His neutral expression makes him worryingly unreadable, while his laser-beam eyes threaten to send me hurtling back against the nearest tree. I freeze and question whether I should close my eyes again, but I feel too entranced. This guy wasn't with us before, was he? There's no way. I would definitely have remembered.

Wait. He looks weirdly familiar. Do I know him?

Handsome Laser-Beam Guy side-eyes Tomm, then comes back to me. With tiny, gentle movements, he performs the universally recognised hand gesture for *wanker*, then he tips me a wink. His big wolfish grin showcases teeth so Hollywood-white that I actually blink. While returning the grin, I find myself wishing I'd devoted way more effort to cleaning my own teeth this morning.

" . . . and Mother Nature, in turn, will look after you. Thanks, everyone. You're beautiful."

As Tomm's poem reaches this limp climax, Handsome Laser-Wolf and I exchange the looks of naughty schoolkids about to be caught. Amusingly, as we join everyone else in applauding, we both remember to squint against the sunlight, as if we've stayed as bat-blind as everyone else for these full fifteen minutes of torment.

Smirky Laser-Wolf and I, we're like *partners in crime.* And now the penny finally drops. This guy is the one I Super-Liked on Tinder, back on Valentine's Day.

The guy who never so much as Liked me back.

"So. Confess . . .'

When Scott whispers these words into my left ear, his breath makes me tingle. "You're dying to get your phone back, right?"

Inside this big tent, our group sits in a circle once again. Always with the circles. Ferrying hot spoonfuls of vegan goulash from bowl to mouth, we engage in low-volume chat.

I never expected to meet someone here, let alone some hot guy I once saw on Tinder. I came to strengthen my resistance to temptation, but now a different kind of temptation has reared its fit, designer-stubbled head.

Could there actually be something between us? During our group's walk across the moors to get here, Scott not only tagged along with me but stayed resolutely by my side. When I asked where he'd appeared from, on the second day of this retreat, he explained that he'd been forced to cancel yesterday after a client had made him "an offer I couldn't refuse". This segued nicely into a spirited discussion about the *Godfather* trilogy. Conversation already flows more smoothly between us than it ever did with any guy I've met through a dating app.

Scott and I, we're dancing this fun little dance. The rest of the group are mere bystanders now, their faces blurred, their voices muffled and distant. Outwardly, he and I are going along with all these mindful activities, but our true focus is on each other.

Right now, I'm focused on lying to Scott, who won't get a confession out of me that easily. "I'm really not thinking about my phone. Never engaged with social media at all. To be honest, I got the distinct impression it was going to be bad news."

Oh, Kate Collins, you dirty rotten hypocrite. What a stupid, extreme lie. Pretty soon, Scott will find this out and then he'll run a mile. But what was I supposed to say? *My name is Kate Collins and I'm a hopeless addict who must never touch a smartphone ever again*? That would never do. Let's not be putting the hot guy off me within mere hours.

Against all odds, despite having shown manifold signs of intelligence, Scott takes my claim at face value. "Impressive. So what made you want to do this retreat?"

"Oh . . . I've always been aware that I'm too much of a city person, so I thought I'd try something different." Must bounce the ball right back at him. Get rid of the damn ball. "How about you?"

"I'm much the same," he says. An invisible layer of connection forms between us. "Although we do see quite a lot of nature down in Brighton."

Oh balls, why does he have to live so far away? Tinder never did show me his distance. "Brighton, eh? Nice. I'm in Leeds."

"Wow. I'm visiting Leeds in a couple of weeks."

"Oh, cool. Business or pleasure?"

Hmm. Probably came across like a customs official there. And did I strictly need to give the word *pleasure* that kind of tongue-in-cheek sultry emphasis? Oh, dear God.

"Business," he says. "Have to nip up there for work sometimes. I'm in IT, by the way. Try not to fall asleep."

Should I suggest we meet up in Leeds? No. Too soon. Must stay breezy, verging on nonchalant. "Well, I mean, I'm no technophobe. With the whole social media thing, I really didn't mean to come across like one of those people who makes a big deal of not having a TV . . ."

Scott's bowl whistles as he runs his spoon around the inside. "Not at all," he says. "That's the decision you made, based on your instinct. And you were right. The internet can be a real hellhole."

"My friends tell me Twitter's the worst," I say. "Apparently, it's become like one big circle-jerk, in which no one ever gets to come."

Scott screws up his eyes and slaps the back of his hand against his mouth, presumably to stop goulash from flying out. Can't help feeling pleased with myself for (a) making him properly laugh and (b) smuggling sex into our conversation. Kind of breaks a barrier. The fewer pesky barriers there are between the two of us – such as clothes, for instance – the happier I'll be.

"I'm doing my best to cut down on social media and phone use in general," Scott says between coughs. Seems a piece of goulash ended up down the wrong pipe. I try not to think about how stray food can aspirate in the lungs and lead to conditions like pneumonia. "It's surprisingly tough."

"Why's that?" I ask, innocence personified.

He thinks this over. "Oh, I don't know. Sometimes I'll find myself scrolling through, you know, whatever, and I'll catch myself . . . and I'll wonder what the hell I was even doing. It ends up being just . . . mindless. It's like you get sucked in, you know?"

Oh, honey-bunch, trust me – I know all too well.

"I did an offline January this year," he goes on, "and it was harder than any dry January I've ever done. My hand kept going to my pocket."

My brain wants to fire back a dirty joke, but I can't quite get there, so I stay quiet, nod and listen some more.

"For the phone!" he adds with a laugh, having read my face. "Drag your mind out of the gutter."

"No idea what you mean," I protest, with a trace of a smirk. Oh yeah, my smirk brings all the boys to the yard.

All the boys with low standards. You don't stand a chance with this one.

Maybe, brain, maybe not. We'll see tonight, won't we, when it's time for everyone to go to bed. That's when I'll bring out my killer seduction moves.

Possibly.

IZZY
has he txted u back yet

KATE
Jesus, are you all still in the pub? It's half-one.

IZZY
yeah trevor's v drunk . . . he just tried to have a piss against the bar so we called him a taxi . . . has scott txted yet

KATE
Has he fuck.

IZZY
try not to worry babe and get some sleep . . . everything's gonna be funeral

KATE
Funeral?!?

IZZY
fuckin autocorrect . . . *fine . . . everything's gonna be funeral

IZZY
FFS! FINE NOT FUNERAL!!!!!

KATE
You should probably get some sleep too.

CHAPTER SIX

3 October

Somewhere north of twenty-four hours since Scott was in touch, my sleep isn't so much broken as shattered.

I've made the classic schoolgirl error of keeping my phone by my pillow, so I keep checking it. This I do, despite suspecting that even the screen-light of this old Nokia messes with the melatonin that controls sleep.

To make things worse, I keep *dreaming* the buzz of incoming texts from Scott. When I wake up and check the phone, of course, there's nothing.

Ghost texts, received via the dream world.

When Izzy texted me just now, I had a brief joygasm, thinking it was Scott.

How very pathetic.

Before bed, I sent my first aggro-text to Scott. Feels so weirdly formal, calling him by his actual name. "Scott, I'm moving in tomorrow. We haven't agreed a time for me to turn up. Where the hell are you?"

My first draft had simply read, *Where the fuck are you?* but restraint prevailed.

An entirely unfiltered text would have read, *I AM FUCKING PETRIFIED. Stop being weird and shutting me out, because I am horribly head over heels with you and I don't want to be left all alone. Also: please, please, please don't be dead.*

One o'clock has slowly become two.

Two o'clock merges into three, with only shallow pools of sleep in between.

Somewhere around four, love no longer feels like a positive force in the universe. Love feels like some pernicious disease to avoid at all costs.

Come seven, a couple of hours before I wanted to wake, there's no way any further sleep will happen. Bleary-eyed, I stumble towards the bathroom to splash cold water on my face, toppling a whole stack of my moving boxes on the way.

The Beardie Boys are booked to collect all this stuff later and ferry it down to Brighton. What happens then? What if me and my hirsute hipster removal guys all arrive outside Scott's place and he's still nowhere to be seen? I don't even have the bloody keys to his flat.

Should that have been a big red flag, the fact that he didn't actually give me keys? Maybe I don't have keys yet because he forgot to give them to me, or I haven't really needed them, or he'll simply *be there* when I arrive. I need to stop being such a damsel in distress, pull myself together and think hard. I need to blow all this negative fog away and act.

Okay, then. Yes. I'm going to have breakfast. Then I'm going to leave the keys to this flat with the removal guys and drive down to Brighton, way ahead of them. When I find that handsome idiot Palmer, I'll punch him on the bicep and everything will be dandy again.

Must start my day as I always do, with three gratitudes, inspired by various life coaches. So, what are today's three?

I'm grateful that I have my health. Not fitness, exactly, but at least I can see and hear and move and all those rather useful things.

I'm grateful that I have Izzy, my best friend, even though I haven't always repaid her kindness, to say the very least.

Lastly, I'm grateful that, despite the weirdness and uncertainty of this situation with Scott, I have a plan. I will face this situation with strength, dignity and courage.

My God. Does this flat feel bigger than it once did, or do I feel so very small?

CHAPTER SEVEN

1 June

Crunch time. Will we or won't we?

Scott and I are climbing the grand staircase of Grayson Manor, an imposing building whose outer walls are choked with ivy and lichen. As we make our way towards the residential floor where everyone has their own room, there's something in the air between us. We're still dancing the dance . . . or are we? For a guy with such open and hopelessly blue eyes, Scott's proving hard to read.

The night ended with everyone drinking organic wine on the manor's back patio. Could it have been sheer coincidence that Scott and I ended up on the sole two-seater bench? In fact, I'm pretty sure we made a beeline for this thing, which was small enough for our upper thighs to just . . . about . . . touch.

Come on, Kate. Best not to assume this guy fancies you. There's a reason why your default relationship status is single.

Scott may be the politest gent on Earth, but he did seem

genuinely into the snatches of chat we managed to grab when we weren't forced to humour dull, jabbering people. We established we're both vegetarian, which is very cool – and have I only imagined us stealing ever-longer periods of eye contact? Especially now we've had a few glasses of red, it seems we're holding each other's gaze for as long as we can without our mutual attraction becoming completely blatant.

Dear OKCupid dating app: I'm afraid that when I answered the profile quiz question *Would you be prepared to sleep with someone on the first date?* with the response *No*, I lied in order to weed out the fuck-boys. Sorry, not sorry.

By the time Scott and I reach the top of this enormous staircase, finally alone together, my killer seduction moves have forsaken me. I need some flimsy pretext for intimacy, but nothing springs to mind. Why isn't there any tempting booze in my room? No one wants coffee at 2 a.m., unless they live in Soho or New York . . . do they?

We arrive in the long corridor dotted with the doors to people's rooms. Here we are in Last Chance Saloon, but we're chatting total small talk, about how *fun* and *interesting* the day's been – conversational ground that we've covered before. We're locked into a holding pattern, but who knows where we'll land? Time to find out.

Scott chuckles. "This corridor reminds me of *The Shining*." Gazing along the length of it, I briefly imagine those creepy twins from Kubrick's film and fail to suppress a shudder.

"Reddd rummm," I croak. Our laughter peters out, and then we're slap-bang in that moment when it's time to either say goodnight or carry on in my room or his.

Fuck it. You only live once and then you're dead forever.

My cheeks flush, even as I say the words. "Weirdly, I don't feel all that tired. Do you?"

Scott breaks our precious eye contact, and a certain awkwardness in his smile concerns me. Shyness? I didn't have him down as shy, but people can be shy in many different ways. There are probably names for different types of shyness, as there are for phobias. This year, for instance, I learnt the word *nomophobia*: the fear of losing your phone. How appalling that the word even needs to exist.

"I must admit . . ." he begins, as I resign myself to my friend-zone fate, "I had such an early start today, I'm fading. I'd rather we carried on talking when I can give you the best of me."

As brush-offs go, this is actually pretty nice. *Talking*, though. Is that really all he wants to do? Oh, relax and go to bed, Kate. What will be, will be.

"That's absolutely fair enough," I say, cursing these rather stiff words. Then I move in for an air-kiss and wince as I make the exaggerated *Mwah!* sound.

Jesus! Definitely bedtime for me.

To my surprise, Scott doesn't go along with the air-kiss. Instead, he kisses me tenderly on the cheek. Tingles envelop my whole head, then fleetingly migrate south.

Convinced that my entire head has become a beetroot, I pull away and wonder if he might lean in for more. When he only smiles and steps back, I manage a painfully bashful *Goodnight*, before sloping off to my room.

By the time I roll onto the bed, I discover that I'm genuinely not tired. My thoughts race and I actually feel a touch giddy. I should enjoy this feeling and this moment, regardless of whether there truly is any connection between me and the intriguing wolf who's loped into my life from the bewildering . . . wilderness.

The bewilderness.

So! Kate, Kate, Kate. Here you are again, back in the darkness. Alone.

I wonder if other people internally heckle themselves. Surely this can't be normal. Thinking back, I suppose I developed the habit of self-criticism so that Mum never had a chance to get in there first. She never even knew, but she was robbed of the advantage of surprise.

As usual, this rabbiting voice of negativity takes some silencing, but eventually I drift away towards sleep.

The sound of scratching jerks me right back out of myself.

What the hell? Something is scratching at my window.

My fourth-floor window.

Should I be glad the curtains are closed or feel even more weirded out?

Could be anything out there. Anything at all. One of the floating vampire kids from Salem's Lot, *for instance. Why don't you take a look? Prove to yourself you really aren't afraid.*

I scrunch the bed covers around my head in the vain hope that the scratching will stop. Finally, pissed off with my own fear, I sweep them aside and head over to the window.

I inflate my chest with air, grip one curtain in each hand, then wrench them apart.

Two shiny black eyes stare in through the grimy glass.

As the squirrel races back off along the tree bough, I can't help wondering which of us had the bigger fright.

2 June

The early afternoon sun cooks the back of my head as Lizzie hands back my Nokia. Here's that familiar rush of grim excitement as I wonder how many calls and texts I've missed over the past two days. And here's the balancing downer of remembering how few real-life friends I have left. Everyone but Izzy and select social media pals backed away slowly in March, during The Great Rudolpho Trauma.

Historically, I'm Johnny-No-Mates anyway. From the playground of my first school onwards, I've developed an abrasive attitude that creates a lousy first impression and drives people away . . . because of course that makes total sense for someone who's terrified of being alone. Bravo, Kate, bravo. Keep on rejecting people before they have a chance to reject you.

Time for the grand parting of the ways. We've all done the morning nature ramble and worshipped the sun, both of which only exacerbated my hangover. The real night owls among us have eyes like piss-holes in snow.

We've had the farewell vegan lunch, so here's the crunchiest crunch time of all, given that Scott and I haven't exchanged contact details. What if he walks off into the sunset forever, like some desperado gunslinger who only ever works alone?

As Scott receives his phone back, he eyes my Nokia with amused respect. "You really weren't kidding. Old school."

I nod at his slick, black smartphone, housed in its protective case. "Feel relieved to get your baby back, do you?"

Shit. His baby. What if he's married with kids, and just fancied a harmless flirt this weekend? I've assumed so much here.

His brow dips as he considers my question. "Yes and no. I reckon you've made me think about a few things."

Have I, Scott? Have I, indeed . . . ?

"Oh yeah?" I say. "Good things, I hope."

"Definitely," he says. "I'm going to strictly ration my usage. Heard about this app that tells you how often you use your phone every day."

I can't help laughing. "What does it say about us all, that we now need an app to tell us that?"

"I know, it's proper deranged."

Everyone else is saying goodbye, thanking Lizzie profusely and heading to their vehicles. Scott's shrugging on his faux-fleece-collared jacket. Say something, Kate.

"So," I say, the absolute epitome of nonchalance, "did you mention that you're going to be in Leeds at some point?" I fake a puzzled frown. "Was it *you* who said that?"

That killer grin blinds me as he says, "Yeah! We should get together and celebrate being back in the city."

I can't help but notice that he says this as a statement, rather than a question. I like that. Confidence is hot and arrogance is not, but Scott has so far shown no trace of the latter. This feels refreshing in such an objectively good-looking creature.

My nod is breezy, easy, bordering on bored. "Yeah, perhaps we should."

"Are you on Facebook?" he says, then remembers. "Ah, no, you're not on anything."

"I do have this brand-new, experimental thing called SMS texting," I offer. "Also, the ability to project my voice over this device known as a telephone?"

"That sounds a bit cutting-edge for me, but I'm happy to give it a spin. What's your number?"

CHAPTER EIGHT

3 October

The cinnamon-sugar tang of fresh-cooked doughnuts collides with salty sea air. This heady brew wafts in through my window as I hit the roundabout in front of Brighton's Palace Pier.

Driving down here was easy enough. Once you've steered an ambulance at top speed through major cities, a steady flow of motorway traffic feels like small potatoes, but how I longed for the magic siren that makes everyone fuck off out of the way.

With my brain, hands and feet on auto, my mind has been free to get on with the important business of worrying itself sick. I became mentally absent on the M1, and during my lunch rest-stop, I questioned how much I really know about Scott Palmer.

Surely I know *enough*, don't I? I know how we connect so well. I know we have lots in common and our conversation never falters. I know we have the kind of sex that makes me fret about his neighbours complaining. And yet . . .

And yet . . .

Dark zones lurk outside our airtight bubble – huge areas of Scott's life that I've yet to fathom. The more I think about this, I realise he does evasiveness very well whenever I broach certain topics. It's like he senses what I'm about to ask, whether the question concerns friends, family, his past or . . . Jesus, practically anything personal at all.

I don't even know where he was born.

If the Kate-and-Scott bubble is Planet Earth, then the rest of Scott's life is the galaxy, vast and unknowable.

Shit.

Shit-fuck.

Shit-fuck-*shit*.

I know next to nothing about the man I'm supposed to be moving in with.

Traditionally when I arrive at the Palace Pier, my stomach does a happy flip. This is partly because I've always loved piers and seagulls and doughnuts, but mostly because it means I'm about to see Scott. This afternoon, my stomach flips through raw nerves.

I had already come to think of Brighton as my new home. Now that Scott's fallen out of contact, though, this city feels weirdly forbidden. Why do I feel like such a madwoman? I'm doing nothing wrong here. My boyfriend and I agreed I'd move in with him today, and here I am, albeit early. Surely my Stalky Psycho Rating has to be pretty low at this point. I mean, I'd estimate a mere three out of ten. It's Scott who's either being a useless dick, or is trapped under heavy furniture, or . . . or . . .

. . . is stone-cold dead.

Apparently, I now have my own parking space in the lot beneath Scott's apartment block, but of course he's not around to show me where it is, or how to get in. So I park up on the seafront and pay the meter. I cross Madeira Drive, heading for Marine Parade, where the Van Spencer building awaits me.

All curvy chrome and glass, this big sea-facing brute reminds me of a 1930s cruise ship. Despite having been here many times, I still have no idea which of the building's front windows and balconies correspond to Scott's place. Most of these flats are in darkness, but there are a few patches of light.

Guess I'll have to try the front entryphone, like every other random visitor.

Hello, moment of truth.

CHAPTER NINE

17 June

The third time I see Scott Palmer, his face is hideously distorted.

Having bagged us a table on the outside terrace of the River's Edge bar, he's draining the last of his ale from one of those old-fashioned jugs with handles. Because his face is all but obscured by the panelled glass, I recognise him only by his fleece-collared jacket.

This brick-walled warehouse-conversion struck me as a potentially romantic venue for our date, without being outrageously so, just in case this isn't actually a date. The River Aire lazily wends its way past the terrace, making for pleasant views. Admittedly, I could have chosen somewhere closer to my flat, not least because I might have crossed Leeds faster and actually got here on time. So now I'm wearing a thin film of sweat to complement my best date-jeans and somewhat low-cut top.

Scott says, "Ah, there she is." He puts down his drained glass and stands, his smile worryingly thin. Seems that my lateness really has pissed him off, until his grin breaks like sun through cloud. "I was *just* starting to wonder if I'd been blown out."

"Really sorry," I say, air-kissing him. No kiss on the cheek back this time – no doubt his impulse back at the retreat in Wales had been inspired by red wine. Sigh. "Let me get you another pint . . . unless you're about to flounce off?"

He scoffs at the suggestion. "Now you're actually *here*, I'll have a Crafty Fox."

As the drinking begins, we both seem on best first-date behaviour: all enthusiasm, positivity and wit. Can't help noticing, though, that Scott seems less cheery and carefree than he was during the retreat. That smile of his remains present, but doesn't always reach the eyes. Could he be more stressed now that he's back in civilisation – back in work mode? Now that it's just the two of us, he might feel as nervous as me, if that's even possible.

Or maybe you've already bored him with your talk of unpredictable working hours.

Silence, brain. He did *ask* about my job. Besides, neither of us seem overly concerned with discussing anything of great importance. Right now, we're talking about the fact that we both wear contact lenses.

Scott carefully removes his pint of Crafty Fox from our wobbly table. "Here's a fun fact for you," he says, between sips, "although you probably know this already. The average disposable contact lens user, over a period of fifteen years, ends up with an average of ten lost lenses permanently stuck to some part of their eyeballs."

"To be honest, that sounds distinctly . . . untrue."

Scott shakes his head, gently insistent. "It's a fact, I swear. A good friend of mine's an optician."

Could this actually be true? My own pint of Crafty Fox has already fuzzed my head. Really should've had more than a vegan sausage roll on the way here. Blinking rather a lot, I'm very conscious of the fact that (a) I've used lenses for almost twenty years, and (b) I'm now trying to detect anything chafing between my eyeballs and my eye sockets. "Jesus. Is that . . . ten on each eye?"

He seems to consider placing his pint back on the table, then puts it on the ground beside him instead. While using a folded beermat to fix the wobbly leg, he says, "No, five on each. I mean, it's an average. But it makes you think about all the times you've come home after a few shandies and only thought you'd removed your lenses. Oh! And most of those lost lenses end up around the *back* of the eye."

"Fuck off," I say, aware that this is watershed moment. Is Scott the kind of guy who minds being told to fuck off in public, even in disbelieving jest? Happily, he seems unfazed. We talk some more about whether contact lenses stuck to the back of your eyeball could actually have any negative health impact, then thankfully turn to films.

"So, Mr Palmer," I say, excited, hopeful, "what would be your favourite film ever?"

Sitting back in his seat, Scott goggles at this, quietly appalled. "Wow. That's pretty hard to narrow down. Do you know yours?"

"Of course. But I asked first."

"I'm still trying to think. It's between three or four movies. Maybe five."

"There can be only one," I insist. "And no, mine isn't *Highlander*. I mean . . . what's your ultimate desert-island movie?"

A flotilla of ducks drifts past our terrace as Scott stares into space. Lines multiply across his forehead until they resemble the front grill of a truck.

"I'm going to have to put the clock on you," I prompt, while thinking, *Please say* True Romance. *Please say* True Romance.

Scott makes a sound like a goose being strangled. Then he says, "*True Romance*."

I got chills, they're multiplyin'. "Jesus, that's mine too!"

He looks sceptical. "Really? You're not just saying that?"

"Why wouldn't it be my favourite film? It's got everything a person could ever *need*."

There follows an energetic burst of *True Romance* discussion. We rave about everything from the scene between Christian Slater as Clarence and Gary Oldman as drug-dealing pimp Drexl, to Dennis Hopper and Christopher Walken's big face-off, to the relative merits of the theatrical and alternate endings.

One drink later, Scott's phone rings. Sheepish, he pulls it from his pocket, apologising, but then we both laugh.

Scott's ringtone is Hans Zimmer's main orchestral theme from *True Romance*.

Well, spank my ass and call me Alabama, if Scott couldn't yet be my very own Clarence Worley.

The drinks and the conversation flow beautifully for the rest of the night. The eye contact becomes more and more lingering . . .

And then confusion reigns all over again.

Poor Izzy, having to hear all my crap in the early hours of the morning.

KATE
Sorry to be texting so late. Had to talk to someone! And you're always the first person I think of.

IZZY
no problem babe . . . was my fault for not muting my phone . . . haha . . . so did mr mixed messages not even kiss u tonight

KATE
Oh he kissed me all right . . . but only on the cheek.

IZZY
u do mean the cheek on your face right n not yr ass

KATE
Yes, sadly I do mean my facial cheek. Izzy, I have no idea if that was even a date.

IZZY
ok think i need the whole story

KATE
So after the bar, we were standing outside, doing that weird thing where you keep talking while waiting for one person to suggest going to a place with a bed. He didn't invite me to his hotel, so I thought fuck it, this isn't 1953, and I asked if he wanted to walk me home.

IZZY
jesus like u should even have to ask

KATE
Well, he did at least seem glad I asked . . . I think . . . and we walked across town. One good thing with Scott is, the chat never runs out. The only awkward moments come at the very end of the nights.

IZZY
so what happened when u got home

KATE
More awkwardness. We talked outside my flat for about TWO YEARS, and then I decided to grab the nettle.

IZZY
u decided to grab what

KATE
Grab the nettle. Have you never heard that expression?

IZZY
no

KATE
Why have you never heard of any expressions I ever say?

IZZY
cuz you make em up

KATE
I do not. Anyway, I decided to take the bull by the horns – you heard of that one?

IZZY
yes

KATE
I asked him in for a drink. And that's when he pulled his phone from his pocket, as if it had buzzed, but I didn't hear a buzz. He read the screen, looked apologetic and said he'd been "called". Apparently he's on a 24-hour call with his job, apparently, so he had to go back to his hotel.

IZZY
u just wrote apparently twice btw

KATE
That's rich, coming from someone who barely writes in English.

IZZY
haha . . . hmm ok n he just so happened to get "called" when u asked him in

KATE
What does it mean, Izzy? I think I know, but . . .

IZZY
what do u think it means

KATE
I'm one of those girls who guys sort of like, but not enough. I've had that before – when I can tell a guy can't fully decide if he fancies me.

IZZY
fuck off girl ur drop dead gorgeous

KATE
We both know that's not true. But what do you think happened there?

IZZY
hate to say it but maybe he has a gf/wife

KATE
Shit. Yeah, that did occur to me too. I'm gonna wait for him to get in touch next, if he even does. If we meet again, I'll either suss him out some more or just ask.

IZZY
straight talkin i like it . . . sounds like a plan

KATE
It does. But is it really an actual plan? WAIT, hold on . . .

IZZY
what what what

KATE
He just texted me . . . !

IZZY
tell me what he said right now bitch don't make me hobble over there

CHAPTER TEN

3 October

My hand actually trembles as I open the wooden box that houses the wall-mounted entryphone panel. Could I convincingly write off this tremble as being down to the cold?

Feels as if I'm about to ring the entryphone of a total stranger. I have the deeply weird sense that reality itself has shifted and Scott no longer exists – or no longer wants me to move in with him, which would amount to much the same thing.

Having entered the digits for Flat Twenty-Three, I hit Call and stare at the entryphone's speaker grill. A ringtone pipes out through this cluster of tiny holes in the stainless steel.

My heart fills my mouth.

Three rings later, Scott's wonderful warm voice bursts out of those holes.

He blurts, "Kate? Thank God! I'm so sorry, there's been this whole crazy thing going on where my phone totally stopped working. The whole thing just *died* and your number was only on my phone, nobody actually remembers numbers these days, do they, and . . . and . . . Anyway, *sorry*, come on up!"

Buzzzzz, clunk. Door opens electronically. Hooray, we live happily ever after.

Except none of this actually happens. This was only a stupidly optimistic scenario in my head.

What really happens is the entryphone keeps on ringing. Such a cold, empty, soulless sound.

How big is Scott's flat? I picture his bedroom, the part that's furthest away from the entryphone. I picture how long it would take for him to cover the L-shaped hallway corridor that leads to the door so he can grab the cream-coloured plastic handset off the wall-mounted cradle. Twenty seconds, max?

What if he's in the shower, or lounging in the bath?

Oh, you sad, sad person. Next, you'll seriously consider how he might be trapped under a fallen wardrobe.

The ringing stops and so does my breath. Did Scott pick up?

Nope, because now there's only this dead tone. The system must disconnect the line after a limited number of rings. The small LCD screen has reset itself to await new requests.

What the hell do I do now?

Could there really have been some kind of vastly coincidental comms breakdown – one that even includes the functionality of Scott's entryphone? He did mention deadlines when we last spoke, so he may have buried his head so deep in the sands of work that he's forgotten what day it is. And his entryphone could be on the blink.

Look, he's dead or he's dying or he hates you.

A powerful pocket of icy wind swoops in from the beach, as if urging me to leave right now. Maybe the wind even wants me to cancel The Beardie Boys, who've texted to say they're en route down from Leeds with all my boxes, and save myself any further embarrassment.

No. I'm sure there's still a perfectly good explanation for all of this.

Two, Three, Call.

The entryphone's ringtone witters on, while my fertile mind enters overdrive. What if Scott is secretly a druggie? Cocaine might be his bag, or even heroin. Yeah, what if he's a great big smackhead who's trying to quit but decided to have one more blowout for old time's sake before I moved in? And what if he got a little too enthusiastic while riding that horse and OD'd himself into oblivion?

Ack. Here's where my job's a real bitch. Because of course now I'm thinking about all the dead junkies I've encountered while at work. And that's just in the office.

Ha ha. Hello, I'm Kate Collins and I make jokes to stave off bad thoughts. Right now, though, that method isn't working so well because my brain presents me with a delightful dead-junkie montage video.

Cold, pale flesh. Blue lips and fingernails. Sightless pupils, the size of pinpricks.

Come to think of it, Scott did look pretty bloody pale, last time I saw him. What if he didn't really have a virus, like he claimed? What if he actually had the raging heroin-hungers and couldn't wait for me to leave so he could chase that dragon?

Keen to stem the panic that wraps sly tendrils around me, I stare at a seagull violating a sealed black rubbish bag with savage tugs of its beak. God, I admire seagulls so much. They care about nothing except food, squawking and flying about. A seagull would surely not give two feathery fucks if another seagull invited it to move into a nest then enigmatically disappeared.

An explosive clunk jangles my nerves as the front door bursts open.

A thin, jittery woman in her early thirties is leaving the building. She's pushing two babies in one wide pram, so I hold the door open for her. Having shredded the bin bag, the seagull delves inside. Time for me to do the same with the Van Spencer.

"Good timing," I say with a smile, and make to enter.

She holds up a hand to block my path. "I'm really sorry, but we have to keep strangers out."

A stranger. That's what you are here now, and that's all you'll ever be.

"Otherwise, homeless people get in," she goes on, "and drug people, and . . .'

Who does this woman think she is: Gandalf? *You shall not pass?* Her voice trails off and she looks awkward, as we both consider her implication that I resemble one of those people. And in truth, I don't look my best. Before leaving the Leeds flat, I'd pulled on the first practical, drive-comfy clothes that hadn't already been boxed. My favourite jumper with the big holes in it, saggy jeans and the most knackered trainers known to man. And now that my mascara's all runny from the rain, I probably resemble The Joker.

I approximate what I hope is a reassuring grin. "I'm sure you can make an exception for me, since I'm moving in today." But I speak these words with zero conviction, because I don't fully believe them. This sounds, for all the world, like the desperate ploy of someone who secretly needs to take a really big dump in the stairwell.

"Sorry," she says primly, "it's just the rules. I have to stick to the rules." Then she clunk-slams the big door, and her pram wheels rattle off along Marine Parade.

Fuck you, Gandalf. My quest ain't over yet.

CHAPTER ELEVEN

28 June

Soon as I emerge from the ticket barrier at Brighton train station, Scott slides one hand around my waist and presses his lips against mine.

Our first ever kiss really fucks me up, even though I totally knew it was going to happen.

Thanks to our nightly sext-a-thons, Scott and I have established our kissing preferences. We both like that gentler, teasing approach, the one that builds up to something hotter and hungrier. I suppose that's something in dirty digital comms' favour: you can work things out beforehand, rather than have the awkwardness of trying stuff the other person doesn't like.

Admittedly, sexting does rob you both of *that* super-special first night when you stay up together until 5 a.m., wondering if sex will happen. Mind you, those nights always stressed me out. I'm too old for them. And besides, Scott's tongue has brushed my top lip and my body's responding in no uncertain terms.

Couldn't care less how many commuters tut and growl as

they're forced to swerve past us. When you're falling for someone, it's like you shift into another dimension. Nothing else matters, besides staying there.

Did I just say *falling for someone*?

Careful, Kate. You might just be Scott's bit of fluff, or even his northern mistress.

Our sext-life began in the early hours of 18 June, when Scott texted to thank me for our apparently *awesome* date in Leeds. Having sunk a few drinks, and feeling I had little to lose but my dignity, I decided to test the temperature of the water between us. The salacious screen-tapping started moderately enough, when I instigated a general discussion of bedtime behaviour. The importance of kissing, for instance, and how it's as intimate as sex itself.

Only a few exchanges later, the floor of our politeness collapsed, plunging us both into a swamp of depravity.

One minute we were indulging in fairly witty oral sex innuendo, the next it was all *take you deep* this and *push your legs apart* that. This chat provided much-needed relief in more ways than one, because I finally knew Scott was into me.

How weird to share intimacy from afar, before it actually happens in the flesh. When you next meet the person, you feel as though you've already slept with them. And if the true value of a relationship lies in the mental connection, which it clearly does, then for all intents and purposes you really *have* slept with them.

One thing's for sure, it's the safest sex you can get.

After our first sext-fest, I asked Scott why he hadn't already tried to do all these lewd things to me in person. There followed a five-minute gap between messages – the kind of pause that would be downright bizarre in person – before he replied, *I suppose I'm a bit of an old-fashioned guy*.

Hmm. Not a bad answer, so I let that pass. Especially as he then asked if I fancied *a visit to the seaside*. Apparently I was *very welcome* to stay at his place. Given the utter filth we'd hurled at each other, this made me cackle. All of a sudden, we were back to being quite formal. After typing *fuck yessss* at the climax of our little chat, Scott had remembered his manners.

At least we resisted the temptation to swap pictures of body parts. You really do have to hold something back for an actual up-close-and-personal meet.

I mean, the cleavage shot I sent him obvs doesn't count.

A stocky businessman with the classic alcoholic's nose storms through the ticket barrier. On his way past us, he rams into Scott's shoulder and mutters, "Out of the way." Having been spun around a quarter turn, Scott throws this suit the evil eye . . .

. . . *the eye of the wolf* . . .

. . . then returns his attention to me. It takes a moment for those eyes to cool down and regain their twinkle, as he slips his fingers between mine.

"Welcome to my city," he says. "I've alerted the mayor, who's granted us full use of the keys this evening."

Travelling light, I only have a backpack, but Scott carries it anyway. He leads me to a road that slopes down beneath the station forecourt itself. After passing through a faintly magical rainbow-lit subway, our short walk to a lovely pub called the Foundry is punctuated by stolen kisses and increasingly keen hands.

Scott surprises me by having booked an astonishing three-course vegan Italian meal, cooked to perfection by chefs Two Wolves. Wow, this all feels very much worth the wait. Mr Palmer's old-fashioned approach may have its merits after all.

The streets blur as we walk hand in hand to the Basketmakers Arms. Here, we seek out corner seats that allow us to sit as close together as humanly possible. Small but perfectly formed, this place has ancient tobacco tins stuck to the wall. Inside these tins lurk various handwritten messages, left behind by patrons. You never know what you're going to get. Could be anything from a crudely drawn cock 'n' balls (sometimes with jizz arcing up from the head, sometimes not – it all depends on each artist's individual sensibilities) to a deeply profound philosophical statement, most likely committed to paper somewhere around last orders.

Stupid though most of these messages are, something about their physical nature, together with the atmosphere of the night, feels like the true antidote to living inside my phone. More than ever, I'm convinced I was right to embrace the humble Nokia.

Scott pops open one of the tins, then goggles comically at the message inside.

"Well," he says. "This is new."

He turns the paper around to show me. Spidery writing announces: *You Will Die*, accompanied by a badly drawn skull.

We laugh uproariously, what with being four or five drinks down.

"Not exactly the most incredible prediction," I say. "Technically it's true." Oh yes, you can always rely on Kate Collins to infuse any given hot date with a reminder of death's inevitability.

Scott nods, and rips up the message. "Wouldn't want anyone else seeing this," he says. "Might freak them out." He places his hand over mine on the table. "But even if I did die tonight, I reckon I'd be a happy man."

"No one's dying here," I say, trying to downplay my reaction to his drunkenly romantic gesture. "We're in the prime of our lives."

Of course, as we clink our ale jugs, my brain decides to show me a rapid-fire montage of all the people I've seen who've died in the very prime of their lives.

Scott arches an eyebrow. "So, if I've got a few years left in me yet, that means there's no hurry for us to get back to mine and get more comfortable . . . right?"

I become the human embodiment of the pondering emoji. "Actually, you do look peaky. Trust me, I'm a paramedic . . ."

CHAPTER TWELVE

3 October

When I reach Floor Five, the lift stutters to a begrudging halt, as requested. The door makes three abortive attempts to open, as if testing my nerve, before finally giving way.

I scurry outside before the lift changes its mind. Determined to ignore all the foreboding I feel, I yank open the fire door that leads to Flat Twenty-Three. Beyond this door, the darkness forms a solid block until overhead lights auto-flicker on.

During the short walk to Twenty-Three, I pass two silent flats, one of which has an Amazon package propped up against the door. Here in the mid-afternoon, most people are still at work. When I dialled random flat numbers from outside and pretended to be a courier, I was lucky to find one resident who sounded too jaded to argue and buzzed me inside.

Could Scott really be doing the Unbelievably Pathetic Man Thing of holing himself up and hoping I'll eventually get the message? How could he possibly think that hiding away will work? He knows I'm travelling 265 miles with all my stuff. Yeah, if he really has done the UPMT, then this will plumb new depths of pathetic.

My mouth dries up as the door comes into view. Styled like a wolf, the metal knocker looks stolen from some gothic mansion. A thick ring dangles from the lower jaw.

Remember how cool you thought this was, the first time you saw it?

I grab the metal ring again and bash it against the door, making a sound like a machine gun. *Rat-a-tat-tat-tat-tat-TAT.*

Hurricane Collins, in the house.

As I wait for a response, I notice the spyhole lens at eye-level. Can't help imagining Scott tip-toeing up to the door to peer out, and silently mouthing the words *Oh fuck.* And now he might be frozen there on the other side of the wood, like a Fyre Festival organiser, praying I'll go away if he simply waits this out.

Not gonna happen, my friend.

What if he seriously is dead in there? What if I'm *rat-a-tat-tatting* to Scott's corpse, all twisted up in rigor mortis, having expired the day before yesterday?

My attention drifts down to the letterbox.

Here's a magic portal, offering me the power to see inside the flat.

My brain wants to look. My heart remains undecided. My stomach is clearly dead set against the idea.

The brain wins. Age-old minor injuries jangle me as I kneel in front of the door and place one hand on either side of the letterbox's polished silver metal flap. Come on, Kate: pretend you're on duty. This may as well be any other job.

Only problem is, my hands won't work. I tell them to lift the flap, but they can't or won't. I'm too scared of what I might see inside.

For fuck's sake. I have nothing to be afraid of. For the last time: the guy's not dead; he's almost certainly just a dick.

Dick, not dead.

Fine, not funeral.

Breathe in through the nose, then out through the mouth.

I place one thumb on each side of the metal flap, then hinge it all the way up.

Two keen, bright eyes stare back at me from inside.

Two *human* eyes. No fucking squirrel.

Somewhere overhead there's a soft *click*, then all the lights die.

Rigid with fear, I shove myself hard away from the door.

This loud, harsh *clap* sounds like the letterbox swinging shut.

This strangled cry seems to be coming from me. Hope so, anyway.

Having fallen back through total darkness, I land on the small of my back. The word *coccyx* flashes uselessly through my head, even as dull sparks light up my spine.

Fuck. *Fuck.* Who was that inside? That didn't look like Scott. And why was this person so ready for me to look through the letterbox? Like they were waiting there . . .

Hate this darkness, fucking hate it, but I need to get a grip. This is nothing more than a temporary absence of light.

Yes, but it also reminds you of the coma. You'll never be free of that memory, no matter how hard you try.

Shut up, brain. This is no time to bring up the whole coma thing.

I reach around, trying to find a wall. Something to help me get my bearings. Up above, another soft *click* heralds the lights flickering back on. This building's management company must be so hell-bent on cutting costs that their system kills the lights if you don't move for a certain period of time. Wonderful.

Those looked very much like a woman's eyes, didn't they? Well, she's messing with the wrong stroppy bitch.

Even if she turns out to be Scott's wife?

Back on my feet, I feel even more stupid than when I arrived. And feeling stupid always makes me angry, so I smash the wolf ring against the door until it dents the wood. Then I get straight back onto my knees, like an actual adult who isn't scared of what they might see inside, or of the stupid dark that might return.

I do not hesitate in yanking this damn flap all the way up.

Shit! The eyes again. Staring right at me.

I'm about to open my mouth, to say Christ knows what, when those eyes blink at the same time as mine.

Oh.

My.

God.

These eyes blink at the same time as mine, because they're *my own fucking eyes*.

The letterbox consists of two metal flaps, one on either side of the door. The inner flap is still down, and the polished metal reflects my idiot stare right back at me.

This mirror face of mine contorts into a hysterical gurn because I'm actually laughing. Silent, mad, incredulous mirth at how ludicrous I've been.

There never was some maniac on their knees on the other side of this door.

Well, actually, there still could be. You haven't lifted the inner flap yet.

Oh, do fuck right off.

Lift both flaps, then. Go on, I dare you.

I press my forehead up against the outer flap, to keep it hinged upright. Then I shove my fingers through the letterbox and prise open the inner one.

On the other side of the door, no eyes lie in wait for me. So that's something.

Inside, the lights are off. The hall runs straight ahead, away from this door, and halfway along its right-hand side there's an ornate archway that leads to the living room. The balcony curtains must be open through there, because the piss-yellow of street lamps drizzles in through this arch to splash the opposite wall. If it wasn't for this faint external light, I might have seen nothing at all through this letterbox. Beyond the arch, the hall continues all the way to the dimly visible bathroom door, before turning off to the right.

This really does look and feel like no one's home. But if Scott freaked out, and/or became lost in some personal crisis, and he knew I was coming, he would turn out the lights and curl up in a ball somewhere. Wouldn't he? Is that something Scott Palmer would do?

I don't know. You tell me – you're the one who thought you knew the guy well enough to move in with him, for Christ's sake.

I study the hallway with intent. Something's different here, but I can't put my finger on what.

I scan for any movement at all. Any tiny change in the shadows or the light. Any signs of life.

Oh, the number of times I've done this exact thing while on the job. Calling through the letterbox to people who live by themselves. People who've phoned us but now aren't answering their door and have gone worryingly quiet, or—

What was that? What the fuck was that?

Something *moved* on the left-hand wall. The one facing the sea.

One of those shadows moved. No doubt about that.

Stop shivering! Mostly likely, a seagull swooped past outside and briefly obscured one of the street lamps. I mean, what did you think this was, jackass: one of those spooky ghosts *you don't believe in?*

Wow. I've barely even thought about ghosts since I was a petrified little kid in my room. When you're small, the night is alive with possibility and shadows can hide anything. Then you grow old, you become a paramedic and reality chases any thought of the paranormal right out the door. You become less concerned about the shadows in the corners of rooms and worry much more about the shadows in the soul of man.

A new *click* from above heralds the second death of the lights out here.

I could wave my arms around to turn them back on, but there's no need. This is only darkness and I do not fear it.

Not sounding nearly as tough as I wanted them to, my words sail through the letterbox and into the gloom of the flat. "Scott? Look, are you in there? It's . . . me . . . obviously."

Such heroic work. Why don't you just bleat at him, like the lost lamb you are? Yeah, why don't you go right ahead and bleat, Please don't leave me all alone*?*

Again, I eagle-eye the corridor walls for signs of movement. This time, there's nothing.

Nothing at all. May as well be calling into a crypt.

Inspiration strikes. I pull out my Nokia, then speed-dial Scott's number. If he's hiding inside, his own phone might ring and give him away.

My phone's crude onscreen animation confirms it's calling Scott. Dumping the handset on the carpet beside me, I listen intently through the letterbox.

No ringing from inside. Of course, he could have muted his phone.

The harsh hiss of Scott's voice makes me jump half out of my skin.

Cursing myself for being so skittish, I pick my phone back up from the floor and shove it against my ear. This outgoing voicemail message is one I've heard all too many times since Scott went incommunicado. He sounds crisp, professional, generic.

Very little like the funny guy I'd planned to spend forever with. *I can't answer the phone right now, but please blah blah blah.*

Injecting steel into my voice, I yell through the letterbox. "Scott, I swear to Christ, if you're hiding in there . . ."

There follows an intensely silent pause.

I add, "This is your last chance to open the door. You've got ten seconds."

Has he really? What are you going to do, exactly? Kick the door in?

You know what, brain? I fucking will. I don't consider myself bound by the same rules as I am while working – the rules that forbid us from forcing entry into someone's home, unless we can physically see someone's collapsed and breaking in might save their life, or if they stop crying for help, or if we see something like blood through the letterbox.

Those may be my work rules, but this is my life. My boyfriend could be slowly bleeding to death, all over that polished wooden living room floor. His final breath could be imminent. So, however much this act might boost my Stalky Psycho points, it's entirely possible that breaking into Scott's flat might be in his best interest.

Stepping back a few paces, I stare at the door as if trying to psyche it out.

I shift my weight back onto my left foot, then slam the heel of my right boot above the lock, just as the lights die again.

CHAPTER THIRTEEN

28 June

Chock-full of ale and fresh sea air, I feel truly in the moment. As Scott and I approach the super-impressive Van Spencer building, I'm aware of every gull's cry. Every gust of wind, heavy with the acid reek of vinegar. Every thump of techno from the rainbow-festooned bar next door.

Mindfulness can be achieved post-1980, after all. Certainly, as we pilot the lift up towards Scott's man-cave, I'm very much mindful that we are finally going to have sex.

Yeah, tonight's the night. Hopefully not in a *Dexter* way, though. If I walk into Scott's flat and see the walls and floor covered in plastic sheeting, I'm straight on the next train back to Leeds. Also: if he turns all *old-fashioned* on me for a third time and offers to sleep on the sofa, there will be ructions.

Without warning, Scott leans in for a kiss. Pressing me up against the mirrored wall, he breathes hot against my neck and slides one hand down the front of my jeans.

Whoa, that escalated fast. Is he about to pull the movie trick of stopping the lift between floors? Does he actually want to have sex in here?

Do I want to have sex in here?

As great as this hand – and specifically these fingers – might feel, probably not. Apart from any other considerations, this lift hardly offers the most flattering light in which you'd want someone to see you naked for the first time.

We reach the fifth floor, the doors go *ping* and Scott whips his hand out of my jeans, like we're about to get caught in the act by a traumatised vicar astride a bicycle.

Keys jangle in his hand as he leads the way to the door to Number Twenty-Three. When I catch up, he's unlocking the deadbolt. Then he sticks another key into the smooth silver door handle. With his face still flushed from our lift play, he says, "You ready?"

Can't say I care for him treating me like some wide-eyed *Pretty Woman* hooker. *Okay Scott, I get it, you live in a fancy flat by the sea*. But I'm also horny, so I meet his smile and raise him a smirk. "Ready for what?"

A very cool wolf knocker glares at me from the door, as if providing the answer.

Scott opens up to reveal a long corridor punctuated only by a fancy archway and an elegant table that holds an abstract marble sculpture.

Together, we take a right-turn through the arch, and what I see takes my breath away.

CHAPTER FOURTEEN

3 October

I take a right-turn through the arch, and what I see takes my breath away.

Behind me in the hall I've busted into, the door hangs open. Must have been on the latch, because it gave way easily and without damage.

So the only thing broken here is my heart.

How am I supposed to process what I'm seeing?

CHAPTER FIFTEEN

28 June

The warm night hugs me. I'm wearing only my favourite oversized post-sex T-shirt and my face still prickles warm. The muscles in my legs feel like they barely exist as I drink in the incredible, panoramic view that stole my breath, what, two hours ago now? Who knows, who cares.

Out here on the decking of Scott's open-air balcony, the volatile sea feels a mere stone's throw away. A gull flies past, heading over to the far right, where the Palace Pier juts out over the water in all its attention-grabbing glory. Wind hauls the bird off target, aiming it instead towards the far left, where an audience has assembled at a big-screen beach cinema. I can catch enough snippets of the movie to identify it as *Jaws*. Ha, nice.

Swept backwards but not to be deterred, the gull ends up flying off over the zip-wire tower that sits directly across from this flat. A white spiral staircase corkscrews up to the scarily high platform.

Scott's balcony comfortably holds a table, two garden chairs and an old barbecue. The ceiling is provided by the underside of the balcony above. The cigarette smoke of Saturday night revellers somehow manages to waft five floors up here from Marine Parade.

Behind me, through a whole row of floor-to-ceiling windows, the flat's interior continues to impress. Throughout the living room and the adjoining open-plan kitchen, dimmer-switch spotlights make the chrome and marble wink. There's so much empty space across those wooden floorboards, you could ride a bike around in circles.

A huge slimline TV hangs on the wall. Swish cordless speakers have been stationed around the whole room, for the full 7.1 experience. Strictly curated Perspex racks display favoured Blu-rays and DVDs. A gooseneck lamp cranes over the back of a cream faux leather sofa, as if waiting to spy on the occupant. Every single object in the living room serves a specific purpose, which makes me kind of hate Scott for his organised restraint. He must never ever visit my flat before I've carried out a major tidy-up job.

Rejecting such a stressful thought, I lose myself in the sea and this gorgeous floaty feeling. Oh yeah, the stud Scott Palmer was worth waiting for. He certainly didn't seem so old-fashioned when we snogged on the sofa and then ended up on his bed.

Beyond the orgasms, though, lay something else. Something that immediately felt deeper and even more intimate.

Behind me, the window-door that connects the living room to this balcony slides open. Brief footfall on the decking heralds Scott's arrival before he hands me a drink, wraps his arms around my waist and plants his chin on my right shoulder.

We *fit together*, don't we? This kind of dovetail match feels so unusual for a new coupling. So very promising.

"Do you trust me?" he whispers in my ear, then hums Celine

Dion's "My Heart Will Go On". We share a chuckle at our *Titanic* recreation, then slip into a shockingly comfortable silence. Together, we watch the black ocean explode onto the beach, over and over, powered by a crescent moon.

My very own Leo DiCaprio may cement the end of my digital addiction. Everything seems so perfect, right down to us having met so randomly at the detox retreat. Like it was all meant to be . . .

Let's not carried away, though. We've had sex, not a wedding. Let's keep everything in perspective here.

Ah, fuck that – I demand to embrace the moment.

I demand to embrace this night.

I'm the queen of the world.

CHAPTER SIXTEEN

3 October

What I am, is the queen of WTF.

The queen of the bewilderness.

The queen of churning guts.

Scott's flat always had a minimalist look. And yet, little more than three months after our cheeseball *Titanic* moment, this place looks minimalist to the nth degree.

Swaying beneath the archway that connects the hall to this wide living space, I am a delicate Victorian dame in need of smelling salts.

I would sit heavily on Scott's faux leather sofa, but I can't, because it's not here anymore. I would perch on one of his high-backed chairs, but there are none of those to be seen either.

There is *nothing here*.

Zero. Nada. Zilch.

Every stick of furniture, the TV, the desk, the PC, all of Scott's possessions . . . they're gone, all gone. Only the fixtures and fittings remain.

I seize upon the idea that all this emptiness must be a weird optical illusion perpetrated by the ailing sun and the salmon-pink sky. So I flick a switch on the wall, but none of the lights come on. When I try another switch, back through the archway, the hall stays drenched in black. Here, I realise what had seemed different when I peered in through the letterbox. The display table and its marble sculpture have gone.

This must be what people mean by an out-of-body experience. Feels like only my mind is moving around the flat, while my body stays put in the living room.

Reaching the L-shaped bend in the dark hallway corridor, I float inside the large bathroom and take in the bare sink. The metal rails where towels once hung. The parched, empty mouth of the medicine cabinet. I tug a long dangling cord by the door, but the overhead bulb fails to respond.

The flat is cold, and yet I feel hot, too hot by half. When I spin one of the sink taps and water pours out, I gratefully splash some on my wrists, then the back of my neck.

Out in the hall, the airing cupboard greets me with four blank, white shelves. Which only leaves the bedroom to check.

Gingerly, I grasp the door handle, then hesitate in darkness.

Droplets of cold water trickle down my spine as variants of Scott's corpse present themselves to me.

Scott, hanging by his neck from the overhead Mediterranean-style fan, his tongue bulging grotesquely between his lips.

Scott, blue in the face, slumped stiff on the carpet with a syringe hanging out of his arm, wearing the shocked grimace of a man who did not expect to die today.

Scott, murdered in countless ways, all straight out of OTT horror films. Bludgeoned to death. Strangled until his eyes popped out. Beheaded with an axe . . .

Or this may be worse than anything you ever saw, in reality or onscreen.

Stop. Please stop. Let's open the door and get this over with.

I clear my head to the best of my ability.

Then I twist the handle, push the door inwards and reveal the room.

CHAPTER SEVENTEEN

28 June

This no longer feels like a room at all. This space has become the eye of a storm.

The perfect storm.

Inside me for the first time, Scott thrusts hard enough to shunt the bed against the wall. My calves cushion his bare shoulders, even though I didn't know I could achieve such flexibility. Go, me.

Without breaking rhythm, Scott eases my legs back even further, so that his face is directly over mine. Sweat drips from his forehead and lands on my cheek.

He and I haven't talked about an actual relationship yet, but now our eyes lock and I feel owned. Usually I end up with my eyes closed, afraid to show myself, but straight away Scott and I connect. I mean, we really connect, like we're gazing straight into each other's souls and feeling comfortable with what we see.

This feels a shade unnerving, but also pretty damn awesome.

As Scott pushes me closer and closer to oblivion, a feral smile stretches his lips. His eyes glow. And yet, during those frantic breaths before he follows me over the edge, that wolf mask slips to reveal the vulnerable guy from Tinder.

I can see that he feels owned, too.

CHAPTER EIGHTEEN

3 October

Here's the calm after the storm.

The sole evidence that the bed was ever here comes courtesy of the four carpet marks left behind by those fancy metal feet.

Both side tables: gone.

Walk-in wardrobe: empty.

I can't believe this barren space is the same room in which Scott and I created our bubble. Surely this cannot be the safe haven which rendered the outside world an afterthought. I wonder briefly if I've broken into the wrong flat, but then I remember the unique wolf knocker. Besides, Flat Twenty-Three is definitely the one to which I sent Scott's birthday card, two months back.

Floating back along the hallway, I struggle to comprehend the sheer *nothingness* of the whole flat.

Trying to grasp what's happened here feels like trying to grab smoke.

By the time I've completed my circuit back to the living

room, I'm determined to remain calm and positive. It seems so far-fetched that Scott really would bail on our relationship, especially in such a ridiculously extreme manner. I simply cannot bring myself to believe it. I won't.

My eye flounders around in the nothingness once again . . .

. . . before being lured to the *thing* on the sliding door that leads to the grey, windswept balcony.

CHAPTER NINETEEN

5 July

Out on the sun-splashed balcony, seated on plastic garden chairs, Scott and I mop up the final mouthfuls of lunch. We'd tossed a couple of Quorn burgers onto the old barbecue that sits out here. The metal case may be thinly barnacled with salt after years of sea-facing service, but the grill handles the burgers and buns well enough.

When you gaze at the strips of beach on either side of the pier, you see more bare human flesh than stones. The media are calling this Britain's most extreme heatwave. If I was still on Twitter, I'd see environmentalists using this fact as climate-change ammo, while idiots fire bullets of sheer denial back at them. Two distinct perspectives that can never meet in the middle. Another unwinnable social media war, in which each side tries to show their followers how well they're doing in the argument by retweeting the opposition and adding their own withering putdown. *Look everyone, I'm totally owning this guy! How great am I?* I've used that technique myself, many times. I've returned to my phone endlessly to see how many Likes and RTs I've scored, while awaiting the opposition's latest salvo with a thrilled kind of terror.

Now, though, the very thought of my smartphone resting on our black plastic lunch table and pumping out notifications? Makes me cringe. I'm so happy to be free of that tragic, self-perpetuating insanity.

You protest too much. You're dying for dopamine right now.

I genuinely believe I'll never go back to the insanity, now that I have Scott. He checks his own smartphone a fair deal, but mainly for work, so that's okay.

As we carry our plates back off the balcony and into the flat, I notice faded white marks on the glass of the sliding door, highlighted by sunshine. More sea-salt? No, these marks are on the inside.

Since I don't actually live here, I keep my tone lightly teasing as I say, "Baby, when did you last wipe this door?" Yes, we've already progressed to the affectionate nickname stage of our relationship, even though we've yet to get any more creative than *Baby*.

"That pen's supposed to clean off completely," Scott says. "Maybe I'm skimping on the elbow grease."

Sensing my puzzlement, he adds, "Oh, sometimes I draw on the window during my work breaks. It's really good to shift posture from time to time. Ergonomics and stuff. Plus, it's relaxing. Wanna try?"

Standing right in front of the giant whirring fan that Scott has positioned in the living room, I enjoy the sweat evaporating on my skin. "Oh God, you're kidding, I can't draw for toffee. Couldn't even draw if you offered me fudge. Mmm, fudge. We need to go back to that amazing fudge place in The Lanes."

As Scott dumps our plates into the spotless sink, he says,

"Pretty sure I've still got *two* of these pens I use to draw on the window . . ."

"Seriously," I protest, "I couldn't even draw a square. Please don't make me embarrass myself."

Rinsing off our plates, Scott calls over: "See if there are a couple of big white marker pens on my desk? They're liquid chalk."

With some reluctance, I abandon the fan. First thing I see on Scott's meticulously tidy desk is a pamphlet covered in writing. Looks like an old A-Z booklet that people would once use to physically write other people's addresses on, back in, oh, the 1920s. This one has been repurposed and appears to be covered with . . . a whole load of his online passwords.

Memorise them. Memorise them all.

Hey, brain, stop that shit. I have no need to know my boyfriend's passwords.

Yeah, but need and want can be two very different things . . . Plus, if he's left this info sitting here, he's practically asking for it.

"Can you see them?" Scott's voice yanks me back to what I'm supposed to be doing. Forgetting the password pamphlet, I return to the sliding door with a big white marker pen in each hand. Joining me, Scott takes one. "We can do something where you don't need to be able to draw. You only need to be able to copy, to trace."

He heaves the sliding door shut, muffling the sounds of traffic and the infuriating plinky-plonky musical busker camped out on the seafront. Then he explains that we're going to draw onto the window what we see outside.

I still take some persuading, but Scott makes us both a gin and slimline tonic, then twists the fan around to face the sliding door. The final convincer comes when he strips down to his shorts and encourages me to do the same.

Having begun on the left-hand side of our glass canvas, I draw around the outline of the zip-wire tower, then the wire itself. Must remember not to stick the tip of my tongue out of one side of my mouth. Not sexy.

Scott takes on the more intricate job of etching Brighton Pier, plus the four yacht-like masts that poke up out of the Harvester restaurant. He also handles the jagged line where the sea meets the beach, which I quite fancied doing myself, because I'm rather getting into this.

"Don't do the horizon," I warn him. "I want to do that part."

"Do it together?" he suggests.

As I trace the horizon from east to west, Scott goes west to east. Together, stripped down to our bare essentials and hammered by blissfully cool air, the nibs of our pens finally come together.

Out here in the real world, two different perspectives actually can meet in the middle.

CHAPTER TWENTY

3 October

Drawn with white marker pen on the glass of this sliding door is a rudimentary cartoon face, the size of a dustbin lid. I've only noticed this bizarre vision now because the last gasp of sunset has blazed in through the glass, a fierce orange, as if setting the face on fire.

This face has empty circles for eyes. A scarecrow nose, shaped like a capital "V".

What really hits me, though, is the broad mouth, with the mocking, half-moon grin.

Not feeling quite so calm and positive now, are we? Scott's laughing at you. And you know damn well it was him who drew this.

How I'd love to disagree with myself.

I contemplate this demonic vision for as long as I can bear. What the fuck is this supposed to mean?

Even as I watch, these last embers of light fade, leaving the face a little less Satanic, as if encouraging me to keep an upbeat, open mind. Without even realising, I've placed both hands on top of my head with the fingers interlaced. Self-consciously, I drop them back down by my sides.

Okay. Time to take stock.

My boyfriend clearly hasn't died of a heroin overdose, or I would have already discovered his corpse. And there's surely no way he's been murdered, or kidnapped, or any of that dramatic stuff I'd feared. Not unless his assailants had the entire flat cleared afterwards as an elaborate middle finger to forensic experts.

On closer inspection, the place actually hasn't been cleaned. There's still plenty of grime and dust, plus a few decaying scraps in the fridge. Hold on . . . what if Scott's heroin addiction made him sell everything?

Okay, okay, Little Miss Drama Queen: we can surely abandon the "heroin" line of enquiry, no matter how ropey Scott's looked of late. But what if he's in debt and has felt too ashamed to tell me? This would make me question how much of a connection we really had, but it would also beat him having walked out on me, or yanking the rug out from under my feet with a mean-spirited leer.

What exactly is this face on the sliding door, if not a mean-spirited leer?

Drifting back out through the front door, I pop open a small cupboard to reveal the flat's electrical fuse box. While studying the row of switches, hoping in vain to spot the odd one out, I try to imagine what kind of pressure might have grown inside Scott as my big move neared. What if debt weighed upon him until he ran for the hills, or work tipped him into a full nervous breakdown? He could be in hospital somewhere. Like I told Izzy: who would even know to notify me if Scott was—

A noise like the end of the world blares out of the flat and shakes my bones.

Jesus. This must be the entryphone handset, mounted on the wall inside the front door.

Could this be Scott, buzzing up? Even though we never arranged a time, is it possible that he's sold all his furniture to make room for the few bits of mine I've brought? Maybe he wants us to buy a whole load of new stuff together? Did he want to surprise me with this fresh start?

Yeah, right. So he sold his desk, his PC, all his books and his Blu-rays too – even the towels in the airing cupboard – so that the pair of you can choose new ones. Get real! Also, if this really is Scott, then why would he need to ring the entryphone? Don't tell me: he's lost his own keys?

Oh. I know who this must be. My fucking removal men.

The entryphone blares again.

What do I say to these people, who have faithfully ferried my stuff all the way from a city in which I almost certainly should have stayed, to a brand-new city where I know precisely no one except Scott? Can I really tell them to perform a great big U-turn?

The only person I know who would willingly harbour my stuff for a while would be Izzy, if her place wasn't already so cramped. Besides, I *know* Scott would show up the very minute I gave these people the order.

No retreat, no surrender. I'm going to stay here and find out what the hell's going on.

The buzzer sounds a third time. Drawing on every Zen technique I know, I slam the electrical cupboard shut.

When I pick up the entryphone, I'm still hoping to hear Scott's voice, but nope, it's The Beardie Boys all right. Against all odds, my voice comes out calm and collected, like it belongs to someone else. "Hi, sorry, I was in the shower. Will buzz you in now."

Denial, that's what I need. The magic ingredient to get me through the next hour.

Everything is fine. Everything is great, in fact, because I'm moving into this wonderful seaside flat with my utterly knowable soulmate, who definitely hasn't vanished after daubing Satan on the window.

While waiting for the guys to get up here, I spy a few keys dangling from hooks above the entryphone. Only takes me a few seconds to confirm that two of these fit the door. No doubt a third fits the building's main entrance, so at least something's going my way.

For how long will you need these keys, though? For how long do you plan to stay? Should you even be here right now?

The act of faking a smile and a sunny demeanour, I've read, can trick your brain into feeling happier. So when The Beardie Boys show up, I fire some cheery small talk their way, apologise for the lack of lighting, then disappear. While they haul my boxes up from the foyer, I camp out on the balcony with the sliding door shut firmly behind me. Need to reassemble my head and work out the next move.

The garden chairs and table have gone, of course, so I've dragged one of my boxes outside. Here, on this impromptu cardboard seat, I can contemplate the sea in vague comfort. The barbecue's been taken, too. But for Christ's sake, by whom? If not Scott, then was it bailiffs? Implausibly thorough burglars?

When I dial 100 to call an actual old-school operator, I picture them sitting bored, playing solitaire or a doing a crossword, then greeting the ringing phone with stunned surprise. Feels like I've hopped back in time to the nineties, but thanks to my humble Nokia, an operator is my only means of contacting the local hospitals.

No one's willing to tell me if they have any record of a Scott

Palmer on their wards. Apparently, I've failed to pass their security procedure, despite having given them this flat's correct address and his date of birth. Thought I knew the latter, because we celebrated Scott's thirty-seventh birthday on 3 August, but apparently I was wrong.

Hmm. A guy on Tinder lying about his age? Whoever would have expected that?

Everyone except gullible old Collins here.

With a hollow sigh, I dump the Nokia back on my lap. Sparse tufts of snow drift down over Marine Parade. I'd planned to bring a frosty bottle of champagne, so that Scott and I could sit out here and toast our new domestic union. I'd pictured better weather and an overwhelmingly magical sense of Everything's Finally Going To Be All Right. Moving into this flat was going to fix me like a Coldplay song.

With the benefit of hindsight, I can see this was one big ask. But why couldn't it have happened anyway? Why couldn't something truly great have happened to me?

Because you're not worth it.

Because you don't deserve it.

Because you're never enough to keep any one man hanging around for too long. The likes of Andy, Calvin, Zane, Rory, Rudolpho and now Scott, they all had the true measure of you.

Shut up, brain. This could still be all right. Scott might still turn up and explain everything. He may have temporarily freaked the hell out, then changed his mind. We could still work with that.

Dream on, you worthless sack of shit. Scott Palmer's movin' on up. Eat his dust.

I pull the collar of my jacket tight, trying to forget about my numb face and hands. I should call the police. What if it turns out that Scott really has been abducted, or something equally unlikely, and all I've done is sit here on the balcony until I froze solid?

Still feels too soon to dial 999. The police would only try and gently break it to me that my boyfriend's flown the coop.

Back on the Nokia, I speed-dial Scott one more time. There's no way he'll pick up, but that's not why I'm calling. I need to leave him a new voicemail, in which I take a different approach. Over the last twenty-four hours, the messages I've left have become aggravated, but now I need to assure him that, no matter what, he can speak to me. If he's in trouble, we can work this out together. He doesn't have to hide from me like this.

Sure, go ahead and debase yourself. See if I care.

As the line connects, I rehearse the words in my head. I'm going to sound as calm and as loving as I possibly can. In case it helps, I'll even call him *baby* and I'll—

From out of nowhere, Hans Zimmer's orchestral theme from *True Romance* pipes up and kills my plan stone dead.

Huh? I'm hearing two things at once. Right up against my ear, amplified by the tiny speaker inside my Nokia, my line to Scott's phone has connected. But as it makes that *beep-beep* calling sound, I can also hear the Hans Zimmer ringtone.

Which is really bizarre. Because of course, you only hear a customised ringtone . . .

. . . when the actual phone handset itself is ringing . . .

. . . within earshot.

Oh my God.

Prickles shoot up my back. I didn't hear the sliding door bust open, but it never makes much noise. Could Scott be right behind me, about to inflict one of his surprise *Titanic* hugs? Christ, will everything be great again, once I've abused him for scaring the hell out of me?

Breathless, I spin around.

No Scott.

No one.

Beyond the closed door, inside the flat, a lone, startled Beardie Boy reacts as though I'm pointedly checking on their progress with my boxes. From his perspective, as he gazes out through the glass, my face seems to be demonic and drawn with white pen, which probably doesn't help.

Hans Zimmer's steel drums play on, as I try to work out where this ringtone's coming from. My first instinct is to activate my Nokia's torch, but it doesn't have one.

Then I see it. The unmistakable glow of a phone screen. The handset faces upwards on the ground where the barbecue used to be, concealed partly by an empty bag of nachos and two dead beer bottles.

The handset feels cold as a tombstone. I glimpse the words *Kate Collins Mobile* before the screen goes dark. Quickly, I kill the outgoing call from my Nokia, so as to not leave a voicemail message in which I repeatedly gasp the word *fuck*.

Not that Scott can access his voicemail now, of course, because his phone is *right here in my hand*.

I wipe water off the protective case, one corner of which has incurred spider-web cracks. Without the case, though, this handset would have become a brick.

That might have been for the best, Kate. Because you know what you want to do next, right?

Brain, I simply have no idea what you mean . . .

The Beardie Boys place my final box on the living room floor, with the kind of reverence usually reserved for the Queen's crown. It's conceivable that these people have detected a soupçon of tension in me tonight.

I muster one final grateful smile as they leave, then close the front door and press my back up against the wood.

No, wait. I'd *thought* I was standing, but I somehow find myself seated, with my back against the door and my arms wrapped around my knees, as my heart taps out a conga beat on my ribs.

While down here, I might as well make myself useful, so I rip open the small pile of Scott's mail. It's all spam, apart from a written notification from Unicorn Energy that they're about to cut off the flat's electricity supply due to non-payment. These guys don't make threats lightly.

For some reason, the bristly post-mat I'm sitting on is littered with chips of wood. Seems they've fallen from the door, which has a few chunks missing. Must have inflicted this damage myself, when I needlessly kicked my way inside . . . unless The Beardie Boys were heavy-handed. Gathering these fallen chips, I pocket them. Feels therapeutic. Distracting.

So. I have Scott's phone. I don't know why, but I do, and its random presence on the balcony only deepens my worry. If Scott had left his phone on the breakfast bar or something, this might have signified he was planning to come back. But outside, on the ground? Clearly a mistake and one made in a hurry.

The guy couldn't wait to get away from you.

Scott having lost his phone does explain the lack of contact from him. It's not as if he has any other means of getting hold of me, since I no longer have email, or at least no email I ever check. At one point, Scott and I acknowledged that if one of us ever lost their phone, we'd lose contact . . . but then we never fixed that distinct flaw in our comms. These days, losing your smartphone feels unthinkable, like losing your arm or your leg, or . . . your anything.

What if Scott's mum or dad has died or been hospitalised, and he's driven off in a mad emotional panic to be with them, leaving his phone behind?

That wouldn't explain the hurried flat clearance. Look, Kate, you know it's most likely that Scott's fallen for someone else and has gone off to be with them instead. This may have been his last-minute decision, or he may have always planned to do it, because he's an enormous bastard. And you may never know . . . unless you unlock this handset. And you know that's going to happen.

For once, my brain is right to be so cynical. Behind all this concern of mine lurks a horrid rush. A sick excitement. Having found this phone may well count as some kind of progress, but it also spells danger. This horde of hidden data invites me to return to my bad ways and then some. Still . . . should I really fret over my smartphone addiction when my boyfriend might be in serious trouble, or even danger? What's the worst thing that could happen if I open his phone?

Well . . . have you already forgotten the worst thing that happened, the last time you used a smartphone? Cast your mind back to Leeds and Flat Ninety-Two . . .

I would normally ask Izzy for her opinion on any given problem. Over the last six years since we met, we've plagued each other with every worry under the sun, but she's the wrong person to advise on this matter, for the same reason I ended up with the world's most basic phone in the first place.

This happened through necessity, rather than desire.

This was penance.

Day after day, I repress this memory, but I don't deserve that privilege.

What I deserve is to forever relive the event that ended my days as a dopamine rat.

Before my very eyes, Scott's glum hallway morphs into the far brighter lobby of a high-rise residential building, somewhere on the northern outskirts of Leeds.

CHAPTER TWENTY-ONE

28 March

OUT OF ORDER. ENGINEER HAS BEEN CALLED.

This is precisely the kind of sign that Izzy and I never want to see sellotaped to lift doors at 2.50 a.m., when we need to reach the ninth floor ASAP. Not even the fact that someone has used a Sharpie to add the words THIS IS BANG before the OUT OF ORDER raises a titter from us. As a special extra treat, the air-con's either broken or never existed, leaving the stairwell thick with the kind of heat that makes you crave two showers, one after the other.

We've been called out to Flat Ninety-Two to see what's wrong with a man in his late forties who's complained of severe dizzy spells and nausea. On the face of it, this seems like a pretty straightforward job. All we need to do is get him to A&E to wait three hours and fifty-nine minutes for a check-up. Over four hours is a breach, so that's our standing joke: everyone gets seen in three hours and fifty-nine.

What ultimately transforms this job into a complete nightmare, however, will be me.

Me and my Rudolpho obsession.

Up until the Venezuelan ghosted me, I thought I was a pretty normal online user. But nobody's normal these days, are they? The new normal is establishing itself faster than anyone can track.

These last few weeks I've found myself in Singlesville, stuck watching The Rudolpho Show via social media.

Every time he tweets about a great night out, I'm right there, reading that tweet.

Refresh, refresh, refresh.

Every time he posts on Facebook, there I am. He hasn't unfriended me on FB yet, but that wouldn't even matter, because all his posts are set to public. Much like me, Rudolpho is far from the world's most private or technically proficient person. Which, of course, was fine when he was proudly showing me off as his latest squeeze . . . but now? Less fine.

Refresh, refresh, refresh.

Here he is on Instagram, nursing a drink in a club with his arm around some super-tanned girl, younger than me, with drawn-on eyebrows.

Refresh, refresh, refresh.

What's he doing now? Who's he left me for? What is so very fucking wrong with me?

At the end of each day, I'm still refreshing long after I should be asleep. When I see him post pictures of his latest mad evening out, my nauseous self-loathing only reinforces the insomnia.

At the same time, my own social media use has exploded. Even though I very much doubt Rudolpho has thought about me at all, let alone thought to check my posts, I've gone out of my way to paint myself as enjoying quite the carefree lifestyle.

In bars, I've persuaded hot strangers to pose for selfies with me, our drinks raised to the camera as if we've been partying all night.

I've drunkenly subtweeted about *certain people*, all of whom are clearly Rudolpho.

I've always been a paid-up member of social media's attention-seeking army, but lately I've gone above and beyond. I go all-out in my quest for attention, as if trying to compensate for the shortfall in my so-called life.

I've grabbed and repurposed any Twitter meme I can, in the hope that they'll go viral and people will somehow like me more. I ingratiate myself with celebrities in a transparent bid to get them to retweet my inane gibberings.

Whenever there's an earthquake in LA or some other natural disaster, I post on Facebook about how I hope *all my friends* there are staying safe. I have zero friends in LA.

Tiny squirts of dopamine drag me through my days. I am a lab rat, feverishly pressing a lever, only to receive ever-diminishing returns. A hopeless consumer, who's bought into the illusion that social media means always having company.

I have genuinely tried to focus on my work, first and foremost. I've tried to feed off the adrenaline of the job and the enormous rewards that come with helping people. Some days I succeed, but all too often I end up exhausted after a night of refresh-refresh-refreshment. Rather than allow my work to suffer, I sometimes rely on amphetamine sulphate to see me through a shift. *It happens*, I reassure myself. Lots of paramedics do this.

I know this is wrong. I know I've passed through a bad gateway and fallen into a hole. I know I should block Rudolpho on Facebook and Twitter and everywhere else. I should get on with my life, such as it is. And yet I can't stop watching. In my head, The Rudolpho Show keeps getting renewed, season after season.

This cannot be true heartbreak, because I only fell in love with having someone in my life again.

I fell in love with not being alone.

Tonight at Flat Ninety-Two, three weeks post-Rudolpho, I'm slap-bang in the thick of the madness, checking his socials whenever I can. Sometimes, these glances at my phone become obsessive stares that untether me from reality.

Our Flat Ninety-Two patient is the classic mild-mannered accountant type. He seems perfectly lucid and sensible, until he does that thing of asking where Izzy's from (Leeds), then asking where she's *really* from (also Leeds, but her family roots lie in Kingston, Jamaica, thanks for asking). Despite this annoyance, I believe the man when he insists he'll be fine to take the stairs on foot, provided we all take it nice and steady.

While Izzy performs one last check of the guy's blood pressure out on the landing, I hang back in his hallway and pull out my phone. Time to grab a quick, self-flagellating dopamine fix.

Refresh, refresh, refresh.

Two minutes ago, Rudolpho posted a picture of himself drunk in a club, with his arms around two equally drunk girls. The tweet simply reads, *Decisions, decisions!!!*, complete with a cheeky tongue-out emoji.

Time warps.

The next thing I know, Izzy's at the top of the stairs, guiding the guy down onto the first step. As the danger dawns on me, I call out. I tell her to wait, but it's already happening.

The guy blurts something about feeling weird, and then his body goes slack.

I'm running so fast, out through the guy's front door. But Izzy, being Izzy, tries to drag him back from the brink, despite now having the entirety of his body weight pitted against her.

If this was the two of us, trying to stop his fall, we might stand a chance. But Izzy by herself? Doomed.

I call her name, but gravity doesn't care.

Gravity only wants to assert its authority.

Skidding to a halt at the top of the stairs, I hardly dare look.

Having tumbled at least ten steps, Izzy and the guy now form a twisted, agonised heap on the landing halfway down.

My first reaction, as I call a second ambulance to help us, is angry self-justification. Izzy should've fucking waited! She should never have tried to get the guy down there on her own. But even as my face reddens with this fury, I know damn well that this is a futile attempt to guard myself against the shame.

Don't be paralysed.

Oh my God, Izzy, please don't be paralysed for life.

When I'm confident she isn't looking, I push my phone out through an open window.

Three heartbeats later, the distant tinkle of smashed metal and glass confirms that my brave new world starts here.

CHAPTER TWENTY-TWO

3 October

My mind rejoins my body in Scott's living room. Facing the turbulent sea with a polystyrene box on my lap, I am shovelling chips and curry sauce into my face while perched on a garden chair I bought from the nearby Morrisons.

While reliving the nightmare of Flat Ninety-Two, I'd comforted myself by braving the cold to visit one of the chip shops at the front of the pier. These chips have gone down a treat, despite my mum's shrill voice invading my thoughts: *Oh, you've eaten the whole lot, you little piglet.* Been watching my weight this summer to feel more worthy of Scott, but since he and I really do seem to be over, I can eat whatever I bloody well like. I'm footloose and totally fancy-free once again.

Fancy-free? You haven't even come to terms with losing Scott yet. That realisation is a time bomb, waiting to blow.

I can do anything I like.

Anything, that is, except look inside Scott's phone.

Clearly, that way lies madness. That way lies obsession. That way lies a complete waste of my precious time on this Earth.

More than anything else, it would be a massive betrayal of Izzy, who's been such a saint about being temporarily saddled with a desk job in Control. She even keeps cursing herself for having stubbornly hurried on without me that night, even though I constantly apologise for letting her down. Thank God she didn't see me using my phone before it happened. I don't know if I could bear Izzy full-on blaming me, even though I so deserve her scorn.

Do you, though? I think she ought to shoulder at least some of that blame. Go on, open the phone.

If Scott really has left me . . .

. . . which you know he has . . .

. . . then it's clear that I never really knew him. I have nothing to gain by getting to know the real him in retrospect. All I can do now is learn from this and move on. I need to learn to stop rushing into emotional attachments for the sake of no longer feeling alone. I need to move onwards and head for a brand-new horizon.

For better or for worse, I'm starting my new job tomorrow. There must be no distractions. Tomorrow morning, if there's still no sign of Scott, I'll call the police, but I will not unlock his phone. Just in case something bad really has happened to him, I'll let the police deal with his disappearance. If the handset will aid their efforts, then I'll gladly hand it over.

So that's decided. I will not open Scott's phone.

Hey, seems I can be a grown-up after all.

With an old-school *ping*, a text arrives on my Nokia.

Here's Izzy, impatient for an update. Talk about a timely sign that I've made the correct choice. Opening up the chat, I give her all the latest news from my mad, bad life.

IZZY
whoa slow down slow down . . . how can all scotts stuff be gone

KATE
By virtue of not. Being. Here. Any. More. The electricity doesn't even work.

IZZY
whaaaaat . . . thats crazy . . . so you think hes done a runner

KATE
I honestly don't know what to think, Izz.

IZZY
i dont get whats happened . . . so hes still not replying on his phone . . . obvs not i spose

IZZY
. . . are u still there . . .

KATE
What if something terrible's happened to him?

IZZY
have u checked to see if hes posted on the socials . . . want me to look again

KATE
Ulp. Shit, no, I haven't. Didn't think. Okay . . . Go on, then.

IZZY
k . . . lets have a look

KATE
Don't give me any Sarah Harding fake news this time.

KATE
I'm in serious suspense here, mate.

KATE
Has he posted or not?

IZZY
right . . . call off the cops . . . scotts been tweeting today

IZZY
i can also see a couple of public fb posts . . .

KATE
You have got to be fucking kidding me. What's he posted?

IZZY
a load of old shit . . . mostly shares of jokes . . . cat vids . . . memes . . . 12 mins ago on twitter he posted a pic of a gin n tonic in a bar with the words LOVIN LIFE . . . jesus im so sorry kate

IZZY
what a cold mofo this guy is

IZZY
kate you still there hun

IZZY
kate

IZZY
kate

IZZY
???

CHAPTER TWENTY-THREE

3 October

Rage makes a statue of me. My hands are stone gargoyle claws. Can't move, can't make a sound.

The living room seems to darken, heat up and expand. How incredibly stupid I've been. All because I believed Scott Palmer was the man to banish loneliness for good.

I was in love with not only him but the idyllic picture we'd created. Never wanted to pop that bubble or break that spell – because I might have ended up by myself again.

I needed the illusion. Scott recognised this and decided to milk me for all I was worth. The fucker exploited me.

What to do with all this hatred? My heart may well stop beating, through sheer astonished apoplexy. I want to destroy everything. Melt everything down into one brick and use it to pulp Scott's evil brains.

My hands ball into fists as I cross the floor to punch a wall, any wall. The first impact sends a jarring shockwave up along my arm and through the rest of me. Can't lie, this feels pretty good, so I do it again, and again. I snarl and yell and even treat myself to a banshee-scream, until I'm flat-out jack-hammering the walls with both fists, like the world's least tolerant neighbour.

To think I was actually *worried* about Scott's *safety*!

Even thought the fucker was *vulnerable*.

Scott Palmer, you have screwed over the wrong person. Carry on *lovin' life* while you still can, mate, because that bliss will soon die when I hunt you down and confront you.

Fuck my past and fuck the dangers. Let's have a damn good poke around inside this phone.

As I pace around the cardboard Manhattan of my boxes, Scott's phone shows me numerous missed calls and texts. The front screen's wallpaper image is a photo ofThe Artist Formerly Known As Prince (or Symbol Boy as I used to call him, before he passed away and it no longer felt respectful to do so). Only a few weeks ago, Scott had my picture here instead.

A horribly familiar mixed-bag of conflicting emotions floods over me. The fear, the compulsion, the queasy thrills. The sense of having little control over my actions, as if someone else is calling the shots.

Flying in the face of the sensible decision I made only ten minutes ago feels deeply disquieting. I was too ashamed to tell Izzy that I have Scott's phone, but now that I know he's alive and all too well, my desire for payback cancels out all that crap.

Rage has unlocked my right to unlock this phone.

Could this be how it feels to smoke a cigarette? You know it's going to kill you, but you do it anyway, through some crazed desire for self-destruction?

When I try to skip past the lock-screen, the display transforms into a stern security keypad with numbers from zero to nine. Apparently, I could also gain access with the correct fingerprint, but that won't be an option unless Scott accidentally left one of his digits behind too.

What kind of guess-work can I use to figure out this passcode?

Nothing springs readily to mind. Funnily enough, over the course of our epic three-month courtship, Scott and I never discussed our favourite numbers.

Sitting with a G&T, lovin' life! My face burns and I can't breathe straight.

Numbers, fucking numbers. How do people choose their passcodes? What about Scott's date of birth? Nah. Might have worked, if only the slippery prick had told me his real age. Still, the day and month are likely to be right, aren't they? What could Scott's real age be, if not thirty-seven? Since he lied, then surely he has to be at least forty.

I plug Scott's possible date of birth into the keypad.

Wrong passcode. Okay, so let's try him one year older . . .

Nope.

One more try on this tack. Might Scott be forty-two?

Computer says no. Bloody hell, 3 August might not even be his birthday. He probably just wanted me to make a fuss of him, as if I didn't make enough already. Thinking back, it *was* quite the coincidence that his "birthday" fell on one of my days off . . .

The fucker never even knew when *my* birthday was. Never even asked.

Still pacing, I glare at the phone's impenetrably black screen. Little pig, little pig, let me in . . .

Outside, the snow has become heavy rain. All I can make out are the smeared colours of the pier, the street lamps and the zip-wire tower.

Barely visible in this light, the demonic window-face looks on, mocking me, as I mentally replay conversations that Scott and I had. When this technique fails to dish up any viable numbers, I grab my own Nokia and scroll through every text we ever exchanged.

Painstaking and painful.

The simple act of sitting down on my boxes gives me a jolting reminder, but one that has nothing to do with passcodes. Frantic seconds later, I haul open the sliding door and retrieve the box I'd left out on the balcony. Soaked through with rain, the cardboard and the books inside may as well be toilet paper.

As a pool of rainwater creeps out from around the base of the ruined box, my hope wanes. Like most people, Scott probably chose some arbitrary array of digits that were simple enough to remember. Is it even worth trying 1234? Nah, he's way too tech-savvy for that. But is he even really an IT guy? For all I truly know right now, he might have earned his keep by frying chips on the pier.

With a heavy heart, I try 1234 and notch up another failure. After a few more fruitless attempts to break in, I toss this stupid secure phone aside.

Need a break. Need time to think properly about this passcode.

Not *too* much time, though, because it may have been at least twenty-four hours since Scott left his phone here. When a phone gets lost or stolen, people contact their service provider to get the old SIM card cancelled. Scott clearly hasn't done this yet. Why? Does he think he lost it in his new place, or while en route, or does he believe he packed it into a hurriedly assembled moving box? Whatever the case may be, as soon as he realises the truth it'll be thank you and goodnight. I'll be blocked out of this handset for good.

All this space around me seems to span out forever. Here in this gutted flat, I'm stuck between a vast coastline and a sprawling, rainswept city in which no one gives two rats' asses about me. Hello, deep blue sea. Hello, Devil.

I feel tiny and humiliated and entirely out of control. Desperation surges from my belly to the back of my throat. Abort, abort! I grab the Nokia and make the first call.

This is insane. I need to go back to Leeds and I need to go back there tomorrow. I can take Scott's phone with me if I want . . .

. . . and you know you'll want to . . .

. . . but surely it can't be too late to reboot my old life up north.

From the moment my old boss Patrizia answers her phone, I may as well be trying to walk up a down escalator. "Kate, we filled the position two weeks back. Something might come up, but . . . what's happened, love? You seemed so certain about this move."

"I'm so sorry, darling," says Mr Gluck, the man who I thought would be my last ever landlord. "The contract's signed, the new tenants move in tomorrow."

Can't move forward by opening this phone, and neither can I move back. I'm trapped with an emotional time bomb that's about to blow.

Might it be possible for someone to cry so hard, and for so long, that they die through dehydration?

Woohoo, there's only one way to find out.

CHAPTER TWENTY-FOUR

28 August

Scott and I are on a train from Brighton to London's Victoria station. This is the tail-end of my glorious seaside visit, during which Scott asked me to move in with him. I'm on my way back to Leeds and he has a handily-timed meeting in London, so we get to cuddle up at the rear end of this carriage like teenagers in the back row of a cinema.

An elderly couple occupy the row in front of us, but they've chosen seats across the aisle from each other. Beneath the man's crop of white hair sits a joyless face, as if he's sucking on a plum. The woman displays an equal lack of joie de vivre. Despite the summer heat, she's still bunched up in her fleecy coat as if trying to gain maximum insulation from her husband.

Neither of them has spoken to the other during the first half of this journey. They just sit there, eating salmon sandwiches that stink out the carriage. As Scott and I chat lazily to each other, I can't help but wonder how many secrets, lies and betrayals have divided this older couple over the past decades.

A certain smugness grips me when I compare them to me and Scott, but this is undercut with fear. I never want our bubble to pop.

By the time the old coots unwrap their packed dessert items – tangerines, which at least help to erase the reek of long dead fish – I catch Scott contemplating them too. I lean over and whisper into his ear.

"God. Let's pledge to never be like them, eh?"

He nods gravely. "No salmon sandwiches. Ever."

I laugh, then tickle-jab him under the armpit.

CHAPTER TWENTY-FIVE

3 October

Why did Scott really crack that joke? Could it be that he didn't understand what I meant about the great divide between the old couple on the train? Or did he understand only too well, and simply knew that he and I would barely even last three months, let alone as many decades?

Inside the impenetrable fortress that passed for Scott's head, he may have been thinking about all the secrets he'd already kept from me. All the lies he'd told. The massive bait-and-switch he may already have had planned, as I sat beside him, so deeply smug and naïve.

Who knows? The fucker might even have laughed to himself as we rolled on towards old London town.

I couldn't say how long this great flood has lasted. All I know is that the tears have given way to numb exhaustion. Tomorrow is my first day at work, so I need to rally myself and get practical. If I try to sleep in the bedroom, too many memories will scuttle across the carpet to torture me, so the living room floor will do for tonight.

As I circle my boxes, trying to work out which might contain my bedding, a terrible feeling creeps up on me. Subliminally at first, then with mounting clarity until the unease sinks bone-deep.

I am being watched.

I can't say why or how I know this. I just know.

My skin feels way too tight.

Very carefully, oh so slowly, I turn on the spot, scanning the room for any sign of an electric eye.

What do secret surveillance lenses even look like these days? Exactly how tiny can they be? The size of a pinhead? Smaller?

Could their size be inversely proportional to my paranoia? Am I the pinhead here?

Possibly. But my gut instinct has served me well in the past, apart from when it comes to choosing men. I should trust my instinct now, or at least treat its suspicions with respect.

What if Scott has done all of this for some kind of sadistic enjoyment? He'd want to see your reaction, wouldn't he? He'd want to film you. Thanks to the magic of night vision cameras, he could be watching you right now. Scott Palmer's azure blue eyes burning into you, from some remote location.

These thoughts drag ice up my spine. The man who I thought I knew and trusted, not only abandoning me but actually doing so with glee, like a mean kid watching an angry wasp trapped inside a bottle.

Please tell me I'm not starring in some banal hidden-camera show. Any second now, will a broadly grinning Scott walk in through the front door, joined by cameramen and a goofy YouTube personality? What a hoot that would be.

Actually, I can't decide whether this would be better or worse than my current situation.

When TV spies conduct a security sweep, where do they

search? Under lampshades usually, but there are none, so I just check everything in sight.

Prowling around, I use Scott's phone torch to examine the walls, the skirting boards, plug sockets, curtain rails, light fittings and the dead radiators.

In the kitchen, the boiler has a detachable metal cover. A big red label stuck to this cover declares PLEASE LEAVE FOR YOUR SAFETY, which does little to ease my nerves.

The harder I search, the heavier my eyelids become. Eventually, having found nothing of note, I'm forced to call it a night.

Raising one middle finger, I slowly rotate 360 degrees, to ensure the message gets across to Scott, just in case. This really does make me feel deranged.

I'm so tired of myself and this bear-trap of a day.

Drawing on my last vestiges of strength, I push my three heaviest boxes across the living room floor and out through the archway, then stack them against the front door. Scott used to make me feel so safe and so protected. And yet now, the thought of this man sneaking in here during the night, perhaps to try and recover his lost phone, gives me the creeps.

Please leave for your safety.

Barricading this door feels like taking back at least one iota of control.

Staying fully clothed, I hunker down on the living room floor. I no longer have the will to find my pillow or blanket in these damn boxes, so I'll make do with tucking my balled-up jacket under my head and braving the cold. Feels like a fitting end to one of the longest and worst days of my life.

What I have here, with Scott's phone, is Pandora's Box. Can't stop thinking about what might be inside. Tomorrow, I'll take this thing to a shop and get it opened.

What happened with Pandora, again? I mean, I know she

unleashed all the evils into the world and stuff, but apart from that everything was fine.

Steel drums summon me back up from the depths of a bad dream. Something to do with the zip-wire tower on the beach, but I can remember no more than that.

I've been rudely woken by the incessant noise of a phone. The *True Romance* theme, to be precise.

Groggy, disorientated and cold, I sit bolt upright. A full moon has lent the hard floor a white sheen. Even though I've stayed in this flat so many times, the place may as well be the surface of an alien world.

The more gunk I wipe from my eyes, the more the fierce glow of Scott's phone slides into focus. An incoming call. *Unknown Number.* Do I pick up?

Of course I do. I want to know who's calling Scott.

But what if it's Scott himself?

Why the hell should I worry about that? He's the one who should be afraid. I have nothing to fear.

Not even here, all alone, in a flat with no lights?

Shut up. Look, I'm answering the call, see?

What I hear on the line is the sound of nothing. The sound of low, grey static.

Instinct tells me not to speak first. What if this is Scott's secret other woman, or merely one of them?

In my ear, the nothing-buzz continues.

I really want to ask who this is, but hold my nerve.

This may only be a spammer. One of those infuriating calls that waits to detect that a human has answered the phone before launching its pre-recorded spiel.

Somewhere in the midst of all this static, I'm pretty sure I can hear someone.

Someone breathing. Calm, steady.

Scott?

Pressing the phone harder against my ear, I try to filter through the noise. I try to differentiate between the inhale and the exhale.

The voice of a stranger lunges out from the static, clear as a bell. Beyond the Scottish accent, this guy's voice sounds flat and dark, as if his words have been recorded, then slowed down for playback.

"You're going to love it here."

Before I can prise open my sticky mouth to ask who this is, the static is replaced by a monotonous, dead hum.

Call Ended.

Before the screen can fade to black, I push a couple of buttons in the hope of exploiting some magical loophole to bypass the security system. Taking none of my shit, the phone dutifully locks itself up nice and tight.

Who *was* that speaking? One of Scott's mates, joining in on the fun? If so, what's next on their agenda: knocking on the door, then running away? What a truly risible pack of bastards. Next time someone calls, I'll give them a message to pass on to Scott – one that'll wipe the wolfy smirk clean off his face.

Loathing the sense that I've become the butt of a joke, I get up and wander aimlessly around the room. I try to stretch my aching back, still feeling like an intruder in what was supposed to be my dream home. The rain has eased off, so I head towards the windows, intending to peer outside.

My right foot steps in the pool of cold water, sending chills up my leg. I picture some prick laughing at this slapstick mishap as they watch the live infrared video feed.

Even though I can't see the face drawn on the window, I can feel it grinning at me.

You're going to love it here.

I'm not creeped out.

You're going to love it here.

I am *not* creeped out.

You're going to love it here.

I. Am. Not. Creeped Out.

The enormity of my fatigue finally triumphs over the adrenaline. I curl up on the floor and manage to close my eyes.

One word comes back to me, over and over. *Why?*

Why has Scott done this to me? And why should I spend the rest of my life not knowing? I might not like myself all that much, but even I know I deserve more.

If I'm ever going to be free of all this anger, hurt and confusion, then I need to know the reasons behind Scott Palmer's behaviour.

I'm going to use his phone to learn what makes him tick. I'm going to crush him. Then I'll flick him aside and rebuild my life as something fantastic.

But right now, I am going to do my best not to think about all these eyes watching me from the dark.

CHAPTER TWENTY-SIX

4 October

An evil sandman has packed my eyelids with grit.

Why did I sell my coffee maker before moving down here? Ah yes, because Scott owned an incredible machine: a mighty, silver-spired kingdom that dominated the kitchen. In my fairy-tale picture-postcard world, I should be using that machine right now. I should be sipping cappuccino on the balcony, while Scott rubs my shoulders and wishes me well for this induction day.

Of course, even if I did have my coffee machine, Scott's failure to pay the electrical bill would render it useless.

Three gratitudes would serve me well right now, provided I can drum any up.

I'm grateful that I've woken in a nice flat by the sea, regardless of the circumstances that brought me here. The autumn sun has painted the walls orange. This warms the place up by a couple of degrees, even if the effect is only psychosomatic.

And, uh . . . I'm grateful for having chosen to unlock Scott's phone. Yes, it was probably the worst decision in the world, but at least it was a decision and—

Fuck. Hold the front page. Looks like my third gratitude might be a stormer.

Scott's phone lies face up on the floor beside me. Seen from this angle, sunlight reveals greasy fingerprint marks on the surface of the screen.

Oh wow. Who needs a caffeine buzz when you can spot something like this?

There are four clearly discernible points where Scott's fingertips have tapped most frequently. When I summon the onscreen security keypad, these points correspond to four numbers.

Two, four, six, eight, who do we appreciate? Me, for figuring this out.

The diamond-shaped formation of these numbers makes perfect sense. We so often remember our passcodes in terms of the shapes our fingertips describe on the keypad, more than the actual numbers themselves. We pick a simple shape, then muscle memory takes over. So here's my first guess: Scott would have chosen the numbers to form a nice, easy-to-remember clockwise circle starting from the two.

I tap two-six-eight-four.

No dice. But did I really expect my first guess to work? I should try the digits anti-clockwise, but I'm already nervous. By my reckoning, there are twenty-four possible combinations of this number, and who knows when the phone will lock itself for increasingly long periods of time? I'm reminded of how Izzy's phone once seized up for literally twenty-five thousand hours, because Dwayne, her child's sperm-donor excuse for a dad, tried to crack the code so many times. She had to reset that thing, which meant wiping the contents.

Two-four-eight-six.

Oh dear God, yes! That's the one. With a jittery animation, Scott's passcode screen flies apart to reveal a home-grid of colourful apps to explore.

I'm in like Flynn. Superb work!

Also . . . what the hell am I doing? My triumphant two-second rush gives way to the dread of what I might see on this phone and how obsessed I might become. If I'm going to scour this thing for the truth, then I very much need rules. I must establish clear parameters, so that this dubious investigation doesn't spiral out of control.

You don't think you're already heading right off the chart? Last night, lest we forget, you gave an empty living room the finger.

Okay, here goes. I, Kate Collins, solemnly swear that when I learn the truth about Scott Palmer, I will smash his phone and retreat to my blissfully data-free Nokia.

I also solemnly swear that I will not – repeat, not – use Scott's phone to check on what that dickhead Rudolpho's been up to. Gorging myself on six months of his dumb social media posts would be like re-opening old, healed wounds. There can be no going back to stalking that braindead bison.

Most importantly of all, I solemnly swear that I will *not keep Scott's phone about my person while at work*. Non-negotiable.

Work must come first. In order to function properly as an ambulance-driving paramedic, I must rigidly compartmentalise my life. I must seal my personal affairs in a biohazard box until I come home each day.

Speaking of which: I have to be at the ambulance station really very soon.

What if Scott comes here while I'm at work? Unlikely, but possible.

I single out my most precious moving box, then slide it into one of the kitchen's under-cupboards. This box contains special goods like my passport, a shiny stethoscope the service gave me as a gift and a framed photo of a baby I delivered that ended up being named after me, God help her. I really should have personally driven this box down from Leeds, but clarity of thought hasn't exactly been my specialty over the last twenty-four hours.

Swearing to myself and checking the time, I grab my jacket and drop one phone in each pocket.

Oh, that's interesting. I thought you weren't taking Scott's phone to work . . .

No . . . uh . . . I said I wouldn't keep it on my *person* while working. And I won't, so shut up.

As I head for the front door, something halts me in my tracks.

On the mat beneath the letterbox, there's a new scattering of wood chips.

Closer inspection confirms that these chips have fallen from the door, leaving ugly new craters in the varnished wood. And now that I have morning light to assist me, I can see that these holes are more like *gouges*. They come in batches of five, too, as if ripped out by . . . fingers?

An obviously ridiculous thought. These chips simply fell from the damaged door overnight, and there are far more important things to think about right now. Such as getting a taxi instead of using my own car, so that I can read the fuck out of Scott's phone on my way to work.

"How's your day going then, love?"

"No offence," I tell the back of my cab driver's head, too tired for niceties, "but I'm not up for chatting at all."

His only reply is to turn the radio sports news up a notch.

For the first two streets of this journey to the ambulance station, I found myself paralysed by choice. There are now genuinely two hundred times as many smartphone apps in the world as there are lions. Staring at Scott's home screen, I wanted to look at everything, all at once. I also wanted to see nothing at all. I felt sick with trepidation, yet dizzy and excited, like the kid on their birthday who can't decide which chocolate and cake combo to devour.

And now I'm ploughing bravely through Scott's photos. All *twenty-six thousand* of them. Scott might have more phone memory to play with than I did, but I can't remember him taking all that many pics. Of course, he may not have felt inspired to do so when we were together, what with not giving a damn about me.

These pictures are eclectic. Streets, meals, starlings flying in tight formation around the Palace Pier like an airborne fingerprint, cats, sunsets, the views from train windows. You name it, looks like Scott was keen to snap it, probably to stick on social media. Must brave his Facebook and Twitter apps at some point. Can't wait to slide into those DMs . . . I think.

The driver turns the radio up another notch, and I ask him to turn it back down.

There are many people in these photos, too. Naturally, my mental filter singles out the women. Which of these ladies could have been seeing Scott at the same time as me? Pretty much any. Okay, probably not the smiling, seventy-something woman wearing a purple paper Christmas hat at a dinner table – but hey, who knows how wide-ranging this rogue's tastes might be?

Here's one skinny blonde in her early thirties, with big expressive green eyes, holding a glass of something like Prosecco. Yep, I could certainly see Scott being attracted to her, what with him being male, and human. Same goes for the deathly pale, late-twenties Action Girl looking so triumphant on top of a mountain which she must have scaled. Bright red-dyed dreads burst out from under her climbing helmet like snakes, and a dense tattoo sleeve covers one arm. Hmm, surely Scott couldn't have snuck off on a mountaineering trip with her while dating me, even if we did mostly only see each other at weekends.

Annoyingly, none of these photos have any date attached . . . but here's a picture of me and Scott from August. Smug Kate From Two Months Ago looks like she's won the lottery. I remember him slipping his arm around my back, pressing the side of his head against mine and snapping the photo while we ate in a Thai place on St James's Street.

I pinch Scott's head between my finger and thumb, exactly as I'd love to in real life, then zoom in on his face.

Specifically, I want to re-evaluate his eyes as they fill the screen. I want to gaze into the soul of the man who Smug Kate From Two Months Ago thought she knew so intimately.

I half expect to see some big and terrible revelation in these eyes – some devastating clue as to the nature of the real Scott Palmer – but even in isolation they sparkle. On the face of things, he appears every bit as happy as me.

And the Oscar goes to . . . *La La Land*. Oh no, wait, sorry everyone, it's Scott Palmer.

Tapping the picture back to its original size, I suffer a pang of loss. I yearn to dive back into the idyllic world of this photo and immerse myself in our warm love. To shake off this pang, I remind myself of how Scott's love was nothing but cold make-believe.

Back on the photo-grid, I scroll down to see a whole ocean of bare flesh and pink parts. Please don't let these be two thousand pictures of Scott having sex with other people.

Doesn't look that way. On closer inspection, when I tentatively open some, this is a whole bunch of pretty generic porn.

Phew. Hooray for good old generic porn.

Except you're almost disappointed, aren't you? If you were to see the cold, literally hard evidence of Scott screwing someone else, that would bring closure. It might kill you, but also cure you. Yeah, you won't be happy until you've demolished yourself and then have to rebuild from the ground up.

By flicking my finger up the screen, I reveal a block of pictures that still look filthy but are also entirely different. Completely bizarre, in fact.

My driver's voice is muffled, as if underwater, as he asks whether this is the right entrance.

Seeing this stuff in thumbnail form, I can't even tell what I'm looking at. The colours are different from the previous pinks and tans: now they're pink, blue, green, yellow and more. What fresh hell is this?

Even when I expand one of these pictures to fill the screen, I have no idea of what I'm seeing.

Here's what looks like part of a bare human thigh. Smooth, so it could belong to a woman. The rest of the picture is filled by what might be part of some bulbous green octopus. Except there's a large claw poking into one corner of the screen, vaguely like a crab's. Some kind of mutated giant crab.

What. The. Christ?

The driver repeats his question: is this the entrance I need?

Braving another picture, I'm confronted with a woman's breast that drips with a bright blue substance the colour of food dye. Goo, that's the word for it. Goo.

The next picture is a close-up of a man's open mouth, filled with a multi-coloured *thing* that resembles nothing I've ever seen. Looks like some kind of nauseating cross between a human muscle and . . . and a big insect. This thing has *eyes*, and lots of them. Some kind of stinger protrudes from its rear end and has pierced the guy's tongue.

I still don't know what I'm looking at, but I really, really don't like this.

Hey, Scott must have been watching some dodgy horror film on his phone and taken screenshots so he could share this fucked-up shit with his social media mates. *Look at this, everybody! Retweet, Like, comment, please please love and validate me.*

"Look, love, are you all right? I need to know where you want to get out."

We've arrived outside the ambulance station, so I mutter an apology to the guy and pay up. While waiting for change, I wonder if I dare check out the Videos folder. Video feels even scarier than still photography. Seeing a picture of your boyfriend banging someone else is tough enough, but a moving picture with sound?

Still . . . in for a penny, in for a psychological pounding, that's my motto. So I tap open Videos.

A new grid of thumbnail images assaults my retinas for one solitary second . . .

. . . before the whole screen plunges into black.

Oh, great. The phone's crashed, leaving me with an almost subliminal impression of what I saw.

These thumbnails were mostly quite dark – nothing like those bizarre horror-sex screen grabs. Some had shown people's faces, while others were entirely nondescript. I certainly caught patches of bare, pink flesh. Even though I hardly saw anything, my stomach lurches like a storm-ravaged yacht.

I stab the phone's power button and mentally beg the video thumbnails to return, but nothing happens. All I see is my face in the black mirror.

The driver dumps coins into my hand. Clambering out of the cab, I tap impatiently at the screen, but the blackness persists. Jesus. What if this thing has literally died before my very eyes, never to return? This would arguably be for the best, and yet—

"Oi, look out!" The cabbie's bark yanks me right back to reality.

Big truck! What looks like a ten-wheeler steams towards me, as I stand here in the road with the passenger door wide open.

I'm too close for the truck driver to brake.

As I picture exactly how my crushed corpse will look, my fistful of loose change hits the road and rolls off in all directions.

The truck-horn punches my eardrums.

I flatten myself against the side of the cab and slam the door, just as my driver screams, "*Door!*"

The horn blares on, even as the truck rolls by, right past my face.

Fuck me. Nothing like a major adrenaline spike to prepare you for your first day on the new job.

Back on the pavement, I gather my nerves while apologising profusely to the driver. I hand him an extra tip, even though he'd been more concerned about losing his door than his passenger.

"Why did you have to get out on the *road* side?" is all he can muster, with a sad shake of the head.

Hesitating outside my new workplace, I so badly want to jab the power button on Scott's phone, in the hope of resuscitating the patient.

With the truck-horn still ringing in my ears, I suppress this urge and force myself in through the front doors.

"Bloody hell, mate, the loopy shit I've seen out in the field. Once saw a guy split in half after he got hit by a race car. I mean, his legs were literally in one place and his torso in another. And then I was faced with having to console his wife, who was going nuts. So I hope you're ready for some scary experiences, mate."

With his long dirt-blond hair tied in a high bun, a chunky

metal hand-grenade pendant hanging from his neck and his phone in a belt-holster, Tyler has the looks and physique of a surfer who's taken six months off and let himself go. The kid's twenty-three years old and thinks he'll live forever. Everyone else at the station seems really nice, so why have I been given the resident dildo as a partner?

"This isn't my first rodeo, *mate*," I tell him. Now that my official corporate induction's done, Tyler is giving me the tour. We pass changing rooms, toilets and a shower room, which will be my new best friend, seeing as Scott's flat has no hot water.

"Oh yeah," he says, with a dismissive swing of his hand. "I heard you've done a little time in London and Leeds, and that's going to serve you well here, but you've yet to see West Street on a Saturday night. Oh man, such a clusterfuck. One time, I got so covered in puke, you couldn't see the actual colour of my uniform. Here's another security door. As you can see, the code's written in pen there on the wall."

"I feel safer already."

"Yeah," he sighs. "Code hasn't been changed in the six months I've been here. Wow, it really has been six months now. The sights I've seen . . . '

For all his dick-swinging, patronising alpha-male talk, Tyler is what we call in this game a *microwave*: five minutes and he's done. These kids all think they're amazing and infallible and that real-life trauma is something to get a buzz from. They have yet to learn compassion and empathy, which is the true beating heart of the job.

When Tyler finds me a locker, I make a point of securing Scott's phone inside, even though my dopamine receptors scream in protest. Then I take great pleasure in trying my uniform on for size. When Tyler sees the fifteen-year badge on my lapel, his face is such a pretty picture. *Ha ha, you thrusting young fuck, see my badge of time and feel your stupidity.* His testosterone levels noticeably diminish, even as his irritation grows.

"Guess you already know the procedure for signing out drugs, then," he mutters. "But maybe I can show you how to . . . log into the intranet, right?"

Now that a grudging respect has infiltrated his manner, I decide to go easier on him. Only a little.

"You guys might have slightly different drug protocols," I point out, "so it's probably worth us going over them together."

Tyler nods, looking relieved that he may still have things to show me. As I let him lead the way, the smirk falls off my face. Seriously, what the hell is going on in all those bizarre images on Scott's phone? What else might I find, if I can even revive the handset?

Argh, I'll just have to wait until tonight. Got to stay strong.

CHAPTER TWENTY-SEVEN

4 October

Dice fall, land and scatter all around me, while I enter the passcode into Scott's phone. Thank God, the handset boots back up on this first attempt.

Since Scott's flat has no electricity . . .

. . . and creeps you out . . .

. . . I decided not to go back there after work. Instead, I bought a phone charger and stumbled upon this fun seafront café-bar, Loading, where a surprising number of young enthusiasts huddle around board games and wrestle with stand-up arcade machines.

Something about how grounded these people are, as they focus so intently on actual physical dice, cards and joysticks, makes me feel all the more uneasy when I blank out all of this activity and delve inside the phone. Time to feed the sick hunger I've fought all day.

I also crave beer, but instead I go for a pot of tea. Alcohol really didn't help during The Great Rudolpho Trauma, so abstinence feels like the safest path for now. Without Dutch courage,

I can't see myself venturing inside the most potentially hellish apps like Tinder or WhatsApp, but that's okay. Best to treat this phone like an agonisingly cold pool and wade in slow.

Can't get into either of Scott's banking apps, because they're fingerprint-locked. All I find among his texts are appointment reminders, takeaway delivery notifications and messages from me.

Disappointed again, aren't you? Almost as if you feel you deserve the punishment of discovering some outrageous affair. Still, early days . . .

As I suspected, the list of Scott's calls also offers zero kompromat. His countless contacts tell me little in themselves, mostly showing only first names or nicknames. Several incoming calls, for instance, have been made to Scott by an individual labelled only *Idiot*. For one disturbing moment, I check the number to make sure this person isn't me.

"What a complete idiot," hoots a girl across the room. She's good-humouredly abusing one of her fellow board game players, but the synchronicity puts me on edge. Here's that feeling of being watched, yet again. Maybe even heard.

Oh, you know what? All this paranoia I've been feeling can most likely be explained by fatigue.

Yeah, wouldn't that be nice and neat.

My own contact name in this phone is not *Idiot*. As I'd already seen when the phone first rang on the balcony, I'm down as the hideously formal *Kate Collins*. Scott must have needed to differentiate between me and all the other Kates he was boffing. Beckinsale, Winslet, Moss.

Ah! Scott's email and browser history finally get me somewhere. Feels like I'm only scratching the surface, seeing as most people hide their tracks with private browsers, but nevertheless I make three discoveries in the time it takes me to finish my tea.

Discovery 1: Scott really is in the shit with loan sharks.

Emails tell me he's been chased by the Hazelcrest Group and MMX Inc, two shady-looking outfits whose websites don't even pretend to be friendly and reassuring. Only someone with a lousy credit history would need to darken their doorsteps.

So, it could well be that Scott ran from these companies and felt I wouldn't understand or accept his situation. Who knows, perhaps the mocking face he drew on the balcony window was intended for their bailiffs.

Nah. You know very well the face was intended for you.

Discovery 2: Scott isn't really vegetarian.

I found this out while scanning over a supermarket delivery confirmation email. I'd been looking out for condoms, because if Scotty Boy had bought himself a box of latex friends, they wouldn't have been for use with me, seeing as I'm on the pill. Instead, I find sirloin steak. Unsmoked bacon. *Veal cutlets.*

Wow. Of all the things Scott could have lied about, I somehow did not see this one coming. Must've been me who mentioned being veggie first, at the detox retreat. Handsome Laser-Wolf obviously decided to lie his face off in response. Which only confirms that he never intended to live with me. Because otherwise, what was his plan: sneaking meat into the flat to devour when I was at work?

Discovery 3: Scott's favourite film is not *True Romance*.

Looks like he only saw the film for the first time in the days leading up to our first proper date in Leeds.

My Spidey-senses tingled when I saw he'd Googled for the film's Wikipedia page, one week before our River's Edge Bar evening, then ordered the Blu-ray via Amazon Prime and downloaded the Hans Zimmer ringtone. Why would he do these things, shortly before we just so happened to discuss the movie he supposedly knew so well?

Wait a second… I'd previously gushed all over social media

about *True Romance* being my favourite film. What if Scott checked out those posts before our date? This does seem feasible. Creepy, but feasible.

Pretending to be veggie, pretending we loved the same movie, lying about his age . . . all bullshit to suggest we were two peas in a pod, so he could reel me in. But why did Scott even want to do that? I still have no idea.

So far, the contents of Scott's phone support only two things he told me: his name really is Scott Palmer and he really does work in IT. This latter point I glean from endless email conversations about *AD passwords*, *DHCP servers* and *a serious case of PBCAK*. He's been under real pressure, it seems, with countless people chasing him on deadlines and even cancelling contracts altogether. In one particularly heated email thread, he protests to a disgruntled client that his mum's in hospital, having her left leg amputated below the knee. Since this is the first time I've seen him mention his mother anywhere, this just looks like an excuse. In reality, is she even still alive?

I see you, Scott Palmer, and I'm closing in.

Unlocking his phone was the correct decision, because this process will show me the reality of the man I fell in love with. This process will diminish him and ultimately disperse the smoke-screen.

I daren't return to the Videos folder in case the phone dies again . . .

. . . and in case you see more of the disturbing stuff you glimpsed there . . .

. . . but those thumbnails are bothering me, and so are the bizarre horror-porn photos. I should at least research where Scott got the latter. A hive-mind would really help right now, so I summon Facebook in his browser. Takes me a while to remember my email address, let alone the password, but finally I reactivate my account. Facebook's welcome-home message carries more than a hint of *We knew you'd be back, ya big sap.*

"Hello, everyone!" I type in my first FB post since March. "Yes, yes, I'm back. Only for a short while, but it's nice to see you all. And in the meantime, I need my horror-fan pals to identify which film these stills came from. Please don't report them to FB for indecency. Ha! Cheers."

I attach a few of the less sexually explicit stills, then fire my post off into The Zuckerberg Machine. If the algorithm's in a particularly good mood tonight, it will be seen by all 324 of my FB friends.

Rudolpho springs to mind. I wonder what that arsehole's been up to . . .

Nope, nope, no. Back away from the Facebook, Miss Collins.

The thought of opening Tinder still makes me feel sick, as does the prospect of tomorrow's super-early first shift in the new ambulance.

Coward.

Uh-uh, brain, you just mispronounced the word *professional.* Time to whip my charger out of the wall, leave all these rolling dice behind me and slope across the road to the Van Spencer building. Anxiety dictates that I check all my boxes are okay. Anything could have happened in the flat while I spent hours barely enduring Tyler's chest-beating mansplainery. If Scott really is messing with me on some hardcore level, then why wouldn't he go the whole hog and steal my boxes, then dump them in the sea?

Slowly, oh so slowly, I twist the handle of the door to the flat.

Locked. Even so, Scott could still be inside.

Behind me, another door bursts open and I almost wet myself.

An old guy in a flat cap is leaving Flat Twenty-Two. He looks me over, trying to work out who I am. When I grin and say hi, he smiles, nods and heads towards the lift. No doubt he's used to seeing strange women coming in and out of here . . .

I twist my key in the lock so very carefully that the final clunk makes me flinch.

Scott's dark hallway greets me with a stony silence, as if trying to say, *You shouldn't be here. Please leave for your safety.* Just inside the door sit three of my boxes in a pile – the ones I used to barricade the door last night. But did I leave them stacked like this?

Maybe I did. Maybe I didn't.

What if Scott's in here, waiting for me?

Clutching a bunch of flowers, no doubt, desperate to explain everything. Yeah, right.

I creep along the hall. Peering through the archway into the living room lit only by street lamps, I glimpse the man standing there and jolt back into the hall with my heart thumping.

My brain soon catches up with my highly strung reflexes. What I've done here is mistake the highest tower of my boxes for a person. Well done, Kate. Still, at least the boxes are still here.

Further along the hall, I can't help listening out for the whir of tiny, hidden camera lenses.

Using Scott's phone as a torch, I check the bathroom, then enter the bedroom.

The closed walk-in wardrobe door gives me pause. Can't help picturing Scott in there, waiting with a grin, confident that I won't check inside.

If he is, then I'm about to prove him wrong.

When I tug open the door, my breath stays held until torch-light demystifies every single corner of the space.

Okay, no one's home except me. If I really can call this place home.

I light all six of the taper candles I bought, position them around the living room, then sit on the garden chair to take another look around Scott's home screen. One unfamiliar app speaks to me: TrooSelf. Could any phrase sum up my mission more succinctly than wanting to discover Scott's true self?

The app's start-up screen runs a twee animation of a human heart being placed inside a heavy-duty safe. Above the safe, in some kind of Courier font, materialise the words *TrooSelf: the private diary that stays private*. Further down, it adds: *Document the real you, 100% secure.* Then, at the bottom of the screen, a progress bar says *Loading . . .*

Could this diary document the inner workings of the real Scott Palmer? If so, I've hit the motherlode early, but here's that fear again. Who knows what I'm about to see? I should probably shut down the app, shut down the phone, chuck it off the pier and get on with my life.

Transfixed, I watch the progress bar fill. The front screen gives way to a list of what I presume are the titles of diary entries.

The first title, for an entry dated 9 February this year, sends my imagination shooting off in all directions:

I Am Possessed

All righty, then. What in the name of God's fat balls is that supposed to mean?

And damn, here's an aggressive pop-up window. TrooSelf requires *two* passwords before it will show me the diary entries? I really hope Scott told his phone to save these passwords. Most people never really expect their handsets to get broken into, do they?

While I wait in vain for the empty password fields to auto-populate, a candle dies for no apparent reason. Big deal, there are five more. But here I am again, with no clue as to what either password might be. Where is Scott's amazing pamphlet full of passwords when I need it? If this app really does live up to its security claims, I can expect it to lock up after three attempts. Five at the very most. So I stop trying.

Still, at least the titles of the other six diary entries remain visible. These are:

Out, Demon, Out

My Sweet Saviour

I Am In Love With V

Burning New Pathways Into The Brain

Joining The Death Grip Cult

The End

Fucking hell, this is one big barrel of WTF.

Out, Demon, Out? No idea.

Burning New Pathways Into The Brain? What. Does. That. Even. Mean.

Joining The Death Grip Cult? Very worrying indeed. When I Google for *death grip cult*, the results include an article from 2010 about an update issue with the iPhone 4, the Wiki-page for a 2012 martial arts movie called *Death Grip* (about a Satanic cult, apparently) and a Merriam-Webster dictionary definition. The latter offers an example of the term *death grip* in a sentence: *the cult leader had such a death grip on his followers that all orders were carried out without the slightest objection.* Thanks, Merriam-Webster: that hasn't freaked me out at all . . .

Another candle dies. Must be a draught getting through those windows.

Or the death grip cult might be messing with you.

Oh God, pipe down.

I Am In Love With V? Since my name doesn't begin with "V", this particular missive must be about some other woman. How delightful. Especially as this particular entry is dated 7 June, which fell between the detox retreat and our Leeds date.

Will keep an eye out for names beginning with V when I finally wade through Tinder and the like. Forewarned is forearmed, or something.

Wow, though: Scott was in *love* with somebody else, back in June? Having assumed him to be a serial shagger, I didn't even consider this possibility. As soon as he realised he was in love with someone else, why would he carry on dating Kate Collins? Am I really that good in bed?

I *am* pretty good in bed.

Hmm. Could Scott have been referring to the 1980s sci-fi series *V*? Doubtful.

This final entry, *The End*, feels ominous. Particularly as this one comes straight after *Joining The Death Grip Cult* and was written a mere three days ago on 1 October. Jesus, what if Scott killed himself? The thought makes me feel ill. Why would he do that? Who knows? Over the years at work, I've consoled so many friends and relatives of people who decided to leave this planet without having displayed a single warning sign.

Frustrating that I can't get inside this thing. So frustrating. What now?

Bed, that's what. Time to clean my teeth.

The air in the bathroom tastes stale and stagnant. There's no external window, only a small, ineffectual air-con grate up by the ceiling. The glossy shower curtain's gone, but there's a delightful mildew scent that I'd never noticed before. Because love.

Here's something handy that Scott showed me: when you flick a tiny switch at one side of the sink mirror, it frames the glass with battery-powered light. I jam my electric toothbrush into my mouth and press the button that treats my gums to the car-wash experience.

I need to sleep, but surely I can just take one more quick

look at Scott's phone once I'm settled down on the living room floor? What possible harm could—

BZZZZZZ.

That crazy entryphone buzzer rocks the whole flat.

Fucking hell, who's this? How I hate being so back-footed, with no clue where I stand in this place. Someone might be coming to kick me out at any time, and I couldn't do a damn thing about it. Where would I go, especially with all these boxes?

Standing in the bathroom doorway with the toothbrush still buzzing my gums, I gaze along the moon-spattered corridor to that handset on the wall beside the front door.

I positively *will* the entryphone not to make that godawful noise again.

BZZZZZZ.

What I hate even more than being back-footed is the fear. The fact that someone *wants in*. Some faceless, invisible person, whose identity I won't know until I tug the entryphone off its cradle.

What if this visitor isn't even human?

WTF, brain? That's ludicrous and far from helpful.

You feel it, though, don't you? You feel that something's wrong here.

Stepping out of the bathroom, I await the third demand for entry.

Seriously, what is wrong with me? I *am* a coward. All that's happening is some human being or other is standing a few floors down, pressing the buttons marked *two*, *three* and *call*.

This is only a human being.

But what if it ain't, coward?

I'm walking now. Closing in on the front door, closing in . . .

I fully expect the entryphone to blare in my face, but somehow the silence screams louder.

Only a human being, I tell myself, feeling so silly as I reach for the handset. This is some flesh-and-blood person who eats and shits and brushes their teeth, just like me.

Oh God, I'm still brushing my teeth. How am I supposed to speak?

I snatch the handset from the cradle and jam it against my ear.

There's nothing. No sound at all.

Hopefully, whoever it was has given up. While I'm here, I feel around on the entryphone wall-cradle for a mute switch, but no, that would be *way* too conv—

Knock-knock-knock from the other side of the door.

I swallow the toothpaste. Totally swallow the lot.

My head spins. I'm wondering why this visitor has refused to take no for an answer while I simultaneously recall online scare-stories about swallowing toothpaste.

Way back along the dark hall, the bathroom's mirror light flickers and makes the front door's spyhole glisten, as if inviting me to take a look outside.

Mint, mint, so much mint. The paste burns my gullet, like radioactive gloop.

Knock-knock-knock-knock-KNOCK.

Only a human being. An infuriatingly impatient human being . . .

Stepping up against the door, I carefully plant my right eye against the spyhole.

Darkness.

All I see is darkness, punctured only by those dim, green emergency lights on the ceiling. How can this be?

The sensor lights must have clicked back off. They do that after a while, remember? That's all this is.

Still, the idea of someone motionless outside the door, unconcerned by the darkness . . . Why don't they wave their hand around to re-trigger the lights?

My horrendous toothpaste throat forces me to croak. "Hello?"

Someone speaks outside. Someone who clearly isn't Scott, what with having the voice of an older woman. "Oh. Who's that?"

I cough, then spit a blob of toothpaste into the corner beside the door so that I'm better able to speak. Classy.

Out through the spyhole, there's still nothing, but irrational fear triggers my sass. "That's not how this works. You've come to my door, so you're the one who has to announce who you are."

The reply comes loaded with indignance. "*Your* door, is it? All right, well, this is Maureen." Before I can run the name Maureen through my own personal search engine, to check if I've ever known a single Maureen in my life, she adds, "Scott's mother."

Shit.

My sass morphs into panic and ingrained British politeness. "Ah yes, of course! Sorry, Maureen, give me a second."

"It's really quite dark out here."

"Try waving an arm around and the lights should come back on." In the time it takes to yell this, I've covered the hallway back to the bathroom. Spinning the sink tap, I take a big mouthful of water, swoosh it around, spit it out, wipe my mouth and check myself in the mirror.

I resemble death itself. A minty-fresh Grim Reaper.

Think, think. What should I tell Maureen about this whole situation? What might she already know? Since I already responded as if I recognised her name, it's too late to pretend I'm a brand-new tenant who just moved in. And yet if I tell her the truth, she might demand that I sod off and cram my boxes into the nearest hostel. So let's play this safe, whatever that means.

"Coming!" I call out, like some swish party hostess. Three lit candles remain in the living room, so I grab one. Deep breath, big smile, open up.

My candlelight bathes the face of a plump woman who might be at the tail-end of her sixties. No more than five-feet tall, she'd be a good few inches higher if it wasn't for the stoop in her posture. Maureen looks like someone who constantly feels life's weight, but she's doing her best to muster a warm, if cautious, smile.

Stretching my fluoride grin from ear to ear, I say, "Sorry for my terrible rudeness. You just took me by surprise."

Her accent differs from Scott's London, with a Cornish tinge. "Oh no, dear, *I'm* sorry. I expected only Scott to be here, you see. Someone let me in downstairs, as they were coming out."

Sensing her preoccupation with my candle, I tell her, "I'm afraid we've got a power cut in here at the moment." Then I quickly add, "Must be affecting the corridor lights too."

"I see," says Maureen. "So . . . is Scott in?"

"He's actually not, but do come in anyway! Sorry in advance for the cold."

What the hell is this great British tradition of feeling obnoxious when you don't invite someone into your private living space? Do I really want her to come in? I don't know, but it's too late now and there's hot wax dripping down my hand.

Maureen hesitates, like a mistreated dog reluctant to step inside its new home. Shuffling past me into the hall, she says, "Um, so . . . you must be . . . uh . . ."

Shall we take this opportunity to count Maureen's legs? Contrary to her son's email claim that she'd had one amputated, I'm counting two, and I'd know a prosthetic on sight.

Just another lie for the growing dossier.

I follow her through the arch into the living room, where she takes in the sight of my boxes, presumably while trying to remember who I am. Chances are, she didn't know I was moving in. Why would Scott have even told her my name when he wasn't planning to hang around?

This is excruciating, but there may yet be an upside. If anyone can shed light on the real Scott Palmer, it must be his dear old mum.

"I'm Kate," I say, extending my hand for a shake which Maureen withholds. Hard to be sure if she even noticed my offered hand in this gloom, but she's palpably relieved to have learnt my name.

"That's it! *Kate*. You know, my memory isn't what it once was. So you're . . . you are obviously . . . Scott's . . . '

Her gaze flicks back across the boxes, then all around the room. Her hands fidget. Once again, here's that acute embarrassment. The bemused disorientation of a mother left out of the loop.

Flitting from one candle to the next, I relight each wick. What should I tell Maureen I am to Scott? My mouth makes the call before my brain gets to offer an opinion. "I'm Scott's girlfriend, yes! It's so exciting to have moved in. Shame you missed him, though – he's away for a couple of nights."

"Oh," she says with surprise, as if Scott never goes away. Which is interesting, given that he presented himself as quite the business traveller. "Where's he gone?"

Well now, Maureen. That's the ten-million-dollar question, and no mistake.

"Leeds. Would you like a cup of tea?"

"Oh . . . I thought you had no electricity?"

Or milk, or tea bags, Kate, you flustered fuck.

"Of course! How silly of me."

Maureen surveys the lack of sofa, proper furniture, TV or anything you'd normally find in a living area. These conspicuous absences form the elephant in this room, trumpeting louder and louder. Feeling like the star of a farcical sitcom, I dash over to grab the garden chair, picking Scott's phone up from the seat and jamming it into my pocket with a bad magician move. Did Maureen see me do this? I think she did, but there's no way she'd recognise Scott's phone in candlelight.

"Scott really wants to redecorate, you see, so all our things are either in the . . . bedroom, or . . . uh . . . in these boxes," I blather. Ferrying the chair over to Maureen, I wince at myself. "I really need to shift these boxes into another room."

Maureen actually settles down in the chair. If it collapses, I'll know for sure that I'm in some kind of virtual sitcom simulation.

She eyes the pristine and perfectly well-decorated walls with a frown. Why, it's almost as if something about my hastily-cobbled story doesn't hang together. "Hope you're not *paying* for this place to be done up, though. All of that should be covered by the landlord."

Whoosh. The word *landlord* sends me hurtling back through time.

CHAPTER TWENTY-EIGHT

12 July

When I ask Scott how long he's lived in his flat, he and I are walking hand in hand along the seafront promenade, like a real couple. We haven't explicitly agreed that we're a couple yet, but I hope one of us has the balls to broach the topic soon, because we already seem so comfortable with each other. I know I'm racing ahead here, but I wouldn't be surprised if Scott and I turn out to be something special.

My third Brighton visit has already been a winner. Following some divine morning snugglefuckery and wonderfully carefree afternoon wandering, we're on our way back from Hove. The late evening is full of that gorgeously vivid twilight you get when the sun's on the wane.

Somewhere around the base of the i360 Tower, we pass a fluffy Pomeranian sitting on the sea wall. Even I, a cat person, can see that this dog is super-cute. Several passers-by have whipped out their phones to photograph and video the hound, as the proud owner laps up all this attention.

Can't help noticing that no one ruffles or even touches the Pomeranian. They simply focus on their upload. As the dog watches them walk away, I swear its eyes go dim through lack of physical attention. This tempers my buzz for a while.

As the distant Palace Pier, zip-wire tower and Van Spencer building edge into view, Scott squeezes my hand. "You okay? Almost home."

"Such an impressive place to live," I say, liking how he's used the word *home* as if we live together. Daren't explain my sadness about the dog, in case he thinks me weird. "How long have you been there?"

"Let's see," says Scott. "I bought this flat at least a year ago. Really couldn't resist the location."

Raising my voice to be heard over the fairground music of the nearby carousel ride, I say, "I can see why. Must be a fair old mortgage, though . . ."

Scott stops walking and groans. Shit, have I been too nosey?

"Indigestion," he says, planting one hand on his chest. "Happens sometimes. I'll pop a Gaviscon when we get back. But I actually bought the flat outright. Works out a lot cheaper in the long run."

Wow. Does IT really pay that well? Glad he felt able to tell me, though. Hopefully means he doesn't see me as the gold-digging type.

Either that, or he doesn't believe you'll be around long enough to dig any gold.

Dear brain: why can't you just let me be happy? Now you've made me want to test our relationship. But dare I?

"Hey, here's a question," I say out of the blue, stopping him in his tracks. "Look . . . I mean, we *are* an actual couple, right?" These last six words barrel out of me so hard, they sound like a threat.

Scott hits me with that unreadable gaze, peppering me with the same uncertainty as when I first saw him in the Welsh glade, except now to the power of ten billion.

Horrifying nanoseconds ooze by.

When he finally grins and wraps his arms around me, only then does my whole body unclench itself.

"I'm ashamed you had to ask first," he says, then he kisses me until I forget all about the Pomeranian.

CHAPTER TWENTY-NINE

4 October

Maureen's looking at me funny. I must've zoned out for a second or two. Flashbacks will do that to a person.

"Oh goodness, yes," I say, suddenly talking like a vicar. "The landlord's paying for everything. He seems like a good sort."

How long will Maureen stay, now she knows Scott isn't here? How much does she intend to quiz her prospective daughter-in-law? But more to the point, how can I use this situation to find out more about Scott? Best to get in there first, before she can open fire with queries of her own.

I perch myself on a box and try to style it out. "So, Scott talks about you all the time . . .'

Literally not once in four months, Maureen. You might as well be thermonuclear physics.

" . . . and now I've finally got to meet you, I'd love to know what he was like as a boy."

No real idea of what I'm gunning for with this line of enquiry. I'd flailed around for any question that wasn't, *So who the fuck is your mad bastard son, really?* Still, a little childhood colour might helpfully contribute to the profile I'm building of my dear departed lover.

Maureen chuckles and visibly loosens up. "Oh! Well, I can't lie, he was a real wild one at school. Had me tearing my hair out at times."

I mirror her laughter, as if my inquisition really is only small-talk fun. "Ah, really? What sort of capers did he get up to?"

Did I say *capers*? Pretty sure that happened. I normally only say that word when ordering pizza.

"He'll kill me for saying this, but he did get into fights."

A real wild one . . . fights . . . I try to square this with the placid, laid-back Scott I thought I knew, then remember the brooding wolf behind those eyes.

"He always told me it was self-defence," Maureen quickly adds. "From bullies, you know. His brother always told me a different story. He said Scotty was sometimes the bully, but you know what brothers can be like. One-upmanship and all that silliness."

Brother? New information alert.

"Oh yes, of course, his brother," I say, then grimace and click my fingers a few times. "What's his name again?"

"Raymond. He's such a good boy." How old is this guy – five? "But I have to admit, Scotty's done quite well for himself too."

She smiles fondly, in the exact same way my own mother never smiles about me. "And now," she adds, slapping both hands down on her thighs. "Scotty's settled down! That's lovely."

I nod and force a grin. Maureen said *settled down* with such happy incredulity that it was basically code for *finally picked one girl*.

Another slice of evidence for my fat dossier.

Before I can ask how often schoolboy Scott kissed the girls

and made them cry, Maureen whacks the ball back into my court. "So how did the pair of you meet? Scotty did mention it, of course, but you know . . . " One hand darts to her temple, by way of explanation, or excuse. Christ, and I thought *I* was a transparent liar.

Well, Mrs Palmer, I first saw Scott on the hook-up app Tinder and Super-Liked him, but he didn't even Like me back.

"We met at a business seminar," I say with a professional smile. "Our eyes met over canapes, and then we were courting for quite a while."

Capers. Canapes. Courting. What ridiculous word beginning with "C" will my brain magic up next?

"Oh, what business are you in?" What's that glint I see in Maureen's eye: is she testing me? Her bullshit detector may be more advanced than I've given her credit for.

Here we are, at another crossroads. Do I lie about my job? No, why should I? It's a good one. And why am I even trying to impress the mother of a man who's abandoned me?

"I'm a senior paramedic," I tell her. "But, you know, there's lots of business involved." Think, think fast, for an example. "So many protocols we have to deal with." Protocols, yes! Brilliantly oblique and dull. Nobody ever wants to hear more information on protocols.

Maureen nods, studying her clasped hands. There follows an eternal silence, during which neither of us knows what to say next. "Well," she says, with a smile that doesn't come anywhere near her eyes, "I suppose I'd better be getting on. Such a pleasure to meet you."

"Likewise," I say, springing up from my box to help her out of the chair. She waves me off, determined to help herself. "Maureen, I'm so sorry I couldn't offer more hospitality. Next time you come, this flat will be a palace."

No, it won't. Either my boxes and I will have gone somewhere else, or only a few will have been unpacked and I'll feed you some crap about how the decorators have delayed the job.

"Have you seen Scott lately?" I ask, light as a feather, as I guide her towards the door.

"Not for a few weeks." She sounds sad about this. "I don't like to bother him on the phone: I always think I'm interrupting work. I wonder if you could ask him to call me, or even pay me a visit?"

"Of course. Do you live nearby, then?"

"Oh, I'm only up in Seven Dials."

"Ah, yes, Scott did say. That *is* nice and close. Lovely." *I have no idea where Seven Dials is.* "Well, I'll certainly badger him to get in touch, Maureen, don't you worry."

As we walk to the door, Maureen scrawls something on a ratty little piece of paper, then hands it over. "That's my home number, just in case you need me."

What's an appropriate farewell, now that we've been introduced? Maureen doesn't strike me as the huggy type. I consider going for the handshake again, but after a quick *Goodbye, dear* she's out the door so fast that the darkness swallows her in one clean gulp.

"Oh, heavens," she says, from somewhere off along the corridor, her voice shrill. "Can't see my hand in front of my face."

"Careful, Maureen! Would you like to take one of my candles?" The fire door thumps shut, placing her out of earshot.

So. I've met Maureen Palmer. What an odd woman. No doubt she's thinking exactly the same thing about me.

Now that I'm by myself once again, her son's phone calls my name. I've barely scratched the surface with this thing, but I'm already awake far later than I should be. Chances are, if I behold evidence of more of Scott's lies tonight, it'll only rile me up and make sleep even more elusive. Besides, simply meeting Maureen has already given me evidence of bonus lies from Scott. Oh, happy day.

Tonight, I will devote more effort to the sleeping arrangements. Having hauled my bedding out of a box, I dump it on my designated spot. My Nokia goes *ping* a couple of times, no doubt because lovely Izzy wants to know how everything went on my first day, but she'll have to wait till tomorrow. I could almost shed a tear of gratitude for the soft familiarity of my trusty old pillow.

Incredibly, all six candles are still burning. The wind must've changed direction. Should I mute Scott's phone, in case another weirdo calls in the middle of the night? No. While I still have access to this handset, I may as well leave myself open to every scrap of information that comes my way. Bring it on, creeps.

There. Done. Let's doze.

Using a technique I remember from a How To Sleep CD, I make my inner voice all slow and drowsy, then count down from three hundred.

Two hundred and ninety-nine . . .

Two hundred and ninety-eight . . .

Two hundred and ninety-seven . . .

Two hundred and ninety . . . can't remember where I was. Back to three hundred . . .

Two hundred and ninety-nine . . .

What's this strange taste in your mouth?

Don't know, don't care. Two hundred and ninety-eight . . .

I think you do care. Tastes like metal. Copper. Could this be blood?

Two hundred and ninety-blood . . . oh God, what *is* this taste?

I stick two fingers in my mouth then check them for blood, but it's way too dark to tell.

Oh. Why is it dark all of a sudden?

Jesus, the candles have died. Every single one. Smoke drifts up from their wicks.

This weird taste grows stronger and my teeth hurt.

Are you feeling what I'm feeling?

No, brain, I'm not. Let's just breathe and—

There's something new in the flat. Some kind of presence.

Keen to rule out blood in my mouth, I reach over for Scott's phone to use the torch.

In the furthest corner of my eye, I catch a glimpse of something and stop dead.

Over in the archway, there's a fierce, pale blue flicker. Quite a big one.

Could this be an ambulance light? Surely not, because I'm on the fifth floor. So what the fuck is it?

Why don't you roll over and take a proper look?

The metallic taste spreads through the soft palate of my mouth, and my dumb heart acts like someone just fired a starting pistol. Flying in the face of rational thought, animal instinct tells me to flee this thing and run out into the fresh air of the balcony, where sanity will prevail.

Fuck that. Sanity dictates that I stay put. This weird shimmer *must* be reflecting in from somewhere.

Then why is it moving towards you from out of the archway?

Somewhere inside me, a panic attack wants out, but I refuse to entertain it.

Sure enough, the flickering blue thing fades away to nothing. Because, of course, there never was any flickering. The metal taste has subsided, too.

Clearly, I've just had a textbook episode of psychosomatic stress. Seen so much of that in my time, and now it's my turn. Stress makes people hallucinate, vomit and, in extreme cases, even go blind, so I'm getting off easy with a little flickering in my peripheral vision. The ambulance-style light even ties in with my job, so it makes perfect sense.

Don't fool yourself. That was no hallucination. This thing came right out of the archway and was an actual entity.

Irritated by myself and my stupid imagination, I go back to counting down from three hundred, determined to ignore this copper aftertaste.

CHAPTER THIRTY

5 October

"Go easy, mate. You're *this* close to clipping a parked vehicle."

"Tyler, I was driving ambulances when you were watching *Teletubbies*."

"Yeah, but this might be a wider truck than you're used to."

"You wanna walk? If so, keep yapping."

Tyler stuffs crisps into his face as I take us north up Queen's Road, an uphill ride from the clock tower to the train station. We are heading for a job in Seven Dials, where our next patient is in some form of panic. "I never, ever watched the fuckin' *Teletubbies*," he mumbles.

How I wish I could still feel the rush that hit me when I first drove one of these beasts. That scary sense of power, when you first actually get to trigger the flashing lights. When all the excitement dies down, being the driver is fifty per cent about taking a break from having to talk to patients when you're too tired to be upbeat and strong for them. The remaining fifty per cent lies in making a lot of noise and waiting for other vehicles to get out of your way.

Here's one positive thing about Tyler: he makes me focus on the road more, because I'm determined to drive so flawlessly that I'm above his criticism. This distracts me from dwelling too much on why the hell I found fresh wood chips on the post-mat this morning thanks to a new set of gouge marks on the inside of the door.

Something inflicted those marks during the night, while you slept, and the culprit may have been the Flickering Thing In The Corner Of Your Eye. You're welcome.

Yes, what I need to do is forget about that . . .

. . . *inexplicable entity* . . .

. . . psychosomatic trick of the retina and concentrate on the road. I need to pat myself on the back, too, for having somehow followed through on my pledge not to bring Scott's phone out on this shift. While I'm at it, I'll remind myself of this morning's three gratitudes: my health, my job and my sanity. Even if the third one might be debatable.

Tyler gabbles about the steering, and I tell him to pipe down because I've zeroed in on a mad news story on the radio. In Japan, a select group of rich people have become early adopters of a brand-new smartphone called the Plasma 5000, which doesn't need any kind of electrical power source.

"This controversial handset can be powered solely by the user's own blood," says the newsreader. "One owner was hospitalised last week in Osaka, leading to widespread calls for a ban. It is understood that the hospitalised man used his phone continuously for thirty-eight hours before his reported collapse."

Tyler says, "What a wanker." He tips his crisp packet up, so he can suck down all the tiny salty bits. Then he slings the empty packet onto the dashboard and grabs his phone to check what's happened during the three minutes he's been away.

"That story has to be bollocks," I mutter, while thinking how cool it would be to have a phone you could power with your own body.

The lunchtime traffic's bad. Of course, Tyler has already suggested alternative roads we could take. I should consider those ideas and stop being stubborn.

When I make the magic siren wail, the sea of metal and rubber slowly begins to part. For some reason, my attention gets sharply drawn to the pavement on Tyler's side. My unconscious mind understands why before I do.

Tyler's saying something vapid when I spot the deathly pale woman with bright red dreadlocks.

Holy Hell, she's Action Girl, from one of those pictures on Scott's phone. Her distinctive, hard features are the same ones that had stared out of the phone screen at me. And there's the tattoo sleeve on her arm.

For one insane heartbeat, I want to roll down the window and call her over. I won't, though, obviously. And now I can't, because she's walked into a pub.

Tyler is saying something else. Much louder now.

". . . Kate? What are you waiting for, mate?"

Shit. The road ahead lays so open before us that it might as well be empty. A whole line of obediently shifted cars is waiting for me to fucking step on it. Behind us, someone finally summons the courage to honk their horn, thereby giving others the go-ahead to raise a chorus.

I stomp the accelerator. As we move, I duck my head down, trying to see the name of the pub, but it's already too far behind us.

I spray Tyler with Gatling-gun words. "What's that pub we just passed? Back there on the left. Quick, look now, right now."

The wipe-clean plastic of Tyler's seat squawks as he twists around to look. "The Hope and Ruin. Fucking vegan place. Delete."

I have no idea what the hell I would ask Action Girl, this complete stranger, if I had the chance. All I know is that her picture is on Scott's phone and I won't be able to come back to this pub until our shift ends in two hours.

The Hope and Ruin, eh? Ain't that just me and Scott in a nutshell.

This man foaming at the mouth has to be in his sixties. He has long, grey hair and a neatly trimmed white beard. He is also stark bollock naked.

His hairy belly mercifully hangs down over his groin as he runs into view from around the side of the house. I was about to push the doorbell, but it seems that won't be necessary.

The next thing I notice, after all the nakedness and the running, is the fact that this man is pushing an empty wheelbarrow. When he reaches the garden path that crosses the front of this house – *his* house, presumably, unless he happens to be the gardener, gone fucking loco – he stops dead, maybe ten paces away, and fixes us with comically wide eyes.

My guess is that Tyler's jaw hangs similarly slack, because Tyler is silent and I already know him well enough to grasp that this is unusual.

Deranged Naked Guy's eyes flick from me to Tyler, then back to me. One moment, frozen in time. I picture myself telling this story across a pub table someday, and decide that this will end in victory. I'm a professional. All I need to do is calm this guy down.

As I open my mouth to speak, the man arches his back and unleashes a howl that sounds like his insides are being shredded.

"Shit," says Tyler.

"Please stay calm, sir," I say as Deranged Naked Guy shoves the wheelbarrow aside. This feels unnervingly like he's discarded a toy and we're about to become its replacements.

When DNG shifts posture, I can tell he's about to charge us like a rhino.

"Back to the ambulance," I tell Tyler, leading the way back along the path.

Tyler stays put. "Let me handle this," he says.

"With me, *now*," I tell him, loading the words with all the authority I can muster, "or this won't end well."

Sure enough, DNG launches into the best impression of a sprint that his obese, goose-pimpled body can muster. Heading straight for Tyler.

Either Tyler has decided to trust my instinct, or it's self-preservation that propels him towards me and the ambulance.

Oh, thank God, I left the back door unlocked. Once we're both inside, I slide the clunky latch across.

Tyler calls the police, then falls silent beside me.

During what might be one full minute, we each only utter two words.

Tyler says, "Zombie apocalypse?"

I say, "Shut up."

The whole ambulance shudders, then rocks. I've experienced this sensation twice before, during small riots on the streets of Leeds. This kind of movement signals that someone is climbing on top of the vehicle.

Moving as one, Tyler and I tip back our heads to examine the ceiling.

The ambulance rocks some more. Big naked footsteps thump louder and louder, until they're right above our heads, then they stop.

"The roof's strong, right?" Tyler breathes.

"Not really," I tell him. I'm about to add that ambulance roofs are only fibreglass shells, when I notice he has his phone in his hand like a camera. He's filming.

"Tyler, what are you doing?"

"Evidence," he says. "In case he bloody tries to kill—'

There's a godawful *crack* and the ceiling gives way. Full-on collapses.

Having fallen through the gaping hole he made, DNG somehow lands on both feet, facing away from us. The ambulance sways to absorb the trauma, as blood dribbles from tiny new cuts all over his back.

Panic makes me clumsy as I unlatch the door and bodily shove Tyler back outside.

I'm about to follow him out, when DNG grabs my shoulder.

His hand is slick with blood and mouth-foam, which makes it easier to slip free of his grasp. In a flash, I'm beside Tyler. Lucky I didn't need his help to escape, because he gave me none. Together, we slam the doors shut in our patient's face, then lock them tight.

We stand and watch as the sounds of pure insanity issue from within. The doors shudder and shake, as DNG gives them everything he's got. I'm guessing he's gone insane on a classic like PCP or some wacky new drug with an equally wacky name, like Dogface or something.

Having caught a glint in Tyler's eye, I decide to cut him off at the pass.

"Don't say it," I tell him. "Don't you fucking dare say it."

Tyler frowns. A picture of pure innocence. "Don't say what?"

"You're itching to say 'Welcome to Brighton', aren't you? Like you're in an action movie."

Tyler shrugs. Then he meets my gaze. We hold for a long moment, then burst out laughing. A whole load of tension rolls out on a wave of pure hysteria.

For the first time, I feel as though Tyler might become tolerable.

CHAPTER THIRTY-ONE

5 October

Right away, the Hope and Ruin impresses the tits off me by being one hundred per cent vegan. Interesting retro-tech stuff clings to the walls, interlaced with fairy lights and artfully loose wires. No two lamps match in the whole place. There's a full-sized caravan wedged into one side of the room, inside which a tiny kitchen bustles with activity. The crowd are young, or at least younger than me. In contrast to Loading on the seafront, many of them are reassuringly preoccupied with their phones.

Action Girl isn't among them. As I'd feared, she must have left. I consider leaving too, until the stoner-rock barman asks if I'd like a drink. And now, like a proper old woman, I realise I really could do with a nice sit-down. Some ale too, please. I'll just have to exercise moderation.

Having placed an order for a vegan kebab, I take my pint over to a table that boasts an embedded retro video game screen. While four ghosts chase Ms Pac-Man around an electronic maze, I make my second attempt to infiltrate Scott's TrooSelf diary app.

I try a few of Scott's favourite words – *bamboozle*, for instance – but it's hopeless. Each password is bound to be a combination of letters and numbers anyway. Symbols, too. Pissed off, I impulsively return to the Videos folder on Scott's phone. The time feels right to try again.

What a dick I am. Once again, I'm allowed only the briefest look at those video thumbnail images – a few faces, a few flashes of pink skin – before the phone crashes. I try to take a screen grab before it dies, but there's nowhere near enough time. Seems pretty obvious, then, that this lame device specifically cannot handle even showing me video thumbnails, let alone the clips themselves. The phone may have been damaged when Scott dropped it on his balcony decking, or it's nearing the end of its lifespan.

Frustrating. This phone is a treasure trove of information and yet I'm stuck out here in the stupid real world. I attack my ale, drum my fingers on the table and try the power button every ten seconds. Nothing. This handset feels as dead as . . .

. . . *that thing in the corner of your eye last night* . . .

. . . a dodo skewered on a doornail.

All the chatter in the room blurs into background noise. I morosely fixate on Ms Pac-Man as she chomps her way through endless pills, pursuing a quest for a satisfaction she can never find. The ghosts who chase her so relentlessly, on the other hand? They will always win.

Unlike Ms Pac-Man, I'm not trapped in this maze. I can stop whenever I like.

I really should stop. And yet, even as I consider this, my finger is locked in auto-pilot, poised to try the phone's power button again.

A plastic basket containing my awesome-looking Beelzebab is placed on the table before me. As I thank the server, a passing flash of red draws my eye. By Christ, here's Action Girl with her unmistakable dreads. She's ferrying her pint from the bar towards the front door. Where's she going: outside for a smoke? No. I watch as she hurries out of the small entrance hall, through a door I'd never noticed before. Typical for me and my Grade-Z observation skills.

After a couple of abortive attempts to hear my question over the music, the barman reveals that this door leads up to "the gig venue". Quickly absorbing this new info, I take myself, my Beelzebab and my pint upstairs, then pay five pounds to see The Shit Monkeys.

"What the fuck?" spits Action Girl, doing her best to outpace me on the pavement. Her accent is proper Yorkshire, right down to the *fook* instead of *fuck*. "Are you seriously gonna follow me all the way home?"

"Yes," I say, feeling more than a little bit crazed.

"I wouldn't advise it, nobber."

Action Girl had refused to speak to me while The Shit Monkeys were purveying their foolishly loud industrial-punk racket. I was, after all, a wild-eyed stranger clutching a pint and a kebab. So I waited patiently, only for her to refuse to speak to me afterwards too. And here we are.

"Look," I tell her. "All I want is to ask you something."

"Yes, and I have asked *you*, several times, to get fucked. I go to gigs to chill out, not to be given a fuckin' asthma attack by someone tapping on me shoulder."

"That's not unreasonable," I say, falling into step beside her. "Although The Shit Monkeys aren't exactly my idea of a chill-out band."

"Who cares what your idea of owt is?"

"I'm honestly not a crazy person or anything." Could anything sound much more ominous than those opening words? "It's just . . . my ex has a picture of you on his phone. And I wonder if you know him."

Action Girl's glance could freeze the sun. "What *type* of fuckin' photo?"

"Oh, no, don't worry! Not *that* type. You're fully clothed."

"Why don't you ask *him* if he knows me? What's all this shit about?"

Do I open my heart to this woman who might be involved with Scott? For all I know, if he's moved elsewhere in Brighton, she could be heading to his new place right now.

I hold up Scott's phone. "Please, take a look at the picture."

When Action Girl sees Scott's photo of her on that mountain peak, her derisory glance becomes the classic double-take, and now she's interested.

"Where'd you get that?"

"Well," I say. "That's the thing. I'm assuming you know a guy called Scott? Scott Palmer?"

She doesn't reply verbally, but her face tells me she doesn't. There isn't even a flash of recognition that she quickly conceals. Okay, but who took the picture, if not Scott? Just in case she knows Scott by an alias, I show her his Tinder pic.

"For fuck's sake," Action Girl says, but now she's less vehement. Spittle no longer flies out of her mouth when she talks at me. "I don't know the guy from Adam. Is that okay? Can I go now?"

We're halfway up a hill, outside a pub called The Battle of Trafalgar. A gust of stale ale drifts out of the front as someone leaves.

"Look," I tell her, nodding towards this door of opportunity. "Five minutes of your time gets a drink on me. Okay, two drinks."

Turns out Action Girl isn't her real name. Who knew?

Ali downs one of her two vodka shots, then slams the glass

on the ancient wooden surface between us, like we're in some Wild West saloon. The surrounding landscape of vacant tables and chairs is interrupted only by the odd group of drinkers.

I'd feared she might neck both drinks, give me the finger and leave, but there's intrigue in these dark brown eyes. "Maybe this Scott bloke was shagging Gwyneth, then? Or still is, for all I know?" Seeing my face tighten, she adds, "Sorry, mate . . . was this a recent split?"

This photo of Ali on top of the County Down mountain Slieve Donard was actually taken by her half-sister Gwyneth two-and-a-half years back, shortly after the two women reached the peak together.

Ali has shown me a picture she took of Gwyneth that day, up on the peak. Her sister has a face so distinctive that I'm convinced I've yet to see her on Scott's phone. Her harsh, bony face is dominated by a fiercely pointed nose and framed by dark curls.

So why does Scott have Gwyneth's own picture of Ali on his phone?

Thanks to vodka, I can't be bothered with fabricating some story for Ali's benefit. "Scott did a runner on me. Could've gone off to be with your sister . . . but actually, that doesn't make sense."

Ali cocks her head, defensive. "Why not? She's a fucking stunner."

"That's not what I mean . . . it's a picture of *you* he's got on his phone." As I say this, I pat my pocket where Scott's phone lives. Ali notices.

"Hold up," she says, looking at me like I'm an escaped lunatic again. "That's *his* phone?"

"He left it behind. And . . ." Sod it, Ali's so drunk she won't even remember this chat. "And I unlocked it to have a look inside."

Ali weighs me up, stony-faced. Then she says, "Good on you, if he's fucked you about. I'd probably do the same. Weird, though, that he has that picture. Ah, you know what? Gwyn *tweeted* it from the top of the mountain. That could be why."

Ah yes, Twitter. A mostly public space. But why would Scott want that picture? He fancied Ali?

"Is he into mountaineering?" she asks, as if following my train of thought.

"I have no clue what he's into," I say, knocking back my second vodka shot to drown the humiliation. "So, if I haven't been too much of an arse-pain already, could you maybe ask your sister if she knows Scott? I just want to find out what kind of guy I almost moved in with, and where he might be, and—"

Ali halts me with a flat palm. "I haven't spoken to my sister since July."

"Oh. Did you guys fall out?"

To my surprise, Ali looks bewildered. "I don't even know. She seems to have kind of . . . disowned us. Even our mum. To be honest, it was on the cards for a while, because we always argued."

"Oh dear."

"Yeah. Gwyn won't even reply on Facebook or owt now. Mum's convinced she's run off to join a cult or summat."

A dark bell rings in my head. *Joining The Death Grip Cult.*

"That's so strange," I say. "And such a shame."

Ali shrugs a little too hard. "Her choice, innit. You can't force people to stay in your life. But yeah, it really *is* a shame. You grow up with someone, and then suddenly your only window into their life is their fucking Twitter feed."

"Tell me about it. Do you ever think it might be better not to look?"

Ali nods. "Don't know why she didn't just block us."

Her tortured expression tells me everything I need to know.

She knows she should stop looking, but she can't seem to follow through. When temptation waits permanently on a screen, twenty-four-seven, while constantly updating itself, what can you do to avoid that? Take down the entire internet?

After being confronted with her own online addiction, Ali has had enough. She downs her second shot and makes for the door, her face and voice lemon-sour. "Well, this has been fun. Good luck with stalking your ex, but me babysitter needs paying."

"What's your surname?" I blurt. "Maybe . . . I'll . . . see you on Twitter?"

"McBeal," she says, then heads for the door.

I piece her alleged full name together in my head, remember the TV show *Ally McBeal*, then call out, "And what's your *real* surname?"

She laughs. "Cooper. Now sod off."

I smirk back at Ali Cooper as she leaves, then I order another shot. These cheeky little drinks are well moreish. Pulling out Scott's phone, I fruitlessly check for new calls or texts – nothing – and launch Twitter to search for Ali and Gwyneth. Even as the app opens up, my heart sinks. Ali Cooper sounds all too much like the rock star Alice Cooper. Did she feed me another fake name?

Brilliantly, her full name genuinely is Alice Cooper. Her Twitter bio says, *No, I'm not that bloke who bites the heads off bats*. I wonder why, in all her time on Twitter, none of the platform's resident *Um actually* brigade have popped up to tell her the bat-biter was Ozzy Osbourne, then I see she only has twenty-one followers.

Despite Alice and Gwyneth being half-sisters, they share the same surname. Here's Gwyneth Cooper's unmistakable face on her Twitter profile, wearing a big friendly grin. Below this pic, there's a slew of tweets, mainly sharing memes and animal abuse petitions. Gwyneth makes no mention of Alice, or how great her new life in a cult might feel. All I see is the usual pile of inconsequential shite that people post in a bid to stave off the daily boredom and grab some attention.

What to make of this whole Cooper sisters thing? Could Scott really have swanned off to be with Gwyneth? Did they bond over their penchant for shutting out family members? I'm pretty sure Maureen hadn't seen or heard from Scott for even longer than the fortnight she claimed.

I spend ten minutes burrowing down the rabbit hole of Scott's social media, for which he uses the same vulnerable-looking profile pic as seen on Tinder. His Twitter bio quite simply reads: *Just another face in the IT crowd.* He has 878 followers. A quick skim through these reveals a high ratio of female faces, none of which are Alice or Gwyneth. They're not among his FB pals either.

Scott's last tweet was today. A retweet, to be precise, involving that meme image of the grinning cartoon dog seated in the burning room, saying, *This is fine. I'm okay with all the events that are unfolding currently*.

Hmm. Why does this image strike a chord with me?

Best not to think about that.

Scott's latest FB post was also today. He's filled in a survey about his personality, namely *Which Historic Royal Would I Be?* and nominated five friends to do the same.

Turns out Scott would've been Henry VIII. Quelle fucking surprise.

The realisation hits me that I'm no longer looking at my own social media accounts. I'm using the apps that take you straight into Scott's Twitter and Facebook. This means I'm actually piloting the fuckers and could therefore post *as Scott*.

That's pretty big.

If I were feeling really vindictive, which I am, I could post something absolutely foul on his behalf and make a social media pariah of him. So very tempting. But what's the first thing someone does when they think they've been hacked? Scott would reset all his social media account passwords, then surely realise his lost phone was to blame. He'd finally get around to changing everything and I'd be locked out. Counterproductive.

While skimming over Scott's tweets and posts, both public and private, what I notice more than anything is the conspicuous absence of me. I'm not mentioned anywhere. Clearly, I only ever registered as a brief anomaly on his radar.

The night melts like Dalí clocks. Before I know what's happening, I'm striding down Queen's Road towards the seafront. Wind and rain team up to punish me, as I finally check out Tinder with the true recklessness of a drunk.

The first thing I see inside Tinder is Scott's face, and my dumb heart swells. The heart does, after all, take longer to process a break-up than the rational mind. You can never kill love outright. You can only leave it to die a slow, lingering death.

Entering self-destruct mode, I open Scott's matches. This is a visual list of the people he's Liked, who have also Liked him right back. Some of these people he has engaged in conversation. Claire from along the coast in Peacehaven, for instance, who has lovingly selected the following three words for her profile bio: *I'm just me!* Thanks for that, Claire, I really feel like I know you already. As far as Scott was concerned, your cleavage made up for your lack of brain cells, because here the two of you are, chatting away one month ago. On 4 September, to be precise. One week after Scott asked me to live with him.

Hey, Scott, what the hell were you doing? If your proposal of domestic cohabitation really was at all sincere, then were you seized by the urge to fill your boots before all that nasty monogamy descended upon you? Was that it? Or were you trying to find someone better?

Reading Tinder can only damage me. And yet, in order to finally kill off any lurking vestige of feelings I have for Scott Palmer, I need to suffer the truth.

Hmm. This probably isn't the best time to ask myself while I'm loaded on ale and vodka, but *do* I still have any feelings left for Scott?

Yes, in a way, I do. But those feelings only apply to the version of Scott I thought I knew. The carefully crafted specimen of manhood that he chose to present to me. In fact, I still love the living hell out of that Scott. He was awesome.

The real Scott, though? The one I'm unveiling on this phone, kilobyte by kilobyte? He can jettison himself so far into hell's bowels that he bursts straight out through the other side and ends up in the Earth's core.

Scott and Claire's Tinder chat doesn't last long before he suggests signing off to head over to WhatsApp. Ah yes, I'd almost forgotten about WhatsApp. Part of me wants to migrate over to that messenger portal so I can follow the rest of their chat that night, while the rest of me would rather go jump in the sea.

Sticking with Tinder, while navigating the seafront towards the flat I laughably call home, I read Scott's conversations with the likes of Holly, Julie . . .

. . . don't forget to look for women whose names begin with "V" . . .

. . . and Emma. These chats all took place between June and October, when Scott and I were seeing each other. I could forgive him for any shenanigans up until 12 July, because we had yet to officially become an item, but anything after that is unforgivable.

Although some of these Tinder chats fizzle and die, others end up switching over to WhatsApp. Given that Scott and I only saw each other once a week at most, and occasionally not for a whole agonising fortnight, he had ample opportunity to hunt down and meet whoever the hell he liked. So did I, of course, but this fact genuinely never crossed my mind.

Finally, I have confirmation. I have certainty. Scott Palmer is what Britney would refer to as a *womaniser*, over and over again.

The guy even liked Crafty Fox ale, for God's sake. The clues were there.

Tinder delivers one last bitter blow. Turns out Scott paid the subscription fee for extra features, including the ability to set his location to anywhere in the world. I find a pictorial grid which gathers the faces of no fewer than eighty-nine women, all of whom told Tinder they Liked Scott. Seems he never got around to either dismissing them from the list or saying he Liked them too. And so these hopeful dames exist in a kind of limbo, neither accepted nor rejected, which is somehow worse than either outcome. These women simply did not warrant any kind of judgement, one way or the other.

And of course here I am, positioned smack-bang in the middle of all the other limbo ladies. Schrödinger's twat. To make matters worse, my avatar pic is shaded blue, to denote that I'd Super-Liked Scott. Clearly, even my OTT act of enthusiasm hadn't inspired him to decide whether he Liked me back.

Was my main Tinder photo really all that bad? Hmm, well, it was the same pic I have on all my socials: me, sticking my tongue out at a jaunty angle. Always best to deliberately make yourself look ugly before someone else can make that judgement.

On Tinder, Scott deemed me unworthy of any judgement at all. And yet, when we happened to meet, four months later in Wales, he gravitated straight to me. Couldn't get enough. Guess I must have struck him as the kind of dimwit he could take for a ride.

At least there was one night in August when I came to question his bullshit.

CHAPTER THIRTY-TWO

20 August

Scott and I have a window table at Food For Friends. Since the most amazing black olive polenta is melting in my mouth, I believe Scott when he tells me this is one of Brighton's greatest veggie restaurants. I love how this is a relatively fancy place, and yet we have nothing special to celebrate except getting to see each other. That's one of the nicest things about a long-distance relationship: every date feels special. Every date feels heavy with meaning and spark.

On this particular evening, however, Scott seems to feel less pressure to make the most of our limited time. His mind has left our table without making its excuses. Having finished his starter, he's checking his phone. After every series of intense taps and flicks, he flashes me a smile, so I don't feel wholly ignored, but I no longer have full access to his mind.

I wonder what Scott looks at most often when he's on that thing. Checking his email, his texts, his WhatsApp, his share prices? How many steps he's walked today?

He could be obsessively checking out an ex's every move. Not that you'd know anything about that, obvs.

Is this unreasonable? Do I really want to be *that* partner who demands full attention at all times? But I mean, fuck, we're having dinner here. Scott's phone siphons away more and more of his attention – especially now that he's upgraded to this fancy new model.

This may simply be the way of all modern relationships. The pleasure of a digital fix will inevitably outshine the pleasure of connecting with your partner. These days, you face the impossible task of vying with the internet for their attention, and that's just the way it is.

Yeah, that's one idea. Or maybe Scott and I only get to see each other once per week at most, and I should speak the hell up.

"Shall we go for a drink after this meal we're having together?" Can't help loading that last part with sarcasm, but it doesn't register. "I like the look of the Mesmerist, across the road."

"Uh . . . " Scott is sitting right across the table, but his brain may as well be in Sydney. "I don't . . . know . . . We'll have to decide in a bit."

"Okay," I say, casual as anything. "Let's talk when you're back in the room." And I glide off to the ladies'. Once inside the cubicle, I breathe deeply and think of a few gratitudes. I tell myself that Scott and I are not, repeat not, going to argue about this issue.

Lost in the heat of argument, we walk the pavement, aimless, almost blind. Our mouths offload all the tension we couldn't shift in the nice, quiet restaurant. Scott is all innocent, hard-done-by eyes – damn those eyes – and earnest spread hands. Me,

I'm caught in that awkward position of not knowing whether I've made too big a deal of this, while feeling obliged to follow my complaint through.

"Baby, you know I've been extra-busy with work lately. I'm sorry I pissed you off, but I do have to keep more of an eye on things than usual."

"You were keeping an extraordinarily good eye on those things, even during our main course. But I'm starting to wonder what sort of things we're talking about here."

I know exactly what comes next from him. This pregnant pause will be followed by the classic utterance made in every couple's argument at some point, the whole world over. Three, two, one . . .

"What's that supposed to mean?"

"Well, how am I supposed to know what you're looking at on there?"

"Oh, Kate, come on. Please. Like what?"

No matter how tightly I fold my arms, my insecurities keep on coming. "How do I know you're not still looking at Tinder?"

This time, the pause lasts for ten steps at least. "Tinder?"

The words almost fly out of me, but I reel them right back in. *Yes, Tinder! Can we finally talk about the place where you fully ignored my Super-Like on Valentine's Day?*

I stop walking and round on him. "I'm using Tinder as an example: most people are on it these days . . . aren't they?"

"I was on there at one point." He doesn't try to escape my gaze, which is encouraging until I realise how political his answer sounds.

"But are you *still* on there, or any other dating places?"

He blinks. "I deactivated Tinder, soon as we became a thing. And that's the only one I ever used."

Unsure as to whether he's telling the truth, I don't know what to do. Ask to look inside his phone? That would stray into obsessive territory. You either trust your partner or you don't.

"I'm getting tired of you spending so much time on that thing when we're together," I tell him. "Can't some of this stuff wait?"

"No," he says. Actually, he doesn't merely say this. He almost growls it, and now a shade of grey has crept into his eyes. A cold grey I rarely see. "It bloody can't. Seriously, I'm under real work pressure at the moment, as I've told you several times."

"Don't patronise me, Scott. Of course I remember you saying, but the question is, do I believe it? You could be getting up to anything while I'm in Leeds."

"So could you," he says, still with that distinct edge, "but you don't see me making a big song and dance about your phone."

"I can hardly do much with that thing, anyway."

Walking again, I hear the angry thud of his footsteps behind me. His voice sounds tight as a steel trap. "Fucking hell, Kate, you know what I think this is really about? I can't believe I'm saying this, but you're jealous of my phone."

Clipping on my finest scandalised, incredulous expression, I laugh in his face.

While so very afraid he's right.

CHAPTER THIRTY-THREE

5 October

Marching home along the beach, I stray as close to the violence of the sea as I can get. The wind mounts one attack after another, no holds barred, as if trying to rip the flesh off my bones. This feels appropriately masochistic.

Okay, so Scott may have had a point about me coveting his phone, but he all-too-smoothly made me believe I was being unreasonable when I should have trusted my instinct that something was wrong. My instinct has, after all, helped save countless lives across the last fifteen years.

By the time we got back to Scott's flat that night, we were laughing about most aspects of our fight. He had apologised for his accusation, but I didn't explicitly apologise for asking him about Tinder. So there's one scrap of self-respect I can cling to.

After some blazing make-up sex, I went to sleep. Roughly one hour after reassuring me that he'd long since deactivated Tinder, Scott then chatted with some floozy named Samantha on that very app. What's more, he'd already exchanged two messages with her that night . . . while we were sitting at the fucking dinner table.

All this rain feels useful, because I can tell myself it's the only source of moisture on my face. After all, if I were crying over Scott Palmer, gaslighter extraordinaire, then what kind of flimsy excuse for a person would I be?

Doesn't matter how much the wind tries to rock me, or how close the sea dares to get to my shoes, because anger sees me through. Anger keeps me walking straight.

I am the rage of each white-crested wave, as it slams onto the glistening stones.

I am the howl at the heart of this gale.

I am the unearthly shriek of each and every gull that flies overhead.

I am the open white and screaming mouth of the moon.

I am a scorned woman with extremely wet feet.

Look out: my pocket is buzzing and here's the *True Romance* ringtone. The screen says *Unknown Number*.

Buoyed by anger and alcohol, I answer straight away.

After what feels like one whole minute of static, an unfamiliar woman's voice cuts through the line. Her voice carries the same flat, dark tone as Mr You're Going To Love It Here. "Listen to me. I don't know how you came to have this phone, but you need to stop using it, right now."

The phrase *red rag to a bull* springs to mind. "No, I really don't *need* to stop – you only *want* me to. Is this Samantha? I'll bet Scott's right there with you, the fucking coward, getting you to do his dirty work. Well, you can tell him from me that—"

She cuts me off. "This is not your phone, so don't use it."

"Why not?"

"For your own fucking good. *Trust* me."

Wow, death threat klaxon! "Am I supposed to be scared or

something? You'll be pleased to know I'm recording this conversation." I'm totally not recording this conversation, but really wish I was. "I suppose you daren't tell me who you are, right? Not to worry, though, I'm sure the police will find out for me."

A dead tone hums in my ear.

I stop to rest in a seafront shelter with my heart pounding, an out-of-shape boxer after a prize bout. Jesus, that was . . . something. This woman was definitely connected to Scott: surely one of his Tinder squeezes. Or could this have been Gwyneth?

By the time I reach the short front path that runs up to the Van Spencer, I'm dying to get inside and pass out. Someone's standing outside the front doors, pressing buttons on the entry-phone panel. A guy, I think, wearing a sharp and rain-spattered suit. His smooth-shaven head reflects the glow of the spotlights that surround the entrance.

If I were a proper resident here, I might be concerned about this random bloke gaining access to the building if I open the door. As it is, I couldn't care less.

Producing my keys, I say, "Excuse me," and he steps aside.

As I jam my key into the door, I side-eye the person's face and jump clean out of my skin, because this guy is Scott.

IZZY
wtf so scotts back . . . whats the deal then . . . was it all a big misunderstanding

KATE
No. This person wasn't Scott, but he looks exactly like him.

IZZY
whaaaat some guy who happened to look like your ex . . . u need glasses or have u lost it

KATE
This guy looked like Scott because he was his brother, Raymond. He much prefers Ray, though.

IZZY
jesus okay but . . .

KATE
his twin brother

IZZY
jeeeeezus woman . . . u could really be in trouble now . . . whatever u do dont bang this twin too

KATE
Too late.

IZZY
whaaaaaaaat tell me ur fuckin jokin

KATE
Okay, I'm joking.

IZZY
phew

IZZY
. . . but are u really joking tho

KATE
Yes, of course I'm bloody joking. What do you think I am?

IZZY
a slut lol . . . so what happened . . .
paint me the rest of the picture hun . . .
u jumped like fuck and then what

KATE
Well . . . I'm having a drink with him right now. He's coming back from the loo, gotta go.

CHAPTER THIRTY-FOUR

5 October

"So you'd like me to dish all the dirt on Scott, is that what we're saying here?"

Ray Palmer sparks a cigarette and winks, actually *winks*. He and I have settled around a heavy stone table in the front beer garden of the Amsterdam Hotel. A short walk from the Van Spencer, this place looks out over the seafront. A huge beer-branded parasol keeps steady rain off us, while an overhead heater fends off the cold.

I'm still recovering from the shock of seeing "Scott" at that front door.

When I laid eyes on Ray's face, I physically recoiled, because the resemblance is un-fucking-canny. He has the same eyes as Scott, which annoyingly means I find myself gazing into them for a little too long. His accent might be more harshly East London than Scott's, but the voice itself is the same, which leaves me with the uneasy sense that I really am talking to my ex. What if Scott went mad for a few days, cut his hair off, joined a cult alongside Gwyneth Cooper . . .

. . . *Joining The Death Grip Cult* . . .

. . . then got brainwashed into thinking he was his own twin? Or what if he's consciously pretending to be his brother? Could this be the next step of his plan to terrorise and humiliate me?

Pah, sheer paranoia. What did I ever do to Scott to deserve such punishment? And besides, it would be ludicrously brazen of Scott to masquerade as his own twin.

Would it be any more brazen than the combined weight of the lies he already told you? How do you know that Scott Palmer isn't a dangerous sociopath – a real wild one?

If so, then he's doing a very convincing job of impersonating his twin. Besides the shaven head, Ray carries himself so differently. His grey suit, snazzy-collared red shirt and pointy shoes all create the look of a Las Vegas pimp, or a poker player fallen on hard times. And whereas Scott's default facial position was an open smile, Ray's natural manner feels far less trusting. From the second we met, he's been shrewdly looking me over, as if trying to work out what makes me tick . . . while blatantly glancing at my chest.

Back at those front doors, there had been awkward introductions. Interestingly, whereas Maureen had clearly never heard of me, Ray actually said, *Oh, Kate! I've heard so much about you.* This could so easily be drunken bullshit, of course. His tell-tale glazed eyes and slurred words belong to a wino straight out of a Laurel and Hardy film.

When Ray inflicted a big, overly familiar hug upon me outside the Van Spencer, I'd made a snap decision to keep my story consistent with the one I told his mum. That story was basically the truth, after all, apart from having omitted the little matter of Scott leaving me.

What I must do here is capitalise on Ray's inebriation and

drill him for info. While taking care not to say too much, I've switched on whatever charm I might have, and used my last reserves of energy to make my eyes all keen and bright and sociable. Ray is enjoying the attention and especially the large Jim Beam on the rocks I've bought him.

He's already surrounded by so much cigarette smoke, it looks like he's on fire. "So how did you guys meet?"

I'm supposed to be asking the questions here. Pretty sure I can turn this one around with only one cunning word. "Guess."

Ray ponders the challenge. "Okay . . . let me see . . . you were in a bar and he sleazed up to you with one of his dodgy chat-up lines? Something like, *Am I dead? Because you look like an angel*?"

The words *Am I dead?* echo in my head, followed by the words *You Will Die*. Shaking them off, I try to summon a convincing image of Scott as a cheesy bar-butterfly. Never saw him that way. When he approached me, after Tomm's poem, it had felt so natural. He'd seemed almost shy.

"Nope," I say. "He can be pretty cheesy though, right?"

Ray sniggers. "He learnt all them lines off a Kindle pick-up manual! But I ain't saying no more. Don't wanna get myself in trouble."

I store the words *pick-up manual* for later use, glug on my G&T, then snap back into focus. "Scott and I actually met at a digital detox retreat."

The wind puffs Ray's cigarette out. "What the bloody hell's one of them when it's up and dressed?"

I can't be bothered to explain. "So, has he mentioned me much?"

He tries to relight the cigarette, without success. "Are you kidding? The legendary Kate Collins?"

Jesus. Scott not only told someone about me but told them my surname? This comes as a genuine surprise. "*Legendary*, eh?"

Ray cups his hands around his smoke and finally fires it back up. "He definitely made you sound legendary when we met for a drink. This was a few months back. The afternoon of our fortieth birthday, in fact. I know you must be shocked to hear I'm forty, but what can I say?"

True age alert! So, Scott hit the big 4-0 this summer. Could this fact have any bearing on his behaviour? People do often lose the plot when they reach a round number. Putting on a pitch-perfect display of casual forgetfulness, I say, "Oh yeah? God, when's his birthday again?"

"Naughty naughty," says Ray, waggling a finger at me. "Forgetting your fella's birthday? It's May the fourth. Scott told me it's easy to remember, cuz of all that geeky *Star Wars* bollocks. 'May the fourth be with you', or something."

Ray must be wrong about Scott having mentioned me back then, because I didn't even meet him in deepest darkest Wales until the first day of June. Ray is, after all, quite tipsy.

When I tune back into the conversation, he's saying, ". . . have to admit, he told me quite a few things that day that he probably came to regret. Drunk as fuck, he was, all confessional like I was some kind of priest. Ooh! Do pardon my language. I really shouldn't have said 'priest'."

He laughs heartily at his own gag, and I chuckle along to keep him on side. "So what was he saying about me that day?"

Ray taps the side of his nose, cartoon confidential. "Now that would be telling. You'd have to buy me a drink."

"Er . . . I already did?"

Ray considers his Jim Beam. "Oh yeah. But I probably already said too much."

"Are you sure it was me he mentioned that day?"

"After a few shandies, he couldn't stop saying your name.

Evangelical, he was! *Kate Collins, Kate Collins, Kate Collins.* Insisted you were gonna sa—'

Forcibly cutting himself off, Ray mimes zipping his mouth shut. Sabotaging my own casual façade, I lean forward, urgent. Damn this drunkenness, robbing me of subtlety. "He insisted I was gonna . . . what?"

Ray's laugh wafts smoke phantoms my way. "Sorry, Kate. Me and Scotty ain't been seeing eye to eye this summer. Don't wanna make things worse by getting indiscreet."

"Ah c'mon . . . you and me, we're family now. There should be no secrets here. Chances are, this is probably something Scott's told me himself anyway."

Ray's zip-mouth mime proves even more irritating the second time around – especially now that he accessorises it by placing the tip of one little-finger against his mouth like Dr Evil, which nobody's done for at least a decade. His cackle deteriorates into a gruesome cough.

"Can I buy you another Jim Beam?" I say, willing to try anything now. Well, almost anything. "I'd like to hear what's up between you and Scott. Perhaps I can help?"

Ray's already checking his flashy wrist-watch. Alarmed by what he sees, he drains his glass. "Sorry, Kate Collins. I've got somewhere to be."

His eyes flit boob-wards once again as he says, "I don't mind saying, my brother's really punching above his weight. Just don't tell him I said nothing about nothing."

I can barely disguise my exasperation. "What did you even *tell* me?"

Ray says, "Don't be a stranger, sweetheart," then swaggers back out onto Marine Parade, as I blurt out how we should swap numbers. Either he ignores me, or the wind scoops up my words to sweep them out over the foaming mayhem of the sea.

CHAPTER THIRTY-FIVE

5 October

Soon as I cross the threshold, the flat feels different.

On a purely physical level, this place ain't getting any warmer. I may as well have walked into a meat locker. The hallway and living room feel eerily still and quiet, but there's something else, too. A kind of tension, like I'm standing on one big loaded mousetrap.

That's because something terrible is going to happen.

The night is a wire, stretched so taut that it might snap without warning. But of course, this oddly brooding atmosphere must be all in my drunk, shattered head. Tomorrow is another early start on the wagon, and I shouldn't have even stayed awake this late, let alone gone out and got loaded.

Screw lighting any candles tonight. Not only am I too pissed to be tooling around with fire, I have no fear of the dark or anything else.

Plus, in the absence of light, you can't see that demon face on the window.

I slump straight down on my makeshift floor-bed, close my eyes, then groan at myself. Sleep, now? Who am I kidding? New unanswered questions make it utterly impossible for me to keep my hands off Scott's phone. On my way back here from the Amsterdam, all I've been able to think about is how an *evangelical* Scott could possibly have spoken to Ray about me in early May, before he even knew I existed.

I'm reminded of what Maureen told me about Scott and Ray's differing accounts of the fights Scott got into at school. So how much of what Ray said about Scott can I trust? Funnily enough, despite Ray having come across like a bad second-hand-car salesman, I feel I can place more trust in him than I ever should have in his twin.

There's one easy way to put this to the test.

The Kindle reader app on Scott's phone previously failed to pique my interest, but now Ray's made his claim about the pick-up book, this thing feels like compulsory reading.

Hey. You didn't check the bathroom or the bedroom, so look over to that archway and the hall. Just one glance to make sure nobody's standing there in the darkness, watching you. Scott, for instance.

Nope. Don't have to look to know there's nobody there.

Oh, really? Or are you too scared to see your ex-boyfriend standing out there . . . possessed?

You might also see another blue, flickering thing . . . right?

Exhaustion makes me twitchy and impatient as I scroll past a load of crime thrillers and unofficial Prince bios. Just when I'm about to give up and confirm Ray's status as a drunken bullshit-artist, here it is: *The Cunning Man's 69-Step Guide To Luring And Keeping Women.*

Well, how delightful. *The Cunning Man. Luring. Keeping.* I feel dirty, just from having seen the book cover.

The table of contents lists the chapter titles, so I skip the author's no-doubt-ugly foreword and go straight to the part about luring all these suggestible li'l kittens. A few pages later, I linger on Step Sixteen, which suggests how to break the ice with the *laydeez*.

The tl;dr version? *Make eye contact with women and find an opportunity to bond over something you agree on.* The author gives an example of mutually tutting over slow service at a bar in order to break the ice, then offering to buy the poor naïve waif a drink.

Bonding over something you agree on? Sounds familiar. Out in those Welsh woods, when Scott and I first made eye contact, we bonded over our shared mockery of Tomm. A deliberate tactic on his part, then.

An important note here, writes the author. *In order to non-verbally express agreement with the woman's point of view, you don't even have to share it. In fact, you can privately disagree. All that matters is the bond made and the hot sex you're getting tonight.*

Prickling and driven by instinct, I search for "Tomm" in Scott's Kindle library.

Three days after the digital retreat, Scott downloaded Tomm Kale's self-published poetry book, then gave it a four-star review on Amazon.

Even our first shared moment has become tainted. Our porcelain castle was built on sleazeball, woman-fearing crap, and I want to hurl Scott into the moat.

Psst! Was that movement, out there in the hall, or did clouds pass over the moon? Go on, take a look.

Kindly fuck off, brain. I only have eyes for this screen.

The wind rallies enough force to rattle the window frames as I meditate on how Ray told the truth about the pick-up manual. Could this mean Scott really did talk about me on their birthday, in advance of the detox retreat?

I search Scott's browser history for "Kate Collins".

Nothing comes up. Propelled by a brainwave, I Google to see if there's any way to dig up his private browser history. Yep, there is. As the instructions warn, this is far from the entire history, or even the entire recent history. But still, these are results I wouldn't otherwise have seen.

Scott's private browsing history is dominated by searches for cheap loans and porn. Hey, might one of these smut sites explain those bizarre screen grabs? Let's head off on a quick tangent. Can't hurt.

When I click on the URLs Scott visited, most of them lead to your standard porn . . . even though he has more of an appreciation of BDSM than I'd realised. He'd dealt me the odd playful spank, but never so much as broached the ball-gags, whips and bunny-tail butt plugs I see in some of these clips. Or indeed, thankfully, the watersports. Some of this stuff's pretty out-there, but nothing like the otherworldly madness in those screen grabs that I'm still really praying were taken from horror movies.

You really should check on that dark hallway now. Anything could be happening through there . . .

Staying on my tangent, I zoom over to Facebook, where none of my friends have convincingly identified those screen grabs I posted. One person vaguely reckons they've been taken from the orgy scene at the end of some lurid 80s horror film called *Society*. This raises my hopes until gore-movie fans queue up to insist that this person is entirely wrong.

Argh. I really should get back on track and solve the riddle of Scott having spoken about me before we met. Then I can sleep. Returning to his private history, I scroll all the way back to May.

Christ almighty, here it is. Scott ran several Google searches for *Kate Collins paramedic.* The first of these searches was on 1 May, exactly one month before we met for the first time in the Welsh woods.

Rattle-rattle-rattle go the windows, challenged by a shrill, unhinged wind. If I didn't know better, I'd swear Mother Nature was laughing hard at my expense.

My mind reels. Scott actually *targeted* me in Wales.

Why, why, why?

For reasons unknown.

How did he even know I would be at the detox retreat? And how am I supposed to sleep now, having learnt this? I'm going to be so fucked in the morning. And to compound the glee, I need the bloody loo.

Ooh, careful. That'll mean going out into the pitch-black hallway.

I can take Scott's phone to use as a torch. Just in case I need it.

Up I get, like a bleary-eyed child instructed to do something against her will. Approaching the archway, step by step, I hate the sense that the hall is practically daring me to set foot out there. Soon as I step through the arch, the whole corridor might come to life. Fast as the paper tongue of a party blower, it could wrap me up and gulp me down.

Please leave for your safety.

Ludicrous. Nevertheless, here I am, still hesitating, one step from the archway.

I actually find myself muttering, "Come on then, if you think you're hard enough."

Kate, major newsflash incoming: you've challenged a hallway to a fight. Calm down, go take a leak and then get some sleep, you absolute nutter.

Here's a fun observation: you haven't pushed all your boxes up against the front door for safety, like you did on that first night. Scott could easily have snuck in while you searched his phone. The wind would have ensured you didn't hear him enter. What if he's lurking unseen, among all those hallway shadows, back to revel in the emotional ruins he left behind and reclaim his phone?

A chill shimmers through me. Angry at this, I push back my shoulders and jut out my chest. My favourite life coach would be proud of the brave body language.

The darkness won't let you see Scott – not until you're close enough for him to reach out and grab you. Or he might say, Hello, Kate *and induce cardiac arrest.*

Without even having to look, I know there's no one standing inside the front door. No one! Not Scott or anyone else. Fuck this.

I stomp through the archway and submerge myself in the oil-slick black of the hall.

Yes, that's it: turn right, straight away. Don't look behind you, towards the front door. Seriously dark here, isn't it? You should use Scott's phone torch. Are you too stubborn to even do that . . . or are you too afraid of what you might see?

Dimly visible, the open bathroom door looks too far away for comfort. I pick up my pace . . . strictly because I really need this pee. No other reason whatsoever.

Definitely not because the taste of copper has crept back into my mouth.

Behind me, something bursts into existence and shoots light along the walls. My heart pinballs down between my knees, then ricochets all the way up to plug my throat.

This light is neither the white of a normal ceiling bulb nor the yellow of the street lamps outside. No, this light is the same colour as that thing I saw in the corner of my eye.

Up ahead, the bathroom's sink mirror reflects my image. Right behind me, hovers a mass of flickering blue light.

Are those . . . does it have eyes?

It does.

With a gasp, I break into a dash for the bathroom.

In the mirror, the blue light melts into black, like a shark darting off into untold fathoms. And yet I can't stop running.

What am I doing? This is crazy.

Ghosts don't care whether you believe in them or not. They don't need your permission to exist.

Even though I don't believe in ghosts, I'm no fan of the unknown . . .

. . . or darkness . . .

. . . but what in the galloping fuck *was* that? Felt like some kind of . . .

. . . go on, think it, there's no harm in only thinking it . . .

. . . some kind of *entity*. I mean, obviously not an entity, because that makes no sense. But . . .

But what?

Barrelling into the bathroom, I slam the door and yank the latch across.

Can't even see my hand in front of my face, but am I bothered? Hell no. This is fine. I am a dog in a burning room, okay with all the events that are unfolding currently.

I'm bone-tired, that's all. Stressed and still drunk. This flicker-thing *must* have been the result of the ceiling lights going haywire. Some kind of power surge, caused by the electricity briefly coming back on. That's exactly what this was.

When I first saw that demonic face on the balcony window, the seed of uncertainty planted itself in a part of my head where rational thought holds no sway. This seed wants me to believe that there's something wrong with this flat. Something . . . off . . . with the very bones of this place.

What does it even mean for a flat to be haunted? Makes no

sense. Flats are essentially boxes made out of wood, stone and glass. How can a box possibly be out to get you?

You're going to love it here.

I Am Possessed.

A real wild one.

Lovin' life.

This flat is *not haunted*. And so I'm going to sit here and take a piss in the dark, like any normal individual would during the night. I desperately need to shrug off the silly fright I've had and sleep.

Come on, admit it, you're seriously creeped out. Why don't you turn on your phone torch, or that mirror light? No one will ever know you caved.

Look, this was a power surge. At a push, it was a stronger hallucination than I experienced last night. That's all! Either way, the case is closed. Now, if you'll excuse me . . .

Fine, stay in the dark. But next time you're watching a scary movie, you're officially no longer allowed to yell, Just turn the fucking lights on! *at the characters.*

I can live with that. Now, while we search around for the toilet seat, let's think about nice things instead, such as a bright future. Let's picture ourselves in love with the man of our dreams. A man who lives in the same town as us, has no secrets worth shouting about and doesn't perform a vanishing act worthy of Keyser Söze.

While we lift the lid, briefly wondering if we might need to throw up, let's note that it will have taken us a while to trust this man. Because, oh sweet Christ, do we ever have raging trust issues thanks to Scott Palmer. But several years into this glorious relationship, we know Mr Perfect would never abandon us for a laugh, or secretly film us, or make us think we're special when in fact we're only a fraction of his grubby Tinder harem.

And as we grace the porcelain throne, let's picture sitting beside Mr Perfect on a blanket in a field. Our child shrieks with laughter as he or she plays with our cute dog. A lovely little terrier with berry eyes, scampering about.

Hey . . . why does Mr Perfect have Scott's face? We've very much moved on from him – haven't we, heart? I'd certainly fucking hope so, given that we now know Scott targeted us from the start.

Yes. And for some reason, he's lured you to this haunted flat.

Shut. Up.

Having erased Scott's stupid enigmatic wolf face, let's be lazy and go with some nice, generic square-jawed guy, straight out of a TV advert. Feels better, doesn't it? Yes. So we'll stay perched on this all-too-cold toilet seat and we'll do our business. We'll wind down, so that when we return to our super-deluxe duvet on the living room floor we can roll directly into sleep's sweet embrace.

Christ, it's so dark. Truly, if I'd gone blind, I wouldn't know the difference till I went back to the living room. But hooray: my business is concluded here. Time for some much-needed sl—

Oh my God, oh my *God*, the fucking *bathroom door.*

Two flickering, corpse-blue hands push effortlessly in through the solid wood. The fingers are rigor mortis claws.

I blink and blink again, desperate to kill the hallucination, but no, this is actually happening. This thing really is *floating in* through the closed fucking door, right across the room from where I sit.

Every hair on my body stands up. Copper fills my mouth and my teeth feel raw, like they've been wrapped in foil. Must have dropped Scott's phone, because it clatters on the floor and skims away.

Between these grasping, spectral hands, a face begins to form. The nose and the chin make their entrance first, followed by the eyes and mouth.

The eyes are twin black holes punched into blue cloth.

The mouth, fixed into the deranged grin of a hunter spotting prey.

This thing . . . this thing, it moves like a crudely animated drawing in a child's flip-book – one with half the pages missing. The further it emerges from the door, the more its strobe dominates the room. Within its shimmering body rages what might be a turbulent electrical storm. Narrow, pulsating forks of white light dart out from its core to illuminate the fingers, the mouth, the dead eyes.

Having left the door behind, the intruder displays nothing but blurred, fizzing mist where its feet should be. The arms and legs move as if independent of the body, performing wild contortions that would cripple any living person.

With a series of angry, spasmodic jerks, this thing wrenches itself through the darkness towards me, as if crossing an ocean bed.

I try to scream, but I'm all seized up inside. I'm dry as dust and copper-mouthed. What good would screaming do anyway? Primal mechanisms take over and I hold my hands out in front of me, but that's just the kind of pointless thing people do before getting splattered across a motorway.

There's nowhere to run and nowhere to hide.

As this thing moves closer, her savage smile becomes all too clear. All too recognisable.

The deathless hands of Gwyneth Cooper reach out for me.

CHAPTER THIRTY-SIX

20 August

Right up until Scott asks me his random question about ghosts, he and I are doing that thing we do. The thing that nauseates everyone around us.

Slouched on deck chairs halfway along the pier, we hold hands in silence. All but ignoring the magnificent view of the sea and the hazy white cliffs to the east, we're lost in each other's eyes. I've never experienced a closeness like this before. For onlookers, the whole spectacle must be truly appalling, but guess how many fucks I give?

Go on, guess.

Every once in a while, the bare-naked romance of these intimate silences becomes so acute that we burst out laughing and talk again, only to lapse back into all the staring. Feels as though we actually enter each other's minds and wander around our shared labyrinth together. In terms of the film *Labyrinth*, which we watched on Blu-ray last night, I am Jennifer Connelly to Scott's David Bowie. Mind you, Bowie's character was pretty evil, so that doesn't work.

This time, Scott's the one who breaks our silence. "Where do you stand on the existence of ghosts? Yay or nay?"

A chuckle rumbles in my chest. "If I'd had to compile a top thousand list of things you might have said next, this question wouldn't have been among them."

He smiles back at me, but says nothing. Looks like he might actually want an answer. I realise that we've never discussed our spiritual or religious beliefs, or lack thereof. For all I know, Scott could be a big old Satanist.

"Spooks get a big no from me," I say. "Seen too many dead people, I'm afraid."

"Same here," he says, before jumping back in to explain himself. "Oh! I don't mean I've seen too many dead people. I just mean, I don't believe in spooks either."

As he gazes somewhere off into the middle distance, I want his eyes back on me. Sometimes the potency of this love drug feels disturbing. "And now," I say, "I can't resist asking what prompted that question . . ."

His faint shrug snowballs into a laugh. "I honestly have no idea. Maybe the ghost train?"

I take a quick look up along the pier. From this position, we can't actually see the Hell Hotel ride. Guess he must have seen it while we strolled up here. Every moment of every day, the mind takes in so much more than we consciously acknowledge.

I open my mouth to ask how many dead people Scott's actually seen, but he squeezes my hand, leans forward in his chair and lays that look on me.

"I'm thinking candyfloss. Yeah?"

As he stands, an alarming noise blasts out of his jeans pocket. The sound is truly bizarre, like some kind of baying, primal animal chorus.

Scott whips out his phone, then quickly presses a button on the side of the case.

The noise stops dead. When he doesn't immediately offer an explanation, my curiosity boils over. "What the bloody hell was that?"

Having stowed the device back away, he laughs. "God knows! Phones have minds of their own. Now, candyfloss? Candyfloss."

CHAPTER THIRTY-SEVEN

5 October

Here in the belly of darkness, on this fucking toilet seat, I've somehow adopted the aeroplane brace position while waiting for something godawful to happen.

Could I open my eyes?

Yeah, sure, I *could* open them. But dare I?

Fuck no. I dare not.

What if the flicker-thing still hangs right in front of my face, biding its sweet blue time?

What if I open my eyes and see the tip of Gwyneth's Wicked Witch Of The West nose one inch away from my own? I might gaze into her eyes and see something that undoes me forever.

Are ghosts really a thing or have I lost my bloody mind?

I. Dare. Not. Open. My. Eyes.

Tears, welling up. So many factors. There's the dread, obviously. The pure dread that makes my stomach feel raw and hollow. I'm rocked by the sense that the train of my life has switched rails and I can never get back on track. There's also no escaping the fact that being scrunched up in this foetal position has dug up memories I prefer to leave buried.

As I retreat inside myself, a single teardrop reaches the end of my nose and then explodes on my bare forearm.

The first time I ever felt alone, I was tucked away inside my mother's womb.

Two different psychotherapists have suggested that I've retro-engineered this memory, based on the way Mum would later treat me. Technically, I know they're right, but in my head this has become real. We paramedics often catastrophise. I don't know exactly why, but we do. Our rampant hypochondria, for instance, has become a running in-joke.

I've certainly never told a soul about this, in case they mistakenly thought I was trying to make some kind of deranged "pro-life" point. But I swear I recall being inside my mother's warm velveteen black womb, and feeling alone. Feeling abandoned.

My mother's heart thumped like a sonic boom, but out of sync with mine. Mum was alive, but she wasn't really there. Nobody was home.

Of course, it wasn't Carrie Collins' fault she was in a coma when she gave birth to me. Neither was it her fault that they had to bring her slightly out of the coma, so that her body could enter the labour process all by itself. And how could it possibly be her fault that she wasn't at liberty to be the first, second, third or even twenty-seventh person to hold me?

None of this was my mum's fault. Instead, we can blame the hod carrier who somehow managed to drop two bricks off a ladder on Tottenham Court Road.

Mum was both unlucky and incredibly fortunate. The first brick missed her entirely. The second, falling from a height of more than twenty feet, could have landed square on her head, pulped her brain and killed us both outright. Instead, this nine-pound fused block of clay and shale clipped the back of her head and rendered her unconscious.

If those awesome paramedics hadn't battled their way through the streets to her in time, she could so easily have died right there on the pavement, with my seven-month-old self inside her. And if those doctors and specialists hadn't known how to induce labour, that would also have been the end of me.

The way my life began robbed my mother and me of any meaningful connection. Had she been able to remember the first three months of my life, she might have developed warmth towards me. It also might have helped if she hadn't been on the way to an ultrasound growth scan when one stray brick changed our lives forever.

Plenty of old photos depict Mum as the life and soul of any party. After the accident, though, her facial expression was mostly blank. Again, not her fault. But on the rare occasion that my own mother looked me directly in the eye, something cold would lurk behind her gaze. I felt convinced she wanted to say, *Kate Collins, this is all your fault. If I hadn't had you, I might still have all of me.*

Soon as I hit sixteen years old, Mum clearly felt she'd done her time by raising me. She jetted off to live in New Zealand with her boyfriend she'd met while on holiday.

I don't want to be back here, inside the coma. I cannot stay in this hellhole space.

I run my tongue around my teeth. Has this copper taste faded? I think so, but can't be sure.

I open my left eye first, because it's my weakest and so won't see Gwyneth so vividly. Fear knows no logic.

There's not a single trace of heart-stopping blue in the room. Only the lush normality of black.

My face and my arms tingle. I've allowed myself to become a human freeze-frame and forgotten to breathe. Like a diver coming up for air way too fast, risking the bends, I suck down all the oxygen I can. I breathe until I feel more level, and yet my panic simmers on.

Could I just stay here all night? If I sit here in the dark, nice and still, then everything will be fine. This, too, shall pass.

It's always darkest before the dawn, right? Florence + The Machine wisdom, don't fail me now.

Only . . . only, *no*. Even if I sit here for hours until the sun rises, all that glorious natural light outside will barely infiltrate this dead space. A thin sliver of weak gold under the door, if I'm lucky.

Still seated, I lean forward to feel around on the floor. If I find Scott's phone, I can switch on the torch. But of course, the damn thing eludes my fingers.

I consider the bathroom door, my only way out of here. But if I approach that door, there's always the danger that incorporeal Gwyneth might float back in through those two inches of corporeal wood.

Got to haul myself together. Got to stand, nice and easy. Got to walk across the room with all the fearless dignity I can muster, find the sink mirror and switch on the light. Fuck toughing it out in the dark any longer. I want these bulbs to fizz and spark and usher safety back into the night.

I can do this.

I. Can. So. Fucking. Do. This.

I launch myself away from the toilet, then fall straight over.

One side of my face slams into the floor. I'd totally forgotten that my jeans were bunched around my ankles and I'm drunk.

My skull drones and throbs as I crawl across the expanse of cold, sticky lino.

A wave of nausea damn near flattens me as I locate the sink bowl, use it to haul myself upright, then feel around the edges of the mirror for the light switch.

Come on.

Come. On.

I've never been so happy to find a switch in my life. With a gorgeous filament buzz, the mirror floods with light that toasts my retinas and kickstarts my heart.

That is . . . until I remember to check the mirror for anyone, or anything, in the room behind me.

There's nothing and no one. Gwyneth really has gone.

I pull up my jeans, then stoop to grab Scott's phone. My throat clogs with relief as I haul open the bathroom door and throw myself outside. I dash along the full length of the hallway, then out of the front door.

Revelling in the auto-triggered light of the communal corridor, I can finally draw down a full, unfettered breath.

What I need to do, more than anything, is think.

I need to reactivate my rational mind. How could this possibly have been a ghost, let alone Gwyneth Cooper's?

More than anything, I need to talk to Izzy. God bless her insomnia.

IZZY
sorry to break it to ya mate but ghosts are real so u probably did see a ghost . . . lucky you were already sittin on the toilet

KATE
You're not helping! You're supposed to be the big voice of reason who tells me I was drunk, or I've gone mad.

IZZY
well both those things are true . . . but u probably also saw a ghost . . . we saw ghosts all the time in my nans house when I was growing up . . . aint no big deal haha

KATE
You saw a ghost?

IZZY
yup more than 1

KATE
What did they look like?

IZZY
spose it was pretty classic ghost stuff . . . like a person but you could see right through them . . . one time at nans i woke up on a sofa n saw this woman across the room

KATE
Was she blue? Did she flicker, with black holes for eyes?

IZZY
no none of that shit she was old skool . . . and i could even see the colour of her eyes bright blue

KATE
Hmmm. Doesn't fit the description of mine, then.

IZZY
well ya know . . . this wuz the 80s . . . ghost fashions change

KATE
What was your ghost doing when you saw her?

IZZY
just standing there looking at me . . . dressed up like a victorian or edwardian or summat . . . like the very sight of a dick would make her faint

KATE
Were you scared?

IZZY
nah she seemed all right had a nice feel about her . . . and ya know . . . me n mum lived near the chapworth estate so we were loads more worried about getting stabbed up than spooks . . . whats so scary about some fuckin echo of a dead person compared to getting killed yourself

KATE
How about a dead person that might kill you? I mean FFS, this one reached out for me. She had this terrible grin like she wanted me dead, and I can't get that out of my head. I have NO IDEA WHAT TO DO.

IZZY
get the leccy company to put the power back on for a start . . . u need lights

KATE
I'd have to start a new contract and it'd be days before they put the lights back on. I don't even want to be here ONE more day.

IZZY
then find somewhere else to live . . . scotts place aint doing ur head any good

KATE
Can't afford a deposit and all those fees. Don't even know anyone down here, so I have no sofas to sleep on.

IZZY
in that case make friends with the ghost

KATE
I'd much rather not see her again. God, this is like seeing a fucking huge spider that disappears. Then you know it's there, but you don't know where . . .

IZZY
oh man dont talk to me about spiders . . . we had two big ones in the bathtub last week . . . fucking brown they were . . . fluffy brown spiders man

KATE
Fuck, Izzy. What am I supposed to make of seeing a "ghost"? While we were on the job, did you ever feel like anybody's soul was drifting off into the great beyond?

IZZY
yeah . . . mine lol

KATE
But seriously . . .

IZZY
hmm . . . dunno yeah maybe . . . just cuz u cant physically see a soul go somewhere else, dont mean it dont

KATE
What's another explanation for this besides a ghost? What if this was a hologram? They're super-advanced now.

IZZY
seriously??? nah babe . . .

KATE
What about a hallucination?

IZZY
people dont hallucinate seeing faces . . . not to that extent . . . unless you have a brain tumour

KATE
Thank you for that suggestion, nurse. Soooo kind. Actually – fuck, please tell me the taste of metal isn't a tumour signifier.

IZZY
um i think it is yeah . . . but everything is these days . . . hey if u hallucinated this ghost then u might have hallucinated Scott as well

IZZY
. . . too soon? Soz . . . u srsly dont have a tumour

KATE
Hmm. Weird thing is, I recognised this thing I saw.

IZZY
who was it

KATE
She's a sort of . . . missing person.

IZZY
shit . . . did u see her on a poster or summat

KATE
Not exactly. It's complicated.

IZZY
aint it always with u babe

KATE
She seems to have disowned her family, but now . . . I don't know, she might be dead. But if that really was her ghost I saw, then why would it appear in Scott's flat?

IZZY
ok is there any connection between him and her

KATE
Yeah, sort of . . .

IZZY
n what would that be

KATE
This girl's called Gwyneth. And her sister is

IZZY
her sister is what

KATE
Well, she's connected to Scott.

IZZY
how

IZZY
u still there . . . how u know theyre connected

KATE
Oh, someone told me.

IZZY
look mate i dont know why but i feel like ur losing a marble or 2 . . . want me to come down there . . . got a coupla days off

KATE
Don't be silly! I mean, thanks, thanks so much, but honestly, I'm fine.

IZZY
u sure . . . was a genuine offer

KATE
Seriously, thanks, but I'm working loads of hours anyway.

IZZY
is there owt ur not telling me tho

KATE
No. You're getting the full exclusive here, practically live! Now go back to sleep, honey. Don't worry about me, I'm fine. Later! X

IZZY
u never say later like that so now im really worried X

CHAPTER THIRTY-EIGHT

6 October

I wake on the roof, buffeted by wind and with a head like a rotten pumpkin.

The Van Spencer terrace offers impressive views over the city and coast. Over by the Marina jetty to the east, light has broken cover from the horizon. The sun bathes a cluster of new-build apartment towers, turning every window into a lantern. Should be safe to return to the flat now, but I'm in no hurry. Especially as there are now even more scratches on the inside of the door.

I came up here in the dark, to get away from the flat and chat to Izzy. After we spoke, sheer fatigue made me lie down across one of these benches. When offered no sleep, the brain tends to take what it needs by force.

Breathless and frozen to the marrow, I check the time. Okay, I only slept for two hours, long enough for me to have a new dream about the zip-wire tower. I remember hanging from the wire and hurtling along, but there was something really odd and disturbing about the whole thing. Something so wrong. Even as I try to remember what, the memory self-destructs.

Why did I have to go and stupidly turn down Izzy's offer of company? I've never felt more alone in my life, but I still don't want her to know about me having Scott's phone. The people who know you best . . . well, they know you best. Izzy would definitely be of the opinion that I'm on a bad path.

My hangover only compounds the fear. As if trying to ease that fear, my rational mind demands an explanation for what happened in that bathroom. I'd only ever half-believed the paranoid idea that Scott was filming me, but what if I really am slap-bang in the middle of the world's most elaborate hidden-camera joke? Or how about an experiment, designed to see how long it would take to make an agnostic paramedic believe in the supernatural?

I picture myself on YouTube, immortalised by infrared cameras in the bathroom. Doomed to perch on that toilet forever, as the comments and cry-laughter emojis pile up.

Feels like a very modern misconception, the idea that the whole world revolves around you. Surely no one's going to build an elaborate hidden-camera prank show around Kate Collins – not even a weirdo like Scott. Are they? But what if I really am getting suckered here?

I'm finding it so hard to discount the evidence of my own eyes. This apparition felt like no trick of the light, or of my mind, or any kind of hologram. It was just fucking *there*. I even *tasted* this thing before it showed up. But who knows what insanity, true insanity, might be like, until you're drowning in the deep blue sea of it? I've seen so many people who've tumbled down between the cracks of social services and barely even know what's up and what's down. Did those people ever consciously pass a threshold that led them to that state of mind, or did every stage of their descent feel like the most natural thing in the world?

Blinking against the molten glare of sunrise, I chew the whole thing over. No matter how real the ghost felt, I need certainty. Either I literally saw someone who'd come back from the dead or I didn't, so how can I nail down the truth?

Until then, I'm going to stay neutral on the whole ghost thing.

Neutral, my arse. You already know that you really saw Gwyneth and she really is dead. What if she used to live in Scott's flat, or elsewhere in the Van Spencer? What if she came to his flat and he killed her?

Whoa there, brain. Killed her? Where the fuck did that come from?

The man's a loon. Remember that night you woke in his bed and he wasn't there? Haven't thought about that since, have you, you big airhead. You haven't thought about how he looked when you finally found him . . .

Enough! I need to focus and get proactive. I need to settle all of this soon, for my own peace of mind, and so I'm taking Scott's phone to work. This is a temporary measure for today, and I'll only use it during breaks.

See? All I've done is swap one pledge for a new pledge. Surely there can be nothing wrong with that.

Now. Before I do anything else, I need to throw up my guts.

Hidden away inside the toilet cubicle, I tap the top of my bare foot until a suitably prickable vein presents itself. Then I go in with the needle, just under the skin.

God knows, I'm not proud of this, especially as it'll mean writing up today's drug administration incorrectly to cover my tracks. But if I don't dose myself, I may end up making mistakes. All things considered, I'd rather abuse drugs than risk lives.

Any member of ambulance staff would spot a recently cannulated vein within fifty yards, so the foot is my best bet. This way, the IV paracetamol, saline and glucose I'm about to give myself will be a slow release. There'll be no risk of a crash later on – only a slow burn to make me human again and get me through the shift.

For a fleeting moment, I was tempted to rejoin the small legion of staff who take uppers to keep them going, then temper the buzz with diazepam. But do I really want to add another bad gateway to my collection? Nope, not again, so this is the most effective means to make sure I can do right by my patients today.

When the foul deed is done, I spend ten whole minutes polishing my boots. No matter how low or exhausted I feel at the start of any given work day, I will always polish these bad boys. When a stranger invites me into their home on one of the worst days of their life, the very least I can do is appear clean, calming and professional.

While making these boots gleam, it strikes me that one proactive thing I can do is find Gwyneth. If she's alive, then I can't have seen her ghost after all. Along the way, I can explore any further links between her and Scott. What else might connect these two people, besides Scott having Gwyneth's photo of Ali on his phone?

Only when I'm on my way out of the cubicle do I remember that I've clean forgotten to do my morning gratitudes. No time – will have to do them later.

I hurry to join Tyler, so that we can load up the ambulance, check the tyre pressure and carry out all the other chores. All goes as normal, until the part of our Vehicle Daily Inspection when Tyler sits in the cabin and works the outer lights so that I can walk around and check that they all work. Confronted with several pale blue strobes, I'm mentally yanked back to being cornered in Scott's bathroom.

Gwyneth's blue grin jerks towards me, relentless, and my lungs fold in on themselves.

You can breathe, Kate. You really can, I swear; it's fine. You've just been triggered, that's all. Now get in the cab and start your shift.

During this first half of our twelve-hour stint, I wait for opportunities when it's one hundred per cent safe to scour Scott's phone for more info. If Gwyneth's ghost *was* real, then there must be a Scott/Gwyneth connection beyond that mountaintop pic, because otherwise her materialisation in Scott's flat would be way too much of a coincidence.

Unless she came to visit you. She may have homed in for some reason . . .

Why would the ghost of a random person I've never met come looking for me?

She may have had something to tell you . . . such as Scott having killed her . . .

Brain, I do wish you'd stop trying to turn this mystery into the supernatural version of some 80s thriller starring either Michael Douglas or Jeff Bridges. Do I really, seriously, believe Scott to be capable of murder?

Do you really, seriously, think that your brain is somehow distinct from you? If I suspect Scott of being a proper psycho, then so do you.

Here's another item on my overall agenda: finally open WhatsApp and discover whether he actually slept with those other Tinder matches. This feels like too big a task to undertake while I'm working, so I stick to smaller missions.

Once I have the ladder-fall builder Malcolm and his broken leg safely strapped to a trolley-bed and hooked up to the IV drip, and Tyler's driving us to hospital, I Google for *Scott Palmer Gwyneth Cooper*. This search produces nothing of note.

Once we've conducted various observations on the elderly Mr Sharma, who fell without injury at home, and we've referred him to a Falls Team, a brainwave leads me to message her on Facebook. Wondering if she'll even see my words there, since we're not friends, I tweet at her for good measure. Both times, I ask her to recommend animal charities around Brighton. Let's not scare the girl off.

Yeah, we wouldn't want her dying of fright.

Once Tyler and I have established that young Sally's toothache doesn't justify an A&E visit, and we've booked a dental appointment on her behalf, I check to see if Gwyneth has replied. She hasn't, so I take a closer look at her recent Twitter output. Once I've got over how much her grin in the profile pic reminds me of *that* grin on the face of the thing I saw in Scott's bathroom, I see tweets protesting China's annual Dog Meat Festival among other animal abuse atrocities . . . and the most recent was posted at seven-thirty *this morning*.

What the actual fuck? Unless ghosts really can tweet, this has to mean she's still alive. I need to see her in person. Today.

While Tyler gruffly persuades Sally to take paracetamol and gargle aspirin, I use the UK electoral roll to track down a history of Gwyneth's home addresses.

Clearly, she has voted before. According to this list of three addresses, she has never even lived near the Van Spencer, let alone inside the building. When I take a screen grab of her allegedly current address, impatience sinks its claws into me. How I hate the idea of having to wait until tonight to pay her a visit.

Yes, because if you can find Gwyneth alive then you no longer have to be shit-scared of her haunting Scott's flat, right? Wouldn't that just wrap everything up with such a delightfully reassuring little bow?

Never gonna happen.

She's dead and she's evil and she wants to fuck you up.

Tyler's gaze burns a hole in the side of my head. "Kate? You ready to leave, or . . . ?"

With a fully unreasonable stab of resentment, I shove Scott's phone back in my pocket, then grab my bag.

As we leave Sally and return to the suburban cul-de-sac where the ambulance is parked, Tyler has another question. "So what's with the two phones? You a dealer?"

"Yes, that is correct. Listen, would you mind if we actually do take our half-hour break today? Got something I really need to do."

"Hmm, I don't know, mate . . ."

The question of whether or not to take the optional break is always a bone of contention among crewmates. These days, if we decide to go without our break, we get extra cash *and* get to leave half an hour early. Tyler's obviously keen on achieving both goals.

"How about if we take our break, and then during the second half, all you have to do is drive?" I say. "I'll take the lead on every job."

Tyler looks tempted. Then, no doubt sensing the power balance in his favour, he performs a sigh. "I don't think so."

"All right, I'll pay you the extra money myself. How's that?"

"What do you need to do during this break, exactly – deliver some fuckin' hashish?"

"Mate, I'm not a drug dealer. Did I really need to clarify that? But I will need to move the truck during this break."

Tyler looks down his nose at me. "You know that's fraud, right?"

"Only technically," I say, even though he's right. When you drive the ambulance during a break, you're no longer insured.

And yet it happens, and I somehow find myself willing to take the risk.

I sneak another look at Google Maps on Scott's phone. "No more than a mile," I add, all too aware that my face has reddened. "We'll be back in the same spot at the end of the thirty, and you can snooze throughout if you want. Come on, Tyler, you look like you could use a power-nap."

"Says Little Miss Bags-Under-Her-Eyes . . . Oh, all right."

It's so much easier to gain entry to a block of flats, even in a rougher part of Brighton like Whitehawk, when you wear a paramedic's uniform and carry a big green bag.

It's also a lot easier to knock on a complete stranger's door and greet whoever opens up with an entirely professional and straight face, even when they're clearly not Gwyneth.

Oh, and when you walk straight into the home of a mid-twenties bruiser with a soccer shirt and a bent nose, you don't get punched. All he does is say, "Whoa whoa whoa."

"Hi," I say, hurrying along the hall. "We received a 999 call from Gwyneth?"

"Not from here you didn't," he says. "This is Flat *Seventeen*, yeah?"

The tiny living room betrays no obvious signs of a female presence. Only empty cider cans, piles of *Men's Health* mags and the distinctive *eau de man*. The bedroom door hangs open, offering more of the same. "Do you recognise the name Gwyneth Cooper at all, sir? Could she be in the building?"

Inside his head, a penny drops. "Actually . . . *G. Cooper*. Shit, yeah." He hands me a stack of letters from off the hall radiator. They're all addressed to Gwyneth. "If you do find this person, tell her to get a redirect or something, yeah? Been two months since I moved in."

When did Ali say Gwyneth dropped off the family's grid: about three months back? Okay, then. Evidently, this guy hasn't bothered to tell the council he's the new tenant, if indeed he ever was on the electoral roll.

Feigning irritation, I perform an about-turn, while stuffing Gwyneth's mail in my pocket. "Great. Seems like another hoax call."

The front door has drifted shut. The closer I get, the more gouges I can see in the wood. This gets my attention. Like the ones in Scott's flat, these gouges come in bunches of five, but they cover the whole inside of the door. No wood chips on the ground, though.

"None of my business," I say, "but do you fire an air rifle in here, or . . . ?"

"Nah. Was like this when I moved in. Landlord hasn't done fuck all about it."

"Landlords, eh? Lying bastards."

"That's what I get for moving to Shitehawk. Hey, don't paramedics usually come in pairs on the telly?"

"The TV lies even more than landlords," I say on my way back to the stairwell. "Sorry to bother you."

"Hi, Maureen! It's Kate here."

Daytime TV buzzes in the background as she tries to remember who I am. "Oh. Oh, yes." Finally, she summons the strength to inject enthusiasm into her voice. "Hello, dear."

"I simply *had* to give you a quick call, because you'll never guess who I bumped into last night. Ray!"

"Oh, how nice. Was he well?"

"You know, it's the strangest thing. I never realised Scott and Ray are twins!"

"Really? That *is* strange. Did Scott never mention that?"

"He didn't, and so I'm going to have words with him. Ha ha."

Maureen grants me the faintest hint of a chuckle. "Well, nice to hear from you, dear. How are you doing with the landlord?"

"To be honest, Maureen, he's giving me the runaround at the moment, but I'm determined to pin him down and get the truth out of him. Have you heard from Scott since I saw you?"

"No, dear. Do tell him to give me a ring, won't you?"

"Of course. Well, I'd better let you go."

All right then, so that's one paranoid idea crossed off the list. Scott was not pretending to be his own twin brother last night.

Really? Just because Scott and Ray genuinely are twins, doesn't conclusively mean that Scott wasn't pretending to be Ray.

Oh, for fuck's sake.

The baby lies on the floor between Jill's legs. A brand-new factory-fresh life, sealed inside its amniotic sac.

Tyler seems particularly happy that we made our pact so that he can stand back and let me deal with this one.

Jill can barely speak through the tears. "Why's he come out like this? What's gone wrong?"

"I promise you, this isn't wrong at all," I tell her. "It's absolutely harmless. Napoleon was an *en caul* birth, and he did all right for himself."

"This guy's already taller than Napoleon," Tyler helpfully chips in.

The sac feels like something between thin tripe, or a really thick sausage skin. The shears I'm using to cut the baby free are the same shears I've used to cut through clothes, seatbelts and shoelaces.

As I dry the burbling newborn down, I notice Tyler's phone in his hand. Which is weird. Not even I, the great smartphone abuser, would do this during a job. Looks like he also has it at a weird angle . . . pointing this way? Soon as he registers my attention, he looks irritated, then pockets the phone. Hmm. Okay.

Jill has lapsed into a post-partum trance. She looks desolate. "He said he'd *be* here when the birth happened. He promised me."

"You're not alone," I tell her, surprised by the swelling in my throat. I feel an almost desperate urge to make Jill happier. "Don't worry, we're here. Your baby's fine and everything's going to be fine. You are *not* alone."

As Tyler steers us through the rain to Hove, towards the seventeenth job of the day, the air in our cabin buzzes with energy waiting to be released.

We've barely spoken a word since leaving Jill. I'm hyper-tense, partly through being angry with him, but mainly because darkness has fallen. As we drive, our lights cast a vivid strobe-glow onto everything around us. I've seen this effect a million times, but now it tweaks me big-style. Houses, fences, road signs, lamp posts, bus stops, the other vehicles, *people* . . . all of them get painted a flickering Gwyneth-blue.

To try and keep my eyes off the road, I alternate between checking for online replies from Gwyneth and ripping open her physical letters. Most of these are circulars, but I do find a curt letter from Prescott & Purvue, the management company which handles her flat. Back in July, they wanted to know why she'd stopped paying the rent.

And here's a bank statement from August to September. The balance on Gwyneth's account is zero, with no financial activity throughout the month. Inside another envelope, a curt letter from the same bank lists all the direct debits that have failed, due to *insufficient funds*. The final letter, a red-stamped bill from a gas company, yells about the debt Gwyneth has accrued over the last three months.

Can't help feeling that these companies won't be getting paid.

Because she's dead.

Not necessarily.

Shoving the letters back away, I reach for other possibilities. Could it be that Gwyneth moved abroad? She might have devoted her life to sabotaging dog meat festivals in China.

She's dead, dead, dead.

She may simply not have told the council about her new address.

She's dead, dead, dead, dead, dead.

Okay. Time to breach the wall of silence in the cabin. The drugs have worn off, leaving me with far less energy for confrontation. Yet I have to address the issue. Can't help remembering how Tyler filmed Deranged Naked Guy's rampage yesterday. Did he repeat the trick in a hideously inappropriate manner?

"Tyler, what were you doing with your phone during that last job?"

His glance lobs a Molotov cocktail my way. "Huh? Nothing. Who are you, my boss? I don't think so, mate."

"I don't think so either, but I *am* your senior crewmate. And if I thought for one minute that you were taking a picture of a patient, or even shooting video . . .'

Tyler steps on the gas and my head punches back against the seat. "For fuck's sake, Kate: are you kidding? I would never do that. You're the one who can't get enough of their phone. Or phones."

"So, for the sake of absolute clarity: if you were to show me your camera roll, I wouldn't see an amniotic sac, is that right?"

Hey, Kate, just FYI: you don't have the automatic right to look inside the phone of every man on the planet.

"No, you bloody wouldn't. And for the sake of absolute clarity: if I was to tell Akeem that you'd moved the truck during a break, exactly how much trouble would you be in?"

Shit, Tyler's checkmated me. How did I allow that to happen?

Does his angry reaction confirm my suspicion? Hard to say. I'll have to keep a close eye on this man-child from now on. And his phone. Who knows what else he's been filming, or have I misjudged him? There's a strong case to be made for my trust levels being low, right now, when it comes to guys and their phones.

Outside, human faces appear in our strobes, then vanish fast, as if they were never there. When seen further away, up ahead, these pedestrians move in herky-jerky steps, just like something out of a child's flip-book . . .

When I can't take any more, I check out Rudolpho's Facebook and Twitter. Even catching up on his latest moronic philandering has to beat looking outside . . . until I notice our strobes reflected on Scott's phone screen too.

The next time Tyler and I speak, it's to discuss how to treat a woman who's collapsed in her bathroom, having thrown up and shat herself.

CHAPTER THIRTY-NINE

6 October

I'm just a girl, hitting a restaurant on her way home from work, that's all.

Just fancied some tapas and there's nothing more to it than that.

Oh, just admit it: you're petrified to go back to that flat, and so you're putting it off as long as humanly possible.

Okay, brain. I do rather wish that I'd found a shop to buy more candles. For the sake of my nerves, I've chosen to believe light would keep Gwyneth away. Yes, shining a light could be like siphoning all the water from a tank. When you do that, all the fish . . .

. . . all those flickering blue sharks . . .

. . . can no longer swim around.

God, I'm so on edge tonight that I'm in danger of falling off myself. No matter how cosy this Casa San Marcos place might feel, I can't stop thinking that anything can now happen in Scott's flat at any given moment. No matter how much I tell myself that Gwyneth is posting on social media, I still fear that something dead or undead could pop up in that place to say hello . . . except when I have candles on the go. Since mine have all but burnt down, the later I can stay out the better.

I'm eating this *patatas bravas* to fuel myself, rather to feed any real appetite. On top of my gut-mashing dread of the Van Spencer, I feel sick from the shame of having bent the system to my own ends today. As much as I tell myself I needed to find out what happened to a missing and possibly dead woman, and that I didn't do anything to put patients at risk, it rankles all the same.

If today's sly investigation had produced solid results, then my perversion of the rules might have felt more justified, and yet the facts remain frustratingly out of reach. Soon as I left work this evening, I looked up Prescott & Purvue online, but their office had closed for the night. Of *course* it had. So now I'll have to wait until tomorrow to go and quiz them on whether their tenant Ms Cooper moved out or died or disappeared.

Gwyneth still hasn't replied via Twitter or Facebook. She has, however, publicly shared a meme gif of a cat leaping dramatically up over the top of a staircase, then landing upon a startled dog. So that's a big bag of lolz, right there.

You know what? I should take a breather from this whole line of enquiry and face WhatsApp instead. The prospect of Scott actually having slept with those other Tinder matches no longer feels so apocalyptic, because Gwyneth feels bigger. Far more significant. Gwyneth draws on both my intrigue and my conscience.

WhatsApp confronts me with a column of mostly female headshots. Some of the names are familiar from Tinder, such as Samantha and Claire, while others are represented only by their phone number.

Look at all this evidence. Once upon a time, people would

plan their cheating affairs by speaking verbally through ye olde telephone landlines. Unless physically overheard, their every filthy utterance would vanish without trace. But now, here's every single incriminating word, laid out like a court transcript. So let's rejoin Scott and Samantha. I'm sure they merely discussed crochet patterns and the like . . .

Not wanting to spoiler myself, I zoom all the way to the top of their conversation, most of which happened while I slept beside Scott in his bed. The pair start by talking politely, like the virtual strangers they are, and then the sex gradually oozes into their chat, as they test each other's boundaries, only to discover there are none. Feels all too familiar.

Scott and Sam's messages become fast and furious, as they express what they plan to do to each other after their imminent first date. Pretty hot and steamy stuff, too. Admittedly, poor Sam screws up when autocorrect makes her accidentally write, *I'm gonna sick on your balls*. That's unfortunate, and she quickly corrects herself with a shocked emoji, before they both post cry-laughing emojis.

Aw, these two were so made for each other. Scott and Sam, eh? Or *Scam* for short.

Munching some nice Manchego, I scroll back down . . .

Down, down, deeper and down . . .

These star-crossed lovers consecrate their beautiful romance by sending each other a close-up picture of their genitals, then trading compliments. Cupid must have felt so flushed with pride that night.

Yesterday, each and every word would have dealt me a gut-punch. Tonight, they barely put me off my stuffed peppers. I now feel more like an autopsy technician, picking through deeply unpleasant remains. What I really want, I suppose, is absolute confirmation. I want proof that Scott actually *did* fuck someone else, during the short time we were together. This now feels more like a curiosity than some sick self-destructive impulse.

Oh. Okay. Scott and Sam's WhatsApp chat ends with her saying, *I'm here! Got a nice table at the back of the bar.* Fifteen minutes later, she says, *You running late?* followed ten minutes later by, *Where are you?* Finally, twenty-nine minutes after she arrived, she says, *I'm leaving. Thx for wasting my time.*

Why do I feel frustrated? That's a pretty weird reaction, isn't it?

Not when it's coming from a freak like you.

Here's another WhatsApp chat with a pretty young thing called Nola. Black hair, big blue eyes, pale skin. This conversation doesn't involve sex. Sweet li'l Nola didn't prove an easy nut to crack like Samantha. Either way, this is one of several chats that originated on Tinder and switched over here, only to shrivel on the vine before a meet could be arranged.

The next chat, with good old Claire from Peacehaven, contains some eye-poppingly feisty sext action. Can't help but begrudgingly admire this slag's creatively intense way with words. I mean, she even mentions *pre cum*. I would never have thought of that, and Scott responds very positively to the notion of Claire *teasing* it out of him. Are they coiled up in bed somewhere right now, laughing at me?

Doesn't look like it. They arranged to meet in front of the Palace Pier for a stroll at 6 p.m., only for poor Claire to end up in the same boat as Samantha. At ten past six, she writes, *Ur still coming, right?* At twenty past, she writes, *We did say the Palace Pier and not the old burnt-out one yeah?* And argh, that's it.

So . . . what happened next? Did he arrive late and they ended up having a torrid one-night stand? Or was she so pissed off with him that she couldn't even bring herself to say she was walking away from the pier alone?

Or did he follow her home and kill her?

Bristling, I crave the kind of unambiguous clarity that WhatsApp seems unable to supply. Why, oh why, can't people have the common decency to make it clear in their private comms whether or not they actually had sex?

That TrooSelf diary app remains Fort Knox.

Burning New Pathways Into The Brain

Joining The Death Grip Cult

I Am Possessed

Still so infuriating to have no idea what these titles signify.

Especially as you're starting to wonder exactly how deep Scott's still waters run, right? You're not ready to admit that to yourself, because it's too frightening.

Hey, what about those videos?

That's right. Change the subject, see if I care.

I haven't returned to try the videos again since my last attempt killed the handset a second time. With a mouth full of omelette, I ponder how to prevent a third shutdown.

Flipping over to Scott's browser, I Google for *how to stop phone crashing*.

Restore to factory settings? Nope, not gonna happen.

Looks like the phone might be all clogged up with data, and I should try deleting some. This is easy enough, and it certainly feels nicely cathartic to ditch all of Scott's favourite Prince albums, even though they'll probably be retained in the cloud.

I also follow instructions to clear something I've never heard of, called the *cache*. Once the phone boots back up, I decide to risk opening the Videos folder again. First, though, I make sure I eat the final tapas dish. There's no telling what I might see in here.

Okay. Videos, do your worst.

A chirrup from my Nokia heralds the arrival of a text from

Izzy. Even though she's the only person in the world I wouldn't ignore right now, I'm still tempted to look at the videos first. Then I remember her broken and screaming on a stairwell landing in Leeds, so I place Scott's phone aside and grab the Nokia.

IZZY
hey im outside

KATE
You're outside what?

IZZY
ur flat . . . well scotts flat . . . whoevers flat this is

KATE
WTF? You're kidding right?

IZZY
r u in the flat

IZZY
hun its raining out here

KATE
Sorry, I'm just in shock. I told you not to come!

IZZY
yeah and as u know i always take orders really well . . . is ur buzzer not working

KATE
I'm not there but I will be in five minutes!

CHAPTER FORTY

6 October

Talk about a conflict of emotions.

I positively *itch* to look at these videos. But at the same time, the thought of having company – someone who actually knows and likes me in Brighton *and* might help fend off a ghost – is incredible. As is the killer hug Izzy administers outside the Van Spencer. My emotional dam cannot help but burst.

"See?" she says, walking on her crutches as I carry her ginormous travel bag out of the lift on Floor Five. "Tears! I knew you needed me. I bloody knew it."

Dabbing my runny nose, I'm determined to keep these waterworks in check. "God, I can't believe you drove all the way down here, with your leg and everything. Where's Jared?"

"He's with Shit For Brains till Thursday," she says, referring to Dwayne. "Wow, this place is *awesome*."

As Izzy takes in the living room and kitchen, I feel so useless. She and Jared should have been visiting me and Scott in our perfect love nest, so they could have a whale of a time in the arcades on the pier and playing crazy golf.

She says, "I mean, more furniture would be cool, but it still rocks. Look at that fuckin' *sea*, man. And hey, look inside my bag. I borrowed this thing from Survival Dave, a couple of doors down. Paranoid apocalypse people really can come in handy."

I tug open the zip on Izzy's bag to unveil a chunky ghetto blaster. She explains how it's a radio and lamp, powered solely by a brilliantly retro hand crank. No juice required.

When we plonk the radio onto my box mountain and press a button, an astonishingly bright light exterminates every shadow in this room. Oh fuck, so much for holding back my waterworks. I'm forced to hug Izzy all over again, but her selfless mission of mercy only intensifies my guilt. Not least because I'm already thinking about how I can steal a good private look at those videos on Scott's phone.

A new spasm of excitement grips her. "So whereabouts did you see the ghost? Oh yeah, you were sitting on the bog."

On our way to the bathroom, I show her the gouge marks on the front door.

"Bloody hell," she says. "Some really big dogs must've lived h—"

I interrupt, brimming over with the need to help her grasp the weirdness of this place. "But these holes are *still happening*. There's more and more of them, every day."

Like a forensic scientist, Izzy uses her own phone torch to take a long, hard long at all these marks. Finally, she says, "This is so cool . . ."

In the bathroom, I flick on the mirror light and re-enact the Gwyneth attack for Izzy's benefit. She even sits on the closed toilet seat, like a detective keen to establish the sequence of events. She can't get enough of this, and I can't get enough of her. How I'd love some of her laid-back attitude towards ghosts to rub off on me.

"That's dead mad, that," she says. "Wish it had happened to me and not you."

"Me too," I say, hugging my arms. Hate being in this room. "Thanks for coming, honey."

Still on the toilet, she says, "So what's the latest? And what's going on? I can only tell so much from texts. I've really wanted to look you in the eye and make sure you haven't gone mental."

Oh Izzy, please don't do that. "I'm fine. Just been trying to work out what the hell happened with Scott, that's all. While getting terrorised by a ghost for no apparent reason, obvs."

My laugh rings so very hollow.

"But you know who this ghost is? The missing person? Gotta tell me all about it."

"I still don't know if this really was a ghost," I say, "but I'll tell you more once we settle down."

"I'm already settled, right here on the loo. So what's been your approach to investigating Scott? What have you got to work on?"

Can't tell her about the phone. Really can't deal with her thinking badly of me. Not tonight. I need one person in my life, only *one*, who doesn't see me as a loser or a soft target.

"Oh, I've asked around the building," I say, "trying to find someone who saw him move out. Stuff like that."

Why haven't I done this, for real? Hardly the worst idea. Still, Izzy looks dubious. "Is that it, Miss Marple?"

"Pretty much. I've been crap."

"To be honest, hon, you don't *look* great. I only saw you a few nights ago, but you're proper pale."

"Thanks. Uh . . . listen, do you want a shower or anything?"

Oh, I am such a bad person. I've offered this shower in order to (a) temporarily halt Izzy's questioning and (b) give me a chance to look at the videos. And Satan rewards me for my cunning ruse, because she says, "I wouldn't mind, to be honest. Meant to get here two hours ago, but the traffic was a proper bitch. Won't it be cold, though?"

Damn. "Ah, yeah, sorry. I've been grabbing showers at work."

"I like a cold shower. Good for the lymph nodes."

Phew. I only have the one towel, but Izzy doesn't mind that either. Of course she doesn't, because she's awesome and I'm a total shit. Soon as I hear the shower start to hiss, I hurry off along the hall, then head through the gorgeous wash of light from Izzy's radio-lamp, while dragging the garden chair out onto the balcony.

Finally! I reactivate Scott's phone and tap the Videos folder.

I'm fully prepared for my cache-clearing remedy to have made no difference whatsoever, but no, we have lift-off.

Here are the videos, for one single second . . . and then another second . . . and then several more. A whole damn matrix of them, and the phone shows no sign of another crash.

My triumph fades fast, now that I'm able to take in these still thumbnails.

What are they?

What the hell *are* they?

Most of the videos look regular enough. The thumbnails show animals, drinks, meals, pleasant views, starlings around the pier. I watch a few seconds of one video in which a cat walks around oh-so-comically on its hind legs. Which is strange, because as far as I'm aware Scott doesn't own a cat. Could be a friend's cat, or Maureen's cat, but none of the people laughing uproariously off-camera sound like Scott or Maureen. Frankly, I doubt if Maureen's ever laughed this hard in her life.

Anyway, forget the other regular-looking videos. There's no time for those, even though Izzy always spends ages in the shower. Because dotted throughout this grid are thumbnails that share a rather unsettling theme.

Only now do I notice that each of these dodgy-looking videos has a running time of between *one and two hours*. That's seriously long, for a video filmed on a phone.

Each thumbnail shows a different person's face and chest, dimly lit. Some are female and some male, and it looks to me as though . . . as though . . .

Yep. Gwyneth Cooper in one of them.

A blood-curdling scream rings out, from inside the flat.

The bathroom.

I leap to my feet and charge towards the balcony door.

Here's a second scream, followed closely by another, and only now do I skid to a relieved halt. These so-called screams are actually whoops of hilarity, as Izzy braves the cold shower. Praise be. I can sit back down and resume work on the phone.

This thumbnail image shows Gwyneth's face, clear as day, with her eyes closed. Also her bare top half.

Finally, I've uncovered the secret connection between Scott and Gwyneth. They *did* have a thing, after all. I feel oddly gleeful about discovering this, because it feels as though part of the puzzle has neatly dovetailed together.

But . . . uh . . . what exactly am I about to see in this Gwyneth video? Probably sex.

Well, poor Gwyneth's dead, remember? So for all you know, this could be a snuff video.

The thought makes me baulk. And yet the threat of Izzy's inevitable reappearance forces me to play the video.

The still image springs into life. Not that there's a whole lot going on. Here's Gwyneth, lying on her back . . . asleep. The camera is being held steady, a good few feet above her. Presumably so that Scott can get her breasts into the frame.

I can tell she's asleep, rather than dead, thanks to the gentle rise and fall of her chest and the rapid movement going on behind her eyelids. So that's a relief, but this woman is almost certainly being filmed without her knowledge, isn't she?

Cool it, Columbo. Gwyneth might have wanted to know if she snored, and Scott was helping her out, like the ever-charitable guy he is. Or they may have had some kinky agreement that he was allowed to film her.

Oh yeah? And all the people in the other thumbnails happened to have the same snoring issue or kink – including the guys? Nice attempt to explain these videos, but you've done nothing to lower your heart rate.

My skin wants to slither off my bones and crawl away. What a true sicko Scott's turned out to be. Standing there at the side of the bed, filming a sleeping woman for . . . how long? Two whole hours? Even if she was his girlfriend, that's utterly deranged.

Inside the living room, the light from Izzy's radio-lamp weakens, allowing shadows to grow back like fungus. My skin tingles, but I have to see the rest of this video *now*. Using the playback slider, I fast-forward through the rest. I am positively unable to breathe, until I know that something terrible didn't happen to this defenceless woman.

Well, she's dead, so don't get your hopes up . . .

On the screen, all sped up, Gwyneth rolls left on her pillow, then right, then lies on her back again.

About sixty seconds before the end, I resume real-time play. Despite my horrid sense of invading the privacy of Ali's lost sister, I have to see what happens. I have to understand what this video was all about.

Gwyneth sleeps on. Oblivious.

With ten seconds left to go on the counter, Scott slowly lowers his phone, keeping himself cleanly out of shot. Not so much as a finger slips into the frame. As he places the phone down somewhere, the screen goes black.

As the video ends, so does the light from Izzy's radio. With my chest tight, I run back inside, taking Scott's phone with me. When I yank the hand crank to revive the lamp, its potent beam forces the shadows to retreat once again.

I feel a strange kind of relief about the video. For a while there, I had a terrible feeling that Scott might have been about to . . .

To do what? Tip rose petals over her? Ejaculate over her? Murder her? What exactly is Scott Palmer capable of?

Even though you didn't see him kill Gwyneth in the video, that doesn't mean he didn't kill her.

Izzy's shower hisses on. I turn the crank harder and faster, until the lamp burns bright, then scurry back to the balcony. I turn my chair to face the sea, so that she won't spot the phone in my hands when she does emerge.

Returning to the Videos menu, I take in another screen's worth of creepy thumbnails. Men and women, all seemingly asleep while being filmed. Some are every bit as naked as Gwyneth was, while others are in T-shirts or nighties. Puzzled by the presence of the men, I realise that I'd never considered the possibility of Scott being bi. I conduct another quick search of the whole phone, but there's no sight of the men-only dating app Grindr.

In another video, I watch a blonde lying on her side, dreaming her little dreamy dreams, her chest thankfully covered by a duvet. Is that Scott's duvet, the one that used to be here? I can't even remember, but the bed looks different to the one in the first video. This could potentially be the girl's own place.

Blondie's face doesn't fit any of those Tinder matches. Once again, I drag the slider forward to sixty seconds before the end, then resume playback. Looks like Blondie is beginning to stir. She frowns, rubs her eyes and senses Scott's presence. At the first sight of this, he chickens out. Here we go again: the phone gets placed back on the bedside table, his recording ends and Blondie presumably stays none the wiser.

What is this behaviour? Some kind of obsessive fetish? Is it actually illegal? You'd hope so, but I have no idea.

How would I feel if Scott had filmed me?

The moment I ask myself this question, the simple act of breathing becomes difficult.

Oh. My. *God*.

No, no, please no.

CHAPTER FORTY-ONE

12 September

Judging by the memory foam mattress and the height of these pillows, I'm not waking up at home in Leeds but visiting my boyfriend in Brighton.

Rolling over, I stretch out an arm to wrap around Scott. Being a contemporary woke couple, we do not conform to rigid *big spoon, little spoon* ideologies, no sir.

My arm does not find him. Instead, it carves through thin air and lands on the undersheet. Scott's side of the duvet has been curled back and vacated.

When I open sticky eyes, Scott's standing there fully dressed, right at the side of the bed. He's staring at me so directly that it makes me reel away, back into the pillow. My reaction is informed by race memory from countless generations back: meeting something's eyes, feeling like prey and wanting to take flight.

"Oh God," he says. "Sorry. I was watching you sleep – but only for a moment!" Now that the rush of self-preservation has passed, I calm down as he sits beside me and strokes my hair, but the impact of the surprise lingers.

"Morning, stalker boy," I murmur.

His laugh feels only a shade awkward. "You *would* have to wake up in the very moment I was appreciating how beautiful you look while you sleep, wouldn't you?"

"Come on, admit it, you're obsessed with me. You've been there for hours, wanking like a sailor at sea. Now get the kettle on."

"Yes, cap'n." He approximates some kind of sailor salute while grabbing his phone from the bedside table. As his footsteps retreat along the hallway, I luxuriate in the sensations of the morning. Scott must have that balcony window-door open, because the flat already feels so fresh and airy. These sheets feel so soft.

And Scott staring at you felt so weird, didn't it?

No, brain, it did not. The man I love was simply passing by when he stopped to appreciate me for a moment.

There's only one door in here and it's not the kind of room you pass by. He was watching for longer than a moment. His phone was on the side table. You came to sense him standing there. That's why you woke up.

Okay, how about this? He may only have just got up himself.

So how come you can feel the living room windows open?

I demand silence from you for the rest of this weekend. Stop trying to create problems where there are none.

When something feels too good to be true, it usually is.

What did I just *say*?

CHAPTER FORTY-TWO

6 October

My heart is a cocktail shaker full of ice.

I scroll back down through the video thumbnails, fast, so fast.

Fucking hell, here's my face.

Ah, okay, it's just a clip of me sitting outside the local Loving Hut restaurant, taken consensually and when I was very much awake.

Scroll, search, scroll, search.

A sliding noise seals up my throat, as Izzy drags open the balcony door. She's wearing only my towel, one of her crutches and the kind of worried look my mother never gave me.

"What you doing out here? It's freezing."

I have to know. I have to be sure that I'm not in one of these videos. And yet here I am, ramming the phone into my pocket. "It's actually quite mild out here now."

"What's that screen?" she wants to know. Casual, yet so not.

"My Nokia," I blurt, standing. "How was the shower?"

Damn you, Izzy, for knowing me too well. And most of all,

damn me for being such a bad liar. As I come back inside, she's eyeing the bulge in my pocket. I don't even have the excuse of just being pleased to see her. Will she let this go?

Pointedly skipping my question, she says, "So how come you're back on Facebook?"

Heading over to crank the radio-lamp, I manufacture a shrug. "Oh, I felt kind of alone down here, to be honest. At least Facebook makes you feel like there's people around, even if most of them don't give a shit about you."

"But you can't get Facebook on your Nokia."

Without missing a beat, cranking faster, I say, "There's an internet café down the road."

Izzy towels her hair. Our swollen silence is broken only by the whir of the radio-lamp. I ask how outrageously cold the shower was, but she lets rip with a heavy sigh that has *profound disappointment* written all over it. "Look, mate . . . if you've got yourself a proper phone again, it's probably not the best idea, but it's no Nazi war crime either. Why can't you talk to me?"

Okay, how the hell do I play this? I need to finish looking through those videos or I'll die of suspense. But what am I gonna do – pretend I need the loo every ten minutes, so I can take sneaky looks? Izzy's so right: why can't I talk to her about this?

Because you and your phone obsession made her fall down some stairs.

I release the crank handle and scratch my elbows hard. "Okay, I did get a smartphone. Not feeling too proud of it, that's all."

"Fuck me, girl, that was like pulling teeth. So have you got a new number, or are you keeping the same one?"

That's really her first question? I expected so much worse, considering what happened the last time I had a proper phone. No two ways about it: Izzy couldn't have seen me messing about on my socials that night. She was too busy taking care of the dizzy guy at the top of the stairs, just like I should've been.

Oh, do stop torturing yourself. Izzy should have waited for you.

"It's the same number," I tell her. Why can't I seem to stop lying?

Izzy gets dressed, without bothering to cover herself. Just us girls here. "So what's the latest on your Facebook thing, where you asked everyone to identify the horror movie those pics came from? Where did you find those pics in the first place – are they something to do with Scott?"

Oh, this is ridiculous. There's a whole bullshit explanation primed to launch off my tongue, about how I was asking for a friend, but should I really insult Izzy's intelligence? The two of us, we've been through so much together. We've teamed up to deliver babies, to make hearts beat again and to shield each other from rocks slung off council estate balconies. We've made each other cry with laughter during night shifts that we thought might never end. I wasn't there for her when she needed me, up on that ninth floor in Leeds, and now I actually have the temerity to try and feed her transparent excuses.

I suck my explanation back off my tongue. "Could you do me a favour, and struggle to get those knickers on for a while longer?"

"And . . . why's that? You enjoying this eyeful you're getting, Collins?"

"It's just . . . I've got *stuff* to tell you. And if your pants are still tangled around your ankles, you can't run over here and slap me."

She listens so patiently. With such uncharacteristic centred silence.

Seated on the garden chair, with me cross-legged on the living room floor in front of her, Izzy could be some all-powerful

Boudicca or Buddha. At some point during my monologue, I get up and pace around, the defence lawyer to her judge. Whenever I feel particularly stressed, I yank the crank of the lamp handle.

Taking in every syllable with her face neutral, Izzy hears how I found Scott's phone abandoned on the balcony, then couldn't resist breaking in. She hears how I used the phone to uncover the truth about everything from his favourite film to eating meat to his debts. How I found his TrooSelf app but can't access it, but have seen worrying diary entry titles.

Crank, crank, crank.

Izzy hears how Scott was talking to other women behind my back while we dated, and even after we agreed to move in together, but I haven't found proof that he'd slept with any of them. She hears how I found those horror-porn images which none of my Facebook friends, or even their friends' friends, can identify. Lastly, she hears how I've now uncovered these insane, epic videos of people sleeping.

Crank, crank, crank, crank.

With every new detail I divulge to another human being, for the first time, the weight on my shoulders feels a little less crushing. And yet I can tell, from every barely noticeable twitch of her face and every slight heave of her bosom, that Izzy is stockpiling Things To Say. My best mate clearly won't be as relaxed about these transgressions as she was about me simply buying a smartphone again. Honestly, people are so judgemental these days. So it's fine to get a new phone, but suddenly it's a *crime* if it actually belongs to someone else?

Crank, crank, crank, crank, *crank.*

". . . and Gwyneth is among the people in the sleep videos," I say, breathless by now in my drive to sell this whole thing. "So that's the connection between her and Scott. But while you were in the shower, I got really freaked out. I'm worried that I might be in one of these videos too."

Izzy studies me for a few beats. Then she says, "You can let go of the handle now, hon. It's pretty bright in here."

I step away from the searing white of the lamp. "Before you lay into me, can I please check to see if I'm in one of these videos?"

Izzy says nothing, recognising the question's rhetorical nature, because I'm already scrolling furiously down through the clips, searching for my own violation.

None of the sleeping faces I've seen so far is my own, but there's still another screen's worth to check through.

"You should sit down," Izzy says, "just in case you're on there. Guys are so weird. It's not enough to fuck a girl, not any more. They need their pathetic little trophy too. A video of them fucking you from behind or summat, to show their mates. Oh my days, man: if this prick filmed you, I am gonna hunt him *down*."

Barely listening, I zip down to check the last video thumbnail. "Jesus! Thank fuck, Izzy, I'm not here."

"That's great," she says, as I check to see if Gwyneth has replied. Nope. "Now, put down the phone. We need to talk this through."

She nods to the balcony. Uh-oh. Here's the part where she tears multiple strips off me. This is going to be like throwing up, isn't it? You hate the process, but you also know it's exactly what you need.

Izzy pulls two glasses from her bag, followed by a bottle of vodka the size of a diver's oxygen tank.

Five floors down, a bunch of rowdy cock-heads yell themselves hoarse. Behind their racket and the ever-present seabird cacophony, the night is punctuated by classic beats from the DJ in the bar next door. Turns out the Scissor Sisters don't feel like dancing today.

Izzy's on the garden chair, with her back to the sea. I'm on a box, facing her. We clink glasses, neck a shot and she very calmly says she loves me. For one long second, I'm stupid enough to think she might approach this whole subject with Zen calm.

"But for fuck's sake, Kate," she snaps. Hard to tell whether this is the sea wind blowing my hair back, or the blunt force of her words. "You really can't help yourself, can you?"

"But I *had* to unlock Scott's phone. Otherwise I would've gone the rest of my life without—"

"Yeah, yeah, you've already said all that, mate. Now it's my turn." As she steamrollers on, I pour myself more vodka and my hand shakes. "I remember how you justified stalking the Venezuelan guy. Some old bollocks about needing closure. Why can't you learn to let go and move on?"

"When I know the whole truth, I *will* move on. Promise."

"Mmm-hmm . . . until the next time. And what makes you think the whole truth will be knowable, anyway? You're trying to water plants that have rotten roots."

I want to congratulate Izzy on her neat metaphor, but I'm finding this tough love harder to take than I expected. My voice sounds annoyingly meek as I say, "I could really do with your support here."

"Real friends ain't always about support. Sometimes they're about home truths, like telling you you're a danger to yourself." I try to speak but she cuts me off, the fire behind her eyes fanned higher by vodka. "When someone dumps you, who cares why? It's *over*, Kate. You and Scott are done, finished, history. Doesn't matter how far you search through this phone or what you find, because that basic fact is never gonna change."

I muster some fire of my own. Or at least a candle's worth. "I know it's over. I do know that, *now*. But there's a hell of a lot more going on here than mine and Scott's break-up. This feels serious. Dangerous, too."

Izzy gives me a careful, steady look. "Does it really feel dangerous, though?"

Truth be told, I'm not sure. The word *dangerous* kind of surged out of my unconscious mind.

That's right. Scott's a psycho and you know it.

Please leave for your safety.

"Come on, Izz, did you not hear all the things I said? Those weird pics on Scott's phone, these videos of sleeping people? I mean, Scott filmed Gwyneth asleep for two whole hours, and now her family can't get hold of her, and I thought I saw her ghost. Does that not seem serious to you?"

Izzy sniffs her vodka like it's merlot. "The ghost might not have been Gwyneth. What if it only looked like her?"

"That was her face," I say, reliving the moment when Gwyneth reached out for me. Since this memory loosens my bowels and makes my brain recoil, this task requires a great deal of concentration, but I picture her in all the detail my mind dares to produce.

Hey, here's something. Gwyneth's blue wrists were encircled by black lines, like intertwining vipers. Bracelets, maybe? No, these lines were too thin, and I'm pretty sure they did not move like bracelets would. Besides, would a spirit retain its jewellery? These things looked much more like . . .

"Tattoos," I say. "This thing had tatts on its wrists. But does Gwyneth?" On Scott's phone, I revisit the only photos I've already seen of Gwyneth. None of these pictures show her wrists. With a surge of impulsive energy behind me, I fire off a question to Ali Cooper on Twitter.

Izzy has that pitying look back in her eye. "Honey, you should probably let this go."

"Okay, you're now saying *probably*, which means you know there's something going on here."

"All right then, let's cut to the chase. Are you honestly saying that Scott's killed Gwyneth? And if he has, then how is she able to post cat memes?"

I still feel stupid for entertaining the idea that I saw Gwyneth's ghost, let alone Scott being a killer. But if I'm reaching here, it's because instinct tells me there's something to reach for. "If you were going to kill someone and wanted to make sure no one realised for the longest possible time, you *might* maintain their online presence, right? Facebook means never having to actually meet most of our friends. Instead, we see their posts and know they're basically all right, even when they're moaning about their life. But for all we know, someone else could be . . . *puppeting* them."

Izzy tips back her head to contemplate the balcony ceiling. Next door, Debbie Harry complains about being left hanging on a phone. "Have you checked up on the other people in these sleep videos? Are any of them 'missing'?"

"I only found the videos a minute before you arrived. But let's take a look at them."

"Oh God, I'm such an enabler."

Excited by the new lead, I flick through the sleep videos.

Wait . . . why is my pulse sky-rocketing? It's not because I'm seeing these videos again. No, that's a more insidious fear, whereas *this* . . . this is a primal, self-preserving rush that makes my heart thump.

Stay calm and think. What's going on? What's changed?

I can taste copper in my mouth, stronger and stronger.

Oh no. Here comes Gwyneth.

I'm fumbling for the words to explain to Izzy what's happening, when she yells the word "Fuck!"

I've never seen her look so scared, not even when we almost drove an ambulance through the front door of a charity shop.

The heel of her good leg pounds the decking, trying to gain purchase with which to shove her chair back and away from whatever the hell she's seeing over my shoulder in the living room.

A faint blue light dances on her face.

Climb down over the front of the balcony and get the fuck away.

Desperate to see what Izzy sees, I swing around and duck down behind my box, like it's a heap of World War One sandbags.

Something incandescent and awful is jerking its way out through the balcony window towards us, with its limbs in constant spasm. The intense colour of its light makes the entire pane of glass resemble the sea on an August afternoon.

Every muscle and ligament in my body has been sewn together, then pulled tight. I hear the feet of Izzy's chair drag hard across the decking. She says "Fuck" again, several times.

Even though this blue, dead-eyed face strobes hard and fast, I can see it does not belong to Gwyneth. This is the face of a roaring man, with a mouth full of shark teeth. Someone make him go away, please someone make him fuck right off.

An ugly *crash* sends a shockwave along the decking and up into the cartilage of my knees.

Izzy. She must have tipped backwards. Might've smashed her head open on the front wall. Might've snapped her fucking neck.

Oh God no, I can't let her down again, no matter what.

Izzy lies face up with her eyes closed, her butt and raised legs still hugging the toppled chair. When I scurry towards her on my hands and knees, it means turning my back on the roaring shark thing. And when I imagine how cold those glacier-blue hands will feel when they grab me, the thought makes me crawl all the faster.

Cradling Izzy's head, I'm relieved to feel no blood on the braids. The back of her falling skull missed the front balcony wall by inches.

My lightning-fast scan of the surrounding balcony and the living room suggests normality and sanity have resumed. The glass of the balcony door has shed all traces of crazed blue. Inside, the radio-lamp fills the living room with warm, steady light as if nothing amiss has gone down.

And yet something did go down. Izzy saw it too. She. Saw. It.

I swipe drool off my chin. The metal taste in my mouth may have diluted, but the frenzied hammer-blows of my heart allow only one syllable out at a time. "Izz . . . I'm . . . so . . . sorr . . . ry . . . are . . . you . . . oh . . . kay . . . can . . . you . . . move?"

I'm horrified to see her face wrinkle into a pained grimace, until I realise she's actually grinning from ear to ear.

"That was a ghost, man. A fuckin' *ghost*. Oh my days, this is the best. Thing. Ever."

CHAPTER FORTY-THREE

19 July

I wake in the still of the night, like that guy out of Whitesnake, to find that Scott is no longer beside me.

Still half-entangled in a nonsensical dream that fades fast, like candyfloss for the mind, I tell myself that he must have gone to the loo. So I wait for a while, keen to drift back off to sleep in his arms. And then I wait some more, and some more, until curiosity pulls me out of bed and into a T-shirt.

This hallway never struck me as creepy before, but there's a first time for everything. The puzzling absence of Scott lends the flat an edge that I would struggle to define.

Behind me, the bathroom sits dormant. Up ahead, on the wall opposite the archway, there's only the palest street-lamp glow.

As I pass through the arch, my T-shirt billows up around me and I slap it back down over my hips. The whole Marilyn Monroe bit feels less sexy when you're alone in the dark . . . but why am I alone? Where is he?

Padding across the living room, my bare feet slap smooth wood until I see him.

A fuzzy, yellow-tinged silhouette, rooted in the centre of the balcony outside.

The closer I get to the open balcony door, the more this silhouette defines itself.

The more bare flesh I see.

The more apparent it becomes that Scott is buck naked.

I've never seen him stand like this before and it makes me weirdly nervous. His shoulders rise and fall in a slow, deliberate, exaggerated manner. With his whole body arrow-straight and his tidy little butt clenched, he looks like a soldier standing to attention.

Or a fucking weirdo standing nude on a balcony in the middle of the night.

As I head past the sofa, another breeze tries to raise my shirt but I'm too quick. I want to call out to my boyfriend and bring this odd moment to an abrupt close, but something stops me – the sense that I'm catching him in a private moment. What do Scott's private moments look like? Here's a rare chance to find out.

Framed by the balcony door, he's as still as a photograph. I daren't even breathe, in case it alerts him that I'm here.

I want to see what happens next.

Craving a closer look, I take two slow steps forward.

Something tiny, but unforgivingly sharp, skewers up into the ball of my right foot, and now I'm hissing and hopping around like a cartoon character.

A gasp punches its way out of Scott's throat. He spins around with one hand outstretched, as if preparing for combat in the Vietnamese jungle, circa 1968. With the street lamps behind him, I can't see his face and find myself hopping back away from him, without fully knowing why.

Breathing hard, Scott slaps one palm against his chest. The sucker-punch severity of his tone makes me feel way smaller than it has any right to.

"Fuck's *sake*, Kate. Why didn't you tell me you were there?"

CHAPTER FORTY-FOUR

6 October

Once Scott had recovered from his shock, our jitters died and were reborn as near-hysterical laughter. He explained that he often wandered out there when he couldn't sleep, but I'd already got over the whole thing. Then I literally got over him, riding cowgirl out on the cool, hard decking. His hands roamed up inside my T-shirt as we fucked the last remnants of weirdness clean out of our heads.

Out of *my* head, anyway. Who knows what messed-up thoughts lurked on in his.

So. What do you now think Scott was really doing out here that night – praising the moon, like a good little psycho? If he'd had a raging hard-on for some imagined lunar goddess, you wouldn't have seen it in that light.

Ugh. The intimacy we allow ourselves to share with people we know next to nothing about. Makes me cringe, to think that Izzy and I are sitting on the exact same spot where I may have cavorted with a killer that night. Am I going OTT with this? I have no clue.

I've shoved my box over to the front of the balcony, so that Izzy is stationed reassuringly between me and the flat. She cannot stop buzzing, and I cannot stop trembling like a dog on Fireworks Night. Not only is there more than one entity in this flat, but the radio-lamp was super-bright when the roaring ghost attacked. This means my "water tank" theory of dealing with ghosts literally holds no water. Light does not deter these flickering blue nightmares after all.

Yeah. If Izzy wasn't here, I'd be spending tonight on the beach.

"That was beyond awesome," she says for the tenth time, using two fingertips to draw calming circles on my back. "So *now* you believe you've seen ghosts, right? Fuck holograms, man. The only other explanation is that we both have exactly the same brain tumour. And I really don't think that girls who work together end up growing brain tumours in sync. It's not like periods."

When I check Scott's phone, Ali Cooper's Twitter reply screams at me. "FUCK PLEASE TELL ME THEY DIDN'T FIND A BODY."

Oh shit. *Not yet, Ali, but they probably will.* What the hell do I tell her? "No, hun, sorry. I just dreamt about her last night, that's all. Sorry for asking."

"FUCKSAKE A FUCKEN DREAM YOU STUPID BITCH SCARING THE FUCK OUT OF ME."

"Sorry. But just to confirm . . . DOES Gwyneth have tribal wrist tattoos?"

"YES SHE DOES MYSTIC MEG NOW FUCK OFF!!!!!!111!!!!"

"So, I don't have a tumour," I tell Izzy. "I really did see a ghost, and it really was Gwyneth."

"Did I not tell you, right from the start? Ghosts are a thing, man."

Hundreds of faces flit through my head. The faces of all those I've seen die. Even though I've never felt able to convincingly reassure people, like Pat up in Leeds, that their late loved ones would live on in some other form, turns out they do anyway. I mean, they might be fucking scary flicker-phantoms with eyes like deep dark wells, full of rage and Christ knows what else, but they're still out there. And sometimes, it seems, they can interact with our plane of existence.

Fuck a duckling, this is huge.

The whole world looks – no, *feels* – different, thanks to my new insight into one of its secrets. While it's impossible not to feel awed by the apparent fact that death is not the end, this does nothing to stem the flow of my fear.

I keep my voice hushed, in case the secret world of evil spirits might hear. "Izzy, why do they keep *coming* for me? Wouldn't mind so much if they only stood there or something, like yours did back when you were young in . . . 1953."

Izzy lightly smacks the back of my head, then resumes her circle-drawing duties.

"Why would Gwyneth's ghost show up here?" I say. "Ghosts tend to hang around the place where they died, don't they? Unfinished business and all that, as they try to come to terms with their deaths? So . . . what if Gwyneth died here?"

"Could both of these spirits have died here and want to tell us something? Wow, a message from beyond!"

"They could be trying to tell us that Scott killed them . . ."

"Mate, seriously . . . what makes you even believe he's capable of murder?"

A swig of vodka scorches my gullet. "I always saw this . . . this thing in him."

I Am Possessed.

"He always reminded me of a wolf," I add

A chill runs through me, as I remember seeing that wild look . . .

. . . a real wild one . . .

. . . in Scott's eyes during sex. Before he peaked, each and every time, was he thinking about how he was going to film me asleep later? Or about how he was planning to kill me?

How about the way Scott shot daggers at that businessman who rammed into him at Brighton train station? He'd looked like he wanted to rip out the big guy's throat.

. . . with his teeth. Because he's a wolfman who barks at the moon.

Izzy says, "If Scott's a killer, then how come he didn't snuff you?"

I have no real answer. "Depends why he killed the others . . . And he might still plan to kill me. Ever since I got here, I've felt watched."

"Hey, this ghost-guy we saw . . . What if he's in one of these sleep videos?"

Again, why didn't I think of this? I hand Izzy the phone so she can flick through the videos herself.

"How come he's got videos of girls *and* guys on there, anyway?" Izzy wonders aloud. She shows me a video thumbnail. "*This* one, right? I'd recognise those teeth anywhere."

I study the sleeping, pudgy-faced man. His open mouth packs a set of fangs that'd put Jaws to shame.

"Oh my God," I breathe. "There is *definitely* something in this."

Izzy fast-forwards through the clip, making the guy's head whip to and fro on his pillow.

"How can we find out who he is?" I ask. "What if he really is missing, like Gwyneth?"

We lose ourselves in thought, long enough for the DJ next door to play one whole Depeche Mode song.

"Google Images," says Izzy, with such conviction that I want to kiss her face. She always knew so much more tech stuff than me. "You can upload a picture to Google Images and it'll show you where else the image has appeared online."

"Except," I say, "a still from these sleep vids won't have been online before . . . Ah, but here's something I can try . . . '

Scott didn't have a picture of Gwyneth on his phone, only the shot of Ali that she took, but Mr Jaws might be a different story. I tap through to the bulging Photos folder and skim through the images.

"Yep," I say. "Here he is."

The big guy's in a bar. Wearing a Mexican hat and a Hawaiian garland, he gurns right at the camera lens. Looks like either a holiday or stag party scenario. Scott's own stag? At this point, we can rule nothing out.

"Izzy, this is exactly how the ghost looked. Like he was roaring at us."

She nods intently. "So go to Google Images and upload that pic."

By the time Gloria Gaynor finishes telling us how she'll survive, we have results. The guy had posted this Mexican-hat picture on his Twitter profile. From here, we get his name: Dieter Keppler. His bio, which notes that he works in diabetes care, includes a helpful link to his Facebook profile.

"Hold on," I tell Izzy, when I've clicked through. "This is really fucking odd."

Izzy peers at the screen and shrugs. "How come?"

"We're not looking at Dieter's profile from the outside, Izz. We're *logged into it*. Look, I can totally read his private messages." My skin prickles. "There! Doesn't this prove that Scott is controlling people's profiles?"

"Okay," she says. "I reckon it . . . might."

Flicking back to Twitter, I see that we're logged into Dieter's account there too.

Back to Dieter's Facebook. Thinking nothing of violating a new individual's privacy, I plough through his messages. Turns out he's one of the few who actually uses Messenger for sexting. Looks like he gets a fair bit of action, too, so I retreat to the safety of his FB wall. His latest post was earlier today, in which he – or more likely, Scott The Puppet Master – posted something about how people don't get Type One diabetes from eating too much sugar.

"Look through his friends," Izzy says, warming to the investigation. "Is Scott there? Is Gwyneth?"

While Lou Reed takes a walk on the wild side next door, I follow her suggestion and find neither of them.

"If you'd killed someone," Izzy says, "and you were controlling their profile, I suppose you wouldn't wanna be on their friends list."

"You also wouldn't want your victims publicly linked to each other as friends." My skin has grown clammy. Up until tonight, the idea that Scott might be dangerously deranged had only skulked around in the back of my mind, but did I actually share a bed with – and plan a whole future with – someone who was not only capable of murder but had already taken multiple lives?

I show Izzy inside the TrooSelf app. "Check this out. *Joining The Death Grip Cult . . .*"

We survey the rest of the list without speaking, while Jarvis Cocker insists that we'll never think like common people.

I Am Possessed

Out, Demon, Out

My Sweet Saviour

I Am In Love With V

Burning New Pathways Into The Brain

Joining The Death Grip Cult
The End

"Looks perfectly normal to me," says Izzy. To my relief, her big eyes confirm she's kidding, not to mention a tad concerned. "Let's look at more people."

I lose all track of time as we cycle through our little process.

Step One: we nominate a likely candidate from one of Scott's sick little sleep-flicks.

Step Two: we find a photo of them on his phone's camera roll.

Step Three: a Google Images search leads us to the person's social media presence.

Three times in a row, we find them.

Three times in a row, we find ourselves logged into their social media accounts.

"So," I say. "Scott filmed these people asleep. He has photos of them. He's controlling their accounts, their online selves. And if someone was to contact these people's families, do you reckon there's good odds that they'll have gone 'missing' and 'disowned' their loved ones?"

Sitting there with Scott's phone in her hand, Izzy just stares at me. She looks dazed, as if the world has spun on its axis. I know exactly how she feels, and now it's my turn to get excited.

"I never thought I'd say this," I tell her. "But I'm actually starting to think *police*. Even though we don't really have proof that anyone's dead, they can look into everything. Izzy, I'm so fucking tired, and what you said was right. It really is time for me to move on."

Ever since I got here, I've based my life around trying to work out what goes on in Scott's head. This means I've been making everything about him. But from now on, everything's going to be about me.

My heart leaps. In the bar next door, Freddie Mercury voices my desire to break free. I can practically smell my new life, back up in Leeds with Izzy, leaving all this Brighton junk broken under my wheels.

Wait. Oh shit.

Something's wrong with Izzy. Very wrong.

Why does she have this intensely serious look on her face, like she's either furious with me or might burst into tears?

"Kate," she says, adopting the gossamer-soft voice that we use when breaking terrible news to patients. "I'm afraid I . . . Well, I've *found* something on Scott's phone."

CHAPTER FORTY-FIVE

28 June

Riffing along with Scott's whole *Titanic* gag, I extend my arms like plane wings and give him my best breathless, girly Kate Winslet impersonation. "I'm flying!"

Over on the pier, a tiny red light at the peak of the helter-skelter flashes in time with my elevated pulse. I could really get used to this place. Especially this balcony. My arms tire, so I let them drop back down by my sides. Still right behind me, pressed up against me, Scott says, "Actually . . . out of interest . . . *do* you trust me, Kate?"

I turn around to face him and he plants both hands on my hips. His expression tells me he genuinely wants his question answered. "That's a slightly odd thing to ask."

"Curious, that's all," he says, but his shrug fails to convince. I search his face for further cues, but find nothing to go on.

"You seem like a really good guy, and . . ."

I'm already falling for you, but would rather jump off this balcony than admit as much.

". . . I like you. But trust you, one hundred per cent, on our second proper date? Ask me again if we're still seeing each other in another two months. Or two years."

Well done, me. That struck the right balance.

"Just FYI, though," I add, "when someone asks if you trust them, it doesn't necessarily make you think, 'Ooh, they must be proper trustworthy.'"

Oh. And now I may have gone a shade too far, on a great night. But he did ask.

Scott nods and smiles. "I get that, yeah. I wouldn't have asked in the first place, if DiCaprio hadn't in the movie! But I don't know . . . Actually, I suppose it's because I've been accused of being *shifty* before. Had a girlfriend, a while back, who didn't trust me, purely because of how I looked. Not that I'm hung up on it or anything!"

There's that flash of vulnerability – the thing that first drew me to Scott. "I don't really get her attitude," I tell him. "You seem pretty honest."

Does he really, Kate? Be honest. Right now, does this guy really seem to be anything but hot?

With a flash of inspiration, I throw in, "She might've grown to mistrust excessively handsome men."

Squeezing my waist, he pulls me against his groin. "Oh, good work. You can come again."

"And again and again, I hope," I say, as I kiss him, tongue first.

Scott pulls back and smiles. Then, without warning, he looks shocked and I wonder what on Earth I've done wrong.

"Christ," he says. "I completely forgot to say . . . and your eyes just reminded me! You know that whole thing about the contact lenses getting lost? That was a wind-up."

I shake his hands off my hips and stand open-mouthed. "*What?*"

A gale of laughter flies out of him. "I'm so sorry! I totally meant to tell you, but then we drank more and ended up on different topics."

"You fucker."

"Let me try and make it up to you, right now? I think I know a way."

CHAPTER FORTY-SIX

6 October

Soon as I realised how effortlessly Scott had lied, I should have run to the hills.

When he told me that contact lens story in Leeds, he even said, *It's true, I swear.* I know it was only a trivial joke, but nevertheless the sociopathic prick *swore* his lie was true. One of many red flags I failed to spot, and now here I am, starring in a little video he made. Running time: two hours and twelve minutes.

Sick to my stomach, with Izzy's hand planted on my shoulder for moral support, I brace myself to watch. She and I have come back inside the living room because the wind's getting up and the temperature has plummeted in all sorts of ways.

Onscreen, my past self lies asleep on her back. Not on a bed, but on the living room floor. My head is resting on my own bunched-up jacket. The only soundtrack on this video comes from gulls and the occasional motorbike engine, car horn or squeal of brakes.

When Izzy and I worked together, she was always the more

thorough one. I like to think this wasn't because I was lazy or didn't care, but she always had the more even temperament. She'd really take her time to study patients, often spotting things I'd missed. In fairness, I'd failed to spot this video during my first skim through because the preview still didn't show my face. The thumbnail was mostly black, because the camera only focuses on my face three seconds into the video. Scotty Boy's direction skills were sub-par that night.

My voice comes out cracked as a desert floor. "Looks like the first night I stayed here. But how did he get in? I had all the boxes pushed up against the door."

For the first time, I study the living room ceiling, looking for trap doors. I want to rush back into the hall and the bathroom and study the ceiling there, too. How could Scott possibly have got in?

"Jesus, Izzy," I whisper, "what if he never left? What if he's tucked away in a crawlspace somewhere?"

Izzy's concern is a tangible thing, hanging in the air between us. "I'm an idiot. Shouldn't have told you about this bloody video."

I clear my throat and wet my lips. "No, no. I'm glad you did."

The video lumbers on. Agonisingly slow and deliberate, it features so little movement that it may as well be a photograph. Only the onscreen counter changes, along with the barely perceptible motion of my chest. Thank God I stayed fully clothed that night. Just because you're paranoid, doesn't mean they're not filming you while you sleep.

Gripped by the urge to break the video's spell, to diminish the power it holds over me, I mumble, "Sleep's really weird, isn't it? When you really stop and think about it, I mean. We take sleep for granted, don't we, and yet that's when we're at our most vulnerable. Our most exposed."

Izzy tries to chip in, but I keep on talking. "You meet someone in a bar, or at a speed dating thing, or even in your home for an impulsive hook-up. You quite possibly fuck them on the first night, and then you allow yourself to fall unconscious in their presence for . . . how long, about eight hours? That is fucking mental when you think about it. This person who you met only hours ago, they could do anything at all to you. You could wake up in the middle of the night gargling blood because your new partner decided to wander into your kitchen, pick the sharpest knife and then slit your throat."

To this, Izzy says nothing. She knows my venting is entirely necessary – some kind of attempt to process what I'm seeing. If we watched the violation of Kate Collins in silence, it might prove unbearable for both of us.

I drag the playback slider. As the video fast-forwards, Past Me's sleeping body jerks to the left, then to the right and back again.

To think that Scott somehow entered the flat that night and stood there, for all this time, filming me. Why two whole hours? And while we're asking questions: why at all? Could this be a power thing, getting off on people's vulnerability? Does he stand there, thinking about all the things he *could* do to us but chooses not to? Does he actually jerk off while filming, or does he wait until he gets home and—

One jarring new thought wipes out all of the above questions. "Izzy, why the fuck didn't Scott take his phone back? Why didn't he take it away with him that night?"

I can see that, for Izzy, this is not a new thought. While I've been held captive by my emotional response to this video, she has applied cold hard logic to the situation. Evidently, she's been left wanting, because she can only splay her hands, at a loss.

"Izzy, why the *fuck* didn't he take the phone?"

Her eyes meet mine. "Either he's the most forgetful bloke on the planet . . ."

Jumping in, I say, "Or he *wanted* to leave it with me. Which almost certainly means he wanted to leave it on the balcony in the first place." I feel light-headed. Disorientated. "You know, I kept thinking how weird it was that he didn't cancel the phone! That's what you'd do if you lost yours, right?"

Izzy says, "Some people have their phones set up so they can delete everything inside, remotely. And Scott is an IT guy, right? Or did he lie about that, too?"

The demonic window-face grins harder than ever. "I'm surprised the fucker didn't tell me he was a hedge fund manager or something. He wasn't a very good IT guy, though, by all accounts. Kept missing his deadlines. Might have been too busy messing with people. Or killing them."

"Why would Scott want to leave the phone here? What if . . ." Here, Izzy hesitates. Oh, how acutely I feel her walk the thin line between doing what's best for me and finding herself drawn into the puzzle. Her puzzle-lust wins – the urge to take this Rubik's cube one twist closer to completion. "What if the phone has some kind of bugging device, babe? What if it's listening all the time? Or . . . I mean, you said you've felt watched . . ."

My vision goes woozy, making the tiny camera lens at the top of the phone wink at me. When will I learn to trust my gut? I felt watched from the moment I moved in here.

No. That's not true, not exactly.

I felt watched after I discovered the phone.

The demon face taunts me from that sliding door, victorious. Those eyes, that cruel smile, they say, *Ah, you finally figured it out, huh? Well done, baby. Lovin' life.*

I spring up to haul my boxes around. I'm searching for certain words I scribbled on the side of one of them roughly ten thousand years ago, when my head swam with endorphins, hope and love. In the background, Izzy is asking what I'm doing and if I'm all right, even though she knows I'm very much not.

I rip the duct tape off the top of the box marked Handy Stuff. Inside, there's an ever-so-handy holdall full of stuff I've lugged from flat to flat during my renting life.

Maybe, Izzy's saying, we're overthinking this whole thing. Maybe the phone isn't really Scott's surveillance device. Maybe I should calm down.

Scott Palmer hacked his way into my heart, then sleazed his way into my life. He stripped away my privacy, including my right to not be fucking *filmed while I sleep*.

I meet the demon face's grin with my own, then rummage around inside the holdall, disregarding the cordless power drill, the spirit level and the battery-powered box that detects the presence of wires in walls. All of these tools are handy for home DIY, there's no denying that, but I'm searching for one item in particular.

Again, Izzy asks what I'm doing. Then, when she sees what I've taken from the holdall, and where I'm going, she yells at me to stop. But not even my best friend, the pal who I owe big-time, can stop me committing this act.

My jaw is locked tight. Every cell in my body is ablaze. Doubt I'd stop marching towards this sliding door even if someone levelled a gun at me.

"Oh yeah?" I bark at the face on the window. "How funny is it now?"

My hammer creates the most gorgeous arc from way back over my shoulder, all the way through to the demon's nose.

The face ceases to exist. Bashed through onto the balcony, it skitters out across the decking in bright, darting shards.

There follows a pause, while the rest of the window comes to terms with what's happened. Two strong arms wrap themselves around my chest, exert a firm grip, then haul me two steps back. Oh God, Izzy must've staggered over to grab me, to save me, without using her crutches.

An almighty waterfall of broken glass cascades down over the spot where I'd stood. The noise is both horrific and so very pretty.

Izzy is the first to get her words out. "Feel better now?"

"Yep. But nowhere near as good as I'm gonna feel. Tell me how I can find Scott."

Together, we wend our awkward way back across the room to the garden chair and her crutches. She's shaking her head, but I'm a dog with a bone. "Izzy, seriously: tell me how I can use the phone to find him. If you don't tell me, I'll find out anyway."

As I settle her down in the chair, she wipes sweat from her eyes and says, "Fuck off, mate. It's not happening. You can come back to Leeds and—"

Spit flies from my mouth as I say, "Fuck that." I know I'm directing my rage at the wrong person, and am still holding the hammer's handle, but I've become a car without brakes. "I'm not walking away. I'm so sick of trying to see Scott through this phone. I'm going to look him straight in the eye and I'm going to do it *tonight*, with or without your help."

"Tonight? You've gotta be kidding. What if he really is dangerous, Kate?"

"Do I not look dangerous right now?"

She glances at the hammer, then mutters, "A danger to yourself, yeah."

I kneel beside the small mountain of broken glass, then place the hammer to one side. Silence reigns, as the energy in the room dissipates.

"I'm sorry, Izz. You're my best mate in the world, but I really am going to find him. So please, please tell me how."

"Do you promise not to break any more glass, you fuckin' madhead?"

"I promise. Well, unless it's over Scott's skull."

Izzy considers Scott's phone on the box beside her, then lets out a heavy sigh.

"I'm guessing you already checked GPS tracking, right?"

Feeling stupid and excited at the same time, I lean forward, all ears.

CHAPTER FORTY-SEVEN

6 October

Now that we're out of the city and into the wild, there are fewer vehicles to contend with but the roads have become way harder to navigate. My headlights illuminate one tight bend after another.

Izzy has Scott's phone on her lap. Paranoia has driven us to wrap both of the handset's cameras and the mouthpiece with several layers of duct tape, in case Scott really has been keeping tabs on us. We have, of course, kept the screen visible. "Next left," she says, consulting Google Maps.

"I've really missed driving on ridiculous missions with you, Izz."

"Focus on the road."

I am way out of Izzy's good books. You can practically hear her teeth grind. On her express instructions, I'm going slow, despite having gulped down two strong coffees on the way. I'd argued that I'd drunk far less of the vodka than Izzy, but she rightly beat me down until I agreed to approach our journey like a Sunday driver. Even then, if we get pulled over, my career will be over. On the face of it, then, this is far from the most ingenious plan, but I know I wouldn't sleep tonight without having found Scott. Especially now that we have a pretty specific idea of where he might be.

I'd been so focused on the actual content of Scott's phone – the words, the media – that GPS tracking never even occurred to me. Yet, as Izzy reminded me, a phone seizes every given opportunity to store the locations visited by its user.

"Left down here," she says. "No, not this one, the next one. And slow *down*."

When we'd opened the list of places Scott had been, not only could we see his footprints across Brighton, Hove and beyond, but each journey bore an ever-so-handy date marker. Before disappearing from the flat and leaving his phone behind, the last place Scott travelled to, on 30 September, was out here in the sticks. In Pulborough, roughly north-west of Brighton, Scott had seemingly visited a spot beside a prehistoric hill fort called Chanctonbury Ring.

Comfortingly, Wikipedia informs us that the Chanctonbury Ring was supposedly created by the Devil himself. Oh yeah, can't get enough of that, especially seeing as it's almost midnight. But apparently, as long as we don't run seven times anti-clockwise around the clump of trees up on that looming peak, we'll be all right.

A turn-off sign bears the words CHANCTONBURY RING. As I swing left into the lane, I can't help also noticing the "dead end" sign.

This lane is little more than one vehicle wide. Rustic homes flash past, most of them with handmade signs out front, telling visitors to stay well clear of their property. Shotguns spring to mind.

The effort required to persuade Izzy to let me come here has stolen vengeful wind from my sails, leaving me drained and edgy. Now that we're here in the thick of the countryside, and potentially heading straight for Scott's hidey-hole, everything feels all the more real. When Izzy wasn't looking, I smuggled the hammer along with me, hiding it under my jacket, but what might I actually do with the thing? And weaponry aside, what am I actually going to say to Scott if I find him?

Dear God: if you really do exist, somewhere up there in all these thick, black clouds, please let Scott be a sad little pervert who hasn't actually hurt anyone, let alone murdered them. Please let him cower before me and beg to be forgiven, so that I may comprehend the full extent of his weakness.

"I've no idea how long this road will carry on for," Izzy says. "The map gets seriously vague from this point."

"Do these even qualify as roads? They're more like lanes."

"You're skating on thin ice as it is, Collins, without bringing pedantry into the equation." She peers out through the windscreen. "Ah, okay . . . here's the end of the line."

When I had Google Street View, I would see unfamiliar destinations long before I physically reached them. And yet here's Izzy and me, parking up at a dead-end turnstile that Street View cameras failed to document. Walking into a territory where even robot cameras didn't fancy going? Oh yeah, baby, where do I sign?

My headlights blast through the turnstile, then smear themselves weakly across the united front of trees the footpath leads into.

"How much battery's left on Scott's phone?" I ask. "Wish we'd thought to bring an actual torch."

"Did we *have* an actual torch?"

"No."

"That'll be why, then. The phone's on thirty-three per cent, but let me ask, one more time – what exactly is your plan?"

"All I'm going to do is creep over to this place, this house, whatever . . . and take a look. Scott's moving boxes might still be piled up inside for me to see . . ."

"Mmm, yes, wouldn't that be convenient. And then what?"

"Nothing. We'll just know this is the right place."

The back of my skull aches. Am I telling Izzy the truth? Tonight, will it really be enough to just know?

Does the Pope shit in the woods?

He probably doesn't, as a rule. But what if the Pope mobile breaks down?

Izzy regards the turnstile like it's a gallows pole. "Can you really picture Scott living out here?"

"Good question, Loyd Grossman. I've no idea. But unless the GPS stuff is way out, he's *been* here for some reason. He might secretly be a dogger. I mean, how accurate does this stuff tend to be?"

Izzy throws her hands up and speaks through gritted teeth. "I've known it to be scarily accurate and scarily inaccurate. Look, why can't we come back here tomorrow in daylight? You know I fucking hate this. Especially as I can't come with you."

Izzy, bless her, she wouldn't even make it over the turnstile. Which suits me fine, because I categorically refuse to place the girl in further danger. This very much feels like a trip I need to make alone. "Tomorrow morning, I'm back at work. And—"

"Yeah, you're back at work if you don't get murdered."

My stomach cartwheels at "murdered", but I conjure my lightest and most reassuring laugh. "I'm not going to get *murdered*, Izz! For all we know, Scott might not even be capable of that."

"You reckon he is, though, don't you. And I might be coming round to the idea. Then again, it's late and we're in the middle of nowhere and I'm really tired."

"First sign of a problem and I'll be back here like shit through a goose. All you have to do is keep one eye open and get ready to start the engine. This bank's full o' cash, Mugsy, I'm tellin' ya."

My crap heist gag, and even crapper Noo Yawk accent, only succeed in making Izzy more doomstruck. "You know who can generally carry out this kind of investigation without getting killed? *The police*."

"True, but they also need a bulletproof reason to visit."

Izzy shudders. "Don't mention bullets. Is there owt I can say that'll stop you doing this?"

"No, honey."

"*Why not*, Kate?"

"Well, because . . . because, I mean . . ."

Clutch at those straws. Go on, grab one.

" . . . what if Scott's kidnapped people, Izz? What if it's a *Silence of the Lambs* type deal? He might have people trapped in a hole out here, telling them to . . . to . . . uh, what's that line in the movie?"

"Put the lotion in the basket," she sighs.

"Lotion! Yes. Police investigations take too long. And like I said, we'd need a really bulletpr— Sorry, *watertight* case for them to come and investigate Buffalo Bill. The lambs are screaming, Clarice."

Even Izzy's seatbelt sounds harsh as she clunks it open. "Okay, okay, I get it, you wanna be the big dead hero. Put Scott's phone on vibrate. If a car turns up or something, I'll text you."

"Got it. Love you."

"Jesus, Kate, don't say that. You never normally say you love me unless I say it first. Makes it sound like the last thing you'll ever do."

"Nope, the last thing I'll ever do is walk into these trees."

"Right. Best you be fucking off, then."

CHAPTER FORTY-EIGHT

6 October

My first mistake was to overestimate the power of a phone torch in darkness this absolute.

Well, actually, if we're being anal about this, my first mistake was talking to Scott in Wales.

My weedy beam of light barely illuminates two steps ahead on this rough-hewn path, littered with small stones, weeds and chunks of chalk. A dense canopy might hide the moon, but it's impossible to miss the shadow-hulk of Chanctonbury Hill up ahead.

My light hits an enormous, towering birch that steals my breath. Serpentine roots sprout in all directions away from the base, each the colour of ash and wide as The Rock's forearm. My torch briefly catches a small nook beneath these roots, stuffed full of twigs.

Blair Witch, Blair Witch, Blair Witch.

Yeah. Let's pretend I never saw that.

Ignoring the fear that wants me for a midnight snack, I rest back on a root-tangle to check the GPS app. Where I'm standing seems pretty close to the spot Scott visited.

A raucous braying noise pins me to the spot.

Please let my black hoodie and jeans render me invisible.

What the hell is that? Some kind of . . .

. . . beast, perhaps a wolf . . .

. . . animal in the undergrowth behind me, and yet I can see nothing back there. Really don't want to see anything, either, so I press ahead much faster than before, feeling more naked with every step.

I dread these animal noises trailing me through the darkness, but thank God they stay put. I'm not being trailed.

Not by anything that makes a sound, anyway.

There's no doubt that this little mission rates high on the stupid-o-meter. But if Scott really does have people bound and gagged in a basement, then my trusty hammer and I might be their only hope. This thought, and this thought alone, stops me trudging back to Izzy, steeped in the mire of defeat.

When the trees finally thin out, the moon kicks down through them to highlight the bungalow cottage ahead. Protected by walls topped with barbed wire, this place backs up against the foot of the hill. Judging by what I can already spy through the wooden bars of the entrance gate, the grounds are expansive but rundown and ramshackle.

Could this be the place? The GPS thinks so. And I could well imagine Scott allowing this kind of land to deteriorate. His are smooth hands, unaccustomed to hoes. Well, hoes of the garden variety, anyway.

Christ almighty. Could the elusive Scott Palmer really lurk within these walls? The very idea makes me feel a little sick. What will I say to him? And what the hell will he say – or do – to me?

I almost muster a laugh when I see how another one-vehicle lane snakes up to this place from around the other side of the hill. If it hadn't been for the vagaries of the map, we could have driven straight here. Then again, whoever's at home might've seen our headlights. Sometimes, things turn out for the best. Right now, I need to believe this.

Even my most careful footsteps sound way too loud as I take a closer look through the gate. The house looks dead in every way. No sign of lights within. Two windows flank the wooden front door, their curtains drawn tight. An unoccupied front drive swerves out of view around the back.

As I wait and watch, a pin-drop silence makes its presence felt. One by one, all those woodland sounds fall away, until I can hear my own breath.

The clock on Scott's phone flicks from 23:59 to 00:00. Something about this drastic switch, the way that all four digits become zero in the blink of an eye, makes me think about death. Specifically, mine.

Reasonably satisfied that no one's home, or at least awake, I bully myself into climbing over the gate before doubt can derail me.

With an ungainly thump, I land on the gravel of the drive, like some drunkard playing ninja. This would be an idyllic place to live – potentially a family home, in fact – were it not for all the neglect. This front garden, and even parts of the drive, are choked with knee-high weeds. Sections of side wall have eroded and collapsed, leaving half-bricks scattered across what should be a lawn. The dark glass of a discarded wine bottle creates the illusion that someone has managed to bottle the moon.

Forget the details. I need to keep my eye out for movement, any movement. A light coming on, a door opening, a twitch of curtain. At the very first sign of anything like that, I need to be back over the gate and out of here. No messing about.

I'm so glad to have this hammer. The harsh metal head rests upside down on my cupped fingers, while the handle hugs my forearm. Thankfully, Izzy failed to catch wind of its presence when I left the car. Guess she never thought to say, *Hey Kate, you didn't bring that potentially lethal weapon along, right?*

Only now do I consider the possibility that security cameras may be dotted around me. The clever money would bet on them being kaput, but I must take no chances. Really hope the hood will conceal my face, even if a light comes on.

Jesus Christ. If security lights actually do burst into life, I will simply keel over. My adventure will very much end here.

I take my first uneasy steps towards the house, the gravel scrunching way too loud under my feet. My conscience screams, *You don't normally do this. You don't normally walk onto other people's property uninvited,* and I have to once again remind myself of the potential stakes here.

By the time I reach the left-hand corner of the house, I can breathe a little easier. From my new position, I can see no vehicles parked further along the drive, which helps.

Edging along with my back to the wall, I arrive at the first window, then crane my neck around to look inside.

Moving boxes, that's what I'm looking for. Boxes and also abductees. Swathed in blacks and greys, this wide open space, a living room, has a ceiling striped with low wooden beams. There's plenty of clutter – way too much furniture and further empty wine bottles – but I can see neither Scott's stuff nor fraught people bound with electrical tape.

The next window along looks into the same room, and the next is all frosted bathroom glass. Can't picture Scott's boxes being stored in there. Can definitely imagine someone chained to the radiator, though.

Aware that the next window could so easily belong to a

bedroom, I devote maximum effort to stealth. And yet, underfoot, every autumn leaf sounds like a whip-crack.

Behind the glass of this next window, the curtains sit almost entirely shut. Could Scott really have chosen these terrible curtains? Yep. I once thought he had taste, but now I can picture him conning some design student into decking out the Van Spencer flat so nicely, then failing to pay them.

Dare I investigate the gap between these curtains?

Ever so slowly, I press my face close to the window, so that my nose almost touches.

Inside, all I see is black. This inconsiderate moon is ill-placed to help me out.

Softly . . .

So very softly . . .

. . . I squash my nose against the window.

An explosion of vampire teeth, savage eyes and gunshot barks jerk me away from the saliva-splashed glass, as if I'm being yanked back by a noose.

My brain knows the Rottweiler is inside the window, but my reflexes don't, so in what feels like one single instant I'm sprinting back to the gate, swearing as I go, in an attempt to process the shock.

When I'm halfway there, the barking stops, but I continue to make like my arse is on fire, in case the beast has been set loose.

The world becomes a clumsy blur of gate and night sky.

Partway up, I lose my grip and fall. My chin snags on a wooden bar, clacks my teeth together and damn near severs my tongue.

Please don't let me hear the sound of paws pounding gravel. Or worse, a shotgun being cocked and someone calling for me to *Stop right there.*

Finally landing on my feet back outside, I cling to the wooden bars and cough hard until a strand of drool connects my mouth to the ground.

By the time I've regained control of my saliva, there's no sign of life from the house. One thing's for sure: if my dog had barked that violently around the witching hour, I would patrol every single window, bare minimum. So that's encouraging.

I feel satisfied that there are no neighbours close enough to hear this dog. Even if they can, they'll only shove those foam plugs deeper into their ears and go back to sleep.

My tongue throbs unhappily as I massage my jaw. Despite the watery ruin of my eyes, I keep them nailed to those front curtains. Not one single twitch over there, far as I can see.

For added safety, I wait until my lungs hold enough oxygen before I tackle the gate again, this time far more systematically. Then I stride back towards the house.

You could break into this place . . . if it wasn't for that pesky mutt. Which doofus failed to bring the diazepam-infused pork chop?

Silly me, eh? Anyone would think I've never done this kind of shit before.

This time, I cover the right-hand side of the house. All but ignoring the first two windows, which will only show me the same big living area, I check out the third. Here, open curtains reveal a small bedroom. Hmm, could Scott's boxes be under the bed? No, it's one of those solid beds with drawers built into the side.

What if he already unpacked his stuff and tossed the boxes? Most normal people do that, you know. And another thing—

A new volley of canine gunshots heralds the arrival of a fast-moving bulk of slobbering muscle. The Rottweiler piles into the room and crashes against the glass as if hell-bent on breaking through and ripping out my throat.

Need to keep my nerve. If this dog could escape the

house, it would already have done so. Moving along, moving along . . .

As I near the back of the house, my attention strays to a big, separate garage that I previously couldn't see. Planted at the very foot of the hill, next to a gentle dirt slope that disappears up out of sight under trees, this behemoth could house two ambulances. A corrugated iron shutter guards the front. Garage or lock-up? There's no need to decide.

Sick of Cujo's racket, I pad across grass to the garage and peer in through one dust-caked, cobwebbed window.

This room looks jam-packed with stuff. Definitely a storage facility, rather than a place where anything gets parked.

I see boxes. Doesn't necessarily mean they're Scott's, but fuck it, I'm going to find out right now.

My heart sinks when I see the heavy padlock that secures the shutter, only to rally when I remember the trick I literally have up my sleeve.

Scott's phone carries a mere eighteen per cent charge. Shit! There's been a text from Izzy. Did she see someone come past her?

No, she only wants to know where the hell I am and how it's going. I'll update her in person as soon as I'm done here.

Switching to the browser, I Google for *break padlock hammer*. Once upon a time, the internet seemed irresponsible for being full of guidelines for doing bad stuff, but tonight this feels awesome.

On the first swing, I bring the hammer down on the very tip of my forefinger, then perform a truly fucked-up pain dance while sucking the bruised nail.

For the second swing, I wise up and whack the metal in the correct place.

The padlock springs open. I tug the bastard free, drop to my haunches, then heave the shutter up into the garage ceiling. The foul, grinding screech only infuriates Cujo all the more.

My phone torch reveals a light switch, but dare I use it? Nope. All this way back here behind the house, I might not hear someone arriving at the gate, and chances are they'd soon notice the glow from these overhead strip-lights.

Everything has been piled up to form a towering block in the centre of the room. Reaching about two-thirds of the room's height, this block leaves enough space to walk around the outside, like a breakfast bar island made from junk.

The phone buzzes my hand. An incoming call. Izzy?

Unknown Number. Does anyone with an actual fucking name ever call this phone? Having quickly considered my options, I rip the duct tape off the top of the phone so that I can pick up and listen.

When the static clears, a man speaks in a grim, flat tone. His German accent distinguishes him from the Scottish guy who told me *You're going to love it here.* As does the fact that he sounds so very afraid.

"For God's sake, don't come in here. Don't let it suck you in."

I find myself taking several quick backwards steps away from the garage, while imaginary insects bustle around inside my clothes.

I peel the tape off the handset's microphone. My tongue and jaw hurt as I say, "Don't let *what* suck me in?"

I catch a *th* sound from this guy, but the rest is smothered by static, and finally the line becomes one continuous tone.

The garage doorway now looks, for all the world, like a gaping black mouth. Waiting for me to dare defy the warning and step inside.

Why can't I stop shaking?

The guy said *Don't come in here*, suggesting he's literally inside this garage. Where the fuck is he hiding, then? Inside one of the boxes? Beneath a hidden trap door, with Scott's other victims? How did he know I was coming inside? Can he see me? Beyond a doorway this dark, several pairs of eyes could be trained on me. They might watch from the walk-space behind this central block of junk, or through spyholes drilled into the concrete floor.

Can't lose the feeling that a ghost is about to fly out of the black at me. The flat, dark, slowed-down tone of this caller's voice and his predecessors' voices had made them all sound . . . almost as if they were all . . .

. . . dead? Time to face facts. The dead have been calling you. And this guy had a German accent – ring any bells?

Dieter.

"Dieter Keppler?" I say aloud.

Somewhere in the trees up on the nearby slope, the spirited hooting of an owl snaps me out of waiting for a reply. I allow the hammer to slide down from my sleeve, then take hold of the handle and swing it to test the weight.

Nice. Because a hammer's gonna be so much use against the dead.

I swipe the hammer to intimidate any human who might skulk within. Scott, for instance. In case they can't see me, I throw in a verbal warning.

"I'm coming in now," I say, doing a surprisingly good job of making my voice fearless. "Try anything and I'll bash your fucking brains in."

Good old Jack Torrance. Always an inspiration.

Spurred on by the stillness of the garage, I step up to the threshold, theoretically poised to strike. Having had first-hand experience of the life-changing impact of blunt force trauma, I doubt I could ever actually harm anyone. How I hope this won't be put to the test.

I shine the phone torch around inside, steeling myself for the sight of a blank-eyed ghoul staring right back at me.

On the back wall, something spindly, the diameter of a coffee cup, scuttles up the back wall, away from the intrusion of my light.

Some of the lower boxes in the central block appear much older; they look crumpled, discoloured and damp. A few have collapsed altogether. Many of the higher, fresher boxes have marker-pen scribbles on the side. Do I recognise Scott's handwriting? Nope, because I never got to see it. Who writes anything by hand these days? Painstakingly composed love letters are long dead and gone . . .

. . . just like whatever's waiting in this garage to suck you in.

My torchlight falls on a box marked BLUE RAYS, right at the top of the pile, on the left-hand side towards the back. Oh Scott, did you really misspell *Blu-rays*? I feel more disappointed by this than by some of your other misdemeanours.

My pulse quickens. Come *on*, this is only a fucking garage. There's no one here. And if this stuff does belong to Scott, I need to take a look before he comes back.

Step into my parlour, said the spider to the fly.

The reek of musk and mould make my nose itch. Edging inside, I walk with a crouch and the hammer raised, heading along the left-hand side of the block. Really bothers me that the boxes are stacked so high that I can't see around the back. Someone . . .

. . . or something . . .

. . . could so easily be standing . . .

. . . or floating . . .

. . . around the far corner I'm moving towards. Need to rule out this possibility before I do anything else.

The breath stalls in my chest as I creep past the assembled junk, towards this rear corner that turns off to the right.

Hey, enjoy these next few steps! They may be your last.

How I'd kill to have a mirror on a stick.

Come on, let's do this. You are, after all, holding a hammer.

I sidle along, my steps tiny, until the rear walk-space inches into view.

There's no one and nothing here.

What if whoever or whatever was back here has moved silently around into the walk-space on the far side of the block? Creepy thought, huh? You're welcome.

I haul the BLUE RAYS box to the ground, while throwing glances along the rear walk-space and back to the open door. This box has no trace of damp. In fact, it feels brand-new. Almost as if it was brought here only a few days ago . . .

I separate the interlocked flaps that seal the box, then haul them open.

Two faces greet me from inside.

Hello, Christian Slater and Patricia Arquette. Here they are on the cover of the Blu-ray of *True Romance*, which sits on top of the likes of *Goodfellas*, *Starship Troopers* and a film called *Eden Lake* that scared the hell out of me.

Okay, so *True Romance* is hardly an obscure indie flick, but could this still be a coincidence? What other films can I recall from Scott's curated collection? Come on, think: what else did we watch while curled up on that sofa?

Ah, *Labyrinth*. The movie we were excited to discover that we both loved, prompting Scott to hurry over and pluck the disc from his shelves for us to view. Of course, in retrospect, he'd almost certainly learnt that I liked *Labyrinth* via Facebook or something, but that's unimportant right now.

Outside, back in the house, the dog's barking again. Big deal, Cujo, you don't scare me – I'm gonna search through your master's *BLUE RAYS* and you can't lift a paw to stop me.

Doesn't take long. Five or six layers down, I discover the faces of David Bowie and Jennifer Connelly on the *Labyrinth* cover.

That's it, then. I've actually found Scott's stuff. When I find his leaflet full of passwords, I might even allow myself a victory dance, but for now I still have a great deal of frenzied searching to do.

My hunt starts with the rest of the Blu-ray box, in case the leaflet happens to be here, but of course that would be way too easy. I close the box back up, place it behind me, then survey the other stuff. Given that I saw the password pamphlet on Scott's desk, what I really need is a box labelled DESK, OFFICE or WORK. I heave one box after another from the block, twisting them around to see what's written on the side.

CLOTHES . . . XBOX/GAMES . . . VINYL. No good. Surely Scott must have dedicated a box to his desk stuff, and this password leaflet would surely be in there.

OFFICE. *Boom*. Let's get stuck in.

The room floods with powerful light, its dingy colour filtered through the grubby windows behind me.

Oh no.

IZZY
howzit going pls

IZZY
kate u said u were just gonna take a look n u been ages

IZZY
Kaaaaaaaaaaaaaate

IZZY
i really need the loo… if you dont reply soon im gonna pee in yr coffee flask

IZZY
i totally peed in yr coffee flask

CHAPTER FORTY-NINE

6 October

Car headlights dominate the room. The low thrum of an engine draws closer, then dies.

Dogs make a fuss for two reasons: intruders and their master coming home. Why the hell didn't I check outside when Cujo started barking again? I have no idea, and now I'm screwed. Where's the hammer?

The headlights blink out. A car door pops open, all too close.

Fucking hell, where is the hammer? Must've put the thing down somewhere to focus on the boxes, but now my phone torch can't find it. I kill the beam, for fear that the new arrival will see my light, if they haven't already.

Mercifully, the open garage door faces away from the car. Whoever this is, I really hope they don't come around to check that no one's broken in. There's no reason why you'd do that, right?

Not unless you'd spotted the light of a phone torch fluttering around inside . . .

From outside: footsteps, heading this way. Shit! It's way too late for me to reassemble the boxes the way they were, and the smashed padlock is lying on the ground outside. Ducking around the corner, I hide behind the junk-stack. Then, for the first time in my life, I pray to God.

Look, I'm sorry for doubting your existence. I'm just more of a believe-it-when-I-see-it girl. You know, like Scully. But if you could do me this one favour and magically make this new arrival head straight towards the back door of their house then I'd be really fucking obliged to you forever. Oh, and sorry for swearing but I'm practically soiling myself.

Everything's gone quiet. No more footsteps. What does that mean? Didn't hear them unlock the door to the house . . .

All I can hear now is nothing.

The brittle glass of silence.

From the garage doorway comes a sharp intake of breath.

And that's me doomed. No hammer, nowhere to run, no chance.

Why didn't I listen to Dead Dieter when he warned me not to come in here? Because I am the cat that curiosity is about to kill, that's why.

I hear the transition that Curiosity's feet make from the grass outside to the concrete floor of the garage. And now a series of clicks, as Curiosity toggles the light switch to no avail. I can't decide whether the lights being out of commission will work in my favour.

Think, think, think. Curiosity will see the fallen, rearranged boxes and head for those first. So I need to back off along this rear walk-space, towards the opposite side of the garage. This, I must do slow and soft, like a cat.

I would feel so much better if I still had the hammer in my hand.

There have been no more footsteps. What I really want to hear, though, is Curiosity picking up a box. Then I'll know he's over there, and I can sneak out the—

Something strikes my left temple, hard.

My brain judders, like a fairground punchbag. My vision triples.

This is it.

This is me, meeting my end in the middle of nowhere. This is me, waking up in half an hour alongside a bunch of my fellow tortured prisoners who have random parts missing.

My legs have gone weak, but there's no time to recover, only time to flee.

Behind me, the silhouette of a person, almost certainly a man, swings another punch at me. Swerving away from the impact rips a muscle in my side.

I run in what I hope is the direction of the fallen boxes.

Behind me, hard and heavy footsteps.

I stumble over a box.

Losing my balance buys me momentum, makes me run faster, while trying to regain control.

I hurtle towards the garage mouth like a freed champagne cork.

Two strong arms seize me from behind. I would scream, but they're squeezing my chest too tight and hauling me back several feet, while Curiosity growls angry, incoherent things in my ear.

A real wild one.

True Romance springs to mind. Having been seized from behind by Drexl's bodyguard, Clarence delivers a backwards headbutt to the big man's nose. This probably only works in the movies, but it's more likely to bring success than trying to stamp on Curiosity's foot.

I bring my chin to my chest, then slam back my skull as far as it'll go.

I feel the sickening crunch of cartilage, and Curiosity's arms fly apart like the head of his padlock.

Miracles happen.

The world goes woozy as I bust out of the garage. Which way? I consider the mental image of Curiosity dragging me off his front gate as I try to climb over and out, then hurling me back down onto the weeds and bricks. Also can't guarantee that he was the only new arrival. If I head back towards the house, others might await me there with open arms. Remembering the end of *Eden Lake* cements my split-second decision to head for the dirt slope covered by trees.

My head might be packed with cotton wool soaked in ether, but at least my limbs work. I'm moving and moving fast, but the trees have devoured me and I can barely see a thing. Lit by patchy scraps of moon, the track has already grown steeper. Really should've seen that coming, given that I'm running up the foot of Chanctonbury Hill, but there's no going back now.

Drenched in sweat, I daren't look to see if Curiosity is pursuing me. And who *was* that back there? Scott? Whoever it was, his nose must be a broken mess, so he'll surely give chase through sheer blind rage. Should I hide somewhere in the darkness and wait? No, he might find me with a torch. I have to keep going.

You'll never make it all the way up this hill in the dark. It's only getting steeper.

Tripwire thorns slice into my ankles and tear the flesh, then hold firm until I fall.

My outstretched hands slam into the dirt, where something spiny and ruthless pierces the webbed flesh between my left thumb and forefinger. Switching on Scott's phone torch might betray my location to Curiosity, but without light I may easily lose my footing and roll all the way back down, snapping my neck in the process.

The phone torch shows me what my feet had blindly tried to figure out for themselves – makeshift steps, provided by tree roots. There's also a tree planted up ahead in the middle of the track, which I might otherwise have walked right into.

My back aches. My lungs heave with lava. My breath sounds like wood being sawn. Shit, is this even a real track? What if this thing gets so steep that I can't go any further?

From below come frenzied growls and barks. These sound way too close for the dog to still be confined in that house . . .

Oh my God.

Curiosity has set his Rottweiler loose, then sent it up the hill after me. How am I supposed to defend myself against a dog like that? Remember that online article about how to defend yourself against violent mutts? Nah. Too long; didn't read.

Torchlight helps me find a fallen tree bough. Using this as a makeshift staff, I heave myself up the slope with renewed vigour.

No matter how fast I move, these barks draw nearer.

Soil gives way beneath my feet and now I'm sliding down the hill.

Jamming my staff into the dirt slows my descent, until I can grab a tree root with my other hand.

Thank you, staff. Fuck you, terrifying hellhound whose scrabbling paws I'm convinced I can hear only a few trees down.

I can never outrun this thing, so I'm going to have to make some kind of . . .

. . . *final* . . .

. . . stand here.

I'm going to have to face the Rottweiler.

Nettles sting my hand as I shove the phone down at the base of a tree. Tilted down, the torchlight half-heartedly reveals a few feet of downward slope, leaving me free to stand here with the staff held tight in both hands, trying to project the impression that I know what in the ever-loving fuck I'm doing.

One thing's for sure: I want to live.

Yes, I want to see another day. Ideally one on which I will make far fewer stupid decisions and quite probably explore my bi side.

The dog's eyes spark into view, the torchlight lending them a rabid glint. Fuck, what if the beast really is rabid?

You mean there's a difference between being torn to shreds, and being torn to shreds and leaving an infected corpse?

Swinging the staff back like a cricket bat, I bare my teeth. My legs are pure jelly.

"Fuck off," I yell. "Fuck *the fuck off.*"

Undeterred, the Rottweiler only races on up the hill at me, its bark now loud enough to stab at my eardrums.

Don't want to hurt this thing. Don't want to die either. Still, a direct strike to the dog's skull would require the kind of perfect timing that I do not possess. So let's show the fucker a warning swipe and try to keep it at bay.

Devoting all my strength to the swing, I hammer the staff into an overhanging tree bough.

The staff snaps in two. The flying, jagged top half smacks me in the face.

Saliva shines on the Rottweiler's jaws as it closes in for the kill.

IZZY
kate please reply im hating this n im scared . . . havent seen another human since you left . . .

IZZY
minds starting to play tricks

IZZY
kate!!!! where the fuck r u

IZZY
ffs . . . ok im gonna leave the car n come find u

CHAPTER FIFTY

6 October

The Rottweiler's eyes are twin burning coals as it tenses its hind legs, ready to leap.

If I try to kick, I'll lose my balance and fall, for sure. All can think to do is pull my fists inside my sleeves, then cross my arms in an X shape, but it's not enough. Can't protect every vulnerable part of my body all at once.

As my whole body stiffens, so does the Rottweiler's. It slides back a couple of steps, then scrabbles around in the dirt. Those eyes now harbour something that looks a lot like fear.

I've no idea why this is happening, but want to strike while the iron's hot. "That's right, you little shit. You *should* be fucking afraid. Now fuck off."

The flailing mutt actually whimpers, then whines as it backs off away down the slope.

Only now do I realise that those carbon-black eyes aren't directly fixed on me.

No, they're looking behind me and up.

Something ripples in my spine. What has a *Rottweiler* seen to put the beast off my tasty flesh?

And now I catch a hint of pale blue reflected in the dog's eyes.

I taste the copper in my mouth.

Leaning against a tree for support, I dare to look up the slope, and oh shit, there it is.

Something distant, but steadily, purposefully, coming down the hill.

Something pale blue. Something that jerks and strobes, a good few feet above the dirt, bathing all the trees with an unearthly shimmer.

With a rush of vertigo, I teeter backwards, waving propeller arms to steady myself. This ghost looks bigger than its predecessors. Can't help but picture this thing flying out of the occult ring of trees that crowns this hill created by the Devil, then sweeping down in search of juicy playthings.

My legs almost give way altogether as the ghost wends and weaves towards me, down through the trees.

Literally *through* the trees, too. It flies behind the trunk of a mighty oak, disappears briefly, re-emerges from the side closest to me, then resumes its smooth descent. Forks of jagged light pulsate through its body like a network of veins.

I want to run, I really do, but I can't take my eyes off this thing. Ten trees away, the phantom has me mesmerised. Some dark and infinitely stupid part of me – some instinct, maybe – wants to see the face.

Never mind the fucking face, put yourself as far away from it as possible.

Eight trees and closing . . .

Scott's phone must still be down at the base of the tree at my feet, but I can't stop watching this phantom.

Six trees.

As this thing jerks closer, I can make out the vague, fundamental features of a face. Eyes, nose, mouth.

Four trees.

What in the galloping fuck am I doing?

I am a startled deer. One that's managed to snap out of the hypnotic sight of its hunter, then turn tail and run.

When I picture myself charging back down through the black with this phantom in hot pursuit, the thought makes me want to burrow six feet beneath all this soil and get it over with. So I snatch up the phone and hold the torch out before me as I attempt to skid back down the hill.

Fear transforms me into wretched, retching, hunted prey. My phone torch flashes crazily around. A pendulum of copper drool swings from my chin.

Dare I risk a glance back over my shoulder, back up the slope?

Best not to know how much ground this thing's gained on me. When the Devil's on your tail, there's no time to check his progress. You assume he's right behind you, and speed the hell up.

"Get away!" I yell through sheer desperation, as if that's going to change a phantom's mind when it didn't even work on a dog. "Leave me alone."

Hey! Look behind you. Check the Devil's progress.

Trees rush past. I am a skier on the world's most narrow and treacherous slalom. I try to keep my feet side on against the slope, to steady myself. When I try to move too fast, I lose purchase and slide down, on the very brink of a fall, before righting myself again.

Go on. Take a look. Surely it's best to know. Yes, you can see the blue light of this thing reflecting on the trees ahead of you, but exactly how close is it?

The question squeezes my heart, makes my blood pump even faster and speeds me up, like I'm trying to escape my own burning tail. Any second now, I know I'll lose control altogether and fall arse-over-tit down the hill.

You'll be fine. One look won't cost you any time. There's no need to slow down. All you have to do is snatch a super-quick glance.

Oh, please let me see nothing. Please let the phantom have vanished into thin air. Life can sometimes be that nice, right?

Preparing for the worst, I look back around as far as I dare.

In the corner of my eye, one ragged breath away, flies a juddering mass the colour of ambulance lights.

My whole body becomes a scream.

Firm ground disappears beneath my feet, and now I'm falling through the big black nothing of night.

My shoulder jars against a tree root. Nerve endings stand up and shout. Back in contact with the dirt, I am a rolled carpet, gaining speed as I descend.

Cruel thorns lash my face. A log clips my head as I pass by.

Something big, hard and immovable punches my guts and brings my descent to a violent and immediate halt.

I've wrapped myself around one of those trees in the middle of the track.

Feels like there's a bowling ball in my stomach and my windpipe's been stapled shut. My sore head fogs up through lack of air.

The phantom. Remember the phantom.

With a broken wheeze, I haul myself around to sit back against the tree. My vision starts to fill with rapidly multiplying patches, darker than the night itself.

Through the gaps between patches, I see the phantom swoop this way, close enough for me to properly make out its face.

Despite the ghost's flickering blue essence and black-hole eyes, I can see that this . . .

Oh my God . . .

I can see that this is the ghost of Scott Palmer.

CHAPTER FIFTY-ONE

6 October

I wake up slow, from a place where dreams are forbidden.

I am a dead fish, drifting towards the surface.

The skin around my eyes feels tight with dried tears. I can't remember why these tears have been shed, and something tells me I don't want to remember.

There's a hard pillow under my head and something wrapped quite tightly around my temples. The room smells of antiseptic cream, cigarette smoke and dog.

Staring at the wooden beams on the ceiling, I try to fill in the blanks. I try to recall what happened on the slope, but first I remember the house at the foot of the hill.

These low ceiling beams . . . that dog smell . . . I must be in the house.

Gripped by the fear that my wrist and ankles are tied to this bed, I raise one weak hand to feel the bandage on my head. My other hand is also free to move, as are my feet, but there's a pressure in my skull so acute that if I move too dramatically I know I'll throw up.

Scott's dead. You saw his ghost. His face, it had that vulnerable Tinder look.

The concept of Scott's death feels too much to handle, like an oncoming flood. My ravaged head struggles to make sense of his phantom and comes up wanting.

A scrawled piece of paper from a tin in the Basketmakers Arms flaps around in my head as if to say *Told you so.*

You Will Die.

But what . . . I mean, seriously, *what*? Scott's dead? Why? How? The ceiling slips in and out of focus as I contemplate the idea that he never walked out on me but was in fact murdered.

I may be crying fresh tears, but at least this time I know why. So if this really is the cottage, how did I get here? And what happens now? Am I a prisoner here, locked in this room?

"She's coming around." I've never been so ecstatic to hear Izzy's voice. Could this actually be some kind of rural hospital? They might actually make them this rustic, and allow dogs in, and let people smoke.

Swallowing down the nausea, I find Izzy, who's using crutches to raise herself from an old wicker chair. Wearing the same clothes as when I left the car, her face is lined with fatigue and concern.

Beside her stands Ray Palmer. Curiosity himself. Holding a freezer bag over his nose, the man's eyes are pure thunder. His dark blue jumper and black trousers are coated in dirt and pieces of leaf. His smooth scalp bears a couple of plasters, presumably earned tonight and applied by Izzy. How did she even get here? Christ, I have this mental image of her hobbling through those woods, all alone, to come and save me. More likely, she drove around the entire hill. Truly, I do not deserve this woman.

Behind them both, across this claustrophobic room, a single

window confirms it's still dark outside. This must be the middle of the night.

"What's . . . what's going on?" I ask Izzy.

"Exactly what I'd like to know," Ray mutters. He groans as he removes the makeshift ice pack from his nose, examines how much blood has smeared itself over the bag, then gingerly pushes it back into place.

"Mr Palmer, please remain calm," Izzy says, "like we agreed you would."

Why's she calling him *Mr Palmer*? But how I love her for taking control of the situation here. Izzy has the strength of a thousand suns.

And now she says, "Miss Collins, when I arrived, Mr Palmer told me he'd had an altercation with an intruder, who'd then taken flight up the hill. It took me a while to explain everything and convince him, but he found you and brought you down here."

"What did you do to Jessie?" Ray demands of me. "She's in my room, cowering under the fucking bed."

Izzy gives Ray a look that appeals once more for calm. She brings a glass of water up from my bedside table.

"Drink," she says.

"Can't get my head up, too sore." I open my mouth like a baby bird and she tips the glass. The water goes down the wrong pipe, so I burst into an explosive and agonising coughing fit as Izzy pulls a sympathetic face.

Once I can speak again, I ask Ray, "So you live here . . . by yourself?"

He nods, sullen, distracted by so many questions of his own. "DI Clarke told me why you broke into my property – and frankly, you're mental."

DI Clarke? Izzy and I exchange one glance, and straight away

I understand what she's done. That old crewmate telepathy, it stays with you forever.

"If my brother finished with you," he goes on, "why couldn't you leave well alone? Coming over here and busting my nose ain't gonna change a thing."

"Sorry about the nose," I say. "I didn't know who you were. I thought you might be your brother."

Scott's flickering corpse-blue face scalds my mind's eye.

Ray fires back, "And I thought you were one of them local thieves. Look, you've got this dumb idea in your head that Scott's vanished, but that's clearly bollocks. Ain't you seen his Twitter lately?"

As Izzy addresses Ray again, my eyes beg her not to mention Scott's phone. "Several other people have also gone missing, Mr Palmer, as far as their close friends and family are concerned, but they're still posting on social media."

I swallow hard. Izzy and I, we'd come to think that Scott might have been behind the disappearance of those people on his phone, but we never took into account that *he'd vanished too*. What if he's one of the people who somebody . . . maybe somebody in this room . . . has made disappear?

Instinct tells me to tread carefully with the next question. I don't, though. "How did all of Scott's stuff end up here?"

Ray tries to fold his arms, then recognises that he can't do this while holding the ice pack on his nose. "None of your business. All you need to know is, my brother obviously don't want to be with you anymore. And when I tell him about this, he'll want you even less."

I study Ray's expression for any trace of lies. What's that giveaway tick people do – is it looking up to the right or the left? Can't remember, but he's talking about Scott as if his brother's still very much alive, without breaking eye contact.

"When did you last speak to him?" I say, aware that I'm sounding a little too much like a murder detective – the role that Izzy has taken on, like the genius she is.

Ray's cold, steady gaze tracks from me, over to Izzy, then back to me. "I'm gonna check on my dog." On his way out of the room, he glances around, as if trying to anticipate any further chaos I might cause.

When he closes the door, I listen out for his footsteps, but hear nothing. So I beckon Izzy down until our noses are mere inches apart, and I whisper, "I saw Scott's ghost. He's dead, Izzy."

She tries and fails to register the news. "You sure about that, mate?"

I give her the firmest and most sincere nod I can manage, then lower my voice even further. "And Scott's ghost was *here*. Why here? All his stuff is in the garage. I mean . . . what if Ray killed him? What if Ray's been making all these people disappear?"

Scott screaming, his face contorted in disbelief, as Ray steals his life away. The image makes me want to get my skull trepanned, so that I can never see it again.

Izzy squints at the door and concentrates, trying to detect Ray standing right outside. "I don't know, Kate. I don't know what to make of any of this shit. I'm so tired. But if Ray's a killer, then why didn't he kill me and leave you halfway up that hill to die?"

I chew this over, grateful that the pain in my head has eased. "Because he doesn't want to kill a copper?"

"Hmm, okay. I guess that might have struck him as a bad move."

"How did you even manage to convince him you were police?"

"Flashed my ambulance ID at him in the dark. And I'd found

an app that makes random sounds like a police radio. The rest was, er, I don't know. Showbiz."

"You are beyond awesome, you know that?"

She shushes me. Side-eyes the door. "Whatever we think Ray may or may not be, this ain't the time or the place to ask him. We absolutely have to take this to the . . ." She mouths the words *real police*.

"I need Scott's password book," I tell her. "It's in this box in the garage marked OFFICE, I know it is. Can you find a way to sneak out there?"

Izzy pulls a face that makes her answer obvious. "Sorry," I say. "Forgot about . . ." I nod at her crutches.

She sighs. "You've had a bang to the head, so I'll let you off."

"How am I looking, doc?"

"Amazingly well, considering."

"Good. Then you won't protest too much when I talk to Ray. Properly talk to him. Right now." Izzy tries to speak, with her eyes all big, but I cut her off. "And before I do that, I need you to go to the kitchen and find the sharpest knife you can."

CHAPTER FIFTY-TWO

6 October

"Kate, you really are fucking nuts. This is harassment and I want you both out of here."

This feels like another authentic reaction from Ray. Now with a bandage across his nose, he's on the other side of his kitchen table from Izzy and me, wreathed in cigarette smoke. Now I've broken the news that I believe Scott to be dead, he's gripping the handle of his coffee cup so hard that it may snap off at any moment. For my part, under the table, I'm gripping the handle of the eight-inch bread knife that Izzy passed me. Pure last-resort self-defence.

When neither Izzy nor I move a muscle, Ray hikes the volume of his voice. "I said, I want you both *out of here*. And you," he says, jabbing a finger at me, "are gonna get sued to shit for breaking into my land."

"You know," I say, "I'm pretty confident there's a really unfair law that states you can't punch intruders, in the head or anywhere else. And if there isn't, there's bound to be one that states you can't set potentially lethal dogs on them." I turn to Izzy. "I'm sure you can help me out here, detective."

Ray shifts uneasily in his seat as Izzy pretends to consult her extensive memory of law. "Yes, if you deliberately set your dog on an intruder and they do suffer injuries . . ."

" . . . including psychological harm," I chip in.

" . . . then you may be liable for prosecution, Mr Palmer. Your dog may be placed under official control, or even destroyed."

The word *destroyed* takes a bite out of Ray's resistance. "That's . . . That is not going to happen."

"Doesn't need to happen," says Izzy, doing so brilliantly, "provided you co-operate with my investigation that Miss Collins has instigated."

Trace levels of scepticism linger on Ray's face. To Izzy he says, "I told you – I want a lawyer present before I talk about anything besides the weather."

"Fine. By all means, I'll be happy to come back and do this later today, with your lawyer *and* several more officers present. Oh, and a search warrant."

Ray squirms in his seat, which feels telling in itself. Why would he fear a search warrant? "Listen, my brother ain't dead. He broke up with this nutter . . . and that's all. He might not have done it in the kindest way, but as far as I know there ain't no law against that."

"When did you last speak to Scott?" I ask again, deriving pleasure from trying to butterfly-pin him to the wall.

Glowering at me, he pulls out his phone. "Tell you what, I'll call him right now, how's that? Don't give a fuck if I wake him. He's brought all this stupidity down on my head . . ."

"Stay *calm*, Mr Palmer," Izzy says.

By the time Ray hits speed-dial, I realise what's about to happen, but am powerless to prevent it.

Sure enough, Scott's phone vibrates in my pocket. In this otherwise silent kitchen in the dead of night, the buzzing sounds like a chainsaw.

I try to talk over the noise, telling Ray that Scott won't answer at this hour, but he follows the sound to my pocket and his eyes narrow.

"Gone to voicemail," he says, ending the call. The vibrations in my pocket stop, too, and a long pause sucks the air out of the room. "Bit of a coincidence, that. Have you got my brother's phone or what?"

"Don't be ridiculous, Ray. How could I?" If this doesn't satisfy him, then we've got a major problem. He'll have to prise this phone out of my cold, dead hands.

My angel of mercy sweeps in to prevent the carnage. "Mr Palmer. Can you explain why your brother's possessions are in your garage?"

Ray's rueful gaze stays fixed on me as he replies. "All right, yeah, fine, I can explain that perfectly well. Scott owed me a shitload of money."

"How did that happen?" Izzy asks. "IT guys earn well enough, don't they?"

Ray shrugs and lights a fresh cigarette. "He never should've taken on that fancy flat. Couldn't afford the bloody rent. Over the summer, he got into the red with a bunch of lenders, so I got him out of all that shit. And then Scott's payments to *me* dragged on for months. I mean, we're talking ten thousand quid, total. Me and Scott, we've never got on all that well." He hesitates, as if realising that he's assigned himself a killer's motive. Then he adds, "I've always been the one who's had to bail him out of trouble, ever since school. Over the years, that takes its toll, okay?"

"So you took all of Scott Palmer's things."

Ray nods at Izzy, unrepentant. "I told him it was time for him to take responsibility and not expect a free handout all the time with no consequences. Then, about a week ago, he came over here with a pitiful amount of cash to offer me, and I s'pose I wanted to teach him a lesson – one he'd never forget. So I said I wanted everything he had of any value. Told him to box it all up, then help me load it onto a van."

"Or," I say, quaking inside, "did you kill Scott, *then* take everything? Did the two of you argue and things got out of hand?"

Ray looks like he wants to lunge across the table and throttle me. I squeeze the knife handle. "My brother *ain't dead.* Stop talking like that."

"Hopefully you're right, Mr Palmer," Izzy says. "I will, of course, need to corroborate your story. So I'm going to take a box of your brother's possessions, which I believe will be key to achieving that. You'll get it all back afterwards."

Ray shrugs, exasperated. "Knock yourself out."

Oh, Izzy Clarke, I would lean over and kiss you right now, if you weren't supposed to be a cop. Also, if I wasn't secretly holding a great big fuck-off knife.

CHAPTER FIFTY-THREE

I Am Possessed
TrooSelf diary entry one of seven
Dated: 9 February
Filed by: SPalm123

Okay then, here goes nothing. I am going to give this app a try, and see if I can get some thoughts down. I'm still sceptical about the supposedly hyper-secure nature of this thing, because if my job has taught me one thing it's that nothing is truly secure these days when it's connected to the internet. If JP Morgan Chase, the Sony PlayStation Network and eBay can get hacked, then how safe can a relative minnow like TrooSelf trooly – sorry, TRULY – be?

It is my belief that files were always safer in physical form, locked up in an actual box. Why are we putting everything precious online, where there's no such thing as an impenetrable digital wall? We load confidential data into a cloud that has the potential to be linked to every other computer in the WORLD, and then all of a sudden that data may as well have been projected onto the sky and we all act all surprised.

Anyway. So, um . . . what am I trying to achieve here? This does feel weird, writing in a cryptic way to myself, but I'm still cautious about this app.

So, here is the first thought that comes to mind, right now.

Sometimes, I feel like I am possessed.

I spiral out of control, like I'm no longer the boss of myself.

I have to finally, finally STOP.

I don't know how I'm going to achieve stopping, but I do know that The Demon is tearing my world apart.

How am I supposed to ever meet somebody, or form any kind of meaningful relationship with them, when I am so tightly BOUND by all of this?

This is an endless nightmare. It is a vicious circle that keeps spinning round and round.

Every morning, when I first enter the bathroom, I look at my reflection in the mirror and say aloud that today I will be myself. My normal self, I mean – the person I used to be.

Every morning, I look myself in the eye, in that mirror, and I make that solemn promise. And then, usually by midday, I have broken that supposedly solemn promise. Often I'll do this without giving the matter a second thought. It's as if somebody else takes over. Somebody else grabs my steering wheel and takes me for a ride into hell.

Afterwards, when it is all over, I feel desperate. The rest of the day is ruined, and I can make all the renewed promises I like, but deep down I know that tomorrow will be exactly the same as today. Doesn't matter how many times I tell myself it will be different.

It is an absolute fucking joke.

I need someone in my life. I need an anchor to drop, so that the wild sea can do its worst but I'll be safely tethered out of temptation's way.

Who am I trying to kid? The way I am right now, I'm never going to meet that person. Vicious circle. Vicious fucking circle.

I am pathetic. Hopeless. Weak.

I am compromised and cursed.

I am possessed.

Well. Can't say I feel any better after writing all this. If anything, it's only deepened the shame and the misery.

I may come back and write another entry or I may not. Only time will tell.

CHAPTER FIFTY-FOUR

7 October

Izzy drives with her whole face crying out for sleep. Here on the motorway, open windows help keep us awake. The first rays of dawn highlight all the snow that's drifted down to settle overnight.

The pair of us driving like this, tired out of our tiny minds, it might even feel nostalgic if my heart wasn't so damn heavy.

On our way out of Chanctonbury, I'd felt like victory was at hand. In Ray's garage, I'd rummaged around inside the box marked OFFICE and had been psyched to find Scott's password pamphlet. I even retrieved my lost hammer.

When we left Ray at his front gate, he'd looked like a guy on the cusp of twigging that he'd been conned. Even as we drove off, I'd half-expected him to come tearing along the base of the hill after us, swinging punches all over again, having phoned the police to check Izzy's credentials. I'm guessing, though, that a wide boy like Ray might never to want to call them for any reason. Whether that reason could be murder remains to be seen.

I soon solved one minor mystery, thanks to Ray calling Scott's phone again, ten minutes after we left. The caller came up onscreen as *Idiot*. Made perfect sense.

Flicking through Scott's pamphlet, I found both of his TrooSelf passwords, which he'd written next to the not-so-cryptic inscription *TS*. Within seconds, I'd stopped talking to Izzy, unlocked the app, and breathlessly accessed Scott's first entry. Not least because the battery was on a mere three per cent.

And now, having read this thing, I don't know exactly how to feel. I'm a mess. Felt so horrendous to read Scott's words, knowing he's dead. And despite my suspicions, it seems he didn't write like some drooling maniac when it was just him and an empty page. In a crazed kind of way, Scott's death might have been easier to deal with if he really had turned out to be a murderous psychopath.

And yet . . . and yet, what was all this talk of shame – and possession? Surely he didn't mean literal old-school possession, did he? Having said that, he did also write the word *Demon*.

How quickly I've adapted to referring to Scott in the past tense. The man who I was so deeply in love with. I can't bear to think of his body lying somewhere unknown, such as a shallow grave back in Chanctonbury. The thought makes me want to sob forever, but I'm trying so hard to keep myself in check.

So if Scott didn't actually believe he was possessed by an evil spirit, then could my original paranoia that he was a drug addict be right? I'm dying to read more, but Izzy keeps asking for directions back to Brighton's seafront. The selfish part of me wants to ask her to open up a satnav app on her own phone, but she's Izzy. So I talk her through the journey, while she tries to talk me out of going to work today.

"You had a really narrow escape last night, mate. You know as well as I do how lucky you are that you don't have a concussion or need stitches. You also know that you need to call in sick and rest up, so I can look after you."

"Izz, I can't do that. To be honest, I'm sorely tempted, mainly because I really want to read all of Scott's diary, but I made a pledge to myself."

"Oh yeah? Well, if that pledge was to avoid doing fucking stupid stuff, I've got bad news for you."

"I pledged that I wouldn't let the whole Scott search affect my work. So I'm gonna go in, get through my shift and *then* you can nurse me tonight, okay?"

"Kate, would *you* want any of your loved ones being treated by a paramedic who's had no sleep?"

"Yes – my mum! Anyway, I did sleep tonight. One of the few benefits of being rendered unconscious."

I don't have to look over to know what Izzy's eyes are doing. "Besides," I add, "there are ways of getting around sleep deprivation."

"Oh no. Please don't go down the 'uppers' route."

"Coffee. More coffee. That's all I meant."

"*Do not* drink from that flask."

CHAPTER FIFTY-FIVE

Out, Demon, Out
TrooSelf diary entry two of seven
Dated: 14 February
Filed by: SPalm123

What in the bloody HELL is wrong with me? A pop-up notification told me I'd been Super-Liked on Tinder, so I took a look to see who it was. Her name is Kate and she is a stunningly beautiful example of womanhood. Her bio comes across as smart and fun and funny – the ideal balance between self-deprecation and confidence.

So Kate Super-Liked me, and yet I couldn't bring myself to even Like her back.

Why, Scott, why? What is WRONG with your ridiculous brain?

The thing is . . . I can't bring myself to Like Kate back, because she surely only hit Super-Like by mistake. If I Like her back, then the outcome can only be really embarrassing, not to mention hugely disappointing, much like me. The fact that this is happening on Valentine's Day only makes the whole thing even more excruciating.

Let's face it: Kate tapped that little blue star by mistake. It's obvious to me that she did, because she is SO far out of my league it's hilarious.

She lives up in Leeds, too. Why would she be interested in me, full stop, but also, why would she be interested in me from all these miles away? As it stands, she thinks I live in London, because that's where I set my Tinder location to be, using the Tinder Gold thing. So I actually live even further away than it appears to her on the app.

How I hate the idea of forcing this poor girl to admit she has no interest in me, or even worse, blank me or block me. I've agonised quite a lot over this, but ultimately feel like it's best all round to leave it. I'd really rather not know.

Here's a question, diary: what happened to my self-esteem? Why am I finding it difficult to even remember a time when the prospect of interacting with women didn't feel like such a big deal? I mean, blimey, years ago I used to date women, and even had GIRLFRIENDS, without having quite so much fucking anxiety about the whole thing.

So what's changed?

Very obviously, it's The Demon.

Yes, over the past few years, The Demon has dug its talons into me, further than ever before, and royally fucked up my self-esteem. This thing never used to be a problem, but now it's shredding my life and I need to get rid of it. This time, for good.

And how many times have I said that? But this time I really mean it.

Valentine's Day has to be the watershed moment. Yes, I will look back on this day as the moment when I got deadly serious and my whole life changed for the better.

Out, Demon, OUT!

CHAPTER FIFTY-SIX

My Sweet Saviour
TrooSelf diary entry three of seven
Dated: 2 May
Filed by: SPalm123

So it's been three months of trying to bury myself in work and shake off The Demon's curse. Also, three months of totally FAILING to do that.

You know what's really weird, diary? You know the one thing that's brought me back to this app, to try and get my thoughts together in some kind of coherent and logical fashion? Try as I might, I simply cannot get this one Tinder woman out of my head.

In the past, I've found that people on dating apps rarely stay in your head for any longer than it takes to make your superficial judgement. Just like the free magazines you get at train stations, they're gone after one quick flick. And yet this girl – Kate Collins, as I've discovered her name to be – keeps coming back to me, all this time after seeing her on Tinder. I mean, she's probably engaged or something by now, but she somehow manages to give me hope.

In her main pic on Tinder, Twitter, Facebook and everywhere else, Kate is sticking out her tongue in a sort of mock defiance. And yet something about those eyes makes me want to wrap my arms around her and tell her everything's going to be all right. Despite the silly tongue thing, the girl has this kind of vulnerable look, and I can't get her out of my head. I want us to sit together in a cosy pub so that I can find out all about her. Thanks to The Demon's influence, I also can't help imagining doing terrible and wonderful things to her. Then again, I don't know: maybe that isn't really The Demon. Maybe that's just me being a typical bloke.

Ha ha ha. *A typical bloke.* A fucking FREAK, more like, who's ruined himself forever.

Anyway, for better or worse, I've turned into a bit of a cyberstalker.

I still daren't respond to Kate's Super-Like because it's bound to have been a mistake. And besides, I can't write for toffee, so I'm crap online. But thanks to this dodgy pick-up book I've read, I feel like I can at least create the semi-convincing impression of confidence in person. With this in mind, I've been trying to work out how to meet her, in a way that seems authentically random. There'll be no chance of her remembering me from Tinder. If I ever even made the most fleeting impression on Kate Collins' brain, then that impression will be long gone.

So, I think I might have found a workable solution. Using information derived from Kate's Tinder bio – mainly the fact she's a paramedic in Leeds – I Googled my aching heart out. I found a local newspaper story about how she heroically saved a young stab victim, by standing between him and a bunch of gang members who wanted to finish him off. That's her in the accompanying photo all right, looking embarrassed to be in the spotlight and have all this fuss made about her. So she's brave *and* humble? That is one heck of a combo, in my book.

Having established Kate's full name, I proceeded to examine Facebook. On 29 March, Kate told her FB friends (in a public post, thank God) that she was quitting her phone and the internet for good, and so wouldn't be on Facebook any more. She told people who had her email to stay in touch, and for anyone who really wanted to stay in touch to PM her. But brilliantly, she also asked if anyone had ever been on a digital detox course before and could recommend one.

I'm so indebted to one of Kate's friends, who piped up to strongly recommend this two-night detox thing in Wales. The latest weekend is due to start on 31 May and Kate said she'd go for it and had already booked. I'm so very grateful for having seen this before the date, or I'd have been so gutted, because I almost certainly wouldn't get another chance. Even if I travelled to Leeds and deliberately got myself knocked over, the chances are that it wouldn't be Kate who arrived in the ambulance to rescue me!

Actually, that scenario is deranged, even for me. In case anyone ever does hack into this thing, *I would never do that. Honestly, I never would.*

And yes, TrooSelf, I know that all of this is seriously weird and creepy behaviour. I know that if I really MUST engineer a meeting between me and a potential mate, they should ideally live in the same part of the country. Hell, even the same end. But sometimes the heart wants what the heart wants – and even though I almost certainly have zero chance with Kate Collins, do I really want to go the rest of my life without confirming that she has no interest in me and I'm a total loser?

Something keeps on whispering in my ear that this woman has the power to save me from The Demon's clutches. That has to be worth a shot.

Roll on 31 May!

CHAPTER FIFTY-SEVEN

7 October

Could my life possibly be any more tragic? No it could not, because I'm crying here in the toilet cubicle at work, while snorting speed.

My God. I cannot get my head around the idea that Scott thought I'd Super-Liked him by mistake. Had he never seen himself in the mirror? But in the same way that chemical depression can be untouched by the good things happening in your life, negative self-esteem can be so firmly rooted in your past that even winning Sex Symbol Of The Year might not have changed how Scott saw himself.

I should know.

All this time, I've cursed Scott's name. I've tried to hunt down this supposed Lothario and bring him to his knees, but it seems I was wrong. Scott genuinely liked me, and he saw the same kind of vulnerability in me that I saw in him. Like he said, his approach was indeed seriously weird and creepy, not to mention dishonest and plain wrong. But . . . I don't know, more than anything else, I'm blown away that he was kind of the opposite of what I'd assumed. What's the betting that Ray bullshitted about Scott being a sleazy ladies' man, thinking it'd make me more likely to hook up with him instead?

And now it's too late. Scott may well have been dead since the day he disappeared. All I can do now is find out who killed him. Might the rest of these diary entries point the finger at Ray? He's been calling Scott's phone all day without leaving any voicemail, but what if he's only covering his tracks – playing the role of the concerned brother? Part of me actually hopes he did kill Scott, purely so I can nail the fucker. Thanks to all of Scott's lies, he and I could never have continued in a romantic mode, but reading these last two entries has left my heart in pieces.

I really hope this amphetamine sulphate pulls me through the shift, but can it also stem the tears? Might make me even more emotional.

I'm dying to read the next entry, *I Am In Love With V*. The title continues to baffle me, and I still have no idea what Scott means by *The Demon*. What the hell is that all about? Infuriatingly, I've run out of time. Tyler has already waited by the ambulance for ten minutes. Got to pull myself together, then use the bathroom mirror to sort my face and check my nostrils for speed-flakes. How I wish I had time to polish my boots and do even one gratitude, but we're already so late.

Hello again, God. I know I asked a big favour of you last night, but here's another request: please don't let me gurn too much. Especially not in front of patients.

Oh, and while I'm asking for favours, please grant me the strength not to sneak a look at *I Am In Love With V* when I'm supposed to be helping people.

I can do this. I know I can.

*

"Why didn't she look where she was going? I'll fucking kill her. Please don't try and stop me or I'll fight you too."

Gently as I can manage, considering that I'm off my tits on drugs, I place my hands on Aisha's shoulders to keep her seated on the grass verge where I've taken her. "Please," I say, "I know this is the worst moment of your life, but I can't have you attacking the driver or anyone else. You also have serious injuries. This arm is broken in at least two places, so I need you to remain very still for me."

Of course, the morning *had* to feature a major accident on this busy stretch of the A23, which the police are now cordoning off. Tyler and I are waiting for more ambulances to arrive. The air is full of horn parps from motorists, probably including some entitled fucks who actually know there's been a serious accident but simply don't care.

When I led Aisha out of her Ford Focus, I tried to position her so that she wouldn't be able to see her husband Doug in the passenger seat, with half of his head missing. She keeps turning to look, though. She may want, or need, to see, to help her come to terms with how the elderly driver of a four-by-four careered into them twenty minutes ago.

"Did you see his head?" she says, her eyes brimming. "Did you see what that evil bitch did to him?"

"Yes," I say. "I saw. And I'm so very sorry for your loss."

I watch, as my confirmation that Aisha has lost Doug corrodes her from within. A full meltdown is imminent and I'd love to join her. Glancing over at what remains of her husband, I wonder if Scott died that brutally or that suddenly. Can there be such a thing as the ideal way to die, when you don't want to go? Passing softly in your sleep? Somehow, I doubt Scott was afforded that mercy.

Got to pull myself together, right now. Got to keep my face in check.

"He's gone somewhere, you know," I say. Aisha is lost in her own devastation, so I doubt she'll notice the slight waver in my voice. "Doug has gone somewhere else. You will see him again, one day."

But hopefully not at ten past midnight, as his strobing blue spirit wends and weaves down a hill towards you . . .

"Do you . . . really believe that," Aisha splutters, as I hand her another tissue, "or is . . . is that something . . . you say to everyone?"

Looking her squarely in the eye, I say, "I swear to you, Aisha. I really do believe."

When you're trying to convey your sincerity, speed truly comes into its own. Hoping that Aisha hasn't noticed my whole "not blinking" thing, I shift into a position that allows me to deliver a gentle hug without adding to the pain in her broken arm.

As Aisha snots all her grief onto my shoulder, I notice Tyler walk past poor dead Doug in the car, closer than he strictly needs to go.

The big ox hangs around the car window, blocking my view of Doug. He glances around, drops his phone into his pocket and walks away.

CHAPTER FIFTY-EIGHT

I Am In Love With V
TrooSelf diary entry four of seven
Dated: 7 June
Filed by SPalm123

The detox retreat went really, really, weirdly well.

Or at least, I think it went well.

I mean, Kate actually seemed to tolerate me throughout almost twenty-four hours! I had to work up so much nerve to break the ice and start talking to her, and then I assumed she'd drift off and mingle with everyone else. She didn't! Hours later, when she and I were still chatting, I honestly expected Lizzie to come over and subtly try to tell me to stop harassing the poor girl.

This may have strictly been all in my imagination, but I can't help feeling Kate considered me to be half-decent company.

Towards the end of the night, the ghost of my old confidence even whispered that Kate might be interested. This seemed unlikely, but there were . . . definite signs, I am sure of this. Come the end of the night, when we stood in the corridor that held everybody's rooms, I almost experienced a will-we-or-won't-we moment!

Not that I would have dared try anything, of course. And even if Kate had dragged me into her room, she would have been sorely disappointed. I can't even function while trying to enjoy The Demon at the moment. This development has scared the living fuck out of me and made me seek urgent online help.

Still! While Kate and I ate goulash in a tent, I mentioned that I was planning to be in Leeds for business in a couple of weeks. This was a lie, but I decided to make it happen if she suggested we meet up. To be honest, diary, I have lost sleep over some of these mistruths I've so shamefully told this woman. If you have to lie to form a connection with someone, then can that connection still be considered real? Almost definitely not, but I can't stop myself. I feel like I need Kate, and in person she is ten times more bewitching than even her Tinder profile suggested.

Anyway. I waited for her to mention Leeds again, which was quite a torturous wait . . . but she finally did when we were saying goodbye on the Sunday! WOW.

Heyyy now, let's not get carried away here. I need to keep this whole thing very much in perspective. The chances are, she'd like to see me again as a friend, because we shared the detox experience. Most of it, anyway, since I almost bottled out on the whole thing. In the end, I only arrived on the second day. Argh, what a tool, but I got there in the end and that's what matters. I ultimately went through with the plan, and as a result I haven't felt this proud of myself in quite some time.

On the unlikely off-chance that sex happens in Leeds, I've been experimenting with a new thing and am loving the results. The side effects aren't great, but they're surely worth it when you consider the embarrassing alternative facing me at the moment.

I very much doubt I'll ever end up on a bed with Kate, but huge thanks in advance anyway to Viagra.

CHAPTER FIFTY-NINE

7 October

Whoa, okay then. V for Viagra.

While unexpected, this also makes sense, given that the drug's side effects include a flushed face and indigestion. Not to mention the fact that my Mr Gaviscon was almost permanently rock-hard between the sheets. Never thought to question this at the time, because it was so very convenient and complimentary.

What cost Scott his mojo in the first place? Still don't understand what he means by *The Demon*.

The ambulance has come to rest outside Asda in the Marina for our half-hour break. By now, I should have confronted Tyler about my renewed suspicion that he's sneakily taking photos of things he absolutely must not . . . but I've been too distracted by Scott's diary.

Alone in the driver's seat while Tyler shops for his latest unhealthy lunch in the supermarket, I'm about to open the next diary entry, *Burning New Pathways Into The Brain*, when I hear the tinkle of an unusual phone notification.

Once I've ruled out Scott's handset and my Nokia, all that

remains is Tyler's phone, which he's left behind on the dashboard. Having checked that Tyler is nowhere in sight, I pick up the handset, because, hey, I'm Kate Collins and this is what I do.

A pop-up notice on Tyler's screen declares, *Way to go, dude! Your upload to SikkFuxx.com has been approved.*

Hoping that Tyler's screen will auto-darken ASAP, I replace the handset where it was on the dash. Back on Scott's phone, I fire up his browser and zip over to SikkFuxx.com.

The site is very much what its charming URL suggested it would be. Pictures and videos of terrorist executions, animal slaughter, queasily violent sex and even worse. Clicking the *Latest Sikk Uploads* tab, I'm shocked, but not entirely surprised, to see a close-up photo of poor dead Doug in his car on the A23, uploaded by user Grenadier666.

Oh, and here's a six-second clip of a newborn baby, still in its amniotic sac.

Here's a video of Deranged Naked Guy invading our ambulance, plus imagery from various other sensationalist scenes from long before Tyler and I teamed up.

What an utterly reprehensible sack of shit. No way am I going to turn my back on this. Tyler is *toast.*

The passenger door opens to reveal the fuckwit himself, his carrier bag no doubt full of sugar-and-salt-based products, plus the wrong sandwich for me.

I should knock his wig off right now with some serious abuse. And yet I tell myself I'll do this later, because we still have ten minutes of our break left. Ten minutes that I need for another purpose. My so-called partner's comeuppance can wait.

Chowing down beside me, Tyler has the sheer unbridled nerve to comment on how obsessed I am with my phone. I roundly disregard him, because *Burning New Pathways Into The Brain* is already drawing me in like a Dyson.

CHAPTER SIXTY

Burning New Pathways Into The Brain
TrooSelf diary entry five of seven
Dated: 21 June
Filed by: SPalm123

Dear TrooSelf, you won't bloody well believe this, but I forgot to take the Viagra.

No, I don't mean I forgot to swallow the tablet – I mean I forgot to take the WHOLE PACK with me to Leeds. I didn't even remember until I left my hotel to go and meet Kate at the River-something-or-other Bar, and of course by then all the chemists were shut. Wouldn't even have needed a prescription, if only I'd realised sooner.

Oh my good God, it felt so awkward when we were outside her house, and I had to make my excuses and leave, like some bloody shady tabloid reporter. The thing was, I actually started to get the impression that she might want more than a coffee, which blew my mind. And needless to say, I couldn't have her attempting to blow some other part of me on her sofa, only for there to inevitably be no lead in the pencil. The very thought mortified me.

Still, our time together out on that riverside patio had been so very heavenly – or at least, it was from my perspective. Once again, I felt really guilty about having swotted up on *True Romance* in advance, even downloading the ringtone to really impress Kate, but I do now genuinely love the film. Along with my childhood love *Labyrinth*, this thing has practically become my all-time favourite movie, so does that make my deception any more forgivable?

I know that I shouldn't be lying to Kate, but I also believe that doing so offers me my only hope of being with her. After all, it was lies, combined with me proactively making things happen, that caused us to meet in the first place.

Oh my God, oh my God! Kate and I have started sexting. This confirms she actually likes me IN THAT WAY, despite how worthless I am. It's funny, I've always known that my actual face is okay, especially the cheekbones. I mean, at least my face isn't fat. And I've known this on a weird kind of scientific level, because Ray obviously has the same face as me and yet he's always had the girls flocking around him. So what has historically let me down is ME. The way I am. The way I carry myself. The lack of comfort I feel in my own skin.

The fact that I know I'm worthless, whereas Ray actually has this maddening self-esteem in his very bones.

For a long time growing up, I thought I felt worthless because Mum and Dad treated Ray as the priority twin. Over the years, though, I've come to believe that he was somehow born with all the confidence, as if having absorbed all of mine while we shared our one sac.

Note to TrooSelf: never, EVER introduce Kate to Ray. She's

so his type, too. This is painfully obvious, because he and I always had the same taste in that way, which is why he ended up stealing Mandy Fuller away from me at high school. He and I have never been the same since then. Which is probably why he's really trying to make me feel bad for this whole debt thing. I swear, he only bailed me out with the loan companies to gain power over me, in order to make me feel bad. But what the hell has he got to feel resentful for? He has everything in life. Dad even left him the Chanctonbury house in his will! What a punch on the nose that was. It still smarts, and it only happened because I never forgave Dad for knocking us around as kids, supposedly to set us *straight*, whereas Ray took that abuse as the cue to become the devoted Daddy's boy, even after our folks split.

If I could afford psychotherapy right now, I would most likely give it a go. But until my finances are back up and running, TrooSelf will have to do.

Anyway! Anyway! Sexting is afoot. And even more astonishingly, today Kate agreed to come down to Brighton. I am thrilled and terrified. For a start, this means I have one week in which to throw out all the clutter and junk in this shithole, not to mention clean the place! Really need to make the flat live up to its true potential, which I should have done before anyway. But when it was only for my benefit, why bother?

Another thing I need to deal with in this place is the Weird Crumbling Door.

A couple of times lately, I've found bits of splintered wood on the inner doormat. At first, I honestly thought one of my neighbours had randomly developed a grudge against me and pushed this stuff in through the letterbox! But no, the door does seem to be falling apart and I've no idea why. This is not a natural way for wood to behave. All I can do is buy a putty knife and some wood-filler.

Demon-wise, I'm not doing well. In fact, I'm doing badly. Sometimes I lose whole mornings, afternoons or whole days to demonic activity and it's really screwing up my work. I'm bending deadlines like nobody's business here and I'm having to start making excuses.

Really need to get a grip on my life! In an attempt to help myself, I've been reading up on demonic addiction.

Fuck it, you know what? From the stuff I've read, I've already gathered that denial about this stuff is no good. So calling this stuff The Demon, even in a super-secret diary, probably doesn't help that cause.

TrooSelf hasn't been hacked in all the months I've been using it, so let's call a spade a spade.

My name is Scott Palmer and I am addicted to porn.

Yes, porn. Porn porn PORN.

Porn is my very own demon. I have been addicted to this stuff in varying degrees, ever since I found a single page from a porn mag, aged eleven.

You know . . . this diary really has made me think about my life and help me put things into perspective. More and more as I grew up, then crossed over into adulthood, smut became my shield. It provided me with my safe place away from the world, while all the time only making it harder to talk to real women.

All the educational stuff I'm reading now makes me realise how much online porn in particular has damaged me and transformed me into a dopamine slave. People don't realise that porn literally burns new pathways into your brain! It makes brand-new connections, in a way that fucks up your physical response to actual naked human beings.

I have to work on my computer all day – or at least, I'm supposed to be working – and yet there's a whole world of porn out there, yelling for me to watch. And when I'm not at my desk, the phone yells porn-notifications at me, too.

Bloody hell. Working with screens all day has to be the equivalent of an alcoholic owning a pub.

The only way out of the whole sorry mess, I'm fast learning, is to reboot yourself. You have to cut porn out of your life altogether, like a troublesome weed, and give your brain at least ninety days in which to rewire itself and return to its default settings.

I'm sceptical, but I'm also game.

And so the challenge begins here. No more porn. And the fact that the amazing Kate Collins, my sweet saviour, is travelling down here to see me in ONE WEEK surely will provide me with the ultimate motivation to do this right.

Come on! Sort yourself out, Scott. A whole new life beckons.

CHAPTER SIXTY-ONE

7 October

Plump grey clouds line the coast, as we rocket along the seafront towards the snow-capped Palace Pier.

Scott is dead.

This afternoon, Madeira Drive lies wide open, straight as a die. Which is just as well, because our damned lights make all this snow on the road resemble blue glitter. Sometimes it can be hard to see past all this glitter to the actual road.

Scott is dead.

Seems a fight has broken out in Nelson's Bar at the end of the pier, and it's been bad enough for the staff to frantically summon us. Bloody afternoon drinkers.

Scott is *dead*.

Now that the drugs have worn off, this fact is sinking in way too deep.

Tyler's engrossed in his phone. I want to toss him a warning, to tell him not to photograph or film *anything* when we reach this bar. I want him to know that I know, but my fatigue barely leaves me with enough energy to drive and ponder those new pathways that Scott burnt into his brain.

So . . . porn, seriously? That was Scott's big bad secret? I mean, I hadn't quite realised porn addiction was such a thing, but he and I could have so easily worked on the problem together. I meet addicts on a daily basis – and we were in love, weren't we? Despite all the other lies he told me, I now know we did have some kind of connection.

Can't help remembering what he said, back in that detox retreat tent. *Sometimes I'll find myself scrolling through, you know, whatever, and I'll catch myself . . . and I'll wonder what the hell I was even doing. It ends up being just . . . mindless. It's like you get sucked in, you know?*

Kills me, to think that he felt unable to talk about this, being so convinced I'd abandon him the moment I discovered the real Scott. And yet, if anything, these diary entries make me like him even more. The Scott I once loved, he now feels like a fake billboard. Some kind of soft-focus cologne advert, concealing the real, three-dimensional, fucked-up Wizard of Oz.

Seems obvious that Scott never meant to leave me. I picture his vulnerable Tinder face, then his dead blue flicker-face, before making myself snap out of it.

Tyler squints over at the pier as it draws closer on the left. With a mouth full of Frazzles, he says, "At least the bar's not on fire. That's gotta be a plus."

The *True Romance* ringtone rises up from the dashboard.

I glance at the phone's screen, expecting to see yet another incoming call from *Idiot*. Instead, it's *Unknown Number.* Oh God, another dead person?

My throat seizes up, as I consider one potential caller.

Tyler is saying something about how familiar this music sounds, when I snatch the phone from the dashboard.

Bouncing my attention back and forth between the blue-glitter road and the glowing screen in my hand, I put the call on speakerphone, then sling the phone back onto the dash.

"Kate," Tyler snaps, "what the hell are you doing?"

I would fire back some cutting retort about people in glass houses and stones, but my head is mush. All I want is to hear whose voice will rise out of the dead static that now issues from the phone.

"Mate, you can't answer your phone when you're bloody—"

"Shut up, Tyler, I'm on the phone."

"Don't tell me to—"

Tyler stops talking as soon as the caller starts. Must be something about how Scott's voice sounds so very flat, dark and dead.

"Kate," Scott says, "get rid of this thing. I'm begging you to throw it away."

Tears blur the road and I swipe at them. "Is that really you? Are you really dead?"

Tyler yells my name and I don't understand why, but then I see the imminent nightmare.

Running across the snow, in the road right in front of us: a small child in blue wellies, chased by a frantic adult.

Too close to brake.

I swing the wheel left. Adult and child fly off to the right.

The whole cab judders as we mount the pavement.

Tyler's voice runs high enough to attract dogs. "Brake, Kate, brake!"

I already fucking have, but now we're skidding on ice. Narrowly missing a statue, we zoom towards the metal rails that separate this pavement from the crazy golf course down at beach level.

I stomp the brake again.

Scott's phone flies off the dash and smacks me in the face.

The van's front bumper comes to a soft rest on the rails. Tyler yells so loud, I'm convinced he must be physically hurt. "What the fuck? What the fuck was that?"

Seeing that Tyler's sustained no damage, I roll down the window and stick out my head, searching for the people we . . .

. . . *you* . . .

. . . almost hit. Please, please, tell me they're okay.

Back across the road, the young mother stands unscathed, physically at least. Her arms are wrapped around the child, whose face is buried in her belly.

Embattled by nausea, I follow Tyler as he marches along the sludge-soaked floorboards of the pier, his bag slung over one shoulder.

I can't speak. I can barely think. All I can do, right now, is feel appalled by myself. I want to turn back time and never go on that digital detox retreat. Or go back even further and never buy a smartphone in the first place. Or best of all, go all the way back to a time when messages were sent by smoke signals and trained birds.

I could've killed both of those people. With an ambulance.

A young mother and her child.

I'm going to do my very best to redeem myself. Could saving a hundred more lives make amends for nearly taking two? No. I doubt I can ever make full amends for such dereliction of duty.

Scott's voice comes back to haunt me. His dead and dismal voice, telling me to get rid of the phone.

Is he still really that desperate for me not to discover the whole truth? What if there's more, beyond the porn?

Enough. Focus on the job. The. Fucking. Job.

An alternative take: could it be that Scott knows his phone has become my obsession? He may have been trying to warn me that disaster lay ahead . . . and as a result he helped to cause this disaster. Fucking hell, that's the kind of irony that would have Alanis Morissette strumming herself.

A snowflake lands on my forehead as I arrive at Nelson's Bar. Need to forget about my impending mental breakdown, strap on my game face and help people.

Tyler, still ahead of me, barges in through the bar's doors, then allows them to slam shut in my face. Following him through, I take in the wide space. The room has emptied, apart from the flustered bar staff and a burly security guard. Several chairs and tables have been up-ended. Broken glass litters the floor, some of it bloody.

"Where are the injured?" Tyler asks the guard.

"They all left," he says. "Did you not see them on your way up here? One of them had blood coming out of his neck."

"How hard?" I ask, feeling like the trainee, desperate to contribute.

Makes sense. Only a trainee would make an insane decision like answering their phone while on the way to a job.

The guard frowns. "What do you mean?"

"How hard is the blood coming out of his neck?" Tyler says. "A gush, a dribble, somewhere in between?"

"More like a paper cut," he says, giving me and Tyler our cue to relax.

When we get outside, Tyler says, "Come with me."

I hate the fact that he's about to rip into me. Much more than this, though, I hate the fact that I deserve it, so I follow him to the far end of the pier. Here, we settle at the railing beside a vertigo-inducing ride called The Booster, which makes me feel even more like throwing up. Beyond the railing, a turbulent sea stretches to the horizon.

With snow resting like dandruff on each shoulder, Tyler says,

"I'm gonna do you one hell of a favour." He holds an object in the air. What is it?

Scott's phone.

Panicked, I slap my pocket where the thing usually lives. How the hell did he get that? Must've grabbed the thing when I left the van to check on the mother and her kid. I've been in such a state that I didn't even think to check where it had landed.

Oh God. Tyler is going to throw Scott's phone in the sea.

"Hey," I hear myself bark, "you'd better give that back, right now."

"Sure," he says. "I could give it back. But if I do, I'll also tell Akeem exactly what happened, back there on the road. And the bloody pavement. *Bang*, there goes your stupid fifteen-year badge."

I present him with the palm of one hand. "Give me back my fucking phone."

This thing isn't even mine. I should let Tyler toss it. This is literally what Scott would've wanted.

"I don't know who that was, calling you," Tyler says, "or why the *hell* you asked him if he was *dead* . . . but you need to take his advice. You never stop looking at this bloody phone and you could have killed all four of us back there. So I'm chuckin' this thing in the drink, love, and— Hey!"

With one cat-snatch move, I steal Tyler's own phone from its stupid belt-holster. He swipes a beefy paw at me, but I hold his phone out over the rail, ready to drop, and he turns to stone.

"So, Tyler . . . bet you were disappointed that the paper-cut guy hadn't been slit from ear to ear, right? You could've scored a few more Hero Points from your fellow SikkFuxx . . ."

Tyler's feral eyes weaken at this, but he keeps Scott's phone raised. What we have ourselves here is a Mexican standoff.

"What I did with the ambulance was actually worse," I say,

"so yeah, you've got me there. But this shit you're doing has to stop, too. Maybe we're both driven by the need for something? I need answers to . . . stuff . . . and you need . . . you need . . . I have no idea what the fuck you need. Why would you upload a picture of someone with half their head gone, for a bunch of gore-hounds to jerk over? Why on Earth would you do that, Tyler?"

His shoulders rise and fall. A fake calm descends upon him, and I can tell that his new smile is designed to humour me while he slyly lowers my defences. "Okay, Kate. Let's keep our heads and explore that question. Bear in mind, by the way, that I bought that phone only recently for five-hundred quid, all right? Your phone looks second-hand." He takes a deep breath. "Okay, I mean, I definitely don't feel great about these uploads. So . . . why do I do it? Uh . . ."

Silence ensues. Convinced he's only pretending to examine his own moral fabric, I step up to the plate. "Let me guess: you think you're not worth all that much. And so sharing sick pictures, these shots that only you can take earns you a micro-dose of power and prestige. It earns you one single gram of leverage in this world. Am I close?"

A single flicker in Tyler's otherwise stony gaze suggests I'm right. "You feel addicted, don't you, mate?" I say. "You're a runaway train. I know, because I feel it too. That's my ex's phone. Ever since he disappeared, I've been using this thing to try and figure out why. And I absolutely cannot stop."

Tyler tries to speak, but I cut him off. "The thing is, Tyler, I do really *need* to stop."

Scott's voice echoes in my head. *Kate, get rid of this thing. I'm begging you to get rid of it.*

Seeing the reckless glow in my eyes, Tyler looks fit to bust a blood vessel. He takes one quick step towards me but doesn't dare make a grab for his phone. "Kate . . . don't do anything stupid."

Scott's voice, again: *Actually . . . out of interest . . .* do *you trust me, Kate?*

"This is the end of stupidity for both of us," I tell Tyler, and I drop his phone into the sea.

CHAPTER SIXTY-TWO

7 October

Izzy pulls the blanket over me, as if I'm a sick child. A perfectly fair assessment.

Thanks to the smashed balcony door, the entire flat plays host to temperatures consistent with Reykjavik, even here in the bedroom with the door shut. Izzy hobbles around the foot of the bed, then climbs in beside me on the other side. God bless her for having persuaded a Freecycling couple to not only deliver this queen-sized delight but carry it all the way in here. She even got a second garden chair for the living room. She's so cool.

Coming home this morning, we found neither wood chips on the floor nor freshly gouged holes in the front door. I'm really hoping this means Gwyneth's and Dieter's ghosts have gone, but what the hell has all this wood-chip phenomena signified? Scott himself experienced it, but why did the door only start to crumble after he and I met, when he'd lived here for much longer? And why did I see the same gouge marks in Gwyneth's old front door in Whitehawk?

While I try to analyse everything that's happened, my fatigue and adrenaline fight for supremacy. Resting on her side, Izzy reaches over to mess around with my hair.

"Losing that phone is the best thing you could've done," she says. "You must know that, or you wouldn't have made the decision."

"It was almost worth it, to see the look on that prick's face."

"But don't forget what it's done for *you*, honey. You're free now."

"Yeah. I am."

So why don't I feel free? I feel . . . weird.

You can't stop thinking about Scott's phone, right? You can't stop picturing that beautiful handset, still packed with so much vital information, lying on the sea bed behind the pier.

Still stroking me, Izzy says, "What did Tyler do, after you chucked his phone? Apart from chuck yours, obviously."

"He grabbed my shoulders and pushed me up against the rails. Then I kneed him in the balls and he kind of folded in half."

"Jesus."

"By that point, people were gathering and pointing, so we called each other very bad names, then ended the shift. Textbook professionalism."

"So what happens next?" she says. "Do you reckon he'll report you for the whole ambulance thing?"

"He might, through sheer spite, because of his five-hundred-quid phone and his bruised nuts. But I can report him, too."

"You *should*. Uploading pics like that, it's gross misconduct. In more ways than one."

"I'm really hoping he's learnt his lesson. I won't report him if he stops, and if he removes all his uploads from that site. I guess he could access his SikkFuxx account from another phone and . . ."

My words trail off as I make a connection that seems both great and terrible. "Izzy, we can still read the rest of Scott's diary, by using a different phone. We still have the passwords. We can use your—"

Izzy pulls back her hand like my hair's on fire. "Oh God, Kate, no. *No.*"

I prop myself on one side to face Izzy and the full heat of her disapproval.

"I know, Izz, I know. But this is about more than me. Scott is dead and may have been murdered. What if—"

"We really don't know for sure he's dead. He even called you on the phone."

"Izzy, I saw his ghost. And on the phone today, he *sounded* dead, just like all the other people who've called me. You're right, we don't know for sure, but I do need to know. I can't get on with my life until I've found" – the words expand to fill my throat – "until I've found his body, all right? And the last two diary entries might help me do that. I really think Ray might have killed Scott, don't you?"

Everything I'm saying, it bounces right off Izzy's stony face. "Kate, if the ambulance crash hasn't made you see that this has to end right now, then I don't know what else to tell you."

"It wasn't exactly a crash," I say, hating how sullen I sound.

Izzy heaves herself upright, like she's about to storm out. Her eyes are windows in a burning house. "Fucking hell, you dick-head, you almost killed people. If I'd been there, I would've stomped that phone straight away. Tyler was actually bloody restrained."

"I will never, ever use a phone while driving again, or even while I'm at work. This was a blip."

"Oh, a blip, is that really all it was? How about all the *blip* sounds that the kid's life-support machine would've made?"

I picture the scene and shudder, but still my mouth won't stop. "I just need to read the last two diary entries and then I promise you, I'm done. Will you help me? Can I use your—"

Izzy shakes her head, slowly and definitively. "Kate, I'm gonna make this plain, okay? If you don't shut up and get some sleep, I'm fucking off back to Leeds tonight. This whole investigation of yours is *over*."

God, I feel so angry. Could this be speed-induced psychosis? "Aren't you even the tiniest bit curious about the last things Scott wrote in his diary? Don't you want to know?"

Izzy gathers herself, then lies back down beside me. This time, when she strokes my hair, it feels patronising. "What I want to know, honey, is that my best friend is safe and *sane*. I want to know that she isn't going to wreck her entire career and life."

Frustration oozes out of me as slow tears. Izzy is my surrogate mum, telling me it's bedtime when I really want to climb a tree. "But we're so close . . ."

With one finger, she gently dabs under my eyes, keeping her voice soft. "I know, honey. I know. Sometimes, you really do have to let go, for your own good . . . and for the good of others. Now please, forget about Scott. Forget about anybody else in the world except yourself and close your eyes."

For now, I'll obey her orders, because my head feels so very heavy. With my drowsy, sunken voice, I say, "You'll still be here when I wake up?"

"I'm not going anywhere. Promise. Now rest."

Well, this is such a shame. I'd really thought Izzy understood me and this whole situation. Somewhere in the back of my head, a new storm warning rings loud and clear.

CHAPTER SIXTY-THREE

7 October

A harsh wind lets me hear Scott yell my name, then cruelly snatches his voice back away across the sea.

He's trapped and I have to find him.

Here at the front of the Palace Pier, I'm flanked by the food stalls outside. The clock tower crowning the entrance declares the time to be 3.33 a.m. The front gates beneath have been locked for hours now, and yet I know I have to get in. I have to save Scott.

Behind me, all around me, there's not a soul in sight. The seafront bars and clubs lie dormant and dark. Over to my left, two revellers have crashed out on the beach, but aside from them I see no signs of life.

I know this must be a dream, despite the fact that I have never felt so cold, and the only clothes I'm wearing are the same T-shirt and pants that I wore to bed. Mud squelches between my bare toes.

Keep telling yourself it's a dream and it might even become true.

High above me, seagulls struggle to get anywhere. Challenged by the wind, most of them appear to hover in the same spot. Some even fly backwards.

Scott calls my name from somewhere far off ahead. His voice carries raw, unfiltered fear, like someone about to meet their maker. With my guts knotted, I prowl the gates in search of an easy way in.

Yes, surely this must all be the product of my sleeping head's imagination . . . despite the fact that the cold air's bite feels so very sharp, so very deep, so very real.

"Kate? Kate! What the bloody hell are you doing?"

This new voice belongs to Izzy. She's calling to me, from back along Marine Parade. Projecting her voice so hard, you can hear the rips in her throat.

This is real. You know this is no dream.

Can't let Izzy stop me from taking action. She wouldn't understand.

Do you even understand what you're doing?

"Kate, please, come back!" Judging by how far away Izzy's voice sounds, she's calling from Scott's balcony. This means she's too far away to catch up with me now. Good. I have to stay focused on the pier, for Scott's sake.

Izzy won't understand. She doesn't get this.

Hauling myself over the locked gates, via one of the gazebo-style towers, costs me a great deal of sweat, but soon my feet hammer down on the other side.

The black carpet of the pier rolls out before me. The only light visible is that single red, flickering bulb on top of the helter-skelter. I really should take this as a warning of danger, but I don't, for the same reason I didn't stop to consider any security cameras back there – Scott needs help and so I'm prepared to accept the consequences.

This place feels like the world's biggest haunted house, daring me to try my luck. *Roll up, roll up, Miss Collins! Find your porn-addict ex alive, or die trying!*

My feet bash the boards as I run. Through the gaps between them, I can make out the surge of the sea.

Izzy's distant cries blend with those of the seagulls, and with the roar of the waves.

The forbidden castle of the front arcade building looms over me, all locked up, but could Scott be trapped inside? I'll break in if I have to. For now, I run around the entire left-hand side, listening out for Scott's voice, then along a central corridor with shuttered stalls on either side. A bulky black shape jolts me, before I realise it's a fake life-sized cow.

If this really is a dream, then it's an extraordinarily lucid one, in which you can properly taste the air and feel the cold sweat spread across your back.

No, you're in a trance. You're being tricked. Lured. Led.

Could I have already passed the spot where Scott's in trouble? Clutching my sides, I stop to listen. In dreams, it isn't usually necessary to catch a breath or massage away a stitch, so this does feel real. Which means I really am trespassing on Brighton Pier in the middle of the night, but Scott needs my help and that's all I can think about.

I wait for the wind to deliver his voice to me again.

Different voices come instead. Two male voices yell loudly to each other. From the front of the pier, two darting flashlights cut through the black. Searchlights, looking for the intruder. Seems there may have been cameras after all. Or that interfering cow Izzy may have made a panicked call. Why doesn't she *understand*?

Scott calls my name twice, heavy with distress. He's still so far away. Somewhere up ahead, among the fairground rides.

When I break into a sprint, the whole pier leaps up and down. Back over my shoulder, those darting flashlights seek me out, catching up all too fast.

Arriving at the end of the pier, the widest section of all, I'm dwarfed by the central domed arcade, the rollercoasters like skeletal dinosaur remains and the ghost train, inside which a horde of mechanical frights await reactivation. Off to my left sits the bar where blood was spilt today.

"—ate! Plea—!"

Scott's voice not only sounds more frantic, but his words are truncated. This makes me picture his head breaking the surface of water, before a relentless current hauls him back under.

The knowledge that Scott may be about to die . . .

. . . again? He's already dead. You're not thinking straight . . .

. . . makes my heart pound my ribcage. I dash past the Wild River ride to the spot by the rails where Tyler and I faced off.

Gripping the ice-cold metal bars, I can make out a small glowing light under the water.

Scott's life force. That's what this must be.

What, wait – why? Don't do this, it's a trick. You'll die.

I have to save him.

I have to do this.

If Scott told you to take a running jump off a pier, would you?

"Stop right there," yells some guy from a good distance behind me. "You're not in trouble."

"Stay calm, miss," says another. "Don't do anything stupid, yeah?"

At this, a ripple of déjà vu passes through me. Both men bark in alarm, but wind blots out their words as I climb fast over the bars and dive headlong into the maelstrom.

CHAPTER SIXTY-FOUR

20 September

The last time I ever see Scott Palmer, he and I talk about suicide.

In the bedroom, I've almost finished packing the rucksack. This will be my last journey back to Leeds before the big move down here.

"Hey, Kate," Scott yells from the living room. "Come and look." The dark urgency in his voice, combined with his use of my actual name, makes me run along the hall. "Looks like someone's jumped off the pier. They must have tried to . . . oh God."

As I hurry through the archway to join him, he slides open the balcony door, filling the living room with the thrum of whirring blades. Up near the clouds, an air ambulance chops through the sky. Two ground crews have parked at the front of the pier.

"You can always tell when something really bad's happened," he says. "Out come all the rubberneckers."

Sure enough, a pack of seafront vultures have assembled to

soak up the drama. *Just like we have*, I think. Wrapping my arms around Scott's waist from behind, I press myself against his back. "Fuck," I say. "I feel like I should be out there, doing something."

He squeezes my hand. There's a fond smile in his voice. "That's you all over."

"But I'm only across the road. I could help out. Time is so precious with things like this."

"Looks like they've got it covered, baby."

"How many times a year does someone jump?"

"Three or four. And yet this person never learns their lesson."

He laughs lightly at his own joke, but as I gaze out over the surging water I can only feel grateful for the gift of breath. The three waterlogged bodies I've seen hauled out of rivers, their faces weren't pretty.

"Drowning really isn't a great way to go," I say.

"Sorry," he says. "I shouldn't joke. It's just . . . depressing, isn't it."

"Oh, don't worry. Some of the jokes we crack on the job would make people's relatives want to lynch us. But we're not laughing *at* the bad stuff. It's like we're trying to flush out our systems. We're trying to stay sane. You either laugh or you cry, and when you're on the job, only one option works."

A pause, and then Scott says, "I think you're incredible, you know that?"

Compliments make me clam up, so I close my eyes and hold him tighter. Finally, someone thinks I'm all right. Someone who isn't Izzy. "Only two weeks to go," I say. "Don't go changing your mind on me, or I will hunt you down and set fire to you."

I feel the vibrations of his laugh from deep inside his chest. "I was about to say the same thing to you. Well, without the whole *hunty fiery* bit."

We watch the helicopter circle the pier, as the coastguard's rescue boat cleaves across the waves to join the search for this poor lost soul.

Standing up here in my ivory tower, cocooned by my perfect new life, I wonder what might possibly drive a person to commit such a sad and desperate act.

CHAPTER SIXTY-FIVE

8 October

The cold black shock swallows me whole.

My T-shirt billows up to hug my face, waterboarding me.

What have I done? I'm going to drown and die.

Don't breathe in. Soon as you get water in your lungs, you're sunk. The average person can last for eighty-seven seconds before the chemical sensors in their brain trigger an involuntary breath. Aren't you glad we stored these handy facts?

I try to move my arms and legs, but the sea exerts too much coercive force. I may as well be a mannequin, bobbing around at the whim of the current. Can't even tell which way is up or down. The water pressure makes it hard to keep my eyes open, but I have to try.

How many seconds have gone already? How long do I have left?

I really don't want to die.

I especially don't want the people left behind to think I killed myself.

Izzy! Oh God, Izzy, I'm so sorry for everything.

Most of all, I don't want my mother to have the satisfaction of thinking she finally drove me to this.

When I manage to yank my shirt back down from over my face, I see a light.

A small glow, rising from the depths to hover right in front of my face.

This must be the light I dove down here to find. Scott's soul. What the fuck made me think that? Insane trance logic. God, I'm so scared.

When I grab hold of this light, a hard rectangle fills my hand. Scott's phone. Christ, this light has been coming from the handset's torch.

Priorities. Look around. My newfound torch illuminates a couple of feet ahead. Tantalisingly close, there's a vertical pole, one of the pier's support beams.

I try to swim in that direction, but the current has other ideas. Pinning my arms to my sides, it jerks me way over to the left and then back again.

Please, please, give me one chance. Even though it's more than I deserve.

Careful what you wish for. Look out, here comes that pole. Fast.

My upper body collides with the metal, bashing my nose and knocking off barnacles. Wrapping both arms around the pole, I grab hold of bolts I can't see.

Incensed by my insolence, the current attempts to haul me away.

How many seconds left? How long before my lungs fill with water and I become another stiff on a mortuary slab?

At least you know there's an afterlife.

Fuck that, brain. Ain't going there yet.

I hook both legs around the metal, then monkey myself upwards.

Why don't you let go of the phone? That would help you to grip.

Inch by inch I climb. My entire being screams for oxygen. I need to get my head above water soon, or any moment now my brain will prise open my mouth and it'll all be over.

The intense cold suggests I'm already dead. When you can't feel your physical self, you may as well be just a soul.

Somewhere above me, up beyond the roiling surface of the sea . . . is that a dim smear of moon?

No, these are *two* lights, and they're roving. Please don't let them be the beckoning lamps of the hereafter.

Don't stop. Come on, you're almost there. Keep going. Do this for Izzy, if no one else.

When the urge for air overwhelms me, I picture Izzy in pieces at my funeral. I picture the tears streaming down her face, as she tells an endless procession of shrinks how her best friend killed herself and she failed to intervene.

My head bursts out into the exquisite and priceless night air.

Spluttering, I grip the pole like it's a child. I can still barely breathe and the cold has sunk fangs deep into my bones, but I'm alive.

What might be any period of time later, someone yells that they can see me and my phone-light torch.

CHAPTER SIXTY-SIX

8 October

"So, Kate. If you're feeling up to it, perhaps you could take a moment to talk me through your mindset last night."

My allotted NHS psychotherapist is Dr Jones, a Chinese man with glasses and a goatee. He exudes precisely the kind of calming vibes I could use right now.

I will never again need to season my food. Both the taste and the lingering feel of salt on my skin are so pervasive that I feel like one almighty hunk of cured meat.

Casting my mind back to the pier triggers mental snapshots I'd much sooner forget.

The violent up-and-down motion of the coastguard's boat. Someone shoving me onto my side so I don't choke on my own copious vomit.

Riding in an ambulance as a patient for the first time in my life. Wrapped in a red cotton blanket, immobilised, spider-strapped to an orthopaedic scoop stretcher. One of the paramedics informing Control that she's *pretty sure the patient is one of our own*, then muttering my name into the radio.

Morning hours blurring and flashing by, thanks to fitful naps on my hospital bed. Whoa, my recurring zip-wire dream came back. This time, the memory's so much clearer: as I hurtled along the wire, I realised I was moving backwards. I knew that when I reached the platform of the tower, something horrendous would happen, but I couldn't stop my ascent . . . and then I woke up.

Probably best not to mention this dream to Dr Jones.

"I'm not sure how to describe what my mindset was," I tell him.

What you mean is, you're not sure whether it'd be best all round if you were sectioned, right? Because that's what might happen if you tell him you were suicidal. Or if you tell him you were trying to rescue your dead ex-boyfriend's drowning soul.

Dr Jones creaks back in his seat and cups the back of his head with both hands, as if sunning himself on a Hawaiian beach. His smile is carefree. Disarmingly conspiratorial. "Well, give it a go and see how you do."

"Okay," I say, deciding to unveil as much truth as I dare. "At first, I . . . I thought I might be dreaming. I thought the whole thing was a dream."

"Ah," he says. "Okay. In my line of work, I'm always loath to put words in anyone's mouth, but would you say you might have been . . ."

"Sleepwalking? Yes, I was, but it was so lucid. I was fully aware of everything."

"So, what was your purpose for entering the pier?"

I try to fight the urge to tell him everything, but I'm not strong enough to keep it all inside. This stuff wants out. I'm also keen to hear the psychiatric take on what the hell I was doing last night.

"My ex-boyfriend has gone missing, and I think he's dead, and I heard him calling me from the pier. So I followed his voice and . . ." A lump in my throat rules out any further speech. The sole coherent thought I seem able to form is that I don't understand anything anymore. Scott's ghost told me to get rid of the phone, which I did – only for Scott's voice to lead me back to the damn thing. Or did I only imagine hearing him?

Dr Jones nods encouragingly, without judgement, as if he hears this kind of wacked-out scenario all the time. "So, from your perspective, why did you jump into the water?"

I'm half grief, half snot. "I thought he was down there. Drowning in the sea."

The full, dizzying extent of everything hits home, as if I'm floating above myself. Scott's disappearance. Scott's ghost. The dead, phoning me for chats. Me, very nearly dying on Chanctonbury Hill. Me, voluntarily leaping off the end of a pier in the middle of the night. My life has become a forest fire, way out of control, and now I'm sobbing into both hands.

Dr Jones pushes a box of tissues across the table to me. "Okay, Kate. It sounds like you're going through a great deal of stress, uncertainty and mental trauma."

Something definitely took over my body last night: could this really have been a manifestation of stress? Chills me to the core, how easily I threw myself off those rails. Didn't even question it, and for what? Almost killed myself, trying to save a guy who was already dead.

Are you really sure it was Scott you were so determined to save?

Christ, what if I *wasn't* hunting for Scott? What if I was actually hell-bent on retrieving the phone?

Have I really fallen so far? Does my obsession seriously run so deep that I would risk my life to find out what happened to Scott?

You know the answer, don't you.

Yes, you know only too well.

Dr Jones says, "Since you're in the medical trade, Kate, chances are you're well aware of the main purpose of our session this evening. So I'm sure you won't mind me asking outright, and answering me as honestly as you can. Were you acting on thoughts of self-harm last night?"

I shake my head. Through the tears, I see him nod as if he believes me.

"Then as far as I'm concerned, unless they want to run any further tests, you can go home for now. As I'm sure you know, I could prescribe you something to help with the anxiety, but you'd probably get addicted. So what needs to happen now, more than anything, is for the police to deal with your missing boyfriend. You should reach out to them. It will help. You should also absolutely reach out to your GP."

Once again, he adopts that Hawaiian beach pose on his chair. "Your friend Isabella is waiting outside to take you home. I sincerely hope you're wrong about your missing ex, and I will cross my fingers for you. In the meantime, you're gonna have to try and chill out, man."

Did Dr Jones really say that? I might not be the most reliable witness at present, but I honestly believe it happened.

Man. Wow.

CHAPTER SIXTY-SEVEN

8 October

"Kate, there's one thing I need to know, more than owt else. Please, please tell me you weren't trying to get the phone back."

Side by side on the living room chairs, both wearing our coats, Izzy and I are gazing out through the smashed balcony door to the horizon, where the clouds inflict one big wide bruise. Halfway through this heavily overcast afternoon, only the pier offers any real light. I used to love that place, but it now resembles a deathtrap and I've positioned the chair to keep it out of my sight.

Overnight, no new wood chips have appeared on the post-mat. Why? No idea. I may have simply been too quick to see supernatural reasons for everything. The door might be old and weak, and Scott's DIY handiwork could have been poor. Sometimes the door crumbles, sometimes it doesn't, and that's that.

Izzy's pupils are fringed with red veins. She carries this haunted look, one that screams, *My best mate has turned out to be a nightmare and I'm struggling to cope.*

I feel one hundred years old, as if imaginary weights have been tied to my limbs. The deep ache in my bones signals that I'm fast falling prey to flu. Every syllable I speak feels like a Herculean task.

"I wasn't trying to do anything in particular. Like I said, it felt like sleepwalking."

"But did you ever sleepwalk before?"

"Yeah, as a kid. I don't know, trauma may have brought it back."

If Izzy and I were sitting face to face, this lie would have required too much energy. Way too much control of all the muscles in my face and repression of those tell-tale ticks. Since we're not, though, I've more lies where that came from.

"Honestly, Izz, I'm going to be fine now. The shrink reckons this has all been down to stress, and I agree. All I need is some rest, so please don't feel like you have to—"

"There's no way I'm leaving you here by yourself, especially after last night," she says. "I've cancelled the next few days at work, so now we can chill the fuck out and sleep for a thousand years."

No, no, no. With Izzy here, how am I supposed to get things done? How am I supposed to finish this? "Thank you."

"I've booked a guy to come over tonight to change the locks on the door. I want us to rest easy, without worrying about Scott or Ray showing up."

"Scott's dead, Izzy."

"Let's not go over that again, yeah? We're both fucked, honey: it's been two nights without sleep and you almost died. If you still feel strongly about all this tomorrow, when we're thinking straight, then the police will have to get involved."

By *we're*, she clearly means *you're*. Could she be any more patronising?

I *am* thinking straight. All I want is to be left alone.

Izzy groans and heaves herself up on her crutches. "I'm going to get some supplies before we crash."

I should tell her to sit back down. I should insist that we get food delivered here instead. And yet I do neither of these things, because I need this time to myself. A little time, that's all, to do what needs to be done. And then we can sleep.

"You are amazing," I tell her.

"I know I am." As she makes her steady progress towards the door, every second feels like one whole minute. This yearning is unbearable. "You're going to be so much better off without that phone now. You know that, right?"

"I do. I swear." *Contact lenses get stuck behind your eyes. It's true, I swear.* "Thank you, honey."

Finally, the front door closes behind her. Oh, blessed, shameful relief.

When I hear both locks clunk, one by one, I have the fleeting sense of being an asylum inmate. Suppose I can hardly blame Izzy for taking no chances.

I don't need to leave the flat, though.

All I need, it's right here in my pocket.

CHAPTER SIXTY-EIGHT

Joining The Death Grip Cult
TrooSelf diary entry six of seven
Dated: 23 August
Filed by: SPalm123

Where to start? It's been a while since I wrote here, even though loads has happened.

First of all, and I can't even believe I'm writing this – I recently had my first ever ghostly experience! The whole thing scared the living piss out of me.

Speaking of piss, it happened when I was on my way to have one, in the middle of the night. Thank GOD Kate wasn't staying here at the time.

I was walking along the dark corridor with my eyes half open, when this blue flashing thing flew towards me. It had a face, a girl's face I think, with these hideous black holes instead of eyes. I completely freaked out and put my hands up to protect myself . . . but then it was gone.

I am still astonished this happened. And now I'm totally

on edge, every single night, in case it happens again. Wasn't sleeping great anyway, but this is really fucking me up. I'm dead tired every day and the fatigue is slowly getting worse, which is the last thing I need.

Since I saw the ghost, Kate has been down to stay. I decided to test the waters by asking her if she believed in spooks, even though I could have guessed her answer. Only a few days beforehand, my own opinion would have been the same. I was so dreading her going to the bathroom in the night and seeing the ghost herself. The last thing I need, right now, is something to scare her off besides ME, her lunatic boyfriend. Yes – boyfriend! Because since I last wrote, Kate Collins is – drum roll, please – my actual girlfriend. But who, exactly, am I trying to fool here? It is self-evident that our relationship will fall apart sooner rather than later.

I still literally cannot believe she agreed we should go "exclusive". We live so far apart and I'm not good enough for her. For a start, she deserves a guy who (a) doesn't lie to her and (b) can get it up without recourse to ED medication. And can I really take Viagra forever without telling her? In my financial dire straits, can I actually even afford to keep on buying the stuff? I've got Ray on my back like a limpet, looking to suck away everything of value that I own. That whole situation has escalated hugely over the summer, after he bailed me out from the loan sharks.

When I dare to imagine Kate finishing with me, it feels like I'm falling down a mine shaft. I don't know how I'm going to face this when it happens. And so this month I've set up dates with other women . . . only to bottle out at the last minute. Didn't have the balls to actually cancel them – I just haven't shown up to meet anybody, which is pretty low. And yet I keep on talking to new women, and I keep on setting up dates, so that when the inevitable happens I'll have formed some kind of bonds with other people. That might allow me to cope with our break-up to some extent.

The cracks are already showing. Three nights ago, we had our first argument after eating at Food For Friends. There was one freaky moment when she accused me of still being on Tinder, which made me think she'd sussed me out, but I think I covered it all right. How many more lies am I going to tell? A few weeks ago, I even pretended it was my thirty-seventh birthday! Guess I wanted to make the most of Kate's attention while I still have her in my life, because there's no way she'll be around for my forty-first "celebrations" next May . . .

Besides her, the other rock in my life is the porn addiction forum I've joined. Feels amazing, yet sad, to realise that there are millions of guys like me, who never realised the negative effects porn would have on them. Men of all ages, from young teens to old men, all rendered unable to get turned on by real people. I've learnt about things like *the death grip* which guys exert on their dicks, making themselves too accustomed to that much hand-friction. Also, our brains crave more and more new things to turn us on, so that we can score the same dopamine hits as we used to. This all rings true to me. What a nightmare.

On this forum, everyone really encourages each other to do the right thing and give up. You can even put a counter on your forum signature, to show how many days you've gone without smut. And so I'm trying, I'm really trying, but I also keep failing and having to reset the bloody counter. Feels like playing a game of Snakes And Ladders, except without any ladders.

Even during the night, I'll often feel the most unbearable urge to watch porn. My latest coping strategy is to get up, brave the Ghost Corridor and then stand out on the balcony, where I do breath exercises to try and shift my sexual energy. Doesn't always work. Oh God, I did this routine in the nude the other night and Kate came out. Scared the living BALLS off me! I totally thought she was another ghost.

My financial nightmare, the inevitability of losing Kate and the unscalable mountain of porn abstinence – they're all ganging up on me and it's really all starting to feel too much.

Been wondering if I should do something counter-intuitive, something crazy. I should fly in the face of all my fears and really try to take the plunge with Kate. What if I ask her to move in with me? If she lived here, that would obviously be incredible in itself, but it would surely reduce my ability to crumble and watch porn. On an intensely pragmatic level, it might also half the rent . . . even though I've lied and told her I own the place. Argh! The more I tangle myself up in this web, the harder it is to see the way out. But Kate Collins may yet prove to be my sweet saviour.

Right, I'm gonna try and sleep. Today, I bought an old-fashioned chamber pot to put by the bed, so I no longer have to leave this room during the night and risk seeing another ghost. Must remember to hide this pot when Kate comes over next.

Thank fuck no one else will ever read this.

P.S. I should make a note here, that I've received a couple of weird crank calls lately. Keep hearing all this kinda . . . grey buzzing . . . and then someone says something I can barely even understand. The first one said, "You're going to love it here." Thanks, random stranger at 2 a.m!

P.P.S. Bits of the front door keep randomly falling off, and I continue to repair them. Sometimes it's the small things that do your head in the most.

CHAPTER SIXTY-NINE

8 October

I am dying to open the final diary entry, but my head overflows with stuff. Need to take a short breath and filter through what Scott wrote.

Bloody hell, so he saw a ghost too? Makes sense, I suppose, if this place has been haunted for a while. Astonishes me, how cool and composed he seemed in person, despite all this turmoil swirling around his head. Porn, debt, ghosts, a hideous case of self-loathing – this guy was a total mess. What I feel for Scott is no longer romantic, so why do I now feel closer to him? The answer feels uncomfortably obvious. He and I had so much more in common than either of us ever knew.

Scott Palmer, where the hell are you? If you really are dead, as I still believe you to be, then where's your body? Could it really be buried on Ray's grounds, or in those woods? Soon, that will be for the police to find out. I'm too weary to take any further direct action, but I still need to know what happened.

A phone rings. My old Nokia. How quaint. Probably Izzy, asking which soup I prefer.

"Hi, Kate," says my supervisor Akeem. "How are you feeling?"

Oh great, here comes the inquisition. I have no time for this. Why did I even answer the phone?

"Not brilliant, to be honest. I'm so sorry I've missed work. If you can wait till tomorrow, I can try and explain what happened?"

"No, no, I wasn't calling about that. Just let me know when you're ready. We all want you well again, Kate."

"I really want to make it clear that I wasn't trying to ki—"

"Don't worry, don't worry. Seriously, that conversation can wait. But I was wondering: have you heard from Tyler today at all? He didn't come into work either."

Okay. The bloke may be lying low, in case I snitched on him. "No, I haven't heard from him at all, sorry."

"Oh. How odd. No worries, I'll try his phone again."

Ah.

"The thing with Tyler's phone is," I say, then take a moment to select the best words – ideally words that aren't *I threw it into the sea*. Since I'm too dog-tired for eloquence, I end up sounding clumsy anyway. "It's not working anymore, basically, so that's probably why you're, uh, having trouble getting hold of him."

"Oh, right. I'll see if we have a landline for him."

With that, Akeem leaves me alone with my rat's maze of thoughts. Could Tyler really have done a pre-emptive runner before he gets sacked? This hardly seems important, when I still have Scott's final diary entry to get stuck into. And Izzy could be back at any moment.

Outside, the storm rises towards the boil. Wind and rain howl through the hole where the glass in the sliding door once was.

I steel myself for disappointment. Chances are, this last part of the diary won't give me any of the answers I've been waiting for. Life doesn't work that way.

Then again, this piece *is* titled *The End*. Shit . . .

With no idea of what to expect, I tap into the unknown.

The beginning of *The End*.

CHAPTER SEVENTY

The End
TrooSelf diary entry seven of seven
Dated: 1 October
Filed by: SPalm123

It's now a mere two days until Kate moves in, and any normal guy would be feeling on top of the world. Not being even vaguely normal, of course, I can't remember the last time my head was this scrambled.

I now NEED to write here. I need to spit out my thoughts before they expand too much and break open my skull. I need to try and swipe victory from the jaws of defeat!

Let's deal with the good stuff first. The GREAT stuff. Kate not only said YES to moving in with me, but she seemed really happy about it! In response, I privately freaked out again and became super-clingy. I even pretended to have a meeting in London, just so I could travel on the train to Victoria with her . . . only to travel straight back to Brighton when she got on the tube. During the journey with Kate, I saw this old couple who seemed so comfortable with each other, they didn't have to say a word. Made me feel all fuzzy. How I would love Kate and I to stay together for that long! And yet, being me, I knew she was bound to come to her senses about the Big Move and leave me tumbling down that emotional lift shaft.

Back on Tinder, I set up more self-defence dates, only to blow most of those off again. The one date I did turn up for, I bought the girl a drink, pretended to go to the toilet, then walked out. What an arsehole I am, albeit an arsehole with some kind of conscience when it comes to infidelity.

Here's a thing: me going on dates behind Kate's back isn't even the worst thing that's happened lately. Are you fucking ready for this, TrooSelf?

Ray broke into the flat last night and filmed me while I slept, using my OWN PHONE. The video he shot was over TWO HOURS long. What a fucked-up thing to do! I'm still shaking at the thought of it.

On impulse, I deleted the video, then regretted it because it could be used as evidence if things get really nasty between me and him. Actually . . . knowing phones these days, it's still lingering in the trash or something. I should check.

CHAPTER SEVENTY-ONE

8 October

Takes me a while to figure out where that trash folder might be, but the video that Scott binned is waiting for me there, among a whole army of porn clips. Really wanted to keep reading *The End*, but the urge to find the video has proved even stronger.

Two hours and sixteen minutes in length, the video plays exactly like the others, but with one key difference. Watching Scott sleep soundly, for what may have been the last time ever, makes me cry myself hoarse. I can barely skim my way across half.

The more I know, the more likely it seems that Ray did film Scott. Which means he probably did the same thing to me, a few nights later. He must have filmed Gwyneth, Dieter and all the others, too.

The case for Ray having killed Scott, among others, has strengthened.

Did Ray deliberately wait outside the Van Spencer building

for me to come home that night? During our small talk between here and the Amsterdam Hotel, he'd asked where Scott was. Did he hope to find out if I had called the police?

Clock's ticking. Must read more.

CHAPTER SEVENTY-TWO

The End

When I phoned Ray to confront him about what he'd done, he completely denied everything. He called me crazy, but I know full well he was trying to intimidate me. Always thought my brother had something missing in his head, but I never realised he was this nuts. Basically, he was conveying a clear message: if I try to run out on the debt between us, he'll find me anywhere. He has POWER over me. The fucker always fancied himself as a gangster or something, and now fantasy has become reality in his head.

The whole debt situation with Ray reached crisis point over the last week, but we have reached a grim settlement. He threatened to get in touch with Kate on Facebook and tell her I'm a penniless porn addict, unless I allow him to take everything of value that I own so he can sell it off and cover a chunk of my debt to him. To reassure his paranoid self that I wouldn't skip town or anything like that, yesterday I drove over to his Chanctonbury shithole and gave him a spare set of keys. Big mistake! That's obviously how he got in last night and shot the video. Can't believe he still did that, despite us having reached an agreement!

Ray's coming over later with the van to pick everything up, so I need to box all my stuff fast. God, how much do I now regret getting so drunk with this idiot, on the one night in years we'd gone out together? Why, of all the people I could have confided in about my problem – such as a pro therapist – did I decide to tell my untrustworthy brother? I should have known he'd hear that information and automatically think, *Aha! Future blackmail material!* On my birthday, too. Well, both our birthdays . . .

What on Earth am I going to tell Kate when she turns up and the flat's been gutted? One excuse could be that I wanted us to make a whole new start together and choose a new TV, new sofa, etc. . . . right down to the towels. Meant to go out and buy WELCOME TO YOUR NEW HOME banners, but I forgot, and they may not even exist. So I am improvising. Used one of my liquid chalk pens to draw a big smiley face on the window, but it looks weird and I can't think of exactly what to write beside it. *I Love You* will do the job, won't it? People always like *I Love You*.

The thing is, I know that my cover story won't wash with Kate. Especially as it's not like I can afford to buy new stuff – I've even fallen behind on the rent! She's already sold her own TV and all the bigger items like that, so this really is shaping up as a disaster of titanic proportions.

Speaking of disasters, I'm doing BADLY with the porn. Even with Kate about to move in, I'm struggling more than EVER to stay clean.

My periods of abstinence have yet to last more than one day, and even those feel like endurance marathons. I have lost so much potential work time to the smut, with people screaming at me over deadlines.

The new phone really isn't helping, either. I never even knew smartphones could pick up viruses, but mine must've already caught one from the dodgy smut sites I've visited. Either that, or the virus has somehow lingered from previous use. When I bought this thing from Gwyneth on Gumtree, the handset was full of someone else's pictures and videos – thousands of them – and it wouldn't let me carry out the reset procedure that would wipe the memory. Hmm, this might explain why Gwyneth decided to sell the phone, and pretty cheaply too. Thinking about it, this may also explain why she didn't want to face me in person and made her nan come over here to deliver it instead. She hasn't replied to any of my follow-up questions, either. Interesting . . .

CHAPTER SEVENTY-THREE

Thoughts racing, I wrench myself out of Scott's diary, flip over to his browser and search for "Gumtree". I want to confirm that the Gwyneth he bought the phone from is the Gwyneth Cooper I know all too well.

Sure enough, here I am on a defunct sales page from mid-August that advertises the very phone I have in my hands. The seller's username is "CoopG".

As I try to digest what Gwyneth's prior ownership of the phone could mean, a pop-up notification wrecks my focus.

Way to go, dude! Your upload to SikkFuxx.com has been approved.

Huh?

A fierce rumble of thunder sounds like the pier caving in on itself. Slanted rain lashes the balcony decking. Some of the water even manages to drizzle the mound of broken glass that I failed to clear up, just inside the window-door.

When I tap the SikkFuxx notification, I'm taken to the browser, where the site opens up. The uploader's name is a random string of letters and numbers, but this registers only subliminally because the auto-playing video already freaks me out.

The camera pans slowly over a burnt corpse, curled up on a scorched domestic carpet. Most of the body has been burned right down to the bone, although the legs appear to be intact. Reminds me of pictures I've seen of supposed spontaneous human combustion cases.

One detail consumes me. Around the corpse's neck hangs a metal pendant, shaped like a grenade.

Oh Christ.

My sandpapered throat refuses to swallow. Outside, the skies unleash a fearsome thunder-crack.

This is beyond me. How did it happen? And why has the video been uploaded from Scott's phone?

Scott's voice comes back in all its urgency. *Kate, get rid of this thing. I'm begging you to throw it away.*

The video ends with a brutal close-up on the open-mouthed terror baked into what's left of Tyler's face. Had it not been for the pendant, I might not have recognised the poor bastard. Likes and comments are already piling in. Feeling horribly complicit, I shut the browser down and fight a strong urge to hurl the phone out into the storm.

Scott bought this phone from Gwyneth and they both ended up dead. What does this tell me?

Stay calm. All I have to do is keep my head together and read.

Tyler threw this phone into the sea and now he truly is toast.

Shut up and let me focus. Let me get through the final chunk of *The End*.

Someone snatches the phone out of my hand.

I cry out, through frustration as much as shock.

"What the fuck, Kate?"

Izzy towers over me, her face quite the picture. All those growls of thunder made sure I didn't hear her coming back. On the floor between her and the archway sit two bags of shopping, right next to my hammer.

"I'm almost *done*, Izz. Let me read the rest."

Izzy hobbles a few steps back, wanting to put distance between us. She goggles at Scott's phone like it's an impossible object. "Bloody hell, this really is the same handset. How the fuck did this thing survive the sea?"

I edge towards her, nice and easy, like someone trying to talk down a rooftop suicide. "The case is really well-made, that's all. It's watertight. Can I have my phone back, please?"

Izzy matches each of my movements with a backwards step of her own. She's looking at me like I'm a bloody stranger. "No, you can't."

"Tyler's dead," I say, so badly wanting her to finally *understand*. "And I don't know how, but a video of his dead body has been uploaded from this phone."

"Serious? Kate, this is all way too fucked. Seriously, I've had enough."

When I speak, it sounds like someone else. "That makes two of us, honey, because I've also had enough – of you trying to tell me what to do."

Her despair gives way to stunned surprise. "Are you kidding? Someone telling you what to do is exactly what you need."

Go and pick up the hammer. Nothing changes the dynamic in a room like someone picking up a hammer.

"What I *need* right now, Izzy, is my phone back. Something *huge* is going on and—"

"If it wasn't for me, mate, you'd still be halfway up a fucking hill. Remember that?"

I give her the same humouring smile Tyler gave me when I

threatened his phone. Poor, deep-fried Tyler. "Sorry, honey. I promise you, I really appreciate everything you've done, but I really need my—"

"I don't think you appreciate owt at the moment, mate. How many addicts have we dealt with over the years? Are you seriously so far gone that you can't hear their words coming out of your mouth?"

I remember how smooth the handle of the hammer feels. "Give me the phone."

"Ray was right, Kate. You just can't handle Scott leaving you, and that's what this whole thing's about. This flat does seem haunted, but he's not dead."

The molten heat inside me melts the smile off my face. "So you're saying I imagined seeing his ghost? Fuck you. You're supposed to be my *friend*."

A full-force tornado flies out of Izzy's mouth. "Oh my *days*, you wanna talk about *friendship*, you stupid bitch? Listen up, and listen so much harder than ever before: I am *never gonna walk again*, okay? I'm on crutches for life. And yes, that's partly my fault, but it's also *yours* because you were fucking around on your *phone* that night."

Oh my. The sheer size of this, it blots out the sun.

"Yeah, that's right," she spits. "I *saw* you, all preoccupied. And I thought to myself, *It's okay, the patient doesn't seem so dizzy now. I can start him off down the stairs and Kate will catch up once she's got her precious update on who Rudolpho's screwing*. So that choice is on me, but you weren't there when I needed you. What's even worse is, I knew you'd feel so guilty, and you're always in some kind of crisis, and I still loved the *bones* of you. And that's why I never told you my diagnosis. But if I'd told you the fucking truth, then none of this Scott crap might have happened."

This must be what they call a moment of clarity.

I have no idea what to say. *Sorry* would feel inadequate.

Izzy cracks open the phone's protective case, then sets about opening the phone itself. "You can have the phone back if you like, but I'm keeping the battery."

Stop her. You have to stop her. Hardly asking for much, are you? All you want to do is read the last few words that your beloved ever wrote.

Yes, but I played a big part in my best mate being disabled for life. And just now, I seriously considered threatening her with a hammer. I've wandered so far off the path, I don't even know how to find my way back.

You have to read the final part of The End.

Too late. Izzy pops the phone's battery out onto her palm. "There," she says.

The intense relief I feel is matched only by the pang of deprivation.

Don't worry. You can read the diary on another phone. Or in a net café. Everything's going to be all right.

A flash of lightning strobes the room.

With Scott's phone in one hand and its battery in the other, Izzy frowns at the screen.

"That's weird," she says. "Why hasn't it died?"

She drops the handset on the floor. "Fucking thing."

The charred corpse of Tyler flashes before my eyes. The guy who threw the phone into the sea, then ended up dead. "Izzy, no! Don't, please don't."

Izzy says, "It's the only way to save you, Kate." She raises one of her crutches, then powers the end down towards the phone.

And now she's gone.

Swept clean off her feet, as if struck by a passing juggernaut, Isabella Clarke has left my field of vision.

My brain flounders, desperate to catch up.

Across the living room, in appalling slow motion, Izzy slides down the wall beside the archway. The impact of her body has dented the brickwork and snapped one of her crutches in half.

Coming to rest on the floor, stunned, with her head lolling back against the wall, she struggles to focus on me.

When she opens her mouth to speak, only blood comes out.

I dash across the room towards her, but I'm nowhere near fast enough.

Something unseen and horribly powerful hauls her back away from the wall and into the air.

When she sails past me, I do my best to catch her, but she might as well be a bullet.

Out through the hole in the window she goes, then keeps on going, off into the storm.

I run headlong out onto the balcony, as if there's still time to save her.

Already so very far away, my best friend's body flies among a flock of gulls. Seen against this torrid purple sky, her silhouette has become indistinguishable from the birds. For one crazed second, I dare to dream that she might fly on with them forever.

My child-logic weakens, along with Izzy's trajectory. She narrowly misses the peak of the zip-wire tower, then plunges out of sight.

Thunder rumbles.

Twin forks of lightning slice right through me.

A cruel wind snakes into my gaping mouth, then burrows down my throat into my chest, as if trying to pulverise what remains of my heart.

How am I supposed to deal with what I saw? I may as well have the entire ocean poured inside my head. And even my powers of denial can't handle a task this gigantic.

The beach and rain-lashed streets are all but deserted. No one may have witnessed Izzy go, which makes this even harder to take. No fucker should be allowed to carry on with their daily routine as if nothing happened. Izzy's death should *matter.* The whole world should stop turning and pay its respects.

I'm one big shapeless tremor. All I seem able to do is stare at the zip-wire tower, at the beach, at the sea, while desperately wanting to look somewhere else, anywhere else.

Why? Why did this happen?

She was about to damage the phone. This cannot be any kind of coincidence – not when Tyler threw the phone into the sea and he died, too.

Something wants to protect this phone. Why?

Might it kill me next?

Not if you behave yourself and look after the phone . . .

I hate looking back over my shoulder into the living room, because I can't bear to see the dent that Izzy left in the back wall, and yet I need to know where the phone ended up. The fucking thing was right there on the floor, but now it's nowhere to be seen. Where did it go? If I've lost the phone, the invisible killer may be displeased and—

There's something in my right hand.

Christ, it's the phone.

Don't even remember picking the handset up, but here it is. Did I really grab it so mindlessly before dashing out here to see what would happen to Izzy?

Probably. You did, after all, try and retrieve the thing by jumping into the sea.

I have no idea what to do.

The same thing you were doing before Izzy grabbed the phone. Let's find out how Scott's diary ended.

I don't know . . . Izzy body's is crumpled up on the beach . . . and I'm supposed to stand here, looking at a fucking *phone*?

This is the safest option and you also know it's what you want. Two birds, one stone.

Shaking from head to toe, I stay put on the balcony as the storm rages on.

Pausing only to wipe my tears off the screen, I read the end of *The End*.

CHAPTER SEVENTY-FOUR

The End

Here is the big, weird problem with this phone. At any time of the day or night, the bloody thing decides to auto-play PORN, of all things! It even tried to start playing this stuff in front of Kate one day, when we were sitting on the pier talking about ghosts. My God, that was such a close call.

This is really fucking mad porn, too. I've never seen anything like it. Women, men and bizarre . . . I don't know how to describe them. Creatures? Things? Slimy beasts with tentacles and tits and insect bodies and serpentine cocks and gaping mouths, making these insane animalistic noises as they have sex with ecstatic humans and semi-humans. I mean, I know it MUST surely be fake, but it looks so astonishingly real, like unbridled filth from another dimension.

The thing is, because my stupid brain has become so accustomed to so many existing forms of smut, this stuff feels so new. As a result, it's been getting me really hard again for the first time in weeks. Jesus Christ. Can't stop myself taking screen grabs for, uh, future use. I really am possessed by this shit and it's making me cry myself to sleep.

There are only two days to go until Kate arrives. I'm broke, hopelessly addicted to porn, my psycho brother's about to come over to take away all my stuff and for weeks now I've felt like I'm coming down with flu. How can I turn any of this into a positive?

Kate talks a lot about various "life guru" blokes. So just now, I watched one of those videos on YouTube, hoping for inspiration. In this video, the guy spoke about making real change happen in your life by (a) getting appalled by your current situation and (b) taking *enormous action*.

I already have (a) nailed, so now it's time for (b).

The root of my problem is the smut, so I've decided to rip these roots clean out. A few minutes ago, I downloaded porn-blocker software for my desktop, which will stop me accessing anything even vaguely suggestive. I wrote down the admin password on a piece of paper, then ripped it up and threw it off the balcony like confetti. That hurt and took serious willpower, but I knew it had to be done. Success!

So what about my phone? Clearly, I can't keep this infected thing, because I'm hooked on the crazy porn it keeps feeding me. So I've been out to a second-hand shop on St James's Street and bought an old Nokia exactly like Kate's. This thing doesn't have a data connection, so that will effectively shut off the other porn avenue in my life.

I am loving this enormous action, but there's one thing left to do. The biggest thing of all.

I'm going to fire up the balcony BBQ. I'm gonna put my smartphone on top and watch the fucker burn.

This is going to be a glorious ritual, and fun too. I'd video the whole thing, if that wouldn't involve using the phone. Ha! I wonder if the handset will explode.

This is a huge moment for me. If I can find the courage to take this final action and change my life, WHICH I WILL, then everything's going to be all right. After I've torched the phone, I'll call Kate on my new Nokia and confess the truth. Yep, I'll tell her the whole, unvarnished truth. She deserves to hear about EVERYTHING. All the lies, the debt, the porn. If she runs a mile, which is very likely indeed, then that will be no less than I've brought upon myself. But if she bizarrely decides to go through with her move, and to help me through this, I'll have shrugged these huge weights off my shoulders and we can have a normal relationship. One that lasts FOREVER.

If there's one thing worth trying for, no matter what the cost may be, then it's living the rest of my life with this incredible woman.

The fire's burning on the barbie, cobber! These flames are hungry for this stupid phone. As soon as I finish this diary entry and it backs up to the cloud, I'm going to thr

CHAPTER SEVENTY-FIVE

Thr? Is that really it?

Scott's words end so abruptly. Clearly, he did not burn the phone . . . so what stopped him?

The same unseen force that stopped Izzy and punished Tyler.

This phone in my hand now feels more like a bomb.

Learn from the mistakes of the dead. Protect this thing and save yourself.

Behind me, the crunch of broken glass. And there stands Scott, just inside the jagged, open mouth of the sliding door.

Of course, it's not really him. This is Ray, back in his pimp suit. Without even trying, he's fooled me one more time.

One last time.

Ray looks and sounds like he's been drinking again. His bandage has gone, leaving the cut on his nose red raw. I also notice he's got my hammer in one gloved hand, keeping it low against his thigh. "Well, that was a fuck-load easier than I expected. Always leave my brother's front door sitting wide open, do you? Eh?"

Ray runs his gaze around the window frame. "Oh dear. Had a little accident, have we? Almost looks like the scene of a *struggle*."

"Get out, right now."

He nods pointedly down at the hammer, then at Scott's phone. "Tell you what. I'll leave when I get my brother's property back. That's a good deal, considering the phone don't belong to you. I bloody knew you had it."

My thoughts trip over themselves. Here's my chance to get rid of the phone. But could I really hand this thing over to someone who doesn't understand the full enormity of what they're taking? Could I knowingly hand over a bomb, even to a prick like Ray?

"Scott's phone doesn't belong to you either," I say. Got to buy myself some thinking time. "Why do you want it?"

Ray stands impassive. The sky flashes twice, highlighting the hard lines of his face. "Because I reckon you think I killed my brother. And if he really is dead, which he'd better fucking not be, then you might plan to stitch me up for it."

"I did suspect you might have killed Scott. But now I don't, okay? You should go."

His dead eyes burn through me. "Like I said at my place: how do I know *you* haven't killed him? Who exactly *are* you, Kate Collins, with your fake copper mate? And how the fuck did you get hold of my brother's phone?"

"When you came here to take all Scott's stuff, after blackmailing him," I say, making Ray's face tighten, "was he actually here, that day?"

He scoffs. "Lazy little sod was nowhere to be seen. Couldn't even get it together to help me load up his stuff. So I decided to teach him an even bigger lesson and take everything. And I *mean* everything. Dumped most of the worthless shit in the skip outside."

I keep my tone even. Reasonable. Some might say, placatory. "Whatever happened to Scott, he and everything else had already gone when I arrived. And he left his phone behind, right here."

I point to the spot on the decking. "You obviously hadn't noticed, or you'd have added it to your stash. So if you must know, that's how I found Scott's phone. I turned up, ready to move in with him and there it was."

Waiting for you . . .

"Whatever," Ray says. He steps over the threshold, out onto the balcony. He's gripping that hammer at waist level now, but I refuse to back away. Can't, won't show fear. Besides, there's nowhere to go. "Here's a good joke for you, Kate. What do you say to a girl with a hammer-smashed face?"

"Nothing," I say, somehow moulding my mouth into a smile. "You already told her once."

Looking irritated that I knew his "joke", Ray draws close enough for me to experience that bourbon-nicotine reek one last time. He holds one hand out in demand. "Phone. *Now*."

Even through the brawl of the storm, I can make out an ambulance siren. My throat contracts. Someone must have found Izzy. I picture her broken body and my eyes sting.

"Ray, please listen. You need to understand the full picture here. There's something going *on* with this ph—"

Ray grunts, then swings the hammer onto my right elbow.

Stars explode. The scream of the ambulance siren becomes my own.

I drop the phone on the decking, then crumble to my hands and knees on top of it.

Before I even have a chance to vomit on the handset, Ray snatches it up and away. There's a real swagger in his voice. "That's right, chuck your guts up, you dumb bitch. Now, if this phone tells me you've had anything to do with Scott going missing, or if you go crying to the police, then trust me: I'll be back to make that elbow seem like a fuckin' graze."

Through puke-tears, I watch him toss the hammer aside

as he re-enters the living room. I try to cradle my smashed elbow with my other hand, but this only makes the joint howl louder.

"Raymond," says a clear and startling new voice from inside. An older woman's voice. "Stop right there, please."

What? That's Maureen, in the living room, perched on one of my boxes. How long has she even been there? Did she come in here with her son?

Hunched forward with her hands clasped around her knees, the woman's face is etched with the weariness I saw when she and I first met.

Crawling off the balcony and into the room, I'm vaguely aware of broken glass carving into my knees and one of my palms. "Maureen, what are you doing here?"

When she silently acknowledges me, the sorrow in her eyes frightens me far more than anything Ray could ever do.

Halfway to the archway, Ray slows his stride. There's an odd distance about the way he assesses his own mother, almost as if he's never seen her before.

Smirking back at me, he says, "Who's this – your bodyguard?"

Struggling to ignore the signals my elbow and hand keep firing to my brain, I say, "How drunk are you, that you don't recognise your own mum?"

Ray's laugh fills the whole space. "She ain't my mum, you fuckin' madhead. Ta ta for now."

What? *What?* If Maureen isn't Scott and Ray's mother, then who is she?

Her voice a cool knife, Maureen says, "Ray, you will hand the phone back to Kate *immediately*. Don't force me to add another regret to my very long list."

"It's okay," I stammer. "Maureen, honestly, it's fine. I don't want it back."

Ray has almost reached the archway. "What you gonna do, Grandma: come at me with your handbag?"

Maureen sighs. Pointing a finger at Ray, she utters one word. "Candle."

Ray stops dead, as if she's used a remote control on him.

The phone falls from his hand and hits the floor. He twitches. He might be trying to move and speak, but something has him glued so very firmly to the spot. All he can do is make alarmed, glottal noises in his throat.

A small orange and yellow flame billows into existence on the top of Ray's scalp, then rushes down to consume his head.

Ray's scream rattles around inside him, unable to escape his mouth.

The vile smell of overcooked pork sends my saliva into overdrive and makes me gag again. I know this reek all too well, from having attended scenes where human bodies cooked on railway lines.

Am I yelling these words or am I only thinking them: *What are you doing? Maureen, what are you doing to him?*

Maureen's voice wavers, her eyes haunted. "I did tell him twice. If it was down to me, people who try to interfere would just go peacefully in their sleep. I'm sorry to say, the master much prefers to see them being burnt or thrown around."

My bubbling guts already know the answer to this question, but I ask anyway. "The . . . master? Who's the master?"

Ray stands silent now. Only his twitching fingers move, and his head has burnt down to the blackened skull. Fire darts across his shoulders, then eats down through the suit on his back. I slap my bloodied hand over my nose, to combat the stench of meat swelling up, splitting apart and seeping fat.

"Maureen, *please*, what's going on? Who are you?"

Still seated on my box, she considers me with something a lot like pity. "The master once claimed me, as it will claim you. Except,

I was given a job to do, as the master's custodian. An insurance policy, I suppose, to make sure it reaches the right people."

My wildly churning brain remembers how Gwyneth's phone was delivered to Scott by her nan. What's the betting this person was really Maureen? "What do you mean, the right people?"

"The master has a keen nose for weakness. It knows what people need."

"Whatever you get out of this, I can offer more. Now *help* me."

Maureen steals a glance at Ray, then shudders, as if repulsed by her own actions. "Nothing's worth more than being allowed my freedom. The master sets me free, to walk this world again and see my daughter, my grandson . . . even though they can't see me."

When Maureen turned up that night, those automatic lights in the corridor didn't detect her. Remember that? Yeah, you remember now, all right. She couldn't feel the cold in the flat and didn't let you touch her . . . in case you realised she was dead.

The discordant symphony in my elbow screeches on as I look from Ray, whose entire torso is ablaze, back to Maureen's infinite melancholy. The words *I don't want to die* loop through my head and my voice is wobbly sludge. "What . . . is . . . going to happen here?"

Movement catches my eye. The phone – Scott's phone, Gwyneth's phone and whoever else's phone before that – now hovers several feet above the floorboards.

This thing floats towards me as if supported by invisible wires.

Ray keels over. Slamming down onto Izzy's shopping bags, his charred corpse pumps fluffy grey ash into the air. The fire has weakened but continues to lap at the last of his flesh.

The phone draws nearer. Close enough for me to notice that the flickering screen carries a pale blue glow.

Out of the corner of my eye, I spot the hammer on the floor.

There's a fat pulse in my head, like a vein's about to pop. I address Maureen, while very much keeping my eye on the phone. "Did you kill Scott?"

"Me, dear? No. I must keep the target alive at all costs, until the master has finished absorbing them."

Absorbing them.

Those sleep videos. People filmed asleep, while the phone hovers over them . . .

It knows what people need . . . such as the most bizarre and compelling porn they've ever seen. Or a huge mystery that provides the perfect excuse to re-embrace a smartphone . . .

Scott, me, Gwyneth, Dieter and whoever came before us. Digital junkies, growing weak and pale . . .

"Only *then* can it destroy the body and consume the soul," Maureen says, her face taut with the effort of remembering. "That's the general gist, anyway. I find the whole thing rather complex."

The phone . . .

. . . the master . . .

. . . . dumps itself on the floor in front of me with a clatter, face up. The words *consume the soul* reverberate in my head.

Maureen says, "I'm so sorry, dear. I know this is a lot to take in. It certainly was for me, all those years ago."

Quick! Destroy this thing, before it destroys you.

My elbow shrieks in protest as I snatch up the hammer.

Maureen has never sounded so lively. "Kate," she cries out, "*don't do that.*"

Her fear only spurs me on. I'm about to swing the hammer down onto the phone, when Scott's face fills the screen.

Staring out through the glass rectangle, he looks like a terrified prisoner. So very, very vulnerable.

Swing the hammer! This is another trick, like Scott's voice on the pier.

Too late. Hesitation has cost me everything.

Can't move a muscle. Can't even blink.

With the placatory tone of someone trying to reassure a cow at the slaughterhouse gates, Maureen says, "Try to relax, dear. This won't hurt *quite* as much as you might think."

The room is lit solely by lightning and the phone's screen, which spins and blurs into a piercing blue whirlpool. As it gathers speed, Maureen continues to say something or other, but her words are lost to me.

You're going to love it here.

This phone can be powered solely by the user's own blood.

This is not your phone, so don't use it. For your own fucking good. Trust me.

Phones have minds of their own.

For Christ's sake, don't come in here. Don't let it suck you in.

Kate, get rid of this thing. I'm begging you to throw it away.

Slowly, but all too surely, my essence is being vacuumed out of my limp shell, but maybe . . . maybe that's all right? My panic has already grown warmer, fuzzier, blurring around the edges. Every nerve ending in my body screams, but all this pain feels like a technicality because my body has less and less to do with me. This death may as well be happening to someone else. Besides, my mother inflicted worse than this, a long time ago. She laid down the path that I chose to follow to get here, step by needy step.

With a ping, a notification window pops up on the phone's spinning screen. An automated reminder set by Scott Palmer, once upon a time.

Kate's bday is two weeks from today! Buy all the presents! ☺

The whirlpool grows to become all I can see, and I become the whirlpool.

CHAPTER SEVENTY-SIX

Outside our perfect bubble, it looks as though heaven wants to break in. The most gorgeous sunlight powers through the balcony windows and soaks the living room and kitchen walls in white gold.

I'm stretched out on the sofa. A nice mushroom risotto sits on the table beside me as I flick through Facebook. Because I have thousands of friends, it takes a while to absorb all their news. Of course, fresh updates are popping up all the time, so this is practically a full-time job. Ha ha! A few of these friends are actually our neighbours, too. There's Gwyneth for instance, and Dieter, who both live . . . oh, somewhere else in the Van Spencer, I suppose, I can't quite remember. We don't go out much. Actually can't recall the last time we set foot outside the door, but why would we ever need to?

Over in the kitchen, Scott perches on a stool with a G&T. His lower half is concealed by the breakfast bar as he checks out the latest porn videos – the ones that make all the crazy animal noises. For some reason I can't explain, I feel like him watching porn all the time should bother me but it doesn't. Everyone is allowed interests and hobbies, even if they aren't necessarily shared by their partner. Besides, I'm busy enough. Need to reserve my energy for all this flicking and tapping. I'm sure Scott and I will have sex at some point or other.

Our beautiful twins, a boy and a girl, lie on their bellies on the floor beside me, each holding a tablet. They chirrup happily with every new achievement they unlock in their games. I can't remember their names at present – the children's names, I mean, not those of the games, which I *do* recall. This does strike me as a tad peculiar, but one of my friends has reposted a three-minute video compilation of shocking near-misses on American roads, which soon diverts my attention and steals my breath. I share the video to Scott's FB messenger, for him to watch later. We send each other links all day long, which feels so very romantic.

When you're falling for someone, it's like you shift into another dimension. Nothing else matters, besides staying there forever.

The afternoon stretches on so peacefully that it feels as though we're on holiday. Actually, come to think of it, *are* we on holiday? I can't remember the last time that Scott or I did any work, but I'm sure we'll soon be back doing . . . whatever it is we do.

I find myself fleetingly preoccupied by the balcony's sliding door. Did that thing get broken at some point? It certainly isn't broken now. We must have got it fixed, if indeed the break happened at all. Sometimes I remember things, little flashes of things that don't make sense, only to dismiss them as the lingering traces of a dream. For instance, I have this dim memory of wearing a uniform and some kind of badge, but this may have only ever happened during REM sleep.

Here's a strange thing, though: I can't remember the last time any of us slept, or even went to bed. Neither can I recall the sun ever having done anything but scorch through these windows, me leaving this sofa, Scott leaving the breakfast bar or ever finishing his G&T, the kids getting up from the floor, or the flat having smelt like anything but hot copper.

I've Instagram-ed my mushroom risotto with a Gingham filter, branding it *to die for*, but my complete lack of appetite means I can't seem to get around to eating the thing.

I'm sure all of these things will happen soon. Or if they don't, that's fine too.

Now, then. If I was a type of cheese, which cheese would I be? I'm going to take this quiz, then compare the results with all my friends. Yay!

You know what? For a while now, this thought has continued to nag at me. So very easy to lose track of time at the moment, because I can't actually remember when the sun last went down, but it might have been days or even weeks.

Our window-door really *was* broken once. Quite a long time ago, I think, but I'm increasingly convinced that this happened.

I have this mental image of me – *me*, of all people – using some kind of . . .

. . . *hammer* . . .

. . . object or other, to smash the glass.

It was a fucking hammer; why can't you remember?

Coupled with this vague recollection is the image of a pile of broken glass that once sat on the floor over there.

Now, why ever would I do such a thing? Makes zero sense.

Remember. Come on, Kate! There's something huge to remember here. Someone was thrown out through the hole in this window.

LOL! Don't cats do the funniest things? I swear to God, they're a law unto themselves.

This person was someone you knew very well. Someone you loved.

Do I merely Like this picture or shall I actually retweet it? How much value would a retweet bring my followers and how much visibility might it bring me? How much pleasure would I gain from a retweet versus a Like?

Fuck this picture of a cat standing upright. Try to keep your eyes off the screen for one second and think hard. Remember why you broke the glass and how you felt. Remember everything.

Remember Izzy.

What is this feeling? This is really strange and I don't like it at all.

I think this is something called *anxiety*, welling up inside me. The growing sense that something is wrong here. Very wrong.

The phone throws several pings at me, but I'm looking at the sliding window-door that I once smashed.

I'm looking at the sun, which burns as brilliantly as it ever did.

Actually . . . I'm looking *directly* at the sun, without even having to blink. Shouldn't that hurt me?

Yes! That's right. This sun could never burn out your retinas, because it's fake. All of this is fake. You know this. There's a major realisation, teetering on the tip of your brain.

Across the room, Scott has his phone in one hand, while pleasuring himself with the other behind the breakfast bar. Thank goodness he behaves like a responsible parent would and only masturbates when he can be sure our children aren't looking.

No, no, this is all wrong. You still can't even remember the twins' names, can you? That's because they're fake, like everything else. Hold onto that anxiety you felt and let it explode, because it's the only way you're ever getting out.

Switching to WhatsApp, I drop Scott a message.

"Baby, I feel weird. Something's wrong here."

I wait a while for a reply, but now I can see he's typing. And then his reply appears. *U ok hun? Let's talk in 5 – I'm just about to shoot.*

My chest coils up, leaving me short of breath. My natural instinct is to reply via WhatsApp, but I force myself to physically speak aloud. "No no, Scott, please listen to me. Everything's wrong. None of this is real. Think! We never had kids – and if we did, you wouldn't be jerking off in the same room as them. We have to get the fuck out of here!"

Scott's reply does not come, but he does. On the other side of the room, his face contorts and his back arches.

The muscles in my legs feel limp, as if they've lain dormant for a long time, but now I'm somehow standing at the balcony door. There are yachts on the sea and people milling around on the pier and around the zip-wire tower, but none of them look real. They're like a matte painting in the background of an old movie. Looks fine from a distance, but on closer inspection . . .

Izzy's body, flying through the air, missing the zip-wire tower, then plunging out of sight.

Oh God. Oh my *God.*

"Mummy," says our little girl, without looking up from her tablet, "what are you doing?"

Tapping intently at his screen, the boy says, "Please come back to the sofa."

"You're not our kids," I tell them. "You're not even real." Cold sweat trickles down my back as I try to slide open the balcony door.

"Stop it, Mummy," says the girl, without raising her voice. "Please stop now."

"You're scaring me," says the boy.

This door is so much stiffer than I remember. Takes my entire body weight, combined with repeated yanks, to even break the seal.

Beyond the inch-wide gap I've created lies a stripe of pure black. The full dark of what could easily be deep space.

This darkness is what you need. Seize your chance! Pull harder.

"Scott," I call out, "please come with me now. I'm begging you. Can't you see that none of this is real?"

There's no reply, but I daren't look back at anybody, in case the illusion regains control. My vital new knowledge feels slippery, as if it could so easily leap back out of my head and send me back into the trance.

Panicked, I wrench at the stubborn door. Every new inch reveals more black.

"Silly Mummy," says the boy. "Why don't you come back, have a nice lie-down and catch up on what your friends have been doing?"

God, that sounds good. I really should close this door and go back to my old life.

No! Your old life is not here. It never was. Your old life, your real life, is somewhere else, through the gap in this door. Somewhere beyond the black.

With a roar of frustration and fear, I yank at the door handle, again and again.

There's a cruel smile in the girl's voice. "Kate, you'll never escape your master. You now exist only to feed me."

One final concerted heave exposes more black. Enough for me to squeeze out through. And then I'm gone.

CHAPTER SEVENTY-SEVEN

The air smells of incense. Lemongrass.

I find myself standing in a bedroom at night. A nearby window tells me this is an upstairs room. Yellow rapeseed fields stretch forever away from the house, with a full moon suspended above them.

I'm pretty sure I've never been here before, but I know I have to get out before something absolutely terrible happens.

My feet barely touch the ground as I fly straight out of the door and onto the dark landing. Here, blue lights activate, making it easier to see where the fuck I'm going.

Seen closer, through the landing window, those rapeseed fields actually look real. They don't have the same bullshit matte painting feel about them as the view from the flat. Have to reach them, and reach them fast.

More lights flicker on all around me as I hurtle down the staircase towards the front door. A stained-glass circle embedded in the wood depicts the multi-coloured head of a horse.

Why does this door look and feel so very familiar? Who cares? All I need to do is get outside. Need to taste the fresh air, smell those rolling fields and everything will be fine. I'll be free forever.

As I make for the door, something throttles my speed. Feels as though my feet are tied to the bed, back upstairs, and the length of rope tethering me has started to run out.

By the time I reach the wood of the door, some kind of force tries to pull me back up the stairs.

Fuck that. I'm never going back to that fake bullshit life of cats and near-misses on American roads and personality quizzes and endless video games and deeply inappropriate masturbation. Hard and fast, as if swimming through glue, I power myself towards the door until my fingernails graze the wood.

Outside, someone presses their shadowed face up against the stained-glass horse's head.

Maureen's mournful eyes gaze at me, through red glass.

The force upstairs exerts a stronger pull, greater than I can bear.

Consumed by the urge to resist and survive, I cling to the door. My fingers gouge through the varnish and into the wood, which cracks and bursts under the pressure.

Only as I'm hauled back away, spraying the doormat with wood chips, do I notice all the other gouge marks. Some of these are identical to mine. Some bear testament to the failed escape attempts of others.

Oh Christ, I've done this before, haven't I? That's why the horse-head door looked so familiar. I've tried to escape, only to get hauled up these stairs like I am now, and I've ended up back inside the belly of the beast. Once I ended up on that sofa with my phone in my hand, I must have forgotten, all over again.

No, no, please, don't let me go back up there.

Don't let me go back into the coma.

And yet back onto the landing I come. My whole body gets twisted around by this force, so that I fly back into the bedroom face-first.

I am a seagull, driven against its will by overpowering winds.

I am a woman going backwards up a zip-wire.

On some level, my brain always knew this was going to happen.

For the first time, I notice the two people in bed. A man and a woman, neither of whom I recognise. On the bedside table beside the guy, sits a phone.

Nope, not a phone. *The* phone, in that same cracked protective case.

The master, drawing me inexorably back inside.

This guy in the bed, he must be the next victim.

Whipping across the room, I catch my own reflection in a wall of mirrored wardrobes and really wish I hadn't.

I am a flickering, airborne, corpse-blue thing.

A crude animation in a child's flip-book.

I struggle to recognise my own eternal eyes, like holes punched into cloth. Then I see the black tongue poking out of my mouth at a jaunty angle. Oh yeah, that's my stupid avatar all right. Looks like I'm stuck with it.

During this whole escape attempt, my feet genuinely never did touch the ground, because I don't have any feet. Those lights on the landing, and on the stairs, they all came from me.

The woman murmurs, "Phil, I got that weird taste in my mouth again." She opens one eye, sees me, gasps, then flinches back against the headboard, waking Phil with a start.

My blue light strobes their silent-scream faces as they haul the duvet up over themselves.

The phone, the master, becomes a whirlpool. The screen spins like a luminous buzz-saw blade as it drags me closer. Very soon I'll go back to the flat, the sofa, a phone, Scott, the twins and our perfect bubble. As I post my latest banal survey results, or a picture of a meal I'll never eat, I'll remember nothing about trying to flee.

Until the next time.

The smell of lemongrass fades, along with the terrified cries of the bed's occupants. Like a spider circling a plughole, my mind scrabbles around, desperate to find even one grain of positivity.

As the master sucks me back in, there's no time for three gratitudes.

Even so, a pretty good one springs to mind.

At least I'll never be alone.

ACKNOWLEDGEMENTS

Having been a music journalist in my time, I was familiar with the concept of That Difficult Second Album, and yet it still somehow came as a surprise when I faced That Difficult Second Novel. Fortunately, I had the world's finest people on my side, starting with my unstoppable and unthinkably dapper agent, Oli Munson at A.M. Heath.

My editor Anna Jackson once again proved a mighty tower of strength and insight, as did spectacular Orbit personnel James Long, Joanna Kramer, Nazia Khatun, Ellen B. Wright, Brit Hvide and copy-editor Maya Berger.

My titanic beta-readers John Higgs, RJ Barker, Helen Armfield, Florence Rees and William Gallagher all offered vital thoughts and support. These people are thoroughly great, as are the ever-encouraging Ray Zell, James Moran, Danny Stack, Sarah Lotz, Louisa Collins, Scott K. Andrews, Kevin Allington, Lee Allington and Esther Dickman.

In terms of research help, no one could possibly have been more helpful than Victoria West. Despite being a virtual stranger, a friend of a friend, Victoria went above and beyond the call of duty to help me make Kate Collins a convincing paramedic. No question fazed her, and God knows I tried. By the way: the Deranged Naked Guy story is based on truth.

Further research assistance came from multiple kind souls including Julie Mayhew, Steve Roberts, Lucy V. Hay, Sara Baroni, Leila Abu El Hawa, Erica Brackenbury, Jordan Paramor, Della Williams, Sammy Andrews, Natasha Von Lemke, Kat Wakefield, Emma Johnston, Sparrow Morgan, Malcolm Franks, Tiff Franks, Dijana Capan, Helen House, Anna-Lou Weatherley, Sarah Jane Harries, Lisa Howells, Amanda Herbert, Sarah Lavender, Eleanor Piper, Tabitha Wild, Claire Lambert, Culzean Driver, Beki Hobbs, Michael Moran and all my other Facebook friends who endured my random questions about phones and dating apps on a semi-regular basis across an entire year.

Some of the Brighton bars and restaurants in this book are real. I can't recommend them all enough as places to visit in the awesome city where I live. So, a big thanks to Sally Oakenfold at the Hope and Ruin, Luke Semlekan-Tansey at Beelzebab (yes, those kebabs do exist – rejoice!), Marion Rees at the Basketmakers Arms (where some of *Ghoster* was plotted out across various evenings, with indispensable help from John Higgs), Food For Friends, James Dance at Loading, Two Wolves Kitchen and the Foundry.

I'm so grateful to Alan Moore, Ron Howard, M. R. Carey, Andy Nyman, David Schneider, Toby Whithouse, Chuck Wendig, Paul Tremblay, Nicholas Kaufmann, Edward Cox, Jamie Sawyer, Kealan Patrick Burke, Kim Newman and Chris Brookmyre, all of whom blew my mind with their praise of my debut novel *The Last Days of Jack Sparks*. And oh my God, I started to write a list of the book bloggers and sites who supported *Sparks*, but we would run out of space here and I'm terrified of forgetting anyone. So please check out the "Jack

Sparks" tab at JasonArnopp.com for a list of those fine people, plus links to their hugely appreciated coverage.

Big love to everyone who follows my Instagram account @jasonarnoppauthor, joined my mailing list legion (bit.ly/ArnoppList) and subscribes to my YouTube channel (bit.ly/ArnoppTube). The biggest love of all, though, must go to those who support me on Patreon (patreon.com/jasonarnopp) and every single reader who bought *The Last Days of Jack Sparks*, then maybe wrote a review or recommended the book to others. I literally could not carry on writing without you incredible people, because my landlord stubbornly resists the concept of letting me live here rent-free, no matter how often I campaign in his back garden at 3.33 a.m.

Right, I'm pretty sure I just felt my dopamine level dip. Time to check my phone for the 268th time today.

Look out for

THE LAST DAYS OF JACK SPARKS

also by

Jason Arnopp

It was no secret that journalist Jack Sparks had been researching the occult for his new book. No stranger to controversy, he'd already triggered a furious Twitter storm by mocking an exorcism he witnessed.

Then there was *that* video: forty seconds of chilling footage that Jack repeatedly claimed was not of his making, yet was posted from his own YouTube account.

Nobody knew what happened to Jack in the days that followed – until now.

www.orbitbooks.net

extras

www.orbitbooks.net

about the author

Jason Arnopp is a British author and scriptwriter. He has written official fiction for the worlds of *Doctor Who*, *The Sarah Jane Adventures* and *Friday the 13th* and co-authored *Inside Black Mirror* with Charlie Brooker and Annabel Jones.

Before *Ghoster* flew out of his tortured brain, Arnopp wrote the 2016 Orbit Books novel *The Last Days of Jack Sparks*. He has also written the likes of *Beast in the Basement*, *Auto Rewind*, *How to Interview Doctor Who, Ozzy Osbourne and Everyone Else*, *From the Front Lines of Rock* and *American Hoarder* – the latter being available for free when you join his mailing list at bit.ly/ArnoppList.

While *Ghoster* and *The Last Days of Jack Sparks* may seem to rail against the online world, they're probably best read as cries for help, given that Arnopp can be found on more than one Instagram account, YouTube, Facebook, Mastodon, Snapchat, Twitter, Medium, LinkedIn, Tumblr, Patreon, Discord, Ko-Fi and of course at JasonArnopp.com.

Find out more about Jason Arnopp and other Orbit authors by registering for the free monthly newsletter at www.orbitbooks.net.

if you enjoyed
GHOSTER
look out for
THE GIRL WHO COULD MOVE SH*T WITH HER MIND
by
JACKSON FORD

*FOR TEAGAN FROST, SH*T JUST GOT REAL.*

Teagan Frost is having a hard time keeping it together. Sure, she's got telekinetic powers – a skill that the government is all too happy to make use of, sending her on secret break-in missions that no ordinary human could carry out. But all she really wants to do is kick back, have a beer, and pretend she's normal for once.

But then a body turns up at the site of her last job – murdered in a way that only someone like Teagan could have pulled off. She's got twenty-four hours to clear her name – and it's not just her life at stake. If she can't unravel the conspiracy in time, her hometown of Los Angeles will be in the crosshairs of an underground battle that's on the brink of exploding . . .

ONE

TEAGAN

On second thoughts, throwing myself out the window of a skyscraper may not have been the best idea.

Not because I'm going to die or anything. I've totally got that under control.

It wasn't smart because I had to bring Annie Cruz with me. And Annie, it turns out, is a screamer. Her fists hammer on my back, her voice piecing my eardrums, even over the rushing air.

I don't know what she's worried about. Pro tip: if you're going to take a high dive off the 82nd floor, make sure you do it with a psychokinetic holding your hand. Being able to move objects with your mind is useful in all sorts of situations.

I'll admit, this one is a little tricky. Plummeting at close to terminal velocity, surrounded by a hurricane of glass from the window we smashed through, the lights of Los Angeles whirling around us and Annie screaming and the rushing air blowing the stupid clip-on tie from my security guard disguise into my face: not ideal. Doesn't matter though – I've got this.

I can't actually apply any force to either Annie's body or mine. Organic matter like human tissue doesn't respond to me, which is something I don't really have time to get into right now. But I can manipulate anything inorganic. Bricks, glass, metal, the fridge door, a six-pack, the TV remote, the zipper on your pants.

And belt buckles.

I've had some practice at this whole moving-shit-with-your-mind thing. I've already reached out, grabbed hold of the big metal buckles on our belts. We're probably going to have some bruises tomorrow, but it's a hell of a lot better than getting gunned down in a penthouse or splatting all over Figueroa Street.

I solidify my mental grip around the two buckles, then force them upwards, using my energy to counteract our downward motion. We start to slow, my belt tightening, hips starting to ache as the buckles take the weight – and immediately snap.

OK, yeah. Definitely not the best idea.

TWO

TEAGAN

Rewind. Twenty minutes ago.

We're in the sub-basement of the giant Edmonds Building, our footsteps muffled by thick carpet. The lighting in the corridor is surprisingly low down here, almost cosy, which doesn't matter much because Annie is seriously fucking with my groove.

I like to listen to music on our ops, OK? It calms me down, helps me focus. A little late-90s rap – some Blackstar, some Jurassic 5, some Outkast. Nothing too aggressive or even all that loud. I'm just reaching the good part of "So Fresh, So Clean" when Annie taps me on the shoulder. "Yo, take that shit out. We working."

Ugh. I was sure I'd hidden my earbud, threading the cord up underneath the starchy blue rent-a-cop shirt and tucking it under my hair.

I hunt for the volume switch on my phone, still not looking

at Annie. She responds by reaching back and jerking the earbud out.

"Hey!"

"I said, fucking quit it."

"What, not an OutKast fan? Or do you only like their early stuff?" I hold up an earbud. "I don't mind sharing. You want the left or the right?"

"Cute. Put it away."

We turn the corner, heading for a big set of double doors at the far end. My collar's too tight. I pull at it, wincing, but it barely moves. Annie and I are dressed identically: blue shirts, black clip-on ties, black pants and puffer jackets in a very cheap shade of navy. Huge belts, leather, with thick metal buckles.

Paul picked up the uniforms for us. I tried to tell him that while Annie might be able to pass as a security guard, nobody was going to believe that the Edmonds Building would employ a short, not-very-fit woman with spiky black hair and a face that *still* gets her ID'd at the liquor store. Even though I've been able to buy my own drinks like a big girl for a whole year now.

I couldn't be more different to Annie. You know how some club bouncers have huge muscles and a shit-ton of tattoos and piercings? You know how people still fuck with them, starting fights and smashing bottles? Annie is like that one bouncer with zero tattoos, standing in the corner with her arms folded and a scowl that could sour milk. The bouncer no one fucks with because the last person who did ended up scattered over a six-mile radius. We might not see eye to eye on music – or on anything, because she's taller than me – but I'm still very glad she's on my side.

My earpiece chirps – my *other* one, the black number in my right ear. "Annie, Teagan," says Paul. "Come in. Over."

"We're almost at the server room," Annie says. She sends another disgusted look at my dangling earbud.

Silence. No response.

"You there?" Annie says.

"Sorry, was waiting for you to say *over*. Thought you hadn't finished. Over."

"Seriously?" I say. "We're still using your radio slang?"

"It's not slang. It's protocol. Just wanted to give you a heads-up – Reggie's activated the alarm on the second floor. Basement should be clear of personnel." A pause. "Over."

"Yeah, copy." Annie says. She's a lot more patient with Paul than I am, which I genuinely don't understand.

The double doors are like the fire doors you see in apartment buildings. The one on the right has a big sign on it, white lettering on a black background: AUTHORISED PERSONNEL ONLY. And on the wall next to it, a biometric lock.

Annie looks over at me. "You're up."

My tax form says that I work for a company called China Shop Movers. That's the name on the paperwork, anyway. What we actually do is work for the government – specifically, for a high-level spook named Tanner.

For some jobs, you need a black-ops team and a fleet of Apache choppers with heat-seeking missiles. For others, you need a psychokinetic with a music-hating support team who can make a lot less noise and get things done in a fraction of the time. You need a completely deniable group of civilians who can do stuff that even a special forces soldier would struggle with. That's us. We are fast, quiet, effective and deadly.

Go ahead: make the fart joke. Tanner didn't laugh when I made it either.

The people we take down are threats to national security. Drug lords, terrorist cells, human traffickers. We don't bust in with guns blazing. We don't need to – not with my ability. I've planted a tracking device on a limo at LAX, waving hello to the thick-necked goon standing alongside the car while I zipped the tiny black box up behind his back and onto the chassis. I've kept the bad guys' safeties on at a hostage exchange – good thing too, because they tried to start shooting the second they had the money and got one hell of a surprise when their guns didn't work. And I've been on plenty of break-ins. Windows? Cars? Big old metal safes? Not a problem. When you can move things with your mind, there's not a lot the world can do to keep you out.

Take the lock on AUTHORISED PERSONNEL ONLY, for instance.

You're supposed to put your finger on the little reader, let it scan your fingerprint, and you're in. If you're breaking in, you either need to hack off a finger (messy), take someone hostage (messy, annoying), hack it locally (time-consuming and boring), or blow it off (fun, but kind of noisy).

My psychokinesia – PK – means I can feel every object around me: its texture, its weight, its relation to other objects. It's a constant flood of stimuli. When I was little, Mom and Dad made me run through exercises, getting me to really focus in on a single object at a time – a glass, a toy car, a pencil. They made me move them around, describe them in excruciating detail. It took a long time, but I managed to deal with it. Now I can sense the objects around me in the same way you sense the clothes you're wearing. You know they're there, you're aware of them, but you don't *think* about them.

If I focus on an object, like the lock – the wires, the latch assembly, the emergency battery, the individual screws on the latch and strike panels – it's as if I send out a part of myself to wrap around it, like you'd wrap your hand around a glass. And then, if I'm locked on, I can move it. I don't have to jerk my head or hold out my hand or screw up my face like in the movies, either. I tried it once, for fun, and felt like an idiot.

It takes me about three seconds to find the latch and slide it back. The mechanism won't move unless it receives the correct signal from the fingerprint reader – or unless someone reaches inside and moves it with her mind. It's actually a pretty solid security system. I've definitely seen worse. But whoever built it obviously didn't take into account the existence of a psychokinetic, so I guess he's totally fired now.

"And we're good." I hop to my feet, using my PK to pull the handle down. I haven't even touched the door.

"Hm." Annie tilts her head. "Nice work."

"Was that a compliment? Annie, are you dying? Has the cancer spread to your brain?"

"Let's just get this over with."

We're on this operation because of a clothing tycoon named Steven Chase. He runs a chain of high-end sportswear stores called Ultra, which just means they're Foot Locker stores without the referee jerseys. If that was all he was doing, he'd never have appeared on China Shop's radar, but it appears Mr Chase has been a very naughty boy.

Tanner got a tip that he was embezzling money from his company. Again, not something we'd normally give a shit about, but he's not exactly using it to buy a third Ferrari. He's funnelling it to some very shady people in the Ukraine and Saudi Arabia, which is when government types like Tanner start to get mighty twitchy.

Now, the US government *could* get a wiretap to confirm the tip. But even if you go through a secret court, there'll be some kind of paper trail. Better a discreet call gets made to the offices of a certain moving company in Los Angeles, who can look into the matter without anything being written down.

And before you start telling me I'm on the wrong side, that I'm doing the work of the government, who are the real bad guys here, and violating a dozen laws and generally being a pawn of the state, just know that I've seen evidence of what people like Chase do. I have no problem messing with their shit.

We're not actually going anywhere near Steven Chase's office. Reggie could hack his computer directly, but it would require a brute-force attack or getting him to click on a link in an email. People don't do that any more, unless you promise fulfilment of their *very* specific sexual fantasies. The research on that is more trouble than it's worth, and you'll have nightmares for months.

Chase is in town tonight. He flew in for a dinner or an awards show or whatever rich people do for fun, and it's his habit to come back to the office afterwards. He should be there now, up on the 30th floor. He'll work until two or three, catch a couple hours of sleep, then grab a red-eye back to New York. Which works just fine for us.

If you can access the fibre network itself – which you can do in the server room, obviously – you can clamp a special coupler right on to the cable and just siphon off the data as it passes by. Of course, actually doing this is messy and complicated and requires a lot of elements to line up just right . . . unless you have me.

The cables from every floor in the building run down to this room. The plan is to identify Chase's cable, attach a coupler to it, then read all the traffic while sipping mai tais on our back porch. Or in my case scarfing Thai food and drinking many, many beers in my tiny apartment, but whatever.

Chase might encrypt his email, of course, but encryption targets the body of the email, not the sender or subject line. If he emails anyone in the Ukraine or Saudi, we'll know about it. It'll be enough for Tanner to send in the big guns.

The server room is even more dimly lit than the corridor. The server banks stand like monoliths in an old tomb, giving off a subsonic hum that rumbles under the frigid air conditioning. Annie tilts her chin up even further, as if sniffing the air. She points to one side of the door. "Wait there."

"Yes, sir, O mighty boss lady."

She ignores me, eyes scanning the server stacks. I don't really know how she's going to find the correct one – that was the part of the planning session where they lost me. All I know is that when she does, she's going to trace it back to where it vanishes into the floor or wall. We'll open up a panel, and I'll use my PK to float the coupler inside, attaching it to the cable. It can siphon data, away from the eyes of the building's technicians, who would almost certainly recognise it on sight.

As Annie steps behind one of the servers, I slip my earbud back in. May as well listen to some music while—

"Shit," Annie says.

It's a quiet curse, but I catch it just fine. I make my way over to find her staring at a clusterfuck of tangled cables spilling out of one of the servers. The floor is a scattered mess of tools and loose connections. A half-eaten sandwich, dribbling a slice of tomato, sits propped on a closed laptop.

"Is it supposed to look like that?" I ask.

Annie ignores me. "Paul, we've got a problem. Over."

"What is it? Over."

"Techs have been in. It wasn't like this this morning; Jerian would have told me."

Jerian – one of Annie's Army. Her anonymous network of janitors, cleaners, cashiers, security guards, drug dealers, nail artists, Uber drivers, cooks, receptionists and IT guys. Annie Cruz may not appreciate good hip- hop, but she has a very deep network of connects stretching all the way across LA.

"Copy, Annie. Can you still attach the coupler? Over."

Annie frowns at the mess of cables. "Yeah. But it'll take a while. Over."

Joy.

"Understood," Paul says. "But we can only run interference for so long on our end. You'd better move. Over."

Annie scowls, crouching down to look at the cables. She takes one between thumb and forefinger, like it's something nasty she has to dispose of. Then she stands up, marching back towards the server-room doors.

"Um. Hi? Annie?" I jog after her, earbud bouncing against my shoulder. "Cables are back there."

"Change of plan." She keys her earpiece. "Paul? Tell Reggie to switch over the cameras on the 30th floor. Over"

"Say again? Over."

"We're going up."

I don't catch Paul's response. Instead, I sprint to catch up with Annie, getting to her just she pushes through the doors. "Are you gonna tell me why we've suddenly abandoned the plan, or—"

"We can't hide the coupler if they got people poking around the cables." She reaches the elevator, thumbing the up button. "We need to go to the source."

"I thought the whole point was *not* to go near this guy. Aren't we supposed to be super-secret and stealthy and shit?"

"We're not going to his office, genius. We're going to the fibre hub on his floor."

"The what now?"

"The fibre hub. Every floor has one. It's where the cables from each office go. We'll be able to find the right one a lot faster from there."

The interior of the elevator is clean and new, with a touch-screen interface to select your floor. A taped sign next to it says that floors 50–80 are currently off limits while refurbishment and additional construction is completed, thank you for your patience, management. I remember seeing that when we rolled up: a big chunk of the building covered in scaffolding, with temporary elevators attached to the outside, and a giant crane in a vacant lot across the street.

When the elevator opens on the 30th floor, there's someone standing in front of it. There's a horrible moment where I think it's Steven Chase himself. But I've seen pictures of Chase, who looks like an actor in an ad for haemorrhoid cream – running on the beach, tanned and glowing, stoked that his rectum is finally itch-free. This guy is . . . not that. He has lawyer written all over him: two-tone shirt, two-tone hair, one-tone orange skin. Tie knot as big as my fist. Probably a few haemorrhoid issues of his own.

He eyes us. "Going down?"

"We're stepping off here, sir," Annie says, doing just that.

He moves into the elevator, mouth twisted in a disapproving frown as his eyes pass over me. Probably not used to seeing someone my age working security in a building like this. I have to resist the urge to wink at him.

I haven't seen inside any of the offices yet, but whoever built this place obviously didn't have any budget leftover for the hallways. There's a foot-high strip of what looks like marble-textured plastic running along at chest height. There are buzzing fluorescent lights in the ceiling, and the floor is covered with that weird, flat, fuzzy carpet which always has little lint balls dotted over it.

"Jesus, who picked out the paint?" The wall above the plastic marble is a shade of purple that's probably called something like Executive Mojo.

"Who cares?" Annie says. "Damn building shouldn't even be here."

I sigh. This again.

She taps the fake marble. "You know they displaced a bunch of historical buildings for this? They just moved in and forced a purchase."

I sigh. Annie's always had a real hard-on for the city's history.

"Yeah, I know. You told me before."

"And you saw that notice in the elevator. They just built this place. They already having to fix it up again. And the spots they bought out – mom-and-pop places. Historical buildings. City didn't give a fuck."

"Mm-hmm."

"I'm just saying. It's messed up, man."

"Can we get this done before the heat death of the universe? Please?"

It doesn't take us long to find the right office. Paul helps, using the blueprints he's pulled up to guide us along, occasionally telling Annie that this isn't a good idea and that she needs to hurry. I pop the lock, just like before – it's even easier this time – and we step inside.

There's no Executive Mojo here. It's a basic space, with a desk and terminal for a technician and a big, clearly marked access panel on the wall. By the desk, someone has left a toolbox full of computer paraphernalia, overflowing with wires and connectors. Maybe the same dickhead who left the half-eaten sandwich in the server room. I should leave a note telling him to clean up his shit.

The access panel is off to one side, slightly raised from the surface of the wall. Annie pops it, revealing a nest of thin cables. She attaches the coupler, which looks like a bulldog clip from the future, then checks her phone, reading the data that comes off it. With a grunt, she moves the coupler to the second cable. We have to get the correct one, and the only way to do that is to identify Chase from his traffic.

There are floor-to-ceiling windows on my left, and the view over the glittering city takes my breath away. We're only on the 30th floor, not even close to the top of the building, but I can still see a hell of long way. A police helicopter hovers in the distance, too far for us to hear, its blinking tail lights just visible. The view looks north, out towards Burbank and Glendale, and on the horizon, there's the tell-tale orange glow of wildfires.

The sight pulls up some bad memories. Of all the cities Tanner had to put me, it had to be the one where things burn.

It's bad this year. Usually, it's some kid with fireworks or a tourist dropping a cigarette that starts it up, but this time the grass was so dry that it caught on its own. Every TV in the last couple of days has had big breaking news alerts flashing on them. The ones tuned to Fox News – you get a few, even in California – have given it a nickname. hellstorm. Because of course they have.

This year's fire has been creeping towards Burbank and Glendale, chewing through Wildwood Canyon and the Verdugo Hills. The flames have made LA even smoggier than usual. A fire chief on one of the TVs – a guy who managed to look both calm and mightily pissed off at the same time – said that they didn't think the fires would reach the city.

"Teagan."

"Huh?"

"You got your voodoo, right?" She nods to the coupler.

"Float it up into the wall."

"Oh. Yeah. Good idea."

The panel is wide enough for me to lean in, craning my head back. The space is dusty, a small shower of fine grit nearly making me sneeze. Annie shines a torch, but I don't need it. She's got the correct cable pinched between thumb and forefinger. It's the work of a few seconds for me to find it with my *voodoo* and pull it slightly outwards from its buddies, float the coupler across and clamp it on. Annie flicks the torch off, and the coupler is swallowed by the shadows.

What can I say? I'm handy.

"Aight," Annie says, snapping the panel shut. "Paul? We're good. Over."

"Copy that. We're getting traffic already. Skedaddle on out of there. Over."

Skedaddle? I mouth the word at Annie, who ignores me. She replaces the panel, slotting it back into place, then turns to go. As we step out of the tech's office, a voice reaches us from the other end of the hallway: "Hey."

Two security guards. No, three. Real ones. Walking in close formation, heading right for us. The one in the centre is a big white guy with a huge chest- length beard, peak pulled down over his eyes. He's scary, but it's the other two I'm worried about. They're young, with wide eyes and hands already on their holsters, fingers twitching.

Ah, shit.